ALL THE RAGE

ALL THE RAGE

A Repairman Jack Novel

F. PAUL WILSON

A TOM DOHERTY ASSOCIATES BOOK • NEW YORK

ALL THE RAGE

Edited by David G. Hartwell

A Forge Book
Published by Tom Doherty Associates, LLC
175 Fifth Avenue
New York, NY 10010

www.tor.com

Forge® is a registered trademark of Tom Doherty Associates, LLC.

Library of Congress Cataloging-in-Publication Data

Wilson, F. Paul (Francis Paul)
    All the rage : a Repairman Jack novel / F. Paul Wilson.— 1st ed.
        p.   cm.
    "A Tom Doherty Associates book."
    ISBN 0-312-86796-4 (acid-free paper)
    1. Repairman Jack (Fictitious character)—Fiction. 2. Drug traffic—Fiction. I. Title.

PS3573.I45695 A79 2000
813'.54—dc21   00-031745

First Edition: October 2000

Printed in the United States of America

0 9 8 7 6 5 4 3 2 1

for Jennifer and John
and their new life together

AUTHOR'S NOTE

The Ozymandias Prather Oddity Emporium may seem familiar to some readers. *Freak Show*, the anthology I edited for the Horror Writers of America, chronicled its final tour. Thanks to Steven Spruill and Thomas Monteleone for allowing their characters from the anthology to appear here.

Readers familiar with the Garden State Parkway may wonder why they've never seen the New Gretna rest stop: you simply haven't looked hard enough.

Thanks to the usual crew for their enlightened and discerning input: David Hartwell, Coates Bateman, Elizabeth Monteleone, Steven Spruill, and Albert Zuckerman.

WEDNESDAY—
APRIL 26

"This is crazy," Macintosh said. "What are we *doing* here?"

Dr. Luc Monnet watched the unkempt younger man breathe into his grimy hands and rub them together as he paced back and forth on the wet grass. It had rained most of the day, but now the skies had cleared.

"You should have brought a jacket, Tom."

"You didn't tell me we'd be standing around in a field at goddamn three in the morning!"

A moonless sky vaulted above them. Nearby, the glowing ribbon of Route 290 lay still and largely empty; beyond it the lights of downtown Chicago lit the horizon with false dawn. Hulking masses of hotels or office buildings rose here and there across the flat land like desert buttes.

"You're the one who wanted to know the source of the molecule," Luc said.

Demanded was more like it, but that was such a loaded term. Luc wanted to keep everything on an even keel for the moment.

"I still do. But what are we doing hanging around a circus?"

"It's not a circus." Luc gestured to the looming shadow of the large oblong tent behind them. "As the sign says, it's an 'Oddity Emporium.'"

Macintosh snorted. "Euphemism for freak show. That still doesn't explain what we're doing here."

"This is the source of the molecule."

11

"Ok, fine. But why are we standing outside cooling our heels? And I do mean *cooling.*"

Luc grinned in the darkness. If Macintosh saw him, he'd probably think it a response to his feeble attempt at humor. But Luc found nothing funny about Macintosh. Nothing likable about him either. Especially his looks. They were such a mismatched pair. Luc's close-cropped, styled brown hair, trim five-nine frame, and tailor-made slacks and sweater next to Macintosh's tall, ungainly torso, his wrinkled shirt, worn jeans, shaggy hair, and wispy goatee.

Truth was, he was glad Macintosh was uncomfortable in the cold. He wished he'd freeze to death right here and now. The swine didn't have much longer to live anyway, and that would spare Luc the ordeal of having him killed.

Killed, he thought, shuddering at the concept. I'm going to cause another human being's death tonight. What would have been unthinkable two weeks ago had become something he had to do. He felt nothing for Macintosh, only a crawling anxiety to have done with it.

"And was all the subterfuge necessary?" Macintosh whined. "Separate flights, separate hotels, you picking me up on the street in the wee hours of the morning to haul me out here to the middle of nowhere. Like some bad movie."

Luc bit back a sharp retort. Didn't the damn fool ever shut up?

"Think about that, Tom," he said, keeping his voice even. It wouldn't do to betray his loathing for this piece of human garbage. Yet. "Just think about it."

Macintosh was blessedly quiet for a moment. Thinking, perhaps? That was something he should have done before he demanded to know the secrets of the molecule.

Macintosh—what had he been thinking when he'd hired this slovenly creature? A brilliant researcher with gaping holes in his intellect. Perfect example: if he'd possessed a lick of common sense he never would have come here.

"Yeah," Macintosh said finally. "I see what you mean. But how much longer?"

Luc lifted his wrist and pressed the illumination button on the rim of his watch. The face lit, revealing 4:11:08. That was Eastern Standard Time. He hadn't bothered resetting it.

"A few more minutes," he said.

In truth, the moment he'd been waiting for had passed. Ten minutes and fifty-four seconds after four had been the mark, but he always liked to give himself a cushion. Just in case.

Canvas rustled behind them and a deep voice said, "We're ready."

Luc turned and saw a tall figure holding back a tent flap.

"Finally!" Macintosh cried as Luc led him toward the faintly lit opening.

"Good evening, Mr. Prather," Luc said to the tall, oddly shaped man holding the flap. The owner of the show had arrived.

"Good evening, Dr. Monnet," Prather said in his deep voice that seemed to echo around him. He pronounced Luc's surname properly, but with an odd cadence.

Ozymandias Prather. An odd-looking duck—nearly six and a half feet tall, with narrow shoulders, a barrel chest, and wide hips. His long, narrow head completed the conical layout of his body.

"This is Dr. Macintosh. I told you that he'd be coming."

"You did indeed," Prather said.

No one offered to shake hands.

The air within was thicker and warmer but only marginally brighter than the starlight outside.

"Didn't they pay their electric bill?" Macintosh muttered as they followed Prather down the midway toward a better-lit area at the far end of the tent. "And what's that stink?"

Luc clenched his teeth. "That's the source."

At the end of the midway, in a pool of wan light, sat a cage. Above the iron bars a chipped wooden sign heralded THE AMAZING SHARKMAN! in faded red letters. Two roustabouts crouched before the cage, struggling with something between them—something long and dark that ended in three taloned fingers.

"My God!" Macintosh said, stopping and gaping at the sight. "What is *that?*"

"That . . . is the source."

He knew what was going through Macintosh's mind: *Sharkman?* That arm cannot belong to a man of *any* sort. It has to be a fake, a muscle-bound performer in a rubber suit with a clawed glove.

That was what Luc himself had thought when he'd first seen the creature that crouched behind the bars. But it had proved to be the real thing. That dark reptilian skin bled when punctured; the talons on the ends of those thick fingers were sharp and deadly.

But Luc was dismayed that tonight it took only two of Prather's

roustabouts to steady the creature's arm. These identical, vaguely canine fellows looked even odder than Prather—muscular, neckless hulks
with close-cropped hair, big square teeth, tiny ears, and dark, deep-set
eyes. When Luc had begun taking samples last year, five of them had
had difficulty restraining the thrashing Sharkman.

He squinted past them into the shadows of the cage but could make
out only a darker blot within. He didn't need to see the creature to
know it was failing. At first he hadn't been sure, but now with each
visit it was more and more apparent that it was fading away. Another
month, perhaps—certainly no more than two—and it would be dead.
The wellspring of the molecule would be gone.

And then what would he do?

The precipitous drop in cash flow would be the least of Luc's problems.

He did his best to shake off the sick feeling crawling through the
pit of his stomach and withdrew the venipuncture kit from his coat
pocket.

Macintosh said, "This is some sort of joke, right?"

Feeling very tired all of a sudden, Luc shook his head. "No, Tom.
No joke."

He unwrapped and inserted the short end of an eighteen-gauge
double-pointed phlebotomy needle into the plastic sheath; with two se-
rum separation tubes ready, he approached the arm.

"W-what are you going to do?" Macintosh said.

"What does it look like? I'm going to draw some blood."

The rank smell of the creature mixed with the wet-dog stink of the
roustabouts, making him a little queasy. Holding his breath, Luc didn't
prep the dark skin, simply trapped a ropy vein between two fingers and
worked the needle point through the gritty epidermis—like stabbing
through layers of sandpaper. As soon as he was into the vein he snapped
the vacuum tube home and watched it fill with dark fluid, much darker
than human blood.

When the second tube was full—always an extra, just in case—he
backed away and the roustabouts released the thing's arm. The creature
snatched it back through the bars, then rolled over onto its side, facing
away from them.

Luc held the tube up to the light.

"That's blood?" Macintosh said, leaning over his shoulder. "Looks
more like tar."

Although as black, the fluid was nowhere near as thick as tar. In fact, this sample was noticeably thinner than the last. When Luc had started drawing the creature's blood, the tubes would fill slowly despite the eighteen-gauge needle. Tonight a twenty-two-gauge would have been sufficient. Another depressing sign that the source was failing.

Macintosh straightened and stepped closer—but not too close—to the cage. He peered into the shadowy interior.

"What *is* it?" he said, his voice hushed.

"No one knows," Luc said, returning the tubes to their padded transport case. "And it's a pity that you don't either."

Macintosh turned. "What's that supposed to mean?"

"Just that if you knew something about it, anything at all, you'd be useful. I'd have a reason for letting you live."

"Heh," Macintosh managed through a wobbly smile.

Luc said nothing; he simply stared at him.

Macintosh licked his lips. "That's not funny, Doc."

Luc took profound pleasure in watching the smile fade and the eyes widen as the traitor came to realize he wasn't joking.

Macintosh glanced quickly around, then made a move toward the midway. But the two roustabouts blocked his way. He tried the other direction, but three more identical roustabouts appeared.

"Oh, God!" Macintosh wailed. "You can't be serious!"

"What did you expect?" Luc shouted. Finally he could vent his fury. "You've tried to blackmail me! Did you think I would stand for that?"

"No! Not blackmail! I—"

" 'Give me a piece of the action or I go to the police.' That's what you said, wasn't it."

"No, really! I didn't—"

"If you'd simply gone straight to the police, I would have been angry, but at least I could have seen you as a well-meaning citizen. But after I'd hired you, provided you with cutting-edge research technology, and trusted you with my records, you try to dip your filthy hands into what is mine, what I discovered and developed. That's despicable—intolerable."

"Please!" Macintosh dropped to his knees, held up his hands, palms pressed together as if in prayer. "Please, I'm sorry!"

Luc stoked his rage. Without it he might not muster the courage to give Oz the signal to remove Macintosh and dispose of him.

"Or if you'd accomplished what I hired you to do, I would have found a way to cut you in. But you've failed me, Tom—as a research-er . . . and as a man."

Macintosh sobbed. "Oh, Jesus!"

Luc glanced at Prather and nodded. Prather cocked his head toward Macintosh. In a single fluid motion, one of the roustabouts stepped up behind the kneeling man, raised a balled fist, and slammed it into the back of his neck.

Luc staggered back as he heard bones crunch like peanut shells and saw Macintosh's eyes bulge in their sockets as if his brain were pushing them from behind. Luc had never dreamed Prather's men would kill the man right in front of him. A surge of bile burned the back of his throat as he watched Macintosh pitch forward, his face landing in the dirt. His hands and feet twitched in time to the tune of his choked gurgling; then he lay still.

Luc swallowed and stared at the roustabouts. The killer had stepped back to rejoin his brothers, and Luc couldn't tell now which one had struck Macintosh, but the power behind that single blow had been . . . inhuman.

He felt weak in his knees. He'd wanted Macintosh gone, but not to watch him die.

A dismissive flick of Prather's wrist set the roustabouts into motion. They grabbed Macintosh's body by its feet and dragged him out like a piece of tarpaulin.

Luc struggled to pull himself together. His life seemed to have been drifting into the Abyss these past months, but with this act he felt he'd accelerated into free fall. And yet, despite his growing despair, he could not deny his relief at no longer having Macintosh's threats hang-ing over him.

"We'll bury him deep," Prather said. "The ground here will be pocked and scarred when we leave Sunday. No one will notice."

Still speechless, Luc removed a thick envelope from his breast pocket and handed it to him. An oily lock of the big man's lank dark hair fell over his forehead as he opened the envelope and fanned through the wad of bills. The wan light made his pale skin look ca-daverish.

"It's all there," Luc said, finding his voice.

"Yes, it appears to be." He stared down at Luc with his icy blue eyes. "Why didn't you have Mr. Dragovic take care of this for you?"

Luc stiffened. "Dragovic? What do you mean?"

Prather smiled—thin, thin lips drawing back over yellow teeth. Not a pleasant sight. "Come now, Doctor. I've done a little research myself. Didn't you think I'd be curious as to why you're so interested in my mystery pet's blood?"

Luc sagged. He could smell another shakedown coming.

"Not to worry," Prather said. "I've no taste for blackmail. Extortion is so sordid. But I can't help wonder why you didn't have your best customer remove this threat to both of you." His smile broadened. "Unless of course you didn't want Mr. Dragovic to know you'd left yourself so vulnerable."

Luc shrugged to mask the bunching of the muscles in his neck and shoulders. Prather had scored a bull's-eye. The last thing Luc needed was for Milos Dragovic to learn that this pig Macintosh had almost blown the whole business. Dragovic must never even imagine that Luc did not have absolute control of his end.

"Just as well," Prather said. "The extra money for removing him will help us meet payroll."

"Business off?" Luc said, trying to steer away from the subject of Milos Dragovic.

Prather nodded. "Bad weather sends people to movies but not to freak shows. And truthfully, some of our attractions become rather . . . ripe in wet weather."

In *wet* weather? Luc thought. How about *any* weather?

"I'll take the next sample on May twenty-fifth," Luc said, paving his way toward the exit. "Where will your troupe be then?"

Prather smiled again. "Virtually in your backyard, Dr. Monnet. We'll be in a little Long Island town that is one of our favorite annual stops. We'll be quite nearly neighbors for a while. Won't that be special."

Luc shivered at the thought of living anywhere near Ozymandias Prather and his freaks. "Well, it will be nice to simply hop into a car rather than fight through the airports."

"See you then, Dr. Monnet."

Relieved to be leaving, Luc turned and hurried along the dark midway toward the exit.

WEDNESDAY—
MAY 24

1

"What did you think?" Gia said.

"Well . . ." Jack glanced around as he gathered his thoughts, not quite sure what to say.

He, Gia, and Vicky had just exited the Metropolitan Museum of Art and now stood atop the high granite steps. The sun had been low when they'd entered and was well gone now. A tiny sliver of moon, a glowing fingernail clipping, hung in the sky. Below them, singles, couples, and groups lounged on the steps, smoking, eating, cuddling, hanging out. Water splashed in the oblong fountains left and right. And beyond the steps and crowded sidewalk, Fifth Avenue traffic crawled along despite the fact that rush hour was long gone. Exhaust fumes wafted up on the evening breeze that billowed the huge dark blue banner suspended above them, trumpeting the Cézanne exhibit.

Jack ran a quick apparel check, comparing his clothing to what the other museum goers were wearing. He'd gone for a slightly more upscale look tonight—light blue oxford shirt, tan slacks, brown loafers—and was pleased to see that he blended pretty well. In a bow to the current trend, he'd had his brown hair trimmed a little shorter than he preferred. He could pass tonight for a teacher or an accountant out for an evening with his wife and daughter. No one worth noticing. And that was perfect.

Jack watched Vicky doing her own scan, but hers concentrated on the sidewalk. Her dark brown hair had been unwound from her customary braids into a single long ponytail for her trip to the museum.

He could read her eight-year-old mind: Where's the ice-cream man? Where's the pretzel guy? For a girl who couldn't weigh more than sixty pounds fully clothed, she could eat like a long-haul trucker.

He turned to Gia and found her pale blue eyes staring up at him as a small smile played about her lips. The breeze ruffled her short blond hair. She looked dazzling in a snug blue silk sweater set and black slacks.

" 'Well' what?" Gia said.

Jack scratched his head. "Well, to tell you the truth, I don't get it."

"Get what?"

"Cézanne. Why he's so famous. Why he's got his own show at the Met."

"Because he's considered the father of modern art."

Jack shrugged. "So they say in the brochure, and that's all fine and good, but some of those paintings don't even look finished."

"That's because they aren't, you ninny. He abandoned a number of his canvases because they weren't going the way he wanted."

"Yeah, well, finished or not, his stuff doesn't do anything for me. How do they put it? It doesn't *speak* to me."

Gia rolled her eyes. "Oh, God. Why do I bother?"

Jack threw an arm around her shoulders, drew her close, and kissed her blond waves. "Hey, don't go getting all huffy now just because I don't like this guy. I liked Monet, didn't I?" He still remembered colors of sunlight so vibrant he'd felt the warmth radiating from the canvases.

"Monet's easy to like."

"You mean a painting's got to be hard to like to be good?"

"Not at all, but—"

"Mommy, look at those men!" Vicky said, pointing down to Fifth Avenue. "They're gonna get hurt!"

Jack turned and saw a couple of middle-aged men in jackets and ties strutting through the slow-moving traffic, seeming to dare the cars to hit them. More than a couple. Jack spotted more—a dozen, maybe two dozen, all well dressed, all in their forties, all swaggering like street toughs.

A car honked and one of the jaywalkers gave the driver the finger as he kicked a dent in his fender. When the driver got out he was jumped by two of the men and pummeled until he ducked back into the car and locked the door. They high-fived each other and continued toward the museum.

On the sidewalk to the right, one of the men snatched a pretzel from a cart as he passed. As the vendor went after him, he was grabbed by three of the well-dressed goons and knocked to the ground. They kicked him a few times and moved on, laughing.

"Jack?" Gia said, and he could hear the unease in her voice. "What's going on?"

"Not sure," Jack said.

He didn't like the looks of this. Unless they were a gang of middle-aged Gypsy Kings on a rampage after knocking over a Barney's—and Jack wasn't buying that—these guys were acting way out of character. For himself he wasn't worried, but he had Gia and Vicky with him.

"Whatever it is, let's stay clear of it."

One of the troublemakers pointed toward the entrance to the museum and shouted back to his buddies. Jack didn't catch what he said, but the others must have thought it was a great idea because they started streaming up the steps after him.

"Let's move over to the side," Jack said, ushering Gia and Vicky away from the center door and closer to the column supports at the downtown end. "Soon as they're in the museum, we're out of here."

But the well-dressed goons were easily distracted. Instead of making a beeline for the door, a number of them stopped to harass people along the way. Fights broke out. Within minutes the formerly peaceful steps of the Metropolitan Museum degenerated into one large multi-centric brawl.

"Oh, Jack," Gia said, pointing directly below them. "Help her."

Jack followed her point, saw a paunchy guy in a blue blazer with some sort of gold crest on the breast pocket. He was trying to nuzzle a young woman who'd been sitting alone on one of the landings, smoking a cigarette. The more she pushed him away, the more aggressive he became.

Jack glanced around. "I don't like leaving you two alone."

"Just chase him off before he does something awful," Gia said. "It won't take you a minute."

"All right," Jack said, heading down. "Maybe you could point out something more interesting to my little friend—like the fountains, say—while I see what I can do."

Jack figured he might have to do something quick and nasty to Mr. Paunch if he wouldn't cooperate. Didn't want Vicky watching.

As Jack trotted down the steps, the slim brunette had risen to her feet and was struggling with the older man who had at least a hundred-pound advantage. The expensive clothes, the good haircut, and the shiny, manicured nails didn't go with the feral lust in his eyes.

Jack was within a dozen feet of them when she shouted, "I told you to get lost!"

"Now, now, sweetie pie," he said through clenched teeth as he pulled her closer. "You don't really mean that."

"Wanna bet?"

She stabbed her lit cigarette at his eye. He jerked back and turned just enough to save his eye, but the burning end caught him solidly on one of his jowls. As he cried out in pain and raised his hands to his face, the young woman landed a forty-yard punt between his legs. The guy's face went fish-belly white as he dropped to his knees, holding his crotch. She kicked him again, in the chest this time, and he pitched sideways and rolled down a few steps.

The woman whirled on Jack, snarling. "You want some of the same?"

Jack stopped and held his hands before him, palms out. "Peace, lady. Just coming to help." He nodded to the battered man, prone on the steps, holding his crotch and groaning. "But you seem to have things under control."

She gave him a quick smile. "Thanks for the thought." She looked around at the melee. "What's gotten into these creeps?"

"Damned if I know. Best if you just—"

"*Jack!*"

The fright in Gia's voice spun him around and he was taking the steps up two at a time before it fully registered that she was struggling with two of the middle-aged yuppies.

"Hey!" he shouted as fire scorched through him.

Vicky batted at one of the men's legs, screaming, "Leave my mommy alone!"

The man, whose round face and pushed-up nose reminded Jack of Porky Pig, turned and shoved Vicky away. "Get lost, kid!"

"No!" Vicky cried, and kicked him in the shin.

His face distorted with rage, the guy grabbed Vicky and lifted her off her feet. "You little bitch!"

Jack's anger turned to panic as the man carried the screaming Vicky toward the end of the top landing. Jack veered away from Gia and poured every ounce of strength into his legs.

"I'll teach you to kick me!" Porky shouted, raising her higher as he neared the edge.

Vicky's terrified wail rose in pitch as she saw the stone steps sloping away before her. Jack reached them just as the man was flexing to fling her. He hooked Porky's elbow, yanked him back and around, turning the guy and Vicky toward him. Jack swung his left arm around Vicky's waist and smashed his right elbow into Porky's startled face.

As the guy staggered back, Jack put Vicky down and advanced on him. With Vicky safe now, Jack's rage had room to bloom. He let the darkness boil out of its cell and take over.

If Porky had had an ounce of sense he would have run. Instead he charged. Jack sidestepped at the last second, drove his fist into the flabby belly—a solid solar plexus shot—doubling him over. And still Porky wouldn't quit. Even bent almost in half, he tried to grapple Jack's waist. Jack didn't have time to dance; he had to get to Gia. He clubbed the guy on the ear, grabbed him by the back of his coat collar and the back of his belt, and gave him the bum's rush toward the end of the landing. At the last second, Jack lifted him and sent him sailing in the flight he'd intended for Vicky. Screaming and kicking and windmilling his arms, Porky hit the granite hard and kept going, rolling and tumbling the rest of the way down.

Jack didn't wait to see him land. Turned and ran back to Gia and her attacker.

"C'mon, babe," this guy was saying as he pawed Gia. "Stop fighting it. You know you want it."

As Jack arrived he spotted a similar crest on this one's blazer. That was about all he had time to notice before the guy slapped Gia across the face.

Something detonated within Jack then and things got fuzzy. Vision constricted to a short, narrow tunnel, sound warped to a muddled roar, and he was grabbing the guy by his blow-dried hair, ripping him off Gia, and slamming his face into the base of the stone columns. Once, twice, and more, until the meaty crunches became wet slaps. Then he threw him against the museum's front wall. As he repeatedly body slammed the man into the granite blocks, Jack became aware of a voice . . . Gia's . . . shouting his name. He released the guy and turned toward the sound.

Gia stood below, on the next landing, clutching her hysterical daughter in her arms. Saying something about getting out of here.

Jack shut his eyes, forced a deep slow breath. Sounds filtered back, rising in volume. Gia's voice, loud and clear.

"Jack, please! Let's go!"

Sirens rose in the distance. Yes . . . definitely time to go.

But as Jack stepped toward Gia and Vicky, he saw alarm widen their eyes. That prepared him for the slam against his back and the arms wrapping around his throat in a stranglehold. The impact knocked him off the top step. Locked together, he and his attacker were pitching forward toward a granite-hard landing. Jack twisted in the air, wrenching the heavier weight of his attacker around to position the other beneath him. The hoarse voice raging incoherently in his ear cut off abruptly when they hit the steps. The other guy had taken the full impact on his back, cushioning Jack.

Jack rolled off and was shocked to see that it was the same guy he'd pulled off Gia and battered against the wall. His face was a bloody mess and he shouldn't have been able to stand, let alone attack. Wasn't standing now—lay sprawled on his back, gasping for air. Had to have at least half a dozen broken ribs. But then he groaned, tried to roll over, and for one incredulous second Jack thought he was going to get up and come at him again. But then he slumped and lay still. Guy was a hell of a lot tougher than he looked, but not that tough.

Looked around at the chaos. People shouting, screaming, punching, kicking, falling, bleeding. The Odessa Steps from *Potemkin* in real life. Thankfully no baby carriages in sight.

What was *wrong* with these guys? Who were they and why were they acting like a Mongol horde? None of them seemed to know when to quit. But what disturbed Jack more was their willingness to hurt. You don't see that in the average person. Most people have a natural reluctance to do damage to a fellow human being. Jack had had that once. Took him years to overcome it, to clear an area within so he'd have a space where that reluctance didn't exist, a place he could step into, a mode he could enter when necessary and find a willingness, an enthusiasm almost, to inflict damage before it could be inflicted, and do so without hesitation. Hesitate and you're lost. Maybe dead. Better to give than receive. Always.

These guys showed none of that natural hesitation. Good thing most of them were doughy and didn't know how to fight; otherwise this would have been a truly scary scene.

Jack took Gia's arm and led her and Vicky to the side and then down. He glanced back to his right and saw Porky at the base of the steps, near the fountain; he was screaming curses as he crawled toward the sidewalk, dragging one leg behind him. Jack wanted to go down there and break a few more of this particular jerk's bones, but no way he was leaving Gia and Vicky alone in the middle of this riot.

When they reached the sidewalk he took the sobbing Vicky from Gia and hustled them downtown. He noticed an adrenaline tremor in his hand as he raised it to hail a cab.

How had such a nice evening turned so ugly?

2

"The bid is eleven-five," the tuxedoed auctioneer said. "Do I hear twelve thousand?"

Dr. Luc Monnet fought the urge to turn and glare at the other bidder; he kept his eyes on the auctioneer. Others around him, elegantly dressed, perched on well-padded chairs arranged in neat rows on the red carpeting, had no such compunction. They craned their necks this way and that, enjoying the auction spectator sport: a bidding war.

Luc did not have to turn to know what was happening. Two rows behind and slightly to the right, a dark-haired man in a blue suit was holding a StarTac to his left ear, receiving instructions from whomever he was bidding for. Luc closed his eyes and sent up a little prayer that $2,000 a bottle was too rich for the other bidder's blood.

He'd come to Sotheby's for the sole purpose of buying the half-case of Château Petrus 1947 Pomerol Cru Exceptionnel offered by the Gates estate. Not simply because it was a fine, fine wine that he wanted for his collection and not because Petrus happened to be his favorite Bordeaux, but because the vintage year had special meaning: nineteen-forty-seven was the year of his birth.

But as much as he desired the wine, he would not allow auction fever to seduce him into an absurd bid. He had set himself a firm $2,000-per-bottle limit before arriving—extravagant, perhaps, but not absurd. Not for Petrus '47.

His eyes snapped open at the sound of a delighted "Ah!" from somewhere in front of him and some scattered applause. That could mean only one thing. Dismay settled on his shoulders like a weight.

"The bid is now at twelve thousand for lot twenty-two," the auctioneer said, directing his gaze at Luc. "Will the gentleman bid twelve-five?"

Hiding his fury, Luc looked down at his bidding paddle, no longer needed now that the bidders had been reduced to two. Who was on the other end of that cell phone? Some billionaire Japanese philistine, no doubt, with Renoirs on the wall and Lafite-Rothchilds in his cellar, a Hun pillaging Luc's culture, whose appreciation of his spoils stopped at their price tags, reducing art and heritage to status symbols.

Luc wanted to grab the phone and scream *You've got your own culture—keep to it! This is mine, and I want it back!*

But he said nothing as he assessed the situation. What if the other bidder had set his own limit at $2,000 per bottle? That was a nice round figure. So if Luc went to twelve-five, that would exceed his own preset limit, but not by much. The price per bottle would be less than twenty-one hundred—exorbitant, but still shy of absurdity.

Luc nodded to the auctioneer and was rewarded by his own chorus of "Ahs" and appreciative clapping.

"And you, sir?" the auctioneer said, looking beyond Luc. "Will you go to thirteen?"

Another pause as his competitor, his foe, his mortal enemy, conferred with the mystery bidder. Luc continued to stare straight ahead.

A loud clearing of the throat and then a voice two rows back said, "Time to separate the men from the boys: fifteen thousand."

Gasps, then applause. Luc could feel his face turning red.

"Sir?" the auctioneer said, looking at Luc with raised eyebrows.

Crushed and embarrassed, Luc could only shake his head. Twenty-five hundred dollars a bottle? The vintage had never gone for that price and he refused to be suckered into topping such an outrageous bid. May the corks be dry and crumbling and leaking air, may the wine have oxidized to vinegar, and may the swine on the other end of the line drown in it.

But Luc knew the wine would be perfect. He'd studied the bottles, how the wine rode high in the necks, how one capsule had been cut to reveal the firm, tight, branded cork.

He rose, placed the paddle on his seat, adjusted the cuffs of his charcoal gray suit jacket, and walked down the center aisle. The weight of the combined gazes against his back from the audience propelled him toward the door.

Time to separate the men from the boys. . . .

Indeed . . . and at the moment he felt as if he were back wearing knickers.

As he passed the grinning winner, yammering into his cell phone, the pig had the bad taste to wink at him and say, "Better luck next time."

Die, Luc thought, ignoring him. Fall down and die.

He pushed through the door onto York Avenue. He took a deep breath of the evening air and consoled himself with the certainty that more bottles of Château Petrus 1947 Pomerol Cru Exceptionnel remained unopened somewhere and that some of those eventually would come to auction and find their way into his cellar.

Yet he still felt a residue of humiliation. He had vied for a prize and was coming away empty-handed. He could afford three thousand, four thousand, five thousand dollars a bottle, but money was not the point. The point was winning. And he had blinked.

He didn't feel like going home right now, so he began walking. He was about as far east as possible without being in the river, so he headed west, walking up stately Seventy-second Street. And he thought about his father. Wine always brought back memories of Papa.

Poor man. If only he had found a way to hang on to the *ancien domaine* in Graves or at the very least cached his wines somewhere before fleeing to America, life would have been so different.

Château Monnet's vineyard had been among the smallest in the Graves district of Bordeaux, but it had provided a respectable living for generations. His ancestors had bottled small lots of their own wine for the family and sold most of the harvest to other vintners. But they'd never quite recovered from the *Phylloxera vitifoliae* plague that attacked the vineyards of Europe in the 1860s. The plant louse wiped out all—not most, *all*—of Château Monnet's vines. Like its neighbors, Monnet had had to replant its acreage with *Phylloxera*-resistant rootstock imported from, of all places, California.

It took years before they were harvesting grapes again. The family fell into debt. Worse, the grapes were never as good as before the plague, so the debt grew. During World War Two, with the Germans in Paris and moving toward Bordeaux, Papa decided to abandon the place—it already belonged more to the bank than to him—and flee to America.

Luc was born in New York and thus a citizen. And by then the bank had auctioned off the Monnet domain to a neighboring château. Unable to face the ignominy of losing the ancestral home, Papa never set foot in France again.

Luc had visited the property a few years ago. He'd found the elegant stone structure that had been the ancestral home still standing, but now converted to an inn. An inn! He'd felt degraded.

Luc had stood in its front hall and sworn that he would buy it back someday. All it would take was money. And someday—soon, he hoped—he would have enough. Then he would drive the money changers from the family temple, move his wine collection back to the land of its origin, and take up where his father had left off.

He looked up and noticed Central Park across the street. Surprised that he'd already walked to Fifth Avenue, he turned uptown. As he reached the Eighties he noticed a blaze of flashing red lights ahead. Curious, he joined the crowd of gawkers gathered behind the yellow tape across the street from the Metropolitan Museum.

Ambulances and police cars blocked Fifth Avenue. Jammed traffic was being diverted. Emergency workers were tending dozens of injured people while cops dragged bloodied well-dressed men into blue-and-white paddy wagons.

"What happened?" Luc said to the Hispanic-looking fellow next to him.

"Some kind of riot." He wore a Mets cap and a Rangers sweatshirt. "Bunch of preppies, I heard."

"Preppies?" Luc said. "I don't see any preppies."

"Not kids. Older guys. Some prep school class was having its twenty-fifth year reunion tonight and decided to go on a rampage."

A premonitory worm of unease began to wriggle in Luc's gut. "Anyone . . . killed?"

"Not that I know of, but I—oh, shit! What's that guy doing?"

Luc squinted toward where the man was pointing. He spotted what must have been one of the rioters—disheveled, bloody, but the crest on his blazer certainly looked preppyish—handcuffed to the door handle of one of the police cars. He squatted there with his face against his handcuffed wrist.

"Oh, Christ!" Luc's neighbor said. "Is he doing what I think he's doing?" He began shouting to the nearest policeman. "Officer! Yo, Officer! Check out that guy over there! By the unit! Oh, man, stop him before he kills himself!"

Luc spotted a growing pool of blood by the handcuffed man's feet. His gorge rose as he realized the man was gnawing at his wrist, as if trying to chew it off.

The cop went over to him, saw what he was doing, and called the EMTs.

"Shit, I heard of trapped animals doing that," said the man in the Mets cap, his voice tinged with awe, "but never a human."

Luc could not reply. His throat felt frozen.

The preppy started kicking and screaming when the EMTs converged on him and tried to restrain him. As they surrounded the handcuffed man he continued to struggle and shout. Luc couldn't be sure but he thought he saw the cop's nightstick rise and fall once, and abruptly the man was silent. One of the EMTs signaled for a stretcher.

Feeling sick and weak, Luc turned and staggered away. What an awful, tragic scene.

And he was to blame.

3

"I think she's asleep," Gia whispered.

She sat on the bed next to her sleeping daughter, holding her hand. Jack stood on the other side.

"About time," he said, looking down at the skinny little form curled under the covers of her bed. He reached out and smoothed her dark hair. "Poor kid."

Vicky had huddled between Jack and Gia in the back of the cab, shaking and sobbing all the way home. Even the safety of her own bedroom hadn't calmed her.

"What kind of human garbage would frighten a child like that?" Gia said.

She hadn't actually seen what had happened, so she didn't know that the guy hadn't been trying simply to frighten Vicky—he'd been on the verge of tossing her down the steps and possibly to her death. Jack saw no point in enlightening Gia. She was already furious. Why make her sick?

"Never seen anything like it," Jack said. "Like they all went crazy at once."

"Who were they?" Gia said, then set her jaw. "No, never mind that; I don't care about the others. I don't care about the one who was pawing me. I just want to know who it was that frightened Vicky like this. And then I want to press charges against him and have him put away."

"Where they'll put him in a cell with a three-hundred-pound serial killer who'll rename him Alice?" Jack said.

Gia nodded. "For life."

"You think that'll happen?" he said softly.

"I'll *make* it happen."

"Can you identify him?"

Gia looked up at Jack. "No. I didn't get a good look at him. But you . . ." She looked away. "No, I guess you can't identify him, can you. Can't have testimony from someone who doesn't exist."

"And you don't want to put Vicky in the middle of all that—making identification, testifying, all for what? At best, his lawyer will get him off with a fine and a suspended sentence."

Gia shook her head and sighed. "It's not fair. He attacks me, scares my little girl half to death—he shouldn't be able to just walk away."

"Well, he's not walking. Looked like he wound up with a broken leg."

"Not enough," Gia said, staring at Vicky's face. "Not nearly enough."

"My sentiments exactly," Jack said. He leaned over and kissed the top of Gia's head. "Gotta run."

"Where are you going?"

"Gotta see a guy about something."

"You've got that look. . . ."

"I won't be long."

She nodded. "Be careful."

Jack let himself out onto Sutton Square and walked toward Sutton Place in search of a cab. Usually Gia would try to stop him, telling him to stay calm and stay put. But not tonight. Someone had frightened her daughter—*touched* her daughter—and she didn't want anyone thinking he could do such a thing and get away with it.

Neither did Jack.

He knew the guy could've killed her, and looked like he'd meant to. Jack tried to keep that fact at a distance, to maintain an oblique perspective. Not easy to do, but he knew if he got too close, if he thought about where Vicky might be now if he'd been delayed a single heartbeat, he'd blow again.

Needed to be cool and deliberate in his approach to this guy. Had to find a way to pound home the message that he must never try something like that again, not to any child, but especially not to Miss Victoria Westphalen. Jack considered Vicky his daughter. Genetically she had another father, but in every other way, in every corner of Jack's mind and heart, Vicks was his little girl. And someone who looked like Porky Pig had tried to kill her.

Bad move, Porky.

4

Mount Sinai Medical Center was right up the street from the museum, so Jack figured that was where the rioters and their victims would wind up. When he got there and saw all the cops and a few handcuffed guys in crested blue blazers, he knew he'd figured right.

The emergency department was in chaos. Doctors, nurses, and orderlies hurrying back and forth, doing triage, seeing the most serious cases first. Injured men, women, and even a few children were milling around or sitting with dazed looks on their faces. Some of the blazered guys were still causing trouble, shouting curses, struggling with the police. A disaster scene.

As Jack wandered around the waiting room, looking for Vicky's attacker, he picked up bits of the story. The wild men were all graduates of St. Barnabas Prep. Jack had heard of it: a rich kids' school located in the East Eighties. Seemed their twenty-fifth-reunion dinner party never got past the hors d'oeuvres. Arguments broke out toward the end of the cocktail hour. Over what? The quality of the canapés? Not enough horseradish in the cocktail sauce? Whatever. The arguments grew into fights that spilled out onto the street and from there escalated to a riot.

They were calling it a "preppy riot." Swell.

But where was the particular Porky preppy he wanted? Jack adopted a confused look and wandered into the treatment area. Peeked behind curtains and saw scalps and faces being stitched up, fingers and wrists being splinted, X-rays being studied, but no sign of the bastard he sought.

A security guard—big, black, with a no-nonsense air about him—stopped Jack. "Can I help you, sir?"

"I'm looking for a friend," Jack said.

"If you're not being treated, you'll have to return to the waiting area." He pointed over Jack's shoulder. "The lady at the registration desk can tell you if he's here."

Jack started to move back toward the waiting area. "I think he broke his leg."

"Then he's probably in the casting room, and you can't go in there."

"OK," Jack said, moving off. "Back to the waiting room."

Halfway there, he stopped a young Asian woman in green scrubs. "Where's the casting room?"

"Right there," she said, pointing to his left, then continued on her way.

You're sharp tonight, Jack thought sourly, staring at the wooden door with the black-and-white CASTING ROOM plaque dead center at eye level. Walked right past it.

He glanced up the hall. The security guard was turned away with his walkie-talkie against his face, so Jack pushed open the door and stepped inside.

And there he was. Dirty, disheveled, his hair matted with blood, he lay on a gurney with a nurse by his side and a doctor wrapping his right leg in some sort of fiberglass mesh. His looked different with his eyes glazed and jaw slackened from whatever they'd shot him up with to keep him quiet, but this was the guy. Porky. Jack felt his jaw muscles bunch. Would have loved, dearly loved, a chance to give the doctor cause to work on the other leg and both arms and maybe carve some bacon off his hide, but the cop watching from the head of the gurney would surely object.

Jack stood statue still, scanning the room. Had only a few seconds before he was spotted. Especially didn't want Porky to see him—might accuse him of tossing him off the steps—but now that he'd found him, Jack wanted his name. Spotted a clipboard atop some X-rays on the counter to his left. Snagged it and stepped back into the hallway.

The top sheet was an intake form, with "Butler, Robert B." printed across the top. A West Sixty-seventh Street address. Jack knew the building—a luxury high-rise maybe twenty blocks from his place. He memorized Butler's unit number, leaned the clipboard against the door, and headed for the exit.

Jack and Robert B. Butler, graduate of St. Barnabas Prep, had been living just a short walk away from each other for who knew how long. About time they got acquainted.

THURSDAY

1

Jack was up early and on his way downtown, enjoying the mild May weather. Too nice a morning to ponder his as yet unscheduled confrontation with the porky prep. Jack hadn't yet figured on the right approach to Mr. Butler, but it would come. Right now he was headed for a meeting with a new customer. Because she was a referral, and because he trusted the referrer, he'd agreed to meet Dr. Nadia Radzminsky on her turf. At this hour her turf was a storefront diabetes clinic on Seventeenth Street, between Union Square and Irving Place, next to a laundromat.

Jack stepped inside and found the front area filled with a jumble of races and sexes, all shabbily dressed. The young mocha-skinned, white-uniformed nurse at the desk took one look at him and seemed to know he didn't belong. Not that he was all that well dressed, but his faded flannel shirt, worn jeans, and scuffed tan work boots were still a few cuts above what everyone else here was wearing.

"Can I help you?"

"I'm looking for Dr. Radzminsky. She's expecting me."

The nurse sifted through the papers on her desk and came up with a yellow sticky note. "Yes. You're Jack? She said to take you right in."

She led him through a curtained doorway, past a pair of curtained examining rooms—he caught a whiff of rubbing alcohol from the one on the right—to a tiny office in the rear. A young woman with straight dark hair cut in a bob sat behind the desk. She glanced up and smiled as they entered. She looked very young—couldn't be a day over twenty. Too young to be a doctor.

"You must be Jack," she said, rising and extending her hand. She stood about five-four and had a compact frame, a stocky build—solid without being overweight.

"And you must be Dr. Radzminsky."

"Nadia, please," she said, pronouncing it "Nahd-ja." "Only my patients call me Doctor." She had a big open face, a welcoming smile, and bright dark eyes. Jack liked her immediately. "Thanks, Jasmine," she said to the nurse.

Jasmine closed the door behind her.

Nadia pointed to one of the chart-laden chairs. "Just put those on the floor and have a seat."

She offered coffee and poured him a Styrofoam cupful from a Mr. Coffee on a shelf.

"We've got sugar and Cremora."

"Two sugars'll do."

"My only vice," she said, sipping from an oversize black ceramic mug with NADJ printed in big white letters along the side. "An indispensable habit you pick up in residency."

"Can I ask you something straight off?" Jack said.

"Sure."

"No offense, but are you old enough to be a doctor?"

She gave him a tolerant smile. "Everyone asks me that. Yes. I'm cursed with a baby face. A blessing if you're a model or an actress, but not when you're a doctor, especially a woman doctor trying to inspire respect and confidence. But trust me, I'm a fellowship-trained, board-eligible endocrinologist."

"That's hormones, right?"

"Right. I do glands—thyroid, parathyroid, adrenal, pituitary, pancreas, and so on. Diabetes is one of the mainstays of endocrinology, which is why I'm here, but my special interest is in steroids."

"Muscle juice?"

Another smile. "Anabolic steroids are just one kind. Cortisone is another; so is estrogen. Remember what that guy whispered to Dustin Hoffman in *The Graduate*?"

"Sure. 'Plastics.' "

"Right. One of my professors did the same thing for me once. He said, 'Steroids . . . the future is steroids.' And over the years I became convinced he was right. Even got to contribute some original research to the field. But enough about me, what about you? Whatever did you do for Alicia Clayton to make her recommend you so highly?"

Jack wasn't going to answer that. "How do you know Alicia?"

"High school. We weren't really friends, but we were both A students so we had advanced classes together. She went away to college, but now she's back and we keep running into each other. We're friends now. I told her about a problem I had and she gave me your number." Nadia cocked her head at Jack, a puzzled look on her face. "She said I could trust you with my life."

Hope she didn't give you any details, he thought.

"Is your life in danger?"

"No. But the way she said it—what on earth did you *do* for her?"

"I'm sure Alicia can fill you in on all the details."

"That's just it. She won't say anything further than it was sometime around last Christmas." Nadia smiled. "She said you were discreet too, and now I see what she meant."

As pleasant as this young woman was, Jack wanted to get to the point. "What can I do for you, Nadia?"

"It's about my boss."

Please, not a sexual harassment thing, Jack thought. A stalker he could handle, but innuendo and suggestive behavior were too slippery.

"The guy who runs this place?"

"No. The clinic is run by a hospital, and I just volunteer here."

"You give these folks insulin shots?"

"No. A nurse handles that. I monitor their charts, test for end organ damage, manage the cases. We treat mostly homeless folk here. Imagine being a homeless diabetic—no place to keep your insulin chilled, no way to check your blood sugar, unable to buy clean needles."

Pretty grim, Jack thought. And now he could see how Nadia and Alicia Clayton had connected. Alicia ran the pediatric AIDS clinic near St. Vincent's, just a few blocks to the west of here.

She went on. "My paying job—which I've only had for a couple of weeks now—is with a pharmaceutical company called GEM Pharma. Ever heard of it?"

Jack shook his head. Merck and Pfizer, yes, but never GEM.

"It's a small company," she said. "Mostly they manufacture and market generic prescription drugs—antibiotics, antihypertensives, and such on which the patents have run out. But unlike most companies of their type, GEM does basic research—not a lot, but they at least make a stab at it. That's why I was hired—for their R and D Department."

"A couple of weeks and already your boss is hassling you?"

"No. Someone is hassling *him*. At least I think so."

Good, Jack thought. It's not sexual. "And why's that?"

"I saw him arguing with a man in the corporate offices. They were down the far end of a hall. They didn't see me, and they weren't shouting, so I don't know what the argument was about, but I saw the other man shove him, then walk out, looking very angry."

"Not a disgruntled employee, I take it."

"No, but the man looked vaguely familiar. It took the rest of the day before I could place him. Then I remembered. He was Milos Dragovic."

Well, well, well, Jack thought, remembering a guy who'd contacted him recently about a beef with Milos Dragovic. Two customers interested in Dragovic in as many weeks. That boy do get around.

Nadia was staring at him. "I can't believe you haven't heard of him." She must have misinterpreted his silence.

"Oh, I have. Everyone's heard of the Slippery Serb."

That was what the *Post* had dubbed Dragovic a couple of years ago. And he lived up to the title. He'd faced indictments for gunrunning, racketeering, procuring, even murder, and had walked on every one. A sharp dresser who hobnobbed with celebrities at all the in restaurants and hot nightspots, Milos Dragovic had replaced John "the Dapper Don" Gotti as the city's chic hood.

"You're sure it was him?" Jack said.

"Totally. I dug out an old copy of *New York* magazine that had a cover story on him. Milos Dragovic, no question."

"And he's pushing your boss around. Any idea why?"

"That's what I'd like you to find out."

"Well, since your guy works for a drug company—"

"He's one of the founders."

"Even better. Doesn't take a genius to figure out that pharmaceuticals of a less than legal nature must be involved. Why not call the cops and tell them the Slippery Serb is shaking down your boss? I'm sure they'd love to know."

"Because Dragovic may have something on him, some secret he's blackmailing him with. And he may already have coerced him into doing something illegal. I don't want to see him go to jail or get hurt."

As Nadia was speaking, Jack picked up on something: a timbre in her voice, a look in her eyes as she spoke about her boss at a job she'd had for only a few weeks. More than just a professional relationship here?

"Just who is this boss you care about so much?"

Nadia hesitated, chewing her upper lip, then shrugged. "Oh, hell. I've gone this far, I might as well tell you: his name is Dr. Luc Monnet."

"Like the painter?"

"Same pronunciation, but with a double *n.*"

There, Nadia thought. I've told him. I hope I'm not going to regret it.

The last thing in the world she wanted to do was cause trouble for Dr. Monnet. In fact, the very reason she'd called this Repairman Jack was to try to protect him.

Relax, she told herself. Alicia had said she could trust this man. And Alicia Clayton's trust was not easily won.

But after the way she'd talked about him, Nadia had expected Jack to have a commanding presence, be six-two at least and built like a fullback. The man sipping coffee on the other side of her desk was a very average Joe—midthirties, good-looking but hardly dazzling, with brown hair, brown eyes, and an easy way, dressed like men she passed hundreds of time a day on the city streets.

I want the man I can trust with my life to be like Clint Eastwood or Arnold Schwarzenegger, she thought. Not a younger poor man's Kevin Costner.

But then she remembered Alicia's warning: Don't let Jack's mild Mr. Everyman act fool you; his bite is infinitely worse than his bark.

"I gather he's more than just a boss to you," Jack said.

The offhandedness of the remark jolted Nadia. Is it that obvious?

She tried to make her shrug equally offhanded. "We go back a ways. He was one of my professors in medical school."

"The one who said, 'The future is steroids'?"

She nodded, glad to note that he'd been paying attention. "He inspired me to go into endocrinology. I owe him for that."

Jack stared at her, as if saying, Go on. . . . I know there's more.

Oh, yes, there was. Lots. But Nadia was not about to confess to a stranger about the mad crush she'd had on Luc Monnet back in med school. His black curly hair, as dark as his glistening eyes, his fine features, his trim body, but most of all his *manner.* With his aristocratic bearing and his delicious, oh-so-faint French accent, he'd simply *reeked* of the Continent. Nadia had been so enthralled that she'd dreamed of seducing him, even worked out a way to go about it. She remembered the old fantasy. . . .

She'd seen herself entering his office and locking the door behind her. She'd never kidded herself that she had fashion model looks, but she knew she was no bowwow either. And on more than one occasion she'd caught Dr. Monnet looking at her, so the thought that she could do it wasn't completely off-the-wall. She'd be wearing a tight short top and a miniskirt worn low to expose her navel. She'd ask him for a clarification on hormone levels and sexual response. She'd work her way around the desk till she was standing next to him, rubbing a hip against him as he reviewed molecular structures. If he didn't take that bait, then she'd simply take his hand and place it on her bare inner thigh. After that, temperatures would rise, clothes would be shed, and he'd take her right there on his desk, demonstrating along the way that he was an expert in the lovemaking art for which the French were famous.

And it had remained pure fantasy until one day near the end of the term. . . .

Nadia shifted to banish the faint tingling in her pelvis. Doug Gleason was the man in her life now—now and forever.

"You owe him enough to play guardian angel?" Jack said.

"Curtis Sliwa I'm not. But what should I do when I think that the man who inspired me toward my life's work and gave me my first job is being coerced into doing something most likely illegal?"

"How do you know it's coercion?" Jack said.

"Come on. If a known thug is physically pushing him around, I've got to believe he's pushing him around in other ways as well."

Jack was nodding slowly. "Yeah. That would follow. So what would you like me to do about it?"

"A number of things." Nadia had worked out an algorithm for the Monnet situation, much like the ones the medical journals worked up for diagnosis and treatment of a given disorder. She pictured the boxes and decision points in her mind as she spoke. "First we have to determine the connection between Dr. Monnet and Milos Dragovic. If it's all perfectly legal—which I very much doubt—then we drop it right there. If it's *not* so legal, then we move on. And if Dr. Monnet is being coerced, I want it stopped."

Jack's eyes bored into her. "And if he's a willing participant in something illegal, with no coercion, then what?"

That was the final leg of Nadia's algorithm, a blank box she hadn't filled in. She hoped, *prayed* she wouldn't have to. She couldn't imagine Dr. Monnet willingly involved in anything illegal. He was already wealthy. He didn't need money.

But then she thought of the sleazy junk bond dealers in the eighties who'd ripped off hundreds of millions in a single year. But did they quit while they were ahead—*way* ahead? No. They wanted still more. The money itself had ceased to matter. It was the high from the risk that kept them pushing for more and more until finally they were caught.

Was Dr. Monnet's aloof demeanor merely a facade? Could a hunger for risk, a need for speed, a jones for adrenaline boil beneath that controlled surface?

This man sitting before her might come up with answers to questions she didn't want asked. But she had to do something. And she had to trust that an important person in her life did not have feet of clay.

She sighed. "I don't think you'll find that. But if you do, I'll make up my mind then."

"Fair enough," Jack said. "I'll need some addresses—his home, the company's corporate offices—phone numbers: yours, his, work, home, and so on."

Nadia pulled an envelope from her purse. "I've got them all right here. I've also written up what I know of his life, his training, his research, plus all I know about the company, GEM Pharma."

Jack smiled. "Efficient. I like that."

"There's just one problem," she said, feeling her stomach tighten. Alicia had told her about the Repairman Jack's usual fee. "Money."

"Yeah, well, I do charge for my services."

"Of course. I can't imagine you wouldn't; it's just that I'm only recently out of residency, and I just started this new job, and I was wondering . . ."

Jack hadn't moved, but she sensed that he'd somehow receded.

"If I'd cut my price?" He shook his head. "I don't haggle, especially when someone like Dragovic is involved. Sometimes I go on a contingency basis, but this isn't that sort of job."

Well, at least I tried, Nadia thought. "Ok, then, can I make time payments?"

He sat there staring at her for what felt to her like an eternity.

"Tell you what," he said finally. "Someone else contacted me about a matter involving Mr. Dragovic—just last week as a matter of fact. If I can find a way to work the two of them together, I may be able to give you a break on the fee."

"And if you can't?"

He shrugged. "I don't do time payments—a guy in my position has no legal means to go after a welsher. But since Alicia vouched for you, I'll make an exception."

Relief flooded her. "Then you'll do it?"

"I'll look into it; that's all I promise."

Nadia drew another envelope from her pocketbook and hesitated. Ten $100 bills crinkled within. A lot of money to hand to a man she'd met only moments ago. But despite his bland looks, she sensed a core of steely determination. All her instincts testified that he was the man.

"All right, then. Here's a thousand as—what? A retainer?"

He smiled as he took the envelope and tucked it away without looking inside. "Retainer, down payment, whatever you like."

"Don't I get a receipt?"

Another smile as he shook his head. "No receipts, no written reports, no evidence that we've ever met." He rose and extended his right hand across the desk. "It's all right here."

She took his hand.

"There's our contract," he said, still clasping her hand. "You trust me to do what I say I'll do, I trust you to compensate me for it."

"Trust," she said softly. "What a concept."

He released her hand and reached for the doorknob. "I'll be in touch."

And then he was gone and Nadia was alone, fighting a sudden wave of apprehension. Anyone watching her hand over a thousand dollars to a complete stranger would have thought her crazy. But money had nothing to do with her worry—although she had nothing in writing, Nadia sensed she had a contract etched in stone.

No, it was a gnawing uncertainty about what she just had set in motion and a premonition that it would end badly.

2

As Jack walked toward Park Avenue, looking for a cab uptown, he heard someone call to him.

"Yo, Jack!"

He turned and saw One-leg Lenny leaning against the wall of the Union Square Theater; he held his crutch in one hand and was rattling the change in the bottom of a Styrofoam cup with the other. His right leg stopped just below the knee.

"Hey, Lenny," Jack said. His real name was Jerry something, but he seemed to prefer the alliterative Lenny. "What're you doing down here?"

"Collectin' unemployment . . . the usual."

Lenny wore a fatigue jacket and his tangled graying hair looked like he'd lost his comb in Nam and hadn't bothered to replace it. He kept a three-day stubble on his weathered cheeks and dressed in raggedy shirts and oversize denims—always oversize. He looked fifty but could have been forty or sixty.

"Not exactly the usual," Jack said, pointing to Lenny's foreshortened right leg. "Every time I've seen you, the left one's been missing. What gives?"

"My hip's been bothering me lately, so I've been switching off."

Jack still couldn't figure how Lenny managed to strap his lower leg up behind him without a noticeable bulge. Had to be uncomfortable as all hell, but he claimed it helped him collect enough change to make it worthwhile.

"Say, listen, Jack," he said, lowering his voice. "I got a fine new product."

"Not today." Jack knew that Lenny dealt to supplement his pan-handling.

"No, really, it's not the usual. This stuff's new and *so* sweet. I'll give you a taste, on the house."

"No, thanks."

"My regulars down here sure like it. Leaves your head clear and don't lay no jones on you."

"Sounds wonderful. Maybe some other time."

"OK. You just let me know."

Jack waved and moved on, forgetting Lenny and reviewing last week's meeting with the customer who'd wanted to see him about Dragovic. Jack had gone all the way out to Staten Island to meet him . . . for nothing.

Jack had started easing back on using Julio's for his meetings, ever since last month when he'd been standing at the bar, sipping a brew, and this guy walked in and asked if Repairman Jack was around. Julio, his usual cool self, said lots of guys named Jack came in and out all day. Was he supposed to meet this Jack here? Guy said no, he'd just heard that this was his hang and he needed to talk to him. Julio had sent him off, telling him he had the wrong place.

Jack didn't want anyplace known as his "hang"—not good for him and maybe not good for Julio. He did his utmost to work his fixes anonymously, but every so often he had to get in someone's face. He'd collected a few enemies over the years. More than a few.

So when Jack got a call last week from someone named Sal Vituolo about hiring him for a fix-it, Jack had made the trip to Staten Island. Turned out Sal wanted him to "whack"—he'd really used the word—Milos Dragovic. Jack explained that he didn't "whack" people for money, and returned to Manhattan.

But now he was thinking maybe he should drop in on good ol' Sal and see if he'd settle for something less than a "whack." Jack might be crossing paths with Dragovic for Nadia anyway, so why not let Sal Vituolo pay some of the freight.

But first he needed to check with Abe, see what he knew about Dragovic.

He raised his hand as he reached Park Avenue South and saw a cab swing into the curb, but it stopped downstream by a woman in a red suit who'd been there ahead of him. As she opened the rear door, a man in a dark blue suit darted up, nudged her aside with his briefcase, and slid into the cab. Jack watched in amazement as the woman, screeching curses, ripped the briefcase from his hand and tossed it across the sidewalk. The shocked and now embarrassed man jumped out of the cab and went after it.

Jack had to smile. Good for you, lady. Serves the bastard right.

Somebody nearby shouted, "You go, girl!"

Jack was turning to look for another cab when he noticed that instead of climbing into the cab, the woman now was going after the ride snatcher. As she rushed up behind him she pulled a pair of scissors from her coat pocket and began doing the Mother Bates thing. He shouted in pain and terror as the scissors rose and fell, jabbing into a shoulder, a thigh, his back. She was going for his neck when the cabbie and a passerby grabbed her and disarmed her. Still screeching, she attacked them with her fists.

Maybe I'll just walk, Jack thought.

3

"You were there?" Abe said around a mouthful of bagel. "At this so-called preppy riot?"

Abe Grossman's Isher Sports Shop wasn't officially open at this hour, but Jack knew Abe was an early riser who didn't have much of a life outside his business. He'd knocked on the window, waved his bag of bagels, and Abe had let him in.

" 'Riot' is something of an overstatement," Jack said, pulling a few sesame seeds off his bagel and spreading them on the counter for Parabellum. Abe's pale blue parakeet hopped over and began pecking at them. "More like a whacked-out brawl. But it had some dicey moments."

Abe, midfifties, balding, his belly straining against his white shirt, was perched on his stool on the far side of the scarred counter. His stock of bikes and Rollerblades and hockey sticks and anything else remotely related to a sport was scattered helter-skelter on shelves, floors, counters, or hung from the ceiling: layout by tornado.

He winced when Jack told him what had almost happened to Vicky. "And this joker . . . he's still upright and breathing?"

"For the moment."

"But you have plans to make adjustments in that state of affairs, I assume?"

"I'm working on it." He didn't want to talk about Robert B. Butler now. "Know anything about Milos Dragovic?"

Abe's bagel paused in midair, halfway to his mouth. "A nice man he's not."

"Tell me something I don't know."

"He got his start in my business."

"Guns?"

Abe nodded. "In the Balkans. A true product of the nineties, Dragovic. Made a fortune with his brother running guns to both sides during the Bosnia thing. They grew up here but were born over there. Their father was in some sort of Serb militia during World War Two so they had ins. The brothers Dragovic came back rich with a small army of Serb vets that they had used to muscle into various rackets—drugs, numbers, prostitution, loan-sharking, anything that turned a profit."

"Midnineties, right? Yeah, I remember a lot of drive-bys and shoot-'em-ups back then. Didn't know it was Dragovic's work."

"Not all of them, of course, but he contributed his share. The brothers then tied themselves in with the Russians and used Brighton Beach as a launching pad against the Haitians and Dominicans. Totally ruthless from what I hear."

"A little local ethnic cleansing, eh?"

"You might say. Then when the Kosovo thing started, Milos and his brother—I can't remember his name—went back to guns, but the brother got killed in some deal that went sour. Milos came back richer and more powerful."

"What's his organization like?"

"He's a control freak. No lieutenant or right-hand man; micromanages everything himself. Not much of an entourage—thinks that shows weakness—and likes the fast lane."

"Yeah, he do love to get his picture in the paper."

"And now a club he's building, so all the beautiful people will come to him. He took over one of Regine's defunct places. And what name, do you think?"

"Milos's Mosh Pit?"

"No. Worse: Belgravy."

Jack had to laugh. "No!"

"But it won't open till the fall, so for reservations you still have time." He looked at Jack over his glasses. "You're getting involved with this man?"

Jack shrugged. "I've found two people in as many weeks with a beef against him."

"Be careful. He's a mean one. Not afraid to get his own hands dirty—*likes* it, I'm told."

"Dirty as in red and wet?"

"Exactly."

Jack blew out a breath. "Well, I wasn't thinking of getting in close."

"Good thinking. With that man, arm's length is too close."

Abe finished his bagel and brushed off his littered shirtfront. The parakeet raced around, gobbling up the cascade of crumbs.

"Look at my Parabellum," he said. "Better than a Dustbuster, that bird." He shook his head. "Listen to me. I'm *kvelling* about a parakeet."

"You've got to get out more, Abe."

"I should go out like a schnook so I can get roughed up by some middle-aged marauders? Feh! I read the papers." He waved a pudgy hand at his stack of newspapers; Abe read all the papers every day—the *Times,* the *Daily News,* the *Post, Newsday,* the *Village Voice,* even the pink-sheeted weekly *Observer.* "A jungle out there. I'm better off at home watching *I Love Lucy* reruns."

"Come on. The city's so safe lately it's practically a theme park."

"So the mayor and his minions say, but I see the shiny mantle slipping. I perceive a contrarian trend. And besides, if the city should be too safe, it could be bad for business."

"It's great for business—except maybe yours."

Abe didn't sell enough sporting goods to pay the rent, let alone make a living. His real stock was hidden beneath their feet: if it fired a bullet, Abe sold it.

"Sales falling off?"

Abe shrugged. "Falling off, no. Flat, yes. But that's not bad. It could mean I'm reaching my goal."

"The polite society?"

Abe nodded. His idea of the ideal society was one where everyone was armed at all times. He truly believed in the Heinlein adage that an *armed* society is a *polite* society.

"What about you? How's demand for Repairman Jack's services?"

"Strong as ever. Probably won't slack off till the system works."

Abe laughed. "Such a bright future you have. But seriously. Did you ever think that maybe the city is too safe and that's why so many people are going *meshugge?* Maybe they were so used to feeling threatened that now that they aren't, all that pent-up, unspent adrenaline is blowing their tops."

Jack stared at him. This was what he loved most about Abe: his crazy theories. But he'd never tell him that.

Abe stared back. "Nu?"

"That's the stupidest thing I've ever heard."

"Then how do you explain all those otherwise law-abiding middle-aged preppies going on a rampage last night? Or how about this?" He looked down at the *New York Post* that lay spread out on the counter between them. "Where was it? I just—oy, Parabellum!"

"Looks like your feathered Dustbuster left you a thank-you note."

Abe grabbed a tissue and wiped up the droppings. He pointed to a column of type. "Here it is. An article about this advertising firm's CEO who hears that their biggest account is being transferred to another shop. What does he do? He picks up a paperweight and starts beating on the account exec who was in charge. Kills him almost. This is normal?"

Jack thought of the murderous rage of the cab lady but didn't mention her. Abe would only say it bolstered his theory.

"It's a big city. Takes all kinds."

"This isn't an isolated incident. All over, I'm seeing it. A trend, I tell you. People flying off the handle for no reason—or for just a little reason maybe. And all because the city is too safe. Pent-up adrenaline. Congested spleens. Something must be done."

Abe was on a roll, and Jack would have loved to hang around and see how far he could ride this, but he had to go.

"Does this train of thought have a caboose?"

"Not yet."

"I know just the thing, then," Jack said, heading for the door. "Start passing a petition for a more dangerous New York. And while you're doing that, I'll go see a new customer."

"Be careful out there," Abe called after him. "Spleens exploding everywhere."

4

Nadia felt giddy as she entered the fashionably retro art deco lobby of the gleaming thirty-story office building on East Thirty-fourth Street, her earlier apprehensions swept away by a surge of anticipation: finally, after two weeks of orientation and acclimation, she would be introduced to the project she had been hired for.

But her euphoria condensed into a cold leaden lump in her stomach when she recognized one of the men sharing her elevator. He looked fiftyish, and his beige-and-charcoal glen plaid suit had to cost a couple of thousand dollars, maybe more considering the tailoring that must have been necessary for the perfect fit around his broad shoulders; his highly polished black shoes were made out of some sort of patterned leather—lizard, rattlesnake, or some other appropriate reptile—no tie, but a diamond stud secured the deacon's collar of his shirt. His gelled jet hair swept straight back from his ruddy face like a glistening pelt, accentuating his high cheekbones, strong nose, and thin lips. His cold dark eyes swept through the elevator cab, lingered briefly on Nadia, then moved on, a raptor cataloging the immediately available rodent population.

Milos Dragovic.

Nadia's mood sank even further when she saw him press the 16 button, already lit because she'd pressed it a few seconds earlier.

He was going to the GEM offices. Why? To shake down Dr. Monnet again? She couldn't stand this. It had to be stopped. She was suddenly glad she'd hired Jack. All lingering doubts vanished. She had done the right thing.

She watched Milos Dragovic out of the corner of her eye. No question he had a commanding presence, sort of what she'd expected from Repairman Jack. He radiated power, a true alpha male who didn't want anyone to forget it. Here was a man who needed to be noticed—*demanded* to be noticed—whereas Jack seemed to prefer invisibility.

Nadia could see why models and starlets and celebrities were attracted to Dragovic. Something primal about his features, his hair, his build, his bearing. If there was such a thing as animal magnetism, Milos Dragovic had it.

She sniffed. The elevator car quickly had become redolent of his musky cologne—probably Eau de Testosterone or the like.

He seemed to be alone. Nadia glanced around. The other half-dozen occupants of the car appeared to be average workaday souls like her. Didn't hoods like Dragovic travel with bodyguards and gofers?

Finally the car stopped at the sixteenth floor, the home of GEM Pharma's corporate offices. Dragovic stepped out ahead of her where he faced a wall of glass etched with the GEM Pharma logo. Claudine the receptionist spotted Nadia through the glass and buzzed her in with a wave and a smile. Dragovic pushed through behind her.

"Excuse me, sir—" Claudine began.

"I have meeting with your bosses," Dragovic said in a deep, sharp, slightly accented voice, never slowing or bothering even to look at her.

Claudine glanced down at her schedule book. "I have nothing about a meeting here."

"That is because *I* call meeting, sweetheart."

Dragovic kept moving. No hesitation—he seemed to know exactly where he was going, striding down the hallway toward the boardroom as if he owned the place.

"I'm not your sweetheart," Claudine said in a low voice.

"Call security," Nadia said.

Claudine shrugged. "What's the point? Nobody ever objects when he busts in."

Nadia watched Dragovic's back, furious. Where did he get off bulling his way in here like this? She was tempted to follow him and see if she could eavesdrop on this meeting. But that could be risky. If she got caught it might mean a one-way ticket back to the sidewalk.

Taking a deep breath, Nadia told herself she was not going to let this ruin her big day. She headed directly for the center of the GEM offices where the stairs down to the research level were located. The company leased two floors in this building: the upper housed most of the corporate business, marketing, and sales offices; the basic research department—Dr. Monnet's baby—was on the lower level and, for security reasons, could be reached only through the corporate floor. The elevator did not make that stop.

She ran her ID card through the magnetic swipe reader and heard the lock click open. She hurried down the stairs and waved to some of the techs and programmers on the way to her office. Once there, she stepped inside, slipped into a white lab coat, then headed for the coffeepot.

Nadia noticed her hand trembling as she poured herself a cup. Too much caffeine, or still-simmering anger at Milos Dragovic?

. . . That is because I *call meeting, sweetheart. . . .*

The arrogance. What kind of power could he have over the GEM officers? She'd give anything to know what was happening in that conference room now.

5

"I do not want excuses!" Milos Dragovic shouted, slamming his hand on the table. He noted with satisfaction how Garrison and Edwards jumped. Monnet, the prick, simply pursed his lips, like he had a sour taste in his mouth. "I want my shipment and I want it now!"

Milos stared down at the three principals of GEM Pharma across the mahogany conference table from him. He knew all about these Harvard graduates: Garrison, Edwards, and Monnet had got together a dozen years ago and started the company. G-E-M—their initials. Cute.

To Dragovic's left sat Kent Garrison, the chubby, red-haired, perpetually wrinkled MBA who oversaw the day-to-day business. Next to him was Brad Edwards, the dark, slim, rich, pretty-boy lawyer who had put up much of the firm's start-up capital; he ran the legal department and acted as comptroller.

And last but not least by a very long shot, dapper Dr. Luc Monnet, head of R and D, one seat away from the other two. Monnet was the partner with both a Ph.D. and an M.D., who published supposedly groundbreaking papers about things only three people in the world could understand.

Monnet . . . simply looking at the man set Milos on edge. Something about him made Milos want to flatten his frog nose. Maybe it was his air of superiority, as if he were royalty or something. Or maybe it was the way he looked at Milos, as if he'd crawled out from under a rock. Milos could stare the other two down in a couple of heartbeats, but Monnet . . . Monnet crossed his arms, leaned back, and matched him eye for eye.

Milos clenched his jaw. I can buy and sell you, Monnet. My folks were immigrants just like yours. We both started with nothing, but I made the big bucks while you were pulling down a teacher's salary, living in genteel poverty. Now you're rich too, but only because of *my* connections. Without me you'd be bankrupt.

And yet he knew Monnet looked down on him, as if he sat high on some pedestal of savoir faire that Milos could never reach.

"Sorry, Milos," Monnet said in that cultured voice of his. "The next shipment of Loki won't be ready until early next week."

"It's true," Garrison said. Ropes of sweat trailed over his pudgy cheeks. Stick an apple in his mouth and he'd look like a roast suckling pig. "We'd give it to you if we had it—you know that."

"A-a-and let's face it," Edwards said. "We don't make any money by *not* shipping, right? But this run is about to turn. We won't be able to start a new run until the weekend."

"Perhaps I don't have your attention. Yes? Is that it?" Milos said, thickening his accent. He turned, lifted a chair, and hurled it against the wall. "Now! Do you hear? I want Loki shipment *now!*"

His parents had brought him here from Herzegovina at age five. His father had been a Chetnik during World War Two who had found it impossible to live under the Communists afterward. He escaped and brought his family to Brooklyn, where they had never felt at ease. Milos had spent most of his childhood and adolescence scrubbing his speech of any trace of his foreign roots. He'd succeeded. By high school he could speak accent-free English. But as he'd moved into quasi-legal circles, he learned that a bit of an accent could be useful—for charming or threatening, depending on the context. So by age twenty Milos Dragovic had backpedaled and begun imitating his father's English.

"It's not there to give you!" Edwards wailed, cowering in his seat.

"Why not? You are selling to someone else? Yes? This is why you don't give me shipment?"

"God, no!" said Garrison. "We'd *never* do anything like that!"

"You damn better not! If I find you give Dragovic's Loki to someone else, I wring your necks like chickens!" He pressed his two fists together, thumb to thumb, and twisted.

Edwards winced.

"So," Milos said, placing his hands on his hips. "If no one else has my Loki, where is it?"

"We don't have it!" Edwards said. He looked like he was going to cry.

Milos hid a smile. He loved torturing these wimps. He knew they ran dry every month, knew damn well they weren't selling to anybody else, but he couldn't resist striking the fear of God—in this case, a vengeful god called Milos—into their blue-blooded hearts.

He looked forward to these little meetings. And this windowless, soundproof, electronically secure boardroom was perfect. He could shout, throw things, and no one outside had a clue as to what was going on. Milos preferred to drop in without notice, sans bodyguards—he didn't want anyone else in his organization knowing the origin of Loki—and terrorize the wimps for a few minutes, then take off, leaving them quaking in their brown-stained undershorts.

All except Monnet.

Keep up the game face, Doctor, Milos thought. I've got something special saved, just for you, something that will wipe that smug expression clean off your ugly little face.

Monnet sighed. "How many times do we have to go through this?

The Loki molecule becomes unstable. When that happens we need to secure a new template. We will have that by tomorrow. We will start running it immediately. We will test its potency and then go into full-scale production."

Milos leaned forward on the table, glaring at the smaller man. "Is Dr. Monnet"—he made sure to mispronounce it Moe-*nett*—"saying that I am stupid?"

Monnet held his gaze. "Quite the contrary. I think you are far more intelligent than you would like us to think. Which makes these transparent displays of ferocity fruitless and redundant."

Monnet's blasé tone made Milos want to rip his head off. But he calmed himself and decided it was time for an about-face. Time to reconfirm their suspicions that he was utterly psycho.

He straightened and flashed them his best smile. "You are right, of course," he said softly, genially. "We should not fight. We are brothers, yes? In my heart I trust you as no others." He clapped his hands once. "So. When should your brother expect his next shipment?"

Garrison and Edwards turned nervously toward Monnet.

"We'll do a trial run of the new template tomorrow, test it late Friday or early Saturday morning. If all goes well, we'll start production immediately. Because of Memorial Day, the first shipment won't go out till Tuesday morning. But it will be a big one."

"Excellent! I will be out of town for the weekend"—he caught the looks of relief on Garrison's and Edwards's faces—"but I will stay in touch."

"Going to Europe?" Edwards said, a hopeful gleam in his eye.

"No," Milos said. "The Hamptons. *East* Hampton. I am having housewarming parties for my new home on the ocean. I would invite all of you, but I know that you will be too busy making my Loki, yes?"

"Absolutely," Garrison said, with Edwards vigorously nodding in agreement.

Milos fixed his gaze on Monnet. As usual, he hadn't been able to rattle him with threats and noise. But he had something special for Dr. Monnet, something he'd saved till now.

"I especially wish the good doctor could join the parties. I will be serving a nice little wine I picked up recently. A Bordeaux. You have heard of Château Petrus, yes?"

He saw Monnet stiffen. His tone was guarded. "Yes."

"But of course you have. It is from your homeland. I am silly. Yes, I bought six bottles of Château Petrus 1947 Cru Exceptionnel last night, and I will be drinking them all this weekend. It is such a shame you cannot be there to have some. I understand it is quite good."

Milos watched with glee as the color faded from Monnet's cheeks, leaving him wide-eyed, livid, and—for once—speechless.

"Have a nice day," Milos said, then turned, unlocked the door, and pushed out into the hall.

6

Luc fought to regain his composure as the door shut behind Dragovic. If he had a gun right now, he would walk out into the hall and shoot the man. He'd never fired a gun before but somehow, with Dragovic as the target, he was sure he could manage it.

At least he would if he could make his legs work. Dragovic's words had left him weak in the knees. Had that . . . that ape been tailing him? That could be the only explanation. One of Dragovic's men must have followed him to Sotheby's and called his boss when Luc started bidding. Dragovic had sat home and outbid him.

Why? Luc wondered. Certainly not because his Slavic palate could appreciate a fine Pomerol. The only reason could be . . . simply to frustrate me.

Again, why? Because I don't tremble whenever he looks my way?

If the wine episode was meant to drive home that Milos Dragovic was not a man to be taken lightly, he'd wasted his money. Luc had been forced to accept that.

Brad Edwards moaned as he stepped to the door and relocked it. "How did we ever get involved with this maniac?"

"You know how," Kent Garrison said. He mopped his florid face on his shirtsleeve. "And you damn well know why."

Brad nodded slowly, sorrowfully. "Yes, I do." He dropped his tidy frame back into a chair. "But what's worse, I don't see how we'll ever be free of him."

"I do," Luc said, finally finding his voice.

His partners sprang upright, chorusing, "You do? How?"

"By not supplying him with any more Loki."

"Not funny, Luc!" Brad said, holding up a manicured hand as if to block the words in midair. "Don't even *joke* about that!"

"I'm not," he said, feeling the dread slip over him. "We may not have a choice."

The sound of Kent's nervous swallow filled the tiny room. "You mean what you said about the source drying up? You don't think that's happened, do you?"

"No. We're safe this time. I would have been informed to the contrary." At least Luc hoped Oz would have called. "But I have my doubts, serious doubts, about next time."

"Oh, God!" Brad said, visibly trembling. "You mean this could be it? In four weeks we come up empty? Dragovic will kill us!"

"Yes," Luc said softly. "He probably will. Or at least try."

But he'll have to find me first, Luc thought.

He could get lost in Provence where no one, especially a Serb swine, would find him. But Kent and Brad . . .

Kent made a noise that sounded like a sob. "We have to tell him, prepare him, convince him that it's not our fault!"

"Do you really think you can do that?" Luc said. "The man is an animal. But despite all his threats we've had nothing to fear from him because we are the world's *only* source of Loki. But once we stop supplying him he'll think we're either holding out for a higher price or we've found another buyer—that's the way they do things in his world. And if he can't have it, he'll finish us. Our only hope is to stabilize the Loki molecule. If we—"

"But you *can't!*" Brad cried, his voice rising toward a wall. "You've been trying to stabilize the molecule since you discovered it and you've failed every time. We spent a *fortune* on that lab of yours. For what? Nothing! And then that Macintosh fellow couldn't do it either. So let's face facts—the Loki molecule can't be stabilized!"

"It can. The problem simply needs a new approach. The new researcher I've hired is quite brilliant and—"

"And what?" Garrison said, his face as red as his hair. "If she's so smart she'll learn too much and then try to blackmail us like Macintosh."

"Nadia is not the type."

When their salesman, Gleason, had mentioned Nadia Radzminsky as a replacement for Macintosh, Luc had been instantly interested. He remembered her for more than that one wild afternoon back in his professor days; she had been a standout student with an intuitive feel for molecular biology. He'd seen her name—second or third in the queue, to be sure—on a number of groundbreaking papers over the last few years. And after her first interview, during which she'd discoursed on his own recent papers so perceptively, he'd known she was their only hope.

"And besides, I've added extra encryption to my personal files. She'll know only what I tell her." He looked around the table. "And we're all onboard about her bonus?"

The other two nodded, Brad a bit reluctantly. "Helluva bonus," he said.

Kent leaned back and ran both hands through his damp red hair. "Worth every cent if she does it." He cast a sharp look at Luc. "And doesn't try to screw us."

Luc wasn't worried about Nadia. Her reverence for him was touching. He'd use that and the bonus—and throw in some warmth and intimacy, just for the delicious hell of it, perhaps—to keep her on track.

"Christ," Brad said. "We only have four weeks. When does she start?"

"I'm introducing her to the Loki molecule today. She'll start work on the new template molecule tomorrow."

"Four weeks," Brad whispered. "It can't be done!"

"It can," Luc said.

It *must*, he thought.

The walls of the small room suddenly seemed to close in on him. Brad had had it built as soon as they'd started dealing with Dragovic. A good idea, too, since all too frequently they had to meet to discuss delicate matters—*felonious* matters—and an electronically shielded, soundproof room fit the bill. But the lack of windows gave Luc a caged feeling, and now the air seemed to be going sour.

He rose and headed for the door. "As a matter of fact, I'm supposed to meet her now in the dry lab."

He unlocked the door and pushed it open slowly in case someone was hurrying down the hall. They'd had to reverse its swing in order to assure a soundproof seal when it was closed. He stepped into the hall and breathed the cooler air. At least it seemed cooler. But still he felt weak.

He leaned against the wall and wondered how it had all gone so wrong.

When Kent and Brad had approached him to be part of a new venture, to lend his name and reputation to the company they were starting up, the future had looked so bright. All things seemed possible. Now it was all turning to shit. He wanted to scream.

To think that an innocent investigation into a strange-looking creature's blood had brought him to this nadir point in his life—a drug trafficker, a murderer. How much lower could he sink?

It was up to Nadia now. He'd tried every way he could imagine to stabilize the molecule but had run up against a wall. Maybe he was too old; maybe his creative juices had dried up; maybe it was the stress dealing with Dragovic and the constant sense of impending doom, the realization that his whole world could implode at any second. Whatever the cause, he'd found himself incapable of breaching that wall.

But a new mind, brilliant, unfettered by such oppressive concerns, might succeed where he'd foundered.

Four weeks . . . Luc squeezed his eyes shut,

You must not fail me, Nadia. Everything depends on you.

7

Nadia sat alone in the darkened room, a bulbous shape floating in the air before her: a molecule of lovastatin, the cholesterol-lowering drug that had gone off-patent; Merck originally had an exclusive on it as Mevacor, but GEM now sold its generic equivalent at a much lower price.

Without taking her eyes off the molecule, Nadia tapped her keyboard, rolled her trackball, and an extra methyl group appeared and attached itself to one end of the larger mass. She rotated the 3-D image 360 degrees in two planes to make sure the new group had the proper orientation, then: *voila*—lovastatin had become simvastatin, Merck's other lipid-lowering agent, Zocor. But Zocor was still patent-protected, so that one was off-limits to the production department. For now, at least.

Nadia loved the dry lab and all its state-of-the-art equipment. No jars of reagents, no pipettes, no ovens or incubators—every experiment and chemical reaction in this small spare room was virtual, thanks to the holographic molecular imager. Nadia knew it had to cost a fortune, far more than any other pharmaceutical company GEM's size would spend. But Dr. Monnet had told her that GEM had made a commitment to original research. They weren't going to be a me-too company forever. The dry lab was ample proof of that.

Nadia sighed. She was restless. She felt she'd had enough practice now. She had the imager down cold. She was more than ready for her first real challenge.

"Hey," said a familiar voice behind her. "Can we play *DNA Wars* on that?"

Nadia gasped and spun in her chair. Her words came in a rush when she saw who it was.

"Doug! My God, what are you doing here! How'd you get in? You'll be fired if anyone sees you!"

Strong arms pulled her from the chair and enfolded her. She wrapped her arms around Doug and breathed in his cologne—Woods, she knew, because she'd given it to him for his birthday. Nadia held him close, loving the solid feel of him.

Douglas Gleason, a fair-haired six-footer with an easy smile and merry blue eyes. A natural charmer whose easygoing manner hid a tenacious, razor-sharp mind. He was dressed for work in his gray suit— the same suit he'd been wearing the day they met.

That had been last year at the annual state medical society convention. Doug had been working the GEM Pharma booth in the exhibit area. Nadia had wandered by with her shoulder bag and her laptop, interested because she knew Dr. Monnet had left his teaching position to co-found the company. She remembered the bolt of electricity that had shot through her when Doug glanced up and smiled. She hadn't meant to stop, but now she had no choice—those eyes, that thick sandy hair . . . A pheromonal cloud enveloped her, drawing her in. . . .

She lingered and listened, barely comprehending a word, as he extolled the virtues of TriCef, GEM's brand-new third-generation cephalosporin antibiotic. When he finished his pitch she accepted a glossy index card and promised to give TriCef a try. But the pheromones wouldn't release her, so she asked about GEM's generic line. When he finally exhausted that subject and nothing was left to say, at least about pharmaceuticals, she thanked him and forced herself to turn away.

"Say, isn't that a 486?" Doug had said, pointing to her laptop. "I haven't seen one of those in a dog's age."

He wasn't letting her go! Nadia remembered feeling giddy with relief.

Playing it cool, she'd told him that at the moment it was an overpriced paperweight. She hadn't been able to get it to boot up this morning. Doug took a break, sat down with her, and within minutes had it up and running, booting faster than she could ever remember. He explained something about her system.ini and win.ini files being "junked up," which meant nothing to Nadia. Computers were like cars to her: she knew how to operate them, could make them do what she needed, but had no idea what was going on under the hood.

They got to talking and she learned that Douglas Gleason thought of himself not as a pharmaceutical sales rep but as a software designer. He even had his own start-up company: GleaSoft; it didn't have a product line yet, but that was why he was working as a sales rep: research. Well, research and a way to pay the rent while he was learning the ins and outs of the pharmaceutical trade in order to program a new tracking software package that would revolutionize how drugs were marketed to physicians.

He'd offered to take her out to dinner—strictly business on his GEM sales account—and she'd accepted. They wound up at Vong, a French Vietnamese place she never could have afforded on her resident's pay. The meal had been fabulous, and their hours together magic. Doug was bright and funny, with wide-ranging interests, but it was his entrepreneurial spirit that captured her. Here was a man with a dream, a need to take control of his life, to call his own shots, and the drive and tenacity to pursue it until he'd achieved it. If he had to be a sales rep for a few years to get started, he'd do it. But he wouldn't—couldn't—do it halfway. He threw himself wholeheartedly into everything he did, and as a result he'd achieved GEM's top sales record.

One dinner led to another, and another, and soon they were sharing breakfast. Lately they'd been talking about marriage.

But right now Nadia was worried for him. She pushed herself back to arm's length.

"Doug, this is a secure area. How did you get in?"

He held up a MasterCard. "With this."

"A credit card? How?"

"It's an old one. I hacked your swipe card and copied the code from its magnetic strip onto this one."

"But that's illegal!"

She'd been worried about him getting fired. Now she was worried about him being arrested.

He shrugged. "Maybe. I just wanted to see if I could do it. And I wanted to get a look at this machine you've been telling me about." He stepped past her and stood before the imager, staring at the 3-D hologram floating above it, a look of sublime wonder on his face. "Oh, Nadj, this is amazing. I'd love to see the code that makes it go."

"Maybe I never should have mentioned it."

Knowing Doug was the compleat computerphile, she'd told him

about the molecular imager. She'd noticed him mentally salivating when she described it. She never dreamed he'd go this far just to see it.

He was slipping around the rear of the workbench, peering at the electronics. "Oh, Nadj, Nadj, Nadj," he was murmuring, sounding a little like he did during sex, "you've got a Silicon Graphics Origin 2000 running this thing! I'd give anything to play with it."

"Don't even think about it. If this thing crashes—"

"Don't worry," he said, returning to her side. "I won't touch it. Wouldn't dare. I just wanted to see it. And see you."

"Me? Why?"

"Well, this is the big day, right? Your first real project? I just came by to wish you good luck, and to give you"—he reached inside his breast pocket and produced a single yellow bud rose—"this."

"Oh, Doug," she taking it and sniffing the tightly coiled petals. She felt lightheaded. Only a rose. How could a single simple flower touch her so deeply? She kissed him. "How sweet of you."

"Let's just hope your project's not the same one Macintosh was working on."

"Why not?"

"Because he said it was—and I quote—'a real bitch.' "

"You knew him?"

"We had a few beers now and again. Tom wasn't the cheeriest guy, and I don't think he had many friends. Wouldn't discuss any details, just kept saying the same thing over and over: 'Real bitch of a problem.' Got so fed up, he just walked out one day and never came back."

My lucky day, Nadia thought. Doug had approached Dr. Monnet and mentioned that one of his own former students was finishing up a residency and might be available to replace Macintosh.

Of course if she'd known what Doug was up to she would have stopped him. And when she did learn he'd been talking to Dr. Monnet about her . . . she'd felt sick. Their fling had lasted one day, one afternoon, really, much too brief to be called an affair . . .

She remembered entering his office at the end of the term, after she'd earned an A—she hadn't wanted him to think she had an ulterior motive—and undressing. He'd watched her with this shocked look on his face, and she couldn't quite believe what she was doing herself, but she'd been wearing only four articles of clothing so there wasn't much time for a change of heart. In thirty seconds she was standing before him in her birthday suit, her nipples so hard they ached, and he'd hesitated maybe two heartbeats. . . .

They'd spent the rest of the afternoon making love against the walls, against the door, and on every horizontal surface in the room. Later he took her out to dinner and told her how wonderful it had been but it couldn't go on. He was married and he'd been swept away, but he hoped she understood that it had to end here.

She'd amazed him and shocked herself by saying she understood perfectly, that a long-term relationship had been the furthest thing from her mind. She'd simply wanted to fuck the most brilliant man she'd ever met.

Nadia still couldn't believe she'd said that—or done it. The whole episode, the wildest day of her life, had been so out of character. She'd never done anything even remotely like that before or since. And maybe that had been it: the urge to let go and do something outrageous. The fact that she'd completed her didactic courses and would never come in contact with Dr. Monnet again must have lent her a sense of security.

Some security. When Doug had said he'd set up a meeting for her with Dr. Monnet, he'd been so excited and proud she just couldn't say no. She'd dreaded seeing him, but Dr. Monnet had been the perfect professional. He'd acknowledged their past together as teacher and student but nothing else. He'd seemed far more interested in her later training than in their brief interlude, quizzing her closely on her contributions to the papers on the effects of anabolic steroids on serotonin levels she'd published with Dr. Petrillo.

As much as Nadia had admired him before, she'd left with boundless new respect for Dr. Luc Monnet.

But when he'd called two days later, he did mention their tryst: He told her he hadn't forgotten their "intimate afternoon," as he termed it, but that was to be buried. He needed someone for a crucial project, and he could allow nothing from the past to interfere. If she could assure him that she would approach her work with a purely professional attitude, the position was hers.

Nadia had been speechless. The man was a prince.

Dr. Monnet had expedited her hiring through personnel and she'd found herself in the GEM dry lab within days.

And even better: Doug insisted on downplaying their relationship. "I told him we were old friends, nothing more," he'd said. "So better keep it that way. They might not like it if they know we're an item. Might think it would get in the way of our work."

That had been fine with Nadia, although she didn't see how Doug could interfere with her work.

"A real bitch of a problem," her predecessor had said before quitting? She knew *she'd* never walk out on Dr. Monnet, no matter how difficult the project. It was too much of a thrill and an honor to be working with him.

The only one who wasn't thrilled was her mother, who didn't think a "real doctor" should do research. She wanted to know when Nadia was going to start seeing sick people, like a "real doctor."

Be patient, Mom, she thought. I'm going to do my damnedest to make a landmark contribution; then I'll go into practice—promise.

"Has Macintosh been in touch with you since he left?" Nadia asked.

Doug shook his head. "Not a word. As I said, not a real gregarious sort."

"Let's just hope he solved that 'bitch of a problem' before he left."

"Even if he didn't," Doug said with that lopsided smile she loved, "you'll just breeze right through it."

"Thanks for the vote of confidence." She held up the rose. "And thanks for this. But now *you've* got to breeze out of here."

"Hey, Nadj, you're talking to their top salesman. They don't want to lose me. Besides, they've gone a bit overboard with the security thing, don't you think?"

"Not a bit," Nadia said. "We're going to be working with human hormones."

"So's everybody else."

"Right. But let's say you find a way to alter estrogen so it doesn't increase the risk of blood clots and breast and uterine cancer but still prevents osteoporosis, hot flashes, and keeps cholesterol down. Or better yet, say we take an anabolic steroid and block all its undesirable side effects but enhance its ability to burn fat. How much would a product like that be worth?"

Doug gave a low whistle. "You could fire the entire sales force. People would be knocking down the doors."

"Right. And that's why Dr. Monnet wants whatever we discover here to stay behind these doors until it's registered with the U.S. Patent Office."

Doug held up his hands. "All right. You win. I'm convinced." He stuck his head out the dry lab door and looked around. "Elaborate as this is, I'd have thought there'd be more to it."

"How so?"

"I don't know how much you know about GEM. It started off selling generic antibiotics but went public a couple of years ago to raise capital to buy the rights to TriCef from Nagata in Japan. GEM would have gone under if TriCef flopped, but luckily the profits are pouring in. And according to the *Pharmaceutical Forum*, it's a top seller. Everybody's using TriCef. I should know—my commission checks show I'm earning big bucks just on that one product. But GEM's not paying dividends. Plus, it's been cutting its sales force. My territory is now so big I can barely keep up with it."

"Just means they're confident in you. Plus they've got a hot new antibiotic, so maybe they don't need to push it so much."

Doug looked at her. "No dividend, cutting the sales force—that sounds like a company on the ropes instead of one that's raking in the profits. Did you see the annual report?"

"Well, no, I—"

"It says the company's pouring most of its profits back into GEM Basic."

Nadia raised her hand. "Hey, that's me." GEM Basic was the research division—right here where they were standing. She pointed to the molecule imager. "There's your proof."

"The amount of money they say they're spending on R and D would fund dozens of these. Makes you wonder, doesn't it?"

Nadia shrugged. "Balance sheets aren't my thing."

"Not exactly mine either. But I figure if I'm going to be an alpha ape in the software jungle, I have to know how a company is run. Damned if I can figure how they're running this one." He smiled. "But that's not my worry. I'll be out of here by this time next year, and in the meantime, let's keep those commission checks rolling in." He pulled her close and kissed her. "Dinner tonight?"

"How about the Coyote?"

"I'm always up for Tex-Mex," he said. "Call you later."

Nadia grabbed his arm as he started for the door. "Whoa! What if you run into Dr. Monnet on your way out? Let me go first and see if all's clear."

She led him back to the security door, passing a tech or two along the way who paid them little attention. They seemed to assume that if Doug had got in and was with Dr. Radzminsky, he must belong.

Nadia stepped through the door and looked around. No one in sight. She motioned to Doug, who hurried up behind her.

"Go," she said, giving him a quick kiss. "And don't do this again."

A smile, a wave, and he was heading down the hall toward the reception area. Nadia turned and nearly bumped into Dr. Monnet.

"Oh, Nadia. There you are. I was just calling the dry lab to tell you I've been delayed. But I'll be down in half an hour and we'll get started."

He looked distracted, frayed at the emotional edges. Dragovic's fault. Had to be. She felt her anger rise. It was criminal for a man of Dr. Monnet's brilliance to be upset by a thug. He needed a tranquil environment to allow him to focus fully on his work.

Don't worry, Dr. Monnet, she thought. I know you're in some kind of trouble, but I think I've found you help.

She wondered if Jack was already working on the case. Would he call it a case? And if he was on it, how was he starting out?

8

The quickest way to Staten Island's north shore was through New Jersey via the Bayonne Bridge. The guy Jack was going to see, Sal Vituolo, ran a junkyard there off Richmond Terrace. Lots of junkyards among the old docks along this stretch of road. Word had it some of them were fronts for chop shops, but Jack wasn't interested in car parts.

When he was a kid, New Yorkers called this chunk of rock the Borough of Richmond and used it mostly as an offshore refinery and garbage dump. Sometime in the seventies it renamed itself Staten Island. A lot of people Jack knew would rather admit they were from Jersey than Staten Island.

He steered his five-year-old Buick Century into the Sal's Salvage, Inc., lot and got out. The air smelled of brine, acetylene fumes, and carbon monoxide. Hopping over muddy puddles, he was making his way toward the office when he heard a voice shout, *"Watch out!"*

Jack turned and saw that someone had backed a forklift into a twenty-foot stack of old tires. For an instant it leaned like the Tower of Pisa but looked like it might hold; then it toppled over, sending tires rolling and bouncing in all directions. Half a dozen came Jack's way, bounding wildly. A scary sight, and he had to duck, dodge, and weave to avoid being hit. He did not avoid getting splashed with muddy water. Once in the clear, he spent an amused moment watching the yard workers chase around like frantic shepherds after a scattered flock, then went inside.

Sal Vituolo did not look happy to see Jack when he stepped through the door. The office was small, cluttered, stuffy, and dim—its two tiny windows probably hadn't been cleaned since La Guardia's day. The man behind the desk was about forty with a low hairline, two days' growth of salt-and-pepper whiskers, and a good-sized gut. Reminded Jack of Joey Buttafuco, but without the class.

"Aren't you the guy from last week? Jack, right?"

"Right."

"The guy that doesn't do what I need done."

"Right."

"So why you back? Change your mind?"

"In a way."

Before Jack could go on, Sal went on a tear. His eyes lit and his hands started stabbing the air. "Yeah? Great, 'cause I've got just the way to do it, see? I know this caterer who's gonna to be doin' the Serb's parties this weekend. I can have him hire you as one of the waiters. All you gotta do is poison the slimeball's food. Easy, huh?"

"Piece of cake," Jack said.

"I'd do it myself if I could look the part, if you know what I'm sayin'."

"I think I do," Jack said, moving a pile of parts catalogs from a chair to the floor and seating himself. "But before we go any further, Sal, I need you to tell me why you've got it in for Mr. Dragovic."

They hadn't got that far last week. When Jack had said he didn't "whack" people for money and Sal had said he'd settle for nothing less, the meeting ended.

"It's that murder thing they had him up on during the winter."

"The one he walked on after all the potential witnesses came down with Alzheimer's?"

"Right. And you know why they suddenly didn't know nuthin'? Because one of the so-called potential witnesses got flattened dead in a hit-and-run in Flatbush a coupla days before the trial."

"So I take it then this guy he was up for killing was a friend of yours?"

"Corvo?" Sal said with a disgusted look. "He was a piece of shit. The world smells better without him. For him, the wrong side of the grass is the right side of the grass, if you know what I'm sayin'. Nah, it was the witness, the potential fucking witness—he was my sister Roseanne's kid, Artie."

"How'd he become witness material?"

"Who knows?" he said, drawing out the second word into a sigh. "Artie got in with a rough crowd. He was headin' for a fall at ninety miles an hour. I warned him, offered him a job here but he was like, 'What? Me work in a junkyard? Fuhgeddaboudit.' Like I was puttin' him on or somethin', if you know what I'm sayin'. Anyway, he happened to be someplace where he wound up knowing something about this killing Dragovic done. And the DA found out, so they was leanin' on him pretty good."

"And he ratted?"

"No way, man. Artie was a stand-up kid." Sal thumped his chest. "He was tough in here." He tapped his head. "A little thick up here, maybe—a real *capatosta*, if you know what I'm saying—but he'd never rat. Dragovic couldn't know that, of course, so he took him out."

That was the word on the street: Dragovic arranged the hit and made sure to be very visible at the 21 Club when it went down. But Jack was curious as to how much more Sal knew.

"You don't know it was Dragovic."

"Hey, I heard from people who saw it go down. Car was aimed right at Artie. When Artie tried to dodge outta the way, the car swerved to hit him. No accident."

"OK. No accident. But as you yourself said, he was in with a rough bunch. Maybe—"

"It was the Serb. Guy was there told me. Won't say nothin' officially, if you know what I'm sayin', but he tells me he recognized one of the Serb's guys at the wheel. So it was Dragovic. I know it, and worse, Roseanne knows it, and every time I see her she looks at me and her eyes say, What're you gonna do about my boy? I'm her little brother, but I'm sorta the man of the family, so I feel I gotta do something. In the old days if you knew someone in the families you could maybe get something done, but those days are gone. So I gotta find someone or do it myself. But this Serb's crazy. I try something and he connects it to me, I'm dead, probably along with my wife and kids to boot."

"You could just let it go."

Sal looked at him. "What kinda guy would I be then?"

"Alive."

"Yeah. Alive and havin' to see Roseanne's eyes lookin' at me every Christmas and Easter and birthday and First Communion, sayin', When, Sal? When you gonna do somethin'?" He sighed heavily. "Bein' the man of the family can really suck, if you know what I'm sayin'."

Jack said nothing. Nothing to say to that.

"So anyways," Sal said, rubbing a hand over his face, "I'm talkin' to Eddy one day, sayin' what am I gonna do, and Eddy says I should call you." He spread his hands and looked at Jack. "And here we are."

Jack remembered Eddy. He'd fixed a problem for him a few years ago. Obviously Eddy remembered Jack.

"Let me float a concept by you, Sal."

"Float away."

"A life for a life balances the scales, sure, but lots of times it can leave you unsatisfied. You're redressing an act that has caused a lot of heartbreak and pain to you and the people you know and love. But when you kill the other guy, it's all over for him. Done. He's gone where he's beyond pain and suffering, but you're still living with the fallout from what he did."

"At least I know he paid for what he did."

"But *did* he pay? *Really* pay? He's pain free and your sister's still hurting. Think about that."

Sal did just that, or appeared to, sitting behind his desk staring at the empty sockets of a plastic pen set. Eventually. . . .

"I take it we're talkin' about something worse than death here, right?"

"Right."

Sal frowned. "Which means, I take it, we're back to you tellin' me you don't kill for money."

"In a way."

"You know, I got to thinkin' about that last week. 'I don't kill for money.' Real funny way of putting it."

"Think so?" Jack wasn't too comfortable with where this seemed to be going.

Sal stared at him a moment, then shrugged. "So whatta you got in mind? Some of the old meat-hook-and-cattle-prod thing?"

"Not exactly. I was—"

"A little amputation action, then. *Wham!* Both legs off at the knees. That'll cut him down to size—in more ways than one." He grinned. "Yeah. Everywhere he goes he's eyeballin' other guys' crotches."

Jeez, Jack thought.

"No, I was thinking about a different approach, maybe coming at him through what's important to him. Dragovic seems to like the lime-light, to be seen with the glitterati, to get his picture in the paper with celebrities and—"

Sal slapped one hand on the desktop and pointed a rust-stained finger at Jack with the other. "Acid in the face! He'll be blind and ugly as shit! That's it! That's it! Oh, I *like* the way you think!"

Jack bit the insides of his cheeks. Maybe this wasn't going to work.

"Acid in the face is always an option," he said, "but it's sort of crude, don't you think? I'm looking for a move with just a tad more style. You mentioned a party this weekend. Where?"

"Out at his new place in the Hamptons. Not one party—two."

"That might be a place to start. Got the address?"

Sal reached for the phone. "No, but my caterer friend will know it. Thinking of torching his place during one of the parties?" Sal said as he punched in the numbers. "Maybe his face'll catch fire and melt. I could go for that."

"Arson is always an option," Jack said, keeping his voice steady.

Sal Vituolo was a shoo-in for Bloodthirstiest Customer of the Year. How was Jack going to come up with something short of death, dismemberment, or disfigurement that would satisfy him?

Maybe a look at Dragovic's new place would inspire him. But if he wanted to avoid the holiday weekend traffic, he'd have to go today.

9

"I call it Loki," Dr. Monnet said.

Nadia stood at his side as he sat at the console and manipulated the hologram of the molecule that floated before them. She'd wondered, feared that being alone with him, being this close, might trigger that old sexual excitement. Thank God, no. She was still in awe of him as a scientist, but that one afternoon seemed to have permanently purged the lust she'd felt.

She concentrated, squinting at the image, not because it was too small or out of focus but because she had never seen anything like it.

"Did you make it?"

"No. I found it."

"Where? On the moon?"

"Right here on earth, but please do not ask me to be more specific. At least not at this time."

Nadia accepted that. Before inserting a sample of this Loki molecule into the imager's sequencer, Dr. Monnet had sworn her to secrecy, insisting that nothing of what she was about to see was to leave this room. Looking at it now, she could see why. This was unique.

Nadia stared at the odd shape. The molecule looked like some sort of anabolic steroid that had collided with serotonin and then rolled around in an organic stew where it had picked up odd side chains in combinations unlike any she'd ever seen.

Something about that singular shape and the way it seemed to go against the laws of organic chemistry and molecular biology as she knew them disturbed her. She felt chilled and repelled . . . as if she were witnessing a crime.

She shook off the feeling. How silly. Molecules weren't right or wrong; they simply *were*. This one was unusual in a disorienting way, and that was all.

And yet . . .

"That can't be stable," she said.

Dr. Monnet glanced up at her. "It is . . . and it isn't."

She didn't see how it could be both. "Sorry?"

"It remains in this form for approximately four weeks—"

"Four *weeks!*" she blurted, then caught herself. "Excuse me, Dr. Monnet, but that structure doesn't look like it would last four nanoseconds."

"I agree. Nevertheless, it does last about twenty-nine days; then it spontaneously degrades to this."

He tapped a few keys and a second hologram took shape in the air a few inches to the right of the first. Nadia felt a trickle of relief when she saw it. This molecule had a much more natural structure. She felt oddly comforted to know that the aberration on the left assumed the more wholesome configuration on the right.

There I go again. *Wholesome?* Where did that come from? Since when do I assign moral values to chemical structures?

"What are its properties?" Nadia said.

"Animal studies are under way. It appears to work as an appetite suppressant."

"We can always use one of those. Any side effects?"

"None yet."

Nadia nodded, feeling a tingle of excitement. A true appetite suppressant with a low side-effect profile would be the equivalent of a license to print money.

"But don't load up on GEM stock yet," Dr. Monnet said, as if reading her mind.

"I won't." Looking at that molecule again . . . Nadia couldn't imagine herself allowing something like that into her system, no matter how thin it might make her.

"Because we have the stability problem to contend with. We can't exploit a product with a shelf life of twenty-nine days, no matter what its effects."

"I take it then that the degraded molecule is bio-inert?"

"Utterly. That's why I call the unstable form Loki."

"Wasn't he some sort of Norse god?"

"The god of deceit and discord," he said, nodding. "But Loki was also a shape shifter, able to assume another form at will."

"Ah. Now I get it. And I'm guessing that's my job: stabilizing the shape shifter."

Dr. Monnet swiveled in the chair and faced her. "Yes. It's an extremely important assignment, a problem we must—absolutely *must*—overcome. The future of this company hinges upon it."

Oh, don't tell me that, Nadia thought as she looked at him. "The future of the company . . . that's . . . quite a responsibility."

"I know. And I'm counting on you to handle it."

"But you have other products—"

"They all pale in comparison to this."

"You think this is doable?"

"I'm praying so. But there's something else you must know about this molecule. It . . . it changes in a manner unparalleled in science."

The intensity in his eyes, the way they bored into her, made Nadia uneasy.

"How so?"

Dr. Monnet licked his lips with a quick dart of his tongue. Could he be nervous?

"What I am going to tell you will sound impossible. But I assure you that I know through personal experience that it is true."

I don't believe this, Nadia thought. He actually looks unsure of himself.

He took a breath. "Once Loki changes to its inert state, any record of its former structure—whether digital, photographic, a plastic model, even human memory of it—changes as well."

Nadia blinked, thinking, Pardon me, Dr. Monnet, but *what the hell?*

"No offense, sir, but that's not possible."

"Exactly what I said the first time I witnessed its degradation. I knew it had changed, knew side chains were missing, but I couldn't remember which ones. No problem, I thought. It's in the computer, so I'll just call up the original structure from memory. But the molecule in memory looked exactly like the degraded molecule."

"How is that possible?"

He shrugged. "I didn't know, and I still don't know. But I figured it must have been a freak occurrence, So I procured another sample—"

"What's the source?"

A grimace. "That, I'm afraid, will have to remain classified for the

time being. But after the change in the molecule and its records occurred a second time, I decided to take precautions. I made hard copy
printouts of the original molecule and filed them away. When the next
degradation occurred, I pulled them out and . . ." He paused and swallowed as if his mouth was dry. "They had changed. They all looked
exactly like the degraded molecule."

"Impossible."

"My sentiments exactly. But there I was, staring at the evidence.
The only explanation I could think of was mischief or sabotage. But
who? So I thought of a foolproof way to overcome this. After obtaining
a fresh sample, I took multiple photos of the unstable form and hid
them in various places in the office and my home; I even went so far
as to build a crude model and lock it in a safe."

"That should have done it."

Dr. Monnet was shaking his head slowly. "No. When I went to
check later, they all had changed: the computer backups, the photos,
even the structural model."

"I know I sound like a broken record, but that's impossible!" Nadia
couldn't believe Dr. Luc Monnet was feeding her this nonsense. Had
he snapped?

He smiled but with no trace of humor. "I kept repeating that word
too, like a mantra. I must have said it thousands of times since I began
working with Loki, but after months I have come to accept the fantastic
as fact. What choice do I have? Its properties are predictable and
replicable. And I have sat here and watched my photos and models
and drawings change before my eyes, felt all memory of the structure
I had been looking at only seconds before vanish like smoke."

"But that's—" No. She would not say the word again.

"You don't believe me," he said, and this time she found a trace
of humor in the twist of his lips. "Good. I'd worry about you if you did.
Were positions reversed, I'd say that you were in dire need of intense
therapy and large doses of Thorazine. This is why I waited until today
to introduce you to Loki. Today is this sample's twenty-ninth day. When
you come in tomorrow morning you will find it all changed, and you
will not remember what the original looked like."

Yes, I will, Nadia promised silently. Oh, yes, I will.

"And then your work will begin. I'll give you a fresh sample—
perhaps the last fresh sample we will be able to secure—and then you

will have twenty-nine days to stabilize it. I'm hoping you will not leave us flat like your predecessor."

"I'm not a quitter."

"I know you aren't. That is why I have high hopes for you."

Not a quitter, no, but she had zero tolerance for looniness. Too much pseudoscience and bad science around as it was, and she would not add to it. A molecule that degraded to a different form was no big deal—but changing all records of its former structure as well? Absurd. Dr. Monnet said this phenomenon is predictable and replicable? She'd see about that. Nadia was going to make copies of the Loki molecule's structure, including a printout to take home with her. Tomorrow morning she'd prove how wrong he was.

"You say it's going to change overnight. Do you know when?"

"I know the exact minute."

"Really? What's the trigger?"

A heartbeat's worth of hesitation. "A celestial event."

Oh, *please*! "Which one?"

"Can I hold that in reserve as well?" he said, sounding apologetic. "I'm not trying to be coy or overly mysterious, but I feel you will be more accepting of all this tomorrow when you've seen—experienced for yourself—the changes I've described."

It was the way he said it that unsettled her—not with the note of someone anticipating vindication, but with the air of a rational man who had been forced to accept the unacceptable.

"This whole thing doesn't make sense. It borders on . . . supernatural."

"I know," he sighed. "That is another reason I christened it Loki. Loki was a god, a supernatural being."

10

"I'm so glad I talked you into this," Gia said.

She was dressed in faded jeans and a pink Polo shirt, and had taken the wheel of the Buick. Legally it was Gia's ride. Jack had bought it, maintained it, and paid its monthly garage fee, but it was registered in Gia's name and hers whenever she needed it. Both of them felt more comfortable riding in a car registered to a real person.

"Me too," Jack replied, but not so sure he meant it.

Gia had been working on a painting when he'd stopped by her place. If he'd had any inkling she'd want to drive out to the Hamptons, he never would have mentioned it. But mention he did, and she'd jumped on the idea with such enthusiasm that he couldn't say no.

It'll be all right, he told himself. Just a cruise by Dragovic's place, maybe a walk on the beach to see the ocean side of his property, and then back to the city. No risk, no danger to Gia and Vicky, just a couple and a child taking in the sights.

"I've never been out to the Hamptons," Gia said. "Have you?"

Flecks of pigment still clung to her fingers as they gripped the steering wheel. Vicky sat in the backseat, engrossed in an old Nancy Drew hardcover Jack had found in a used bookstore. A good night's sleep seemed to have been all she'd needed to recover from last night's scare, although Jack wondered how she'd react next time Gia took her to the museum.

"A few times," Jack said. "Just to see what it was like."

They'd cruised the Long Island Expressway most of the way out, then switched to the two-lane Montauk Highway for the drive onto the south fork. They'd passed though West Hampton, Bridgehampton, This-hampton, That-hampton, and lots of fields between. Farm country out here—the potato fields had been plowed and planted; cornstalks stood ankle-high under the late May sun. All the windows were open and the breeze ruffled Gia's short blond hair, lifting and twirling little golden wings.

"South Hampton College," Jack said as they passed the road sign pointing to the right. "Home of the Fighting Quahogs."

"What?" Gia laughed and glanced at him. "It didn't say that! Did it?"

"Of course it did. Would I make up something like that?"

"Yes. Most certainly yes." She hit the brake. "I'm going to turn around and go back to that sign, and if you're lying . . ."

"OK, OK. I made up the Fighting Quahogs. But if they're not the Fighting Quahogs, they should be, don't you think? That's one tough clam."

"Enough about clams. What about your trips out here? Were you with anyone?"

Jack smiled. Gia was always looking for clues about his pre-Gia love life.

"All by myself. Went all the way to Montauk one time. Put in calls to Paul Simon, Billy Joel, Sting, Paul McCartney, and Kim Bassinger to let them know I was coming—they all live out here, you know."

"I read the papers too."

"Yeah, well, you being from Iowa and all, I wasn't sure you knew. Anyway, they never got back to me. Not a one. Must have been out of town."

"They're busy people. You've got to give them more notice."

"I suppose. But I did stop off to see the Memory Motel—you know, from the Stones song? Walked the dunes. Nothing special except for the size of some of the houses. I guess I'm not much of a beach person."

"I love the beach. Thanks for letting us come along. It's such a beautiful day to get out of the city . . . especially after last night." She glanced into the backseat where Vicks was still absorbed in her book, then at Jack. "Did you find who you were looking for after you left?"

Jack nodded. "Got his name and address. He's got a broken leg."

"Good. What are you going to do?"

"What do you want me to do?"

"Last night I wanted to have him strung up by his thumbs and let the Yankees use him as a tackling dummy."

"Uh, Gia, the Yankees are a baseball team. They don't tackle."

"Whoever then. You know what I mean. I'm saner now. Maybe a broken leg is enough."

"Maybe . . ." Jack said aloud, mentally adding: *for you.*

He still intended to pay a visit to Mr. Butler but wasn't going to be able to work him into the schedule today. Tomorrow for sure.

"Want me to take the wheel for a while?" he said, knowing her answer.

Gia preferred to drive rather than be driven by him—all but insisted on it. Which was fine with Jack since Gia's license was the genuine article.

Gia shook her head. "Uh-uh."

"I thought you might want to enjoy the scenery."

"That's all right. I know you think you've got this perfect depth perception, but you drive too close to things. I'm always jumping, thinking you're going to hit something. Besides, this is an easy drive."

"This time tomorrow afternoon will be a completely different story. Bumper-to-bumper for miles and miles."

Jack rested his hand on Gia's thigh, leaned back, and closed his eyes, wishing every day could be like this—not just the weather, but the ambience, the togetherness, the *peace.*

"Where are we going, Jack?" Gia said.

"East Hampton."

"No, not this afternoon. I mean, in life. You. Me. Us. Where?"

Jack opened his eyes and studied her profile. What a nice little nose she had. "Is there something wrong with where we are?"

She smiled. "No. But sometimes, especially when it's good like this, I have to wonder how long before something goes wrong."

"Why does something have to go wrong?"

"Well, with you doing what you do, doesn't it seem like just a matter of time before a big load of you-know-what hits the fan?"

"Not necessarily. I'm being more careful, more choosy, sticking with fix-its I can handle from a distance."

"But where does it end? You can't be Repairman Jack forever."

How true.

"I know. This isn't carved in stone, but I'm thinking maybe four or five more years and I'm out. I'll be forty then. That's when the reflexes begin to slow and you start needing reading glasses. Might be a good time for my midlife crisis. You know, look around at my life and say,

'Is this it?' and go off and do something radically different and crazy like, I don't know, becoming an accountant or a stockbroker."

"CPA-man Jack," Gia said. "I can see you coming up with all sorts of unique ways to handle an IRS audit."

Jack didn't laugh. The future wasn't funny. Not having an official identity, being a nonentity to the IRS and all the other federal, state, and local arms of the bureausaurus was fine now, but what happened later if he got tired of the constant hiding and dodging and simply wanted to kick back and join Shmoodom? He hadn't thought of that when he'd erased himself from the societal map. Hadn't figured he'd ever get to that point.

And he still might never. Jack wondered if he could ever reconcile himself to the idea of paying income tax. He expended time—hours and days and weeks out of his life—earning his fees, sometimes at the risk of that life, and at its most basic what was life but a struggle against a ticking clock, doing the most with the time you were allotted. To allow then some government bureau to confiscate the product of his time . . . it was like handing over chunks of his life. The way he saw it, once you surrendered sovereignty over part of your life, even a tiny part, you've already lost the war. After that it becomes an issue not of whether you have a right to your own life but of how big a chunk of your life you're going to surrender. And no one asks the giver. The decision is made by the takers.

But still . . . what if the only way to secure a future with Gia and Vicky was to enter their world? He certainly couldn't see them entering his. If he needed to put himself back on the map, how did he do it? He couldn't appear out of nowhere without a damn good explanation of where he'd been all these years.

If it came down to that, he'd figure something out. After all, he still had time. . . .

"Would you be offended if I retired and bought a farm? I mean, you being a vegetarian and all."

"Why would I be offended?"

"Well, I'd want to grow, you know, steaks."

She laughed. He loved that sound. "You can't grow steaks."

"OK, then I'll hunt them—wild filet mignon, free-range T-bones."

"You mean cattle," she said, playing along. "You raise cattle and then you slaughter them and slice up their dead bodies into steaks."

"You mean kill them? What if I get attached to them and can't?"

"Then you've got yourself a bunch of very large pets that go 'moo.' "

Vicky was suddenly hanging over the seat between them, pointing through the windshield as they cruised into another town.

"Look! Another windmill! That's the second one I've seen. Are we in Holland?"

"No," Jack said. "This is still New York. A town called East Hampton. And speaking of which. . . ."

He unfolded a map and figured out where they were. Immediately he realized he should have checked sooner.

"Hang a U-ie when you can. We overshot our turn. We have to get back to Ocean Avenue and then to Lily Pond Lane."

"Thanks, Chingachgook," Gia said as she got them going the other way. "Lily Pond Lane . . . wasn't that mentioned in a Dylan song?"

"Believe so."

"I read somewhere that Martha Stewart lives on Lily Pond Lane."

"Hope she fixed us something good for lunch."

As they wound their way south toward the ocean, the homes grew larger and larger, one more imposing than the next, and the walls and privet hedges and fences around them grew taller and taller, all posted with signs listing the security company that guarded the grounds behind them.

"Who owns *these?*" Gia said.

"The Calvin Kleins and Steven Spielbergs of the world."

"And the Milos Dragovics."

"Yep. Them too. He's supposed to be at the end of Faro Lane— there. Hang a left."

Faro Lane was short and straight; the three-story house at its end blocked any view of the ocean and a good part of the sky. A Mediterranean-style tile roof, but royal blue instead of red, capped light blue stucco walls.

"I think he likes blue," Jack said.

He scanned the perimeter as they passed. A high stucco wall with what looked like broken glass embedded along the top—more aesthetically pleasing than razor wire, he supposed; videocams jutted from the walls of the house, sweeping the grounds. No security service was listed on the wrought-iron gate—Dragovic probably used his own boys as guards—but Jack spotted a German shepherd through the opening.

And then Gia stopped the car.

"Hideous," she said, shaking her head and making a disgusted face as she stared through the windshield. "No other word for it. Of all the colors available, he had to pick those? Whatever look he was going for, he missed."

"No-no!" Jack said. "Don't stop!"

He glanced up, saw a security camera atop the gatepost pointed directly at him, and quickly turned away.

"What's wrong?" Gia said.

"Nothing." Damn! Was that cam used as needed or on continuous feed? Did they have him on tape? "Just keep moving and see if we can find a way to take a walk on the sand."

Should have come alone, he thought. Never guessed she'd stop. But what's done is done. And no point in making too much of it. Who'd be suspicious of an old Buick stopping to take a gander at the big blue house? Probably happens every day.

Gia drove farther west and found a public parking area for Georgica Beach. The three of them kicked off their shoes—Jack surreptitiously removed his ankle holster and jammed the little Semmerling into his pocket—and barefooted it up the dunes. Jack and Gia strolled hand in hand eastward along the higher dry sand while Vicky frolicked along the waterline, playing tag with the waves.

"The water's cold!" she cried.

"Don't get wet," Gia told her.

They trekked up a dune and stopped at its summit to gaze at the blue expanse of Milos Dragovic's twenty-room summer cottage. From this angle Jack could see that it was U-shaped, squatting on the sand like a wary blue crab stretching its claws toward the sea. An oblong free-form pool glistened between the arms, surrounded by a teak deck. A glass-roofed structure that was either a solarium or hothouse huddled in a corner. And all around the grounds men were setting up tables and umbrellas and scrubbing chairs and chaises.

"Looks like someone's having a party," Gia said. "Are you invited?"

"Nope."

"Are you going anyway?"

Jack heard the tension in her voice, turned and saw the worry in her eyes.

"Maybe."

"I wish you wouldn't. He's not a nice man, you know."

"He says he's an honest businessman who's never been convicted of a single crime."

Gia frowned. "I know the rant: everybody picks on him because he's a Serb. But who believes that? What does he do, anyway?"

"Bad stuff, I'm told. I'm not sure of the specifics. I'm waiting for *People* to do an in-depth cover story."

"What are you keeping from me?"

"Truthfully, I don't know much about him. I don't find flashy hoods interesting reading."

"He was accused of murder."

"But the charge was dropped."

"Please don't get on the wrong side of this man."

"Trust me, that's the last thing I want to do. But I do want to get a closer look at his house."

They walked down the dune, scattering a flock of resting seagulls along the way.

"It's even uglier close up," Gia said.

Jack was making a mental map of the grounds. If he were going to invite himself in, he'd have to approach from the beach. He studied the wide open pool area, then looked out to sea. An idea began to form as he watched Vicky gathering shells along the waterline.

"Uh-oh," Gia said. "Looks like we're attracting a crowd."

Jack turned. Two very tall, very broad-shouldered beef jerkies in wraparound shades and ill-fitting dark suits were scuffing toward them across the sand. Both had broad, flat faces and bristly military-style haircuts—one brown and one that had probably been brown once but was now a shade of orange-blond. And Jack could tell from the way their sleeves rode in their left armpits that both were armed.

"Keep moving, folks," said the dark-haired one in a deep, thickly accented voice.

"Yeah," said the other, with the same accent. "This is not place for sightseeing."

"Nice house," Jack said, trying what he hoped was a disarming smile. "Who's the owner?"

Turnip-head smirked. "Someone who does not want you standing in his front yard."

Jack shrugged. "OK." He turned and took Gia's elbow. "Let's go, dear, and let these nice men get back to their work."

"Whoa, whoa, whoa!" Gia said, pulling free of his hand.

Her eyes were narrowed and her lips were pulled into a thin line as she stared at the two guards. Jack knew that look and knew it meant trouble. Once she got her back up, she could be a badger.

"Gia—"

"No, wait. This beach is public property. We can stand out here all day if we please, and we might just do that."

Jeez. This was the last thing he wanted. Up till now he'd been just a guy out for a walk with his wife or his girlfriend who had to be shooed along. Now they'd remember him. And worse, they'd remember Gia.

"Just move on, lady," said the dark-haired one.

"No. You move on. This isn't Kosovo, you know."

That did it. Jack saw Turnip-head's cheek twitch and knew she'd hit a nerve. The dark-haired guard looked Jack's way. Jack couldn't see his eyes behind the black lenses, but the rest of his face said, We both know where this is going, don't we.

Jack knew. He turned, bent, pressed his shoulder against Gia's abdomen, and gently lifted her off the ground.

"So long, gents," he said as he carried her back up the dune.

He heard their laughter behind him and one of them say, "Now there is smart man."

Gia was beating her fists against his back, crying, "Put me *down!* Put me down right now, Jack!"

He did—at the top of the dune. She faced him, furious.

"I don't believe you did that! You carried me off like some sort of caveman!"

"Actually, I was trying to be *un*-caveman and avoid a fight."

"What fight?"

"The fight that would start as soon as the guy with the orange hair shoved you and told you to shut up and get moving."

"If he tried that I'd shove him right back."

"No, *I'd* have to do the shoving, and that would mean facing both of them because I couldn't take on one without the other stepping in, which meant I'd probably get hurt."

"You did OK last night, and besides—"

"Those two aren't a couple of middle-aged drunks. They're not even rent-a-slabs. They've got ex-military written all over them. They're tough, they're in shape, they've probably been in battle, and though they weren't looking for a fight, they were ready for it. It would not have been pretty."

"Well, who said you'd have to step in?"

"Come on, Gia. Some guy lays a hand on you right in front of me and I'm just going to stand there and watch? I don't think so. I'd have to do something."

She threw her hands up. "I'm so sick of this macho shit!"

Uh-oh. A four-letter word from Gia. That meant she was *really* ticked.

"I'm not sure I know what macho is, Gia. I hear that word and I think of somebody named Tony or Hernando in a sleeveless T-shirt, tattoos on his deltoids, and a stiletto in his fist. Is that how you think I am?"

"You know damn well I'm not talking about that. It's this 'a-man's-gotta-do-what-a-man's-gotta-do' attitude. I can't stand it sometimes."

"You want me some other way?"

Sal Vituolo's words of a few hours ago came back to him. *Bein' the man of the family can really suck, if you know what I'm sayin'.*

Yeah, Sal. I know what you're saying.

Gia said, "I want you *alive,* dammit!"

"So do I. That's why I got us out of the line of fire." He held up his hands, making two *V*s with his fingers, and put on his most beatific expression. "You know me . . . a man of peace."

That teased a hint of a smile from her. "You're a piece of work is what you are." She sighed. "It's just that I get so mad when somebody like that tries to push me around."

Jack pointed past her. "And here comes another reason for staying out of a knockdown drag-out."

Vicky came puffing up the dune carrying a horseshoe crab carapace filled with clamshells. "Look what I got!"

They oohed and ahed over her sandy treasures all the way back to the parking area.

As Gia drove the now slightly fishy-smelling car back toward the city, Jack sat in silence, pondering his next move. Since he'd already been made by Dragovic's security, he'd have to work behind the scenes.

They were near Hicksville on the LIE when Jack spotted a sign for the Jericho Turnpike. That made him think of a couple of good old boys whose services he'd employed a few years ago. And that gave him the start of an idea. . . .

"Do you mind if we make a stop?" he said.

Gia glanced at him. "Usually it's Vicky who's got to—"

"Not that. I want to see if some old acquaintances are still in business. Take the next exit."

He directed her off the highway and along a rutted dirt road until he saw the hangar with its red sign: TWIN AIRWAYS.

"Is this the place?"

"Yeah. It's their own private airfield." He pointed to the helicopter and two Gulfstream executive jets on the runway. "They charter those out."

"And why are we here?" Gia said.

"Need to talk to these guys." He got out and started toward the hangar. "Why don't you and Vicks stretch your legs and check out the planes while I check the office."

Luckily, both the Ashe brothers were in—tall, lanky twins in their midthirties. Both had fair, shoulder-length hair, but Joe wore a stubbly beard while Frank sported a droopy mustache.

"Well, well," Frank said in a thick Georgia drawl. "Looky who it is."

Joe stepped up and stuck out a hand. "Where you been keepin' yerself, boy?"

They liked small talk about as much as Jack, so after thirty seconds or so of catching up, Joe said, "What brings you round, Jack?"

"A little business. A couple of quick charters."

"No offense," Frank said, "but since it's you, I gotta ask: how legal we talking 'bout?"

Jack shrugged. "Not terribly *il*legal."

"Not no RICCO-level shit where we could get our assets froze, I hope. That would be a bummer."

"No-no," Jack said. "Not even close. More legal than the last time. Promise."

"Reckon we can handle that," Joe said. "What's up?"

11

Doug Gleason congratulated himself as he left Dr. Alcott's office in Great Neck and walked toward his car. Another once formidable barrier had fallen. He'd penetrated Dr. Alcott's perimeter defenses and actually got to sit down with the man. A coup among sales reps.

Doug had never seen himself as a salesman but had thrown himself into the job to see what he could wring from it. He'd approached it as he would a programming problem, establishing object relationships and then functionally decomposing them. His applied system had met with resounding success.

In Doug's two years on the job, the most important truth he'd discovered was that knowing all the receptionists' first names, knowing the names of all their children and grandchildren, burbling at their baby pictures, smiling for them until you thought your cheeks were going to cramp, did not guarantee you a sit-down with the doctor. You needed the secret weapon.

Food.

A crumb cake or bagels and cream cheese in the morning or pizzas and subs at noon and, for the battle-hardened veterans who manned Dr. Alcott's front lines, the afternoon coup de grâce: chocolate-covered strawberries.

Those had done it. The guardians of the gate had hoisted the white flag and all but demanded that their boss give that nice young Mr. Gleason five minutes.

Doug stowed his sample case in the trunk, then slipped into the front seat of his company car—more of a business office on wheels, actually. In addition to the indispensable cellular phone, he had a cellular fax, a cellular modem for his laptop computer, and a small inkjet printer.

He checked his cell phone—not wanting to be interrupted in Alcott's office, he'd turned it off—and the display told him he had voice mail. The message was from a pharmacist in Sheepshead Bay wanting to know where he could return some TriCef that was going out of date.

Doug wondered about that as he returned the call. TriCef had been out a couple of years now, long enough to start hitting its initial expiration dates, but with the way it was selling, there shouldn't be any of those old batches left.

When he got the pharmacist on the line, Doug identified himself and said, "So what did you do, lose a bottle in the back of one of your cabinets?"

"Not at all," the man said with a vaguely Jamaican-sounding voice. "TriCef simply isn't moving for me."

"Top-selling branded cephalosporin in the country."

"Yes, I read *Pharmaceutical Forum* too, but it's not moving in my place. Same with most of the other pharmacies around here. Only a couple of our docs have ever written for it."

Troubled, Doug gave the pharmacist directions for returning his outdated stock directly to the company and said good-bye.

Was this a trend? Were sales of TriCef slowing? Not according to his commission checks. But GEM commissions were based on dollar amounts shipped rather than number of prescriptions written. And GEM did its own distribution, so it was right on top of product flow. If sales were slowing, his checks would be shrinking.

So Sheepshead Bay had to be an anomaly.

But an anomaly was a glitch, and the programmer regions of Doug's brain abhorred glitches. He opened the pharmacy section of his computer's address book and made some random calls. First three, then five, then a dozen. Each pharmacy had the same story.

TriCef wasn't selling well. Had never sold well.

Unsettling, but only a bit. Because this didn't make sense. *Somebody* was buying it. GEM's profits were on target and the stock price was steady.

He wondered what the head honchos would say about it. As top salesman in a small company, he'd met all three. He didn't particularly care for any of them—and couldn't figure Nadia's near worship of Monnet—but at least they'd been reasonably accessible. Until lately. Over the past months they'd grown increasingly withdrawn, all but moving into their fortresslike boardroom.

Was something going on? Something he should know?

Doug knew this little mystery would keep nipping at his ankles until he solved it. Maybe it was something Nadia should know as well.

Nadj . . . that was another mystery. How had he lucked onto her? Every day he awoke thankful that he'd found her and that she somehow, miraculously, cared for him.

He had planned to knock off early today anyway. Why not spend some of the afternoon looking into it? He had hours before he was to meet Nadj for dinner. That should be enough. He was an expert with the investigating tool he planned to use: his computer.

He was sure there was a logical explanation, but at the moment he couldn't imagine what it could be.

But if it was findable, he'd find it. He smiled as he started the car. This could be fun.

12

"How many old tires can you scrape together?" Jack said into the phone in the Ashe brothers' office.

He'd come to terms with Frank and Joe on the when and how of the delivery; now he had to arrange for the payload. For that he'd called Sal Vituolo.

"Old tires?" Sal said. "Christ, I got tires up the freakin' wazoo. They ain't good for nothin' though, 'cept maybe dumpin' in the ocean."

"I've got another use for them. Can you put together a truckload?"

"You kiddin'? I can put together two or three. What you gonna do with a buncha old tires?"

"Trust me—you're going to love it. Pile them in the back of your biggest truck and I'll be by later to pick them up."

"This got something to do with the little matter we talked about earlier?"

"It do."

"Awright! You got 'em!"

As Jack hung up he wondered what sadistic uses Sal was imagining for those tires. He turned to Frank and Joe.

"It's a go."

Frank grinned through his droopy mustache. "Gotta hand it to you, Jack, you sure do come up with some fun stuff."

"Boy's downright evil," Joe drawled.

They sealed the deal with a handshake; then Jack headed back to the car. Gia and Vicky had seen all they wanted of the aircraft and were waiting for him. He reminded himself to call Nadia when he got back and let her know that her fix-it was being cofinanced by another party, so she'd only have to pay half the usual fee. Sal, however, would pay full fare.

He threw an arm around Gia and kissed her. He was feeling very good about the day.

"Why are you smiling?" Gia said.

"Just glad to see you."

"Uh-uh," she said. "You've got that cat-after-a-canary-casserole look."

"Well, I did just solve a little problem that's been nagging me."

"Does it involve a certain Serb?"

"It do."

"I don't want to know about it," she said, slipping in behind the wheel. "I just want to know if you'll be in danger."

"Not this time. This gig will be strictly arm's length."

At least it'll start out that way, he thought. Things go right, it'll stay that way. But when was the last time everything went right?

13

Doug was not his usual gabby self at dinner. Nadia watched him push his chiles rellenos back and forth across his plate while his Corona went flat. All around them in the Lost Coyote Café people were laughing, talking, calling across the room to friends, but their table was an island of silence.

"Earth to Doug," Nadia said. "Earth calling Douglas Gleason, are you there?"

He snapped his head up and straightened in the seat, ran a hand through his sandy hair, and smiled. "Sorry. Just thinking."

"About what? Something wrong?"

"I'm not sure," he said.

His blue eyes held hers as he told her about the call from the pharmacist this afternoon and the other calls he'd made.

Nadia's last sip of her margarita soured on her tongue. "Is the company in trouble?"

"That was my first thought," he said. "And it occurred to me that maybe it wasn't such a good idea for both of our incomes to depend on the same source. If something goes wrong with GEM, we could both be out of work."

If something goes wrong with GEM . . . She didn't want to think about that. She'd just started. . . .

"But you said that magazine, what was it called?"

"Pharmaceutical Forum."

"Right. Didn't it say that TriCef was tops in its class?"

Doug nodded. "But it's a lie."

Nadia tensed. "How can you know?"

He glanced around, looking furtive, then leaned forward. "My company laptop hooks into the GEM system to let me download my data, email, and new information on the product line directly, and upload my contact reports. I spent a few hours this afternoon using that entrée to hack into other areas of the GEM network."

She gasped and reached across the table to grab his hand. "Doug, you could go to jail for that!"

"Maybe, maybe not. I don't know. It's not as if I was trying to crash their system or anything. My company laptop puts me on the other side of their fire wall, so I'm not really breaking in. But I didn't push things. I was very careful. If I ran into a secure area, I tried to sneak past rather than break through."

"This sounds dangerous."

He sipped his Corona. "But what was I going to do, Nadj? I couldn't just sit around wondering and not do something to find out. You know me."

Yes, Nadia knew Doug. Once he sank his teeth into a problem, he wouldn't let go until he'd solved it. She'd seen him stay up for forty-eight hours straight resolving a programming glitch.

"And obviously you learned something you're not supposed to know."

"Yeah. I broke into the sales master files." He glanced around the little restaurant. "I guess I'm not such a great salesman after all. My sales figures for TriCef stink. The only consolation is that I'm not alone—the entire sales force has tanked on TriCef."

She could feel his hurt. "But your commission checks—"

"Inflated. Just like everyone else's."

"But that doesn't make sense!"

He sighed. "Tell me about it."

"So the company's in big trouble?"

His eyes fixed her again. "That's just it: the company's bottom line is fine. TriCef is a major hit overseas, doing gangbusters business. The dollar amounts are staggering."

"So much so that they can pay you commissions on antibiotics you haven't sold?"

"Apparently, yes. But why the discrepancies between the real and published sales figures? Why are *Pharmaceutical Forum*'s figures so inflated?"

"Obviously to hide the fact that TriCef is a flop in the U.S."

"But it's a monster overseas. What's the point?"

Nadia shrugged. "To protect the stock price?"

"I don't see that. They're operating in the black."

"How about company pride?" Nadia knew Dr. Monnet was a very proud man. But would he involve himself in a deception of this magnitude? Surely he valued his personal reputation more than the company's.

"You might have something there," Doug said after a swallow of beer. He picked up a blue corn chip and dipped it in the salsa. "GEM started as a generic company. TriCef is their first time out competing against the big boys and they want to look like winners."

"I'm sure that's it."

"Well, I'm not *that* sure. I've still got a few questions that need answering." He grinned. "Let's go to my place when we're done. I'll make you into a hacker."

Nadia forced a smile. "OK."

She knew Doug would gnaw this bone till he was satisfied no morsel remained to be gleaned from it, and she had an uneasy feeling she should stick as close as possible to him on this.

14

The front section of Ozymandias Prather's trailer served as the business office for the Oddity Emporium. Luc Monnet sat inside and glanced at his watch. Almost time.

He'd been enormously relieved to learn that the creature was still alive.

He looked around the tiny office: a rickety desk, two chairs, and no room for much else. The rear section, Prather's living quarters, Luc presumed, was curtained off. Curiosity about the lifestyle of this strange man with an even stranger business nudged him to take a peek, but he resisted. He was not a snoop.

Nothing wrong with perusing the walls of the business office, though. It was papered with old posters and flyers, one particularly old one mentioning a Jacob Prather and his "Infernal Machine." Prather's father, perhaps? Behind the desk was a map of the U.S. with a planned route that circled the country.

"Find anything interesting?" said a deep voice behind him.

Luc jumped. He hadn't heard Prather come in. He moved quietly for such a big man. Luc didn't turn but continued looking at the map.

"You've played in all these places already this year?" Luc said.

"That is a future route card," Prather said. "A dream of mine . . . for when I've gathered the proper troupe—the ultimate troupe, one might say—of handpicked performers. That will be the tour to end all tours."

Something in his voice made Luc turn. Prather's eyes were bright under his lanky hair; his grin looked . . . hungry.

Luc glanced at his watch, as much to break contact with Prather's eyes as to check the time. The digits read 8:43. A minute past time.

"Have you got the creature secured?" Luc said.

Prather nodded. "We are ready if you are."

"Let's go then."

"Payment first," Prather said, holding out a wide, long-fingered hand.

Luc hesitated. He'd always paid after he'd drawn the sample. "Is something wrong with the creature?"

"Yes. It is dying, as we both know. But do not fear—it is not yet dead."

Then why did Prather want payment first? Luc stiffened at a terrifying thought—if the creature was near death, if this was to be the last sampling of its blood, then Luc was of no further value to Prather. If they would no longer be doing business, then Luc, a witness to murder, was . . . disposable.

He would never forget how casually Prather had disposed of Macintosh.

"You look frightened, Dr. Monnet," Prather said, baring his teeth in a yellowed grin. "As if you fear for your life."

"No, I—"

"Relax, Doctor. I am a man of my word, forthright in my dealings. I am so because I must set an example for my troupe." He extended his hand closer to Luc. "This is my business office; let us do business."

Luc pulled out the envelope and handed it to him. "I've included advance payment for three of your roustabouts as security when I test this batch."

Prather nodded as he counted the money. "Things got a little out of hand last time, you say?"

"A little."

More than a little. Luc had lost control of two of the test subjects. He chewed his upper lip at the memory. It had been quite nearly a disaster.

Prather sighed as he closed the envelope. "I don't like hiring them out, but attendance is off this tour. In good times people seem less inclined to go and stare at those less fortunate than they—at least those who *appear* less fortunate. So we must make ends meet any way we can." He stuffed the envelope into one of his own pockets. His voice dropped to a whisper, as if he were talking to himself. "Because I *must* keep the troupe together—by any means necessary."

Wondering at the hint of desperation in Prather's voice, Luc followed him out of the trailer and into the twilight. He caught the scent of the Long Island Sound as they followed a path of trampled marsh grass to the main tent.

"You're fairly isolated out here," Luc said, wondering why Prather had chosen this relatively well-off section of the North Shore to set up. "Do you do enough business in this area?"

"Not as much as we might in a more blue-collar location," Prather said. "But we do enough. The owner rents us the land for a reasonable fee, and the truth of it is, we like the town."

"Monroe? What so special about Monroe?"

"You wouldn't understand," Prather said.

Just then a young woman came running toward them across the grass, crying, "Oz! Oz!"

She was short, thin, with a long ponytail trailing from her under-sized head. Luc could see that she was crying. She grabbed Prather's hand and pulled him aside. Between sobs she whispered in a high-pitched voice, her words tumbling out so quickly Luc couldn't catch their meaning beyond something about someone named Rena being "so mean."

He watched Prather nodding as he listened, saw him pat her shoulder and murmur in a reassuring tone. She smiled, giggled, then skipped away as if she hadn't care in the world.

"What was that all about?" Luc said when Prather rejoined him.

"A domestic squabble," the tall man said. "We are a family of sorts, and every family has them."

"And you're the father they come to as mediator?"

"Some of them do. Many in the troupe are quite adept at handling their own affairs and solving their own problems. Lena and her sister Rena, however, have a mental age of about six. Their petty disagreements seem momentous to them. I play Solomon."

"Ah. I thought she looked microcephalic."

Prather nodded. "They're called 'pinheads' in the trade. Lena and her sister are known as 'the Pin Twins' under my canvas."

Luc felt a twinge of revulsion that his face must have mirrored.

"Offended, Doctor?" Prather's mouth twisted into what might have been a smile. "Exploitation of the mentally retarded . . . that's what you're thinking, am I right?"

"Well . . ." That was exactly what he'd been thinking.

"But you know nothing of their life before I found them. Lena and Rena were living in a cardboard box in Dallas, vying with rats for scraps from restaurant garbage bins, being repeatedly raped and otherwise abused whenever it suited their fellow street dwellers."

"Dear God."

"Now they live in their own trailer, they travel the country, and during the show they sing and recite nursery rhymes in close harmony for the customers who stop at their stall. And they are *safe*, Doctor." His deep voice took on an edge. "We watch out for each other here. No one will ever hurt them again."

Luc said nothing as Prather lifted the tent flap for him. What was there to say?

A moment later he was standing before the Sharkman cage. A pair of the vaguely canine roustabouts had one of the dark creature's arms. Luc shuddered as he realized that one of these two could have dealt Macintosh's death blow last month. Their powerful bodies seemed relaxed; they were expending little effort to hold the creature's arm steady. One of them probably would have been enough. Even the creature's stink seemed to have faded since last month.

Luc closed his eyes as the world seemed to tilt beneath his feet.

This is it, he thought. The last sample. The creature is all but gone.

His fingers trembled and fumbled as he prepared his phlebotomy needle, but he managed to find the vein and fill his tubes with the black fluid. When he stepped back the roustabouts released the arm, but the creature didn't even bother to withdraw it into the cage.

Luc held up one of the tubes and tilted it back and forth. The inky fluid within sloshed around like water.

"And next month?" he said to Prather.

"I doubt very much there will be a next month for this poor creature," Prather said. "But if you want to pay a visit, just for old times' sake . . ."

Prather's voice faded, replaced by a vision of Milos Dragovic's rage-contorted features and his coarse voice echoing, *Where is my shipment? Where is my shipment?*

"I don't . . ." Luc's mouth had gone dry. He swallowed. "You will call me if . . . when it happens?"

"Yes," Prather said softly. "We will mourn our brother."

Struck by the note of genuine melancholy in Prather's tone, Luc glanced at him but saw no mockery in the big man's expression.

Feeling as if the tent were collapsing on him, Luc turned to go. He realized too late that he was leaving the back of his neck exposed to the kind of crushing blow that had killed Macintosh. He hunched his shoulders as he hurried for the exit, but no one followed him.

He allowed himself a sigh of relief when he hit the night air but did not slow his pace. No time to waste. He had to get this sample to the synthesizer immediately.

15

"Here," Milos said, patting the cushion next to his thigh. He wore a double-breasted Sulka suit, pure cashmere navy chalk over a pearl gray thirty-three-gauge worsted cashmere turtleneck. "Come sit by me. I want to share something with you."

The young model swayed toward him across the deep carpet of the living room like she was strutting a runway. He didn't know her real name. She called herself Cino—pronounced "Chee-no"—but Milos doubted that was on her birth certificate. She'd probably been born Maria Diaz or Conchita Gonzales or something like that. She'd never tell. And what did Milos care about her given name? All that mattered were the dark, dark eyes under the silky widow's veil of her bangs, the jutting cheekbones, and the jaguar-lithe body.

Milos watched her move toward him now, her slim hips swaying rhythmically within the tight black sheath she wore. He'd met her two weeks ago at a club opening and had been struck by how thin she was—downright bony. She looked better in her photos where the camera did her a service by adding a few pounds to her anorectic frame. Women this thin did not populate Milos's fantasies. In his dreams he preferred sturdier bodies, women with more meat on their bones, flesh he could grab and squeeze and hang onto during the ride. Someone like Cino . . . well, sometimes he was afraid she'd snap like a twig.

But Cino had the look everyone wanted. And if everyone wanted it, Milos Dragovic wanted it even more.

The best of everything, first class all the way—that had become his credo, the rule by which he would live the rest of his days.

The watch on his wrist, for instance: a gold, thirty-seven-jewel Breguet, considered the best watch in the world. Did it tell time better than a Timex? Hardly. Did he need to know the phases of the moon on its face? It said there was a new moon now—who cared? But people who counted would know it cost upward of thirty grand.

Did he need the fifty-inch plasma TV screen hanging like a painting on the wall of the entertainment room? He hated television. But the sort of people who'd be his guests here Sunday would see it and know it was the best screen money could by.

This house and its lot, where waves tumbled onto the beach beyond the sliding glass doors that lined the south wall of the living room, was the absolute best money could buy. But that hadn't prevented certain locals from interfering with its construction. The Ladies Village Improvement Society—he'd thought someone was putting him on, but this turned out to be a real group, with real clout—had objected to his blue tile roof. He'd paid through the nose to bypass them.

But then, he'd paid through the nose for everything connected with this place. He'd overpaid for the land, been overcharged by the contractor who built it, gang-raped up the ass by the crew of fag decorators who had been swarming through the rooms for the past few months, and to top it all off, the place squatted a hundred yards from the Atlantic Ocean, a sitting duck for the next hurricane that wandered too far north.

Milos didn't care. It was only money, and he'd always known how to make lots of money. What mattered was having the *best*. Because if you had the best, that meant that you recognized what was best, and people—at least people in America—equated that with class. They were all jerks as far as Milos was concerned. He didn't know a designer sofa from something from the JC Penny catalog, an antique dresser from a junk store reject, but so what? He simply hired people who did. And what was the only thing you needed to hire anyone? Money.

It all came down to money.

But sometimes money wasn't enough to impress the people who really mattered—the people inside. They demanded more than money. They wanted breeding, lineage, class, celebrity—take your pick. Some computer geek could start a company, sell it for a hundred million a few years later, but he'd still be a geek. He'd still be an outsider. Milos had always been an outsider, but now he was working his way in. It took work, it took smarts, but he was learning the ropes.

His reputation—some called it shady; he preferred *colorful*—actually worked as a plus, lending him an air of dark celebrity. That was a toehold in that other world. He found that certain insiders liked to drop his name. He played up to that. That was why he had invited Cino out for the weekend. She would be his trophy, a decoration on his arm for both parties.

But most important, she would *talk* when she returned to the city next week. The girls always talked. That was why everything she saw this weekend must be first class, the best. Even the sex. Cino was less than half his age but she'd developed some kinky tastes in her twenty-two years; she liked it rough—as long as she didn't end up with any bruises—and Milos was more than happy to accommodate her. She'd talk about the sex and everything else, and he needed her to describe it to her friends and acquaintances as the best. Because they would quote her in their circles and that would spread to other circles and soon all the insiders would know about Milos Dragovic's Memorial Day Weekend parties and wish they'd been invited . . . and they'd vie to be asked to his next gala.

And that vying would spill over to his club. When Belgravy opened in the fall, it would be *the* place to be.

Cino barely dented the cushion as she alighted next to him.

"Share what?" she said, showing perfect teeth that appeared to glow amid the smooth olive tones of her face. "A secret?"

He glanced at her. You want secrets, my dear Cino? I could tell you secrets that would send you stumbling and screaming from the room.

"No . . . no secrets." He gestured to the wide-based crystal decanter on the glass coffee table before them. "Just some wine."

"I don't really like red wine. Champagne's my thing. You know that."

"Of course. Your other lover. Dampierre."

"Not just Dampierre—Dampierre Cuvee de Prestige."

"Of course. And only the 1990 vintage."

"Mais oui. That's the best."

Milos wondered if it was truly the taste of her Dampierre Cuvee de Prestige 1990 she preferred or the fact that it was harder to find and twice as expensive as Dom Pérignon. If it was price and rarity that turned her on, then she'd go absolutely wild for the Petrus.

"I have something even better here." He lifted the decanter and held it up to the light. "A very special red wine, a Bordeaux whose grapes were harvested long before you were born. In nineteen forty-seven."

"Nineteen forty-seven!" she said, laughing. "That's before my *father* was born! Is it still any good?"

"It's marvelous," Milos said. "I've been letting it breathe."

Actually, he hadn't tasted it, but anything this expensive had to be good. He hadn't poured it into the decanter either. Kim had done that.

Kim was further proof of the Milos maxim: you don't have to know shit—you simply have to hire people who do.

And Kim Soong knew damn near everything—about food, about wine, about clothes, about all sorts of important things. How a gook got to know so much was beyond Milos, but Kim had become indispensable. He had done a little dance when Milos showed him the half-case of Petrus 1947. Milos had figured it had to be pretty good stuff if Monnet had wanted it; Kim's reaction had confirmed that. Kim really knew red wines.

But Kim had said to pour this Petrus—he'd pronounced it "pet-*troos*," and Milos had made a note of that—directly from the bottle to a glass would be an insult to the wine. Imagine . . . a wine with tender feelings. It had to be candled and decanted. Milos hadn't the foggiest what the hell that meant, but he'd gone along, and soon he was watching, fascinated, as Kim slowly poured the wine into the crystal decanter while staring through the neck of the bottle at a candle flame on the other side.

And now Milos did the pouring, from the decanter into the pair of wide-mouthed tulip-shaped glasses Kim had set out. Half a glass each. He handed one to Cino, then raised his own.

"To a weekend full of surprises," he said, locking eyes with her.

"I'll drink to that," she said.

Milos took a sip and swallowed. It tasted . . . awful. But he let nothing show on his face. He looked at his glass.

I spent two and a half grand a bottle for this shit?

He took another sip. Not quite as bad as the first, but still awful.

He glanced at Cino who looked as if she'd just spotted a maggot in the bottom of her glass.

"Eeeeuw! This tastes like cigarette ashes!"

"Don't be silly," Milos said. "It's delicious."

Actually, she wasn't far off. It did taste like ashes.

"Blech!" Another face as she returned the offending glass to the table and pushed it as far away as she could reach. "Like sneaker soles."

"Just try a little bit more." Milos forced a third sip. Ugh. How was he going to drink the rest of this? "It's really excellent."

"Tastes like dust bunnies. Where's my Dampierre? I want my Dampierre."

"Very well."

He pressed a button built into the coffee table, sending a signal to the kitchen. Dressed in a crisp white shirt and a black vest, Kim whispered into the room a moment later and did one of his little bows.

"Yes, sir?"

"It appears the lady does not find the Petrus to her liking."

Another little bow. "Most unfortunate."

"Old holy water," Cino said.

Milos wanted to clock her. "Perhaps you would taste it, Kim, and give her your expert opinion."

Kim smiled. "Of course, sir. I would be honored."

He whisked this oversize silver spoon from his vest pocket and poured maybe half an ounce of the Petrus into it. He sniffed it, then slurped it up like hot soup—Milos never would have believed Kim could be such a slob—and rolled it around in his mouth. Finally he swallowed. His eyes rolled up in his head before he closed them. They stayed closed for a moment. When he opened them he looked like someone who'd just seen God.

"Oh, sir, it's wonderful! Absolutely magnificent!" He looked damn near ready to cry. "Nectar of the gods! Mere words cannot do it justice!"

"See," Milos said, turning to Cino. "I told you it was good."

"Laundromat lint," she said.

"Perhaps the miss's palate is not so educated as Mr. Dragovic's. It takes a certain seasoning of the tongue to fully appreciate a well-aged Bordeaux."

You just earned yourself a bonus, Kim, Milos thought. But Cino wasn't the least bit impressed.

"I appreciate Dampierre, aged all the way from 1990. When can I have some?"

"Right away, miss," Kim said, bowing and backing away. "I shall return in an instant."

Furious, Milos rose with his glass and moved away before he throttled her. Cino liked it rough? Cino might get more than she could handle tonight.

He pretended to study one of the paintings his decorators had stuck on the walls. A swirling mass of creamy pastels. What the hell did it mean? All he knew was that it was expensive.

He sipped the wine again. Did Monnet and people like him really enjoy this stuff? Or did they just pretend to?

"You really should give the wine another chance," he said. "At twenty-five hundred dollars a bottle you—"

"Twenty-five hundred dollars a bottle!" she cried. "For stuff that tastes like wet cedar shakes? I can't believe it!"

"Believe it," he said. "And worth every penny." Even if she hated the wine, she'd talk about the price tag.

"Say, who's this?" she said. "He looks like you."

Milos turned and saw her by the bookshelves, holding a framed photo—Milos's sole contribution to the room.

"He should. He was my older brother."

"Was?"

"Yes. He died a few years ago."

"Oh, I'm so sorry." She sounded as if she meant it. "Were you close?"

"Very."

Milos felt a twinge of sadness at the thought of Petar. They had done so well running guns to the HVO in Bosnia, but they fell out during the Kosovar meltdown. Peter hadn't wanted to sell to the KLA. He'd wanted to supply only the Serbs. Oh, how they fought, like only brothers can fight. He remembered Petar screaming that he would die before he supplied the KLA with the means to kill Serbs.

How prophetic.

To this day Milos could not understand his brother's idiotic posturing. They'd always sold to both sides when they could. And the KLA had had a blank check from the Arabs to buy anything they could get their hands on—they'd been willing to pay multiples of the going rate. How could he turn his back on such an opportunity?

But somehow, somewhere Petar had got it into his head that he was a Serb first and a businessman second. Fine. Milos would do the deal on his own. That was when Petar stepped over the line. Bad enough that he would have nothing to do with the KLA, but when he tried to sabotage Milos's deal . . .

Milos still regretted shooting his brother. His only consolation was that Petar never knew what hit him and did not suffer an instant. The point-blank shotgun blast literally took his head off.

Milos had killed before and since—Emil Corvo being the most recent. He'd been careless with Corvo and might have been sent up had he not iced one witness to chill the rest. Who was the one he'd ordered the hit-and-run on? Artie something . . . he couldn't even remember his name.

That was the way it was. A death settled problems, cleared the air, and Milos believed in doing his own wetwork when he could. Not because it was personal—never personal. It simply kept everyone on their toes.

But with Petar it had been personal, too personal to allow anyone else to do. He'd grieved for months, and to this day he missed his older brother.

Ah, Petar, he thought looking at the photo in Cino's hands, if only I could have seen the future then. Had I known of Loki and the millions it would bring, I would not have bothered with the KLA deal, and you would be here with me today to share in the bounty.

Milos's throat tightened as he lifted his glass to the photo. "To my beloved brother."

Wishing to hell it was vodka, he forced the rest of the Petrus past the lump in his throat.

16

Nadia blinked and bolted upright to a sitting position. Dark. Where were her clothes? Where was *she?*

She glanced out the window and saw the underside of the Manhattan Bridge and remembered. She was in Doug's bed—alone.

God, what time was it? The red LED digits on the clock said it was late.

Where was Doug? She called his name.

"Is that Sleeping Beauty I hear?" he called back from somewhere in the apartment.

"Where are you?"

"I'm in the office. Come here. I want to show you something."

She stretched, arching her back under the sheets. She and Doug had returned to his place with the intention of hacking into the GEM mainframe together, but made a detour to the bedroom on their way to the computer. She smiled at the memory. Doug hadn't been the least bit distracted during their lovemaking. She'd had his full attention then.

And afterward, lying snuggled in his arms, she'd dozed off. She never did that. Well, almost never. But she hadn't been getting enough sleep lately.

She slipped out of the bed, pulled on her clothes, and detoured to the kitchen where she found a Jolt Cola in the fridge. She preferred Diet Pepsi, but this would do. She carried it to the second bedroom that Doug had converted to an office.

She found him, dressed only in his boxer shorts, munching cereal from a blue box as he stared at the monitor. She loved the broad wedge of his shoulders.

"Eating something good?" she said, leaning against his back and watching the numbers run across the screen.

He handed her the box without looking up. She was startled to see a familiar cross-eyed propeller-headed alien on the front.

"Quisp?" She flashed back to the cute Quisp versus Quake commercials of her childhood. "I thought they stopped making this ages ago."

"So did I, but apparently it's still sold in a couple of places around the country. I ordered some on the Net."

She tried a few of the crunchy saucer-shaped pieces and nearly gagged. "I don't remember it being this sweet."

"Gotta be ninety-nine percent sugar. But what's even better . . ." He held up his wrist. "Look what you can get."

"A Quisp watch?"

"But wait—there's more!" He handed her a little gold ring set with an image of the cereal's alien mascot. "Will this do until I can get you that diamond?"

She laughed. "You've gone bonkers."

"I think the term is *qwazy*."

She pointed to the monitor screen. "What are you up to now?"

"Trying to get into GEM's financial data. Not the cooked figures they publish in their annual reports, I want the real skinny."

"My God, Doug! They'll trace you!"

"Not to worry. I routed the call through a Chicago exchange."

"Chicago? How—?"

"Old hacker trick."

"Please, Doug," Nadia said, riding a wave of foreboding, "don't do this. It'll only get you in trouble."

He sighed. "You're probably right. But it's eating at me, Nadj. They're paying me commissions on sales that aren't there. The profits they've supposedly allocated for R and D should be enough to fill a ten-story building with researchers and equipment, yet we both know that the GEM Basic division occupies a single floor and that's sparsely populated. The money's going somewhere. If not to GEM Basic, then to what? Or whom?"

"Where the money's going won't help you when you're going to jail."

"I'm being careful."

"Why don't we just say it's a mystery and leave it at that."

He smiled. "You know, I remember in catechism class back in grammar school when I used to ask the nuns all sorts of questions about God and heaven and hell. Lots of times the nuns would say, 'It's a mystery,' and that would be that. Subject closed. That didn't satisfy me then, and it doesn't satisfy me now."

Nadia remembered kids like Doug from her own years in Catholic school. There was always one in every class for whom pronouncements from On High and exhortations simply to "have faith" never cut it. They kept asking questions, kept probing and pushing. Everyone else in the class had already swallowed the latest bit of dogma and was ready to move on. But not these guys—they wanted an explanation. They had to *know*.

"OK, try this: it's none of our business."

"When both of our livelihoods depend on GEM, I think it's very much our business."

Their livelihoods, Nadia knew, were only a small part of it. Even if Doug had won a multimillion-dollar lottery this afternoon, he'd still be picking away at GEM's computer defenses. It was an itch he had to scratch.

She leaned around and kissed him on the lips. "Call me a cab. I've got to go."

"What about your hacking lessons?" he said.

"Some other time. I've got to be at the clinic bright and early."

He picked up his cell phone and ordered her a cab. Doug's apartment was in the DUMBO section of Brooklyn; you could get old waiting under the Manhattan Bridge for a cab to cruise by.

When he clicked off, he reached out and pulled her onto his lap. "If you lived here," he said, nuzzling her throat, "you'd already be home."

Nadia puffed her cheeks as she let out a breath. "We're not going to get into this again, are we?"

"You're going to be living here anyway when we're married." His nuzzling was sending goose bumps down her back. "Why not just move it up a few months?"

"It's over a year. And do you want to convince my mother?"

He laughed. "No thanks!"

She'd moved in with her mother during her residency. It had seemed like such a good idea at the time. She'd been spending so much time at the hospital, it didn't make sense to rent a place when Mom's little two-bedroom rent-controlled apartment on the upper border of Kip's Bay was just a few blocks from the medical center. Might as well pay the rent stipend to her rather than a stranger.

Now she wished she hadn't. Not that they didn't get along. Just the opposite; they got along too well. Mom was seventy and a widow—Dad had died five years ago. She'd come over from Poland before the war. She might be an American citizen now, but she had never really let go of the Old Country. Her accent was thick, and pictures of Pope John Paul II papered her apartment walls.

Except for religion—Nadia had stopped going to Sunday mass while Mom went daily—they got along fine. Well, maybe Mom was skeptical about her daughter the doctor taking a research job instead of practicing medicine like a "real doctor," but that was a minor point.

Moving out of Mom's and into her own place would not be a problem—Mom was independent and could handle living alone just fine. Moving in with Doug, on the other hand, would become an issue. She'd wail about her daughter living in sin and embark on a string of Novenas to try to save Nadia's soul.

What was the point in putting the poor woman through that torment? She and Doug would be married before long. Until then she'd hang in with the current arrangement, which wasn't hard to take. They saw plenty of each other, and living apart certainly hadn't stunted their sex life.

"Didn't want to start anything," Doug said.

"I know," she sighed. Reluctantly she pulled free of his embrace and rose. "Gotta go."

"Call me when you get in."

He always had her call him after she left, just to let him know she got home safe.

"How will I get through if your modem's got the line tied up?"

He held up the cell phone from the desk and hit a button. "I'll leave this on." He blew her a kiss and renewed his attack on the keyboard.

Another wave of apprehension eddied around her as she headed down to wait for her cab. Tonight she wished more than ever that she lived here.

17

Dressed in layers of rag shop clothing, Jack sat on a piece of cardboard in a shadowed doorway of Doyle's auctions across the street from Dr. Monnet's co-op building on East Eighty-seventh Street. He was keeping a low profile, not because he was afraid Monnet would spot him but because his current look wasn't exactly common in Carnegie Hill, especially just a few blocks up from the mayor's digs. The hour was late and traffic was light in this land of upscale shops and high-rise condos and co-ops.

Business must be good in pharmaceuticals, he thought as he checked out the front of Monnet's building. Eight stories—tall stories— the apartments inside had to have ten-, twelve-, maybe fifteen-foot ceilings—with some sort of turretlike superpenthouse or common area on the roof. Three different kinds of brick, and large balconies recessed in the face. Even a small apartment in that place probably had a seven-figure price tag.

Since Dragovic was more secretive and harder to tail—and was probably already out in the Hamptons for the weekend anyway—Jack had decided to stick close to Monnet. Jack hadn't said anything to Nadia, but he wasn't ready just yet to buy into her idea that Dr. Monnet was a completely unwilling participant in any relationship he might have with the Slippery Serb. Guys like Dragovic did their fair share of arm-twisting, but lots of times the arm they were twisting had been offered to them. Jack was curious what else Monnet might be into.

But where was the good doctor? Jack had called his number before coming over, and a couple of more times from the pay phone on the corner. All he'd got was the answering machine.

That didn't necessarily mean the man wasn't home. Maybe he had caller ID and didn't pick up when the readout said "unknown caller." So Jack had parked himself here to keep an eye on the front entrance and see if Monnet showed—either coming or going.

But he'd been at it since nine and here it was almost midnight with no sign of him. No sense in hanging here any longer. If Monnet was in, he'd most likely stay in; if he was out, Jack wasn't going to learn anything by watching him come home. Time to pack it in.

Annoyed at the waste of time he could have better spent with Gia, he rose and folded his cardboard and headed west. He entered Central Park at Eighty-sixth Street and walked across the Great Lawn with his Semmerling in his hand in case some genius got the bright idea that a homeless guy might be an easy roll, but he reached the bright lights of Central Park West without incident.

Back in his apartment he stripped, showered, then set up the projection TV for the start of his Moreau festival—not Jeanne . . . *Dr.* Moreau. Jack had the tapes set up in chronological order. Unfortunately that meant playing the best first. *The Island of Lost Souls* with Laughton,

Lugosi, and Arien was one of his all-time favorites and certainly the best of the Moreaus. Despite the inexplicable Hungarian accent of his man-wolf character, Bela remained unmatched as Sayer of the Law.

"Not to spill blood! That is the law! Are we not men?"

And then the guttural response from dozens of coarse throats not designed for human speech . . . *"Are we not men? . . ."*

But fatigue got the best of him. He dozed off with Charles Laughton complaining through his prissy little mustache and goatee about "the stubborn beast flesh creeping back . . ."

Somewhere in Jack's dreams Sal Vituolo became the Sayer of the Law, crying over and over, "Are we not men? . . . Are we not men? . . ."

FRIDAY

1

"Jesus H. Christ!"

It had changed.

Nadia sat on the edge of her bed and stared at the printout in her vibrating hands.

The diagram of the Loki molecule's structure—it looked different, *was* different. She couldn't say how, exactly, but she knew that some of the side chains present yesterday afternoon were missing this morning. For the life of her, though, she couldn't remember what they were.

She'd meant to check the printout last night when she came home but forgot. Probably because she hadn't thought it worth the effort, or maybe she'd subconsciously believed that Dr. Monnet had been kidding her. In Nadia's world, diagrams did not alter themselves.

Until now.

No-no-no. Don't go there. This is impossible.

Wait. She'd also printed out the empirical formula and memorized it. She pulled the sheet from her shoulder bag and unfolded it. It read "$C_{24}H_{34}O_4$." But that was wrong. She was sure it had been $C_{27}H_{40}O_3$. Or had there been six oxygen atoms? Damn! She couldn't be sure. And that wasn't like her.

She checked the empirical formula against the molecular structure—they tallied perfectly.

She closed her eyes against the queasy, dizzy feeling stealing over her. This can't be happening. It's some sort of trick. Has to be.

Somehow someone had got into her shoulder bag and switched the printouts. But who? And when? She'd made the printouts just before she'd left GEM yesterday, and her bag hadn't been out of her sight since. And why the hell would someone go to all that trouble?

But a switch didn't explain her memory lapse. Even on a bad day she'd be able to remember at least one of the missing side chains, but this morning she was drawing a complete blank.

A strange mixture of unease and excitement started buzzing through her. Something very strange was going on here. That molecule—Loki— was some sort of singularity. It had properties she could not explain but not unfathomable properties; over at GEM she had tools that could help her unravel its mysteries. This would be ground breaking work. She thought of all the papers she could publish about Loki, all the lectures she would give. Barely thirty and she'd be world famous.

Well, famous among molecular biologists.

And best of all, she was getting paid to do what she'd be willing to do for free.

Nadia started pulling on her clothes. She wanted to be in the dry lab right now, but she had to stop by the diabetes clinic first. She'd do a fly-through there, then run straight over to GEM.

As she hurried down the hall toward the front door, passing various portraits of Pope John Paul and loops of dried palm fronds tacked to the walls, she heard her mother's voice call out from the other side of her bedroom door.

"I heard you, Nadj!"

"Heard me what, Mom?" she said, still moving.

"Take the Lord's name in vain. You shouldn't do that. It's a sin."

When did I do that? she wondered. But she had no time and less inclination to discuss it right now.

"Sorry, Mom."

Doug's right, she thought as she swung into the hallway. Got to move out. And soon.

2

Doug's eyes burned from staring at the monitor. He leaned back and rubbed them. He'd spent the whole night chipping away at the defenses in the GEM mainframe. Some he'd overcome—the partners' expense account records, for instance. He'd tooled through those and wasted a lot of time without finding anything unusual or even interesting.

But the defenses around the finances of GEM Basic were giving him fits. He could follow the money trail to the R & D division, but there it stopped. Details of where, when, and how that money was spent were locked in a cyber safe, and he didn't have the combination.

Not yet, anyway. He was making headway, but at a glacial pace.

"Need a break," he muttered as he rose and rotated his aching back.

He walked around the study, stretching, punching at the air to loosen up. He felt tired but wired. He was getting the hang of the GEM security codes. Whoever had set them up was good, but Doug was pretty good too. He'd pulled his share of all-nighters with the computer nerds back in college, hacking into various corporate and academic systems and leaving prank messages in the sysops' mailboxes. Nothing vicious, more like the cyber equivalent of water paint graffiti.

He glanced at the clock. Damn—almost eight and he had a couple of calls scheduled for late morning, plus he was delivering lunch to the staff of a group practice in Bay Shore.

He hated quitting now, but if he didn't get a little shut-eye he'd be useless the rest of the day. But then, why should he worry about sales calls and feeding nurses and receptionists if sales had no relationship to his commissions?

Good question, but it wasn't his style to blow off appointments. And besides, he had tonight and a three-day weekend ahead to complete the hack.

Reluctantly he shut off his laptop and staggered to the bedroom. He set the alarm for nine-thirty, then toppled onto the bed like a falling tree. The sheets still smelled vaguely of Nadj. He dozed off with a smile on his face.

3

"See!" said Abe, jabbing a juice-coated finger at the *Daily News* spread out on the counter before him. "See!"

"See what?" Jack said.

Breakfast with Abe again, back in their customary positions on either side of the counter. Jack had brought a couple of papayas this time. Sipping coffee, he watched as Abe quickly and expertly began quartering and seeding them, amazed that his chubby, stubby fingers could be so agile.

"Right here. More congested spleen being vented. It says some high school teacher in Jackson Heights tossed two unruly students out a second-story window."

"Probably a physics lab and they were having trouble with the concept of gravity."

"One's got a broken arm, the other a broken leg. Four cops it took to arrest the teach. Know what he said when they finally subdued him? 'They were talking while I was talking! Nobody talks when I'm talking! Next time they'll listen!' "

"Somehow I doubt there'll be a next—hey, what are you doing?"

Abe had just dumped a mass of black papaya seeds and their gooey matrix on the sports section of the *Times*.

"What? I should dump them on my nice clean counter?"

Jack wasn't going to get into that—the counter was anything but clean. "What if I wanted to read that?"

"Suddenly you're Mr. Yankee Fan? A jock you're not."

"I used to be a star hitter in Little League. And what if I wanted to know who won the Knicks game?"

"They didn't play."

"All right. The Nets, then."

"They lost to the Jazz, one-oh-nine to one-oh-one."

Jack stared at Abe. He believed him. Abe listened exclusively to talk radio. He'd probably heard the scores a dozen times already this morning. But Jack wasn't giving up. He rarely read a sports section outside of World Series time or Super Bowl season, but a principle was at stake here. He wasn't sure which one, but he'd come up with something.

"But sometimes I like to *read* about a game."

Abe had freed up the orange papaya fruit but left the crescents lounging in their rinds. Now he was cross-slicing the crescents into bite-size pieces.

"You know the score already. You need more? For why? You're going to read some self-styled mavin's postulations on why they won or why they lost? Who cares unless you're the coach. Team A won; Team B lost; end of story; when's the next game?" He gestured at the papaya with his knife. "Eat."

Jack popped a piece into his mouth. Delicious. As he reached for another piece, Abe gestured to where Parabellum was eyeing the gloppy mass on the sports section. The parakeet cocked his head left and right with suspicion, hungry for the seeds but not sure what to make of the goo.

"Such a fastidious bird I've got."

"You kidding?" Jack said. "You plopped that stuff down on George Veczy's column, and now he can't read the end."

Abe fixed him with a silent, over-the-reading-glasses stare.

Jack sighed. "All right then, hand me the *Post*, will you—unless you've messed up *its* sports section too."

Abe's hand started toward it then stopped. "Well, well, well. Here's something that might interest you."

"Something about the Mets, I hope," Jack said.

"A different kind of sportsman—your preppy rioter friends are in the news again."

"Sent to Sing-Sing, I hope."

"Quite the contrary. They're walking—all of them."

Jack's mood suddenly darkened. "Let me see that."

Abe gave the Metro Section a one-eighty spin and jabbed his finger at a tiny article next to the lottery numbers box. Jack scanned it once, then, not quite believing his eyes, read it again.

"None of them booked! Not one! No charges against any of them!"

"Due to 'a new development' in the case, it says. Hmmm . . . what do you think that could mean?"

Jack knew what Abe was getting at: Well-to-do guys, some of them undoubtedly with a connection or two in City Hall or Police Plaza, get a few strings pulled and sail home as if nothing had happened.

And one of them was Robert B. "Porky" Butler. The bastard who'd damn near killed Vicky hadn't spent a single night in jail—wasn't even being *charged* with anything.

"I've got to make a call."

Abe didn't offer his phone and Jack wouldn't have used it if he had. Not with so many people using caller ID these days.

Jack had retrieved Butler's phone number from his wallet by the time he reached the pay phone on the corner. He plunked in a few coins and was soon connected to the home of Robert B. Butler, alumnus of St. Barnabas Prep and attacker of little girls on museum steps.

When the maid or whoever it was answered the phone and asked in West African–accented English who was calling, he made up a name—Jack Gavin.

"I'm an attorney for the St. Barnabas Prep Alumni Association. I'd like to talk to Mr. Butler about the unfortunate incident Wednesday night and his injury. How is he doing, by the way?"

"Very well," the woman said.

"Is he in a lot of pain?"

"Hardly any."

Damn. He felt his jaw muscles tense. Have to fix that.

"May I speak to him a minute?"

"He's with a physical therapist right now. Let me check."

A minute later she was back. "Mr. Butler can't come to the phone right now, but he'll be glad to see you anytime this afternoon."

Keeping his voice even and professionally pleasant, Jack said he'd be over around one.

Scaring Vicky, endangering her life, and then skating on any charges . . .

He and Mr. Butler were going to have a little heart-to-heart.

4

Nadia sat in the sealed, dimly lit room and stared at the 3-D image floating in the air before her. The first thing she'd done upon reaching the GEM Basic lab was light up the imager and call up the Loki structure from memory: the Loki molecule—or rather its degraded form, which she'd begun thinking of as Loki-2—had appeared.

Changed, just like her printout.

OK. That could be explained by someone tampering with the imager's memory. But she had an ace up her sleeve. Before leaving yesterday she had scraped a few particles of the original Loki sample from the imager.

She removed the stoppered test tube from her pocket and dumped the grains into the sample receptacle. Something about the color . . . she couldn't say exactly what, but it wasn't right. She sat back and waited, then punched up the image. Her mouth went dry as the same damn molecule took shape before her.

The dry lab lightened, then darkened again as the door behind her opened and closed.

"Are you a believer yet?"

She turned at Dr. Monnet's voice. He stood behind her, looking as if he hadn't slept last night.

She swallowed. "Tell me this is a trick. Please?"

"I wish it were." He sighed. "You have no idea how much I wish this were some sort of hoax. But it is not."

"It *has* to be. If you were simply asking me to believe that this molecule alters its structure during the course of some 'celestial event,' I could buy that. I'd want to know how the 'event' effected the change, but I could imagine gravitational influence or something equally subtle acting as a catalyst, and I could handle that. But what we've got here—if we haven't been flimflammed—is a molecule that not only mutates from one form to another but substitutes its new structure for all records of its original structure. In effect, it's editing reality. And we both know that's impossible."

"Knew," Dr. Monnet said. "That was what we assumed was true. Now we know different."

"Speak for yourself."

He smiled wanly. "I know how you feel. You are utterly confused, you are frightened and suspicious, yet you are also exhilarated and challenged. And the tug-of-war between all these conflicting emotions leaves you on the brink of tears. Am I right?"

Nadia felt her eyes begin to brim as a sob built in her throat. She wiped them and nodded, unable to speak.

"But it's *true*, Nadia," he said, his voice dropping to a whisper. "Trust me. We are not being tricked. There's something here that challenges our most fundamental beliefs about the nature of the physical world, about reality itself."

And that was what was so upsetting, making her crazy. What if the ability to reorder reality, along with the very memory of reality, were not confined to this one molecule? What if it were happening every day? How many times had she typed or written a word and then stopped and stared at it, thinking it looked wrong, that it was spelled some other way? She'd look it up and find most times that her original spelling had been correct, so she'd move on despite the feeling that it still looked wrong.

"We must know how it works," Dr. Monnet said. "And the first step toward an answer is to stabilize the molecule."

"How can you do that if you can't even remember what it looked like originally?"

He pulled a vial from his pocket and held it out to her. "Because we have a new supply."

Nadia stared at the tube for a heartbeat, then snatched it from him and with trembling hands began preparing a sample of the pale blue powder for the imager. When it was ready she fed it to the machine and waited.

Finally the molecule appeared and she wanted to cheer when she recognized it. *This* was what had been erased from her brain. Now the memory was back and, disturbing though its shape might be, she felt whole again.

"How . . . where did you find the unaltered Loki?"

"From the source. It doesn't change within the source, only after it's been removed from it."

She turned to face Dr. Monnet. "And are you still keeping the source a secret?"

"For now, yes."

Nadia wanted to scream at him to tell her. It had to be organic— a plant? An animal? What?

"And the mysterious celestial event? Does that remain a secret too?"

"I only held back on that until you'd seen for yourself the changes wrought by the event. The event itself is common, occurring a dozen, sometimes thirteen times per year: the new moon."

Nadia wet her lips. "The new moon? When was that?"

"Exactly eight-forty-two last night."

The cycle of the moon, one of the primal rhythms of the planet. And the new moon . . . a time when Earth's celestial night-light was out, blind to what was going on below on the darkest night of the cycle.

A chill ran over her skin.

"I'd like you to get started right away," Dr. Monnet was saying. "We have no time to lose. The Loki source may be . . . unavailable after this, and then we will have lost forever our chance to unlock its secrets."

"Don't you think we should get some outside help? I mean, if we've only got twenty-nine days . . ."

Dr. Monnet shook his head vigorously. "No. Absolutely not. Loki does not leave GEM. I thought I made that clear."

"You did, but—"

"No buts about it." His face paled, but Nadia wasn't sure whether from anger or fear. "Absolutely no outside consultation on this."

Nadia wanted to wail that he couldn't—shouldn't—put all this responsibility on a beginner like her.

"You *are* going to help me, I hope," she said.

"Of course. To save you time, I'll show you all the dead ends I've already explored. After that, I'm counting on you to come up with a new perspective."

Uncertainty tickled her gut. "I don't know if you should count too heavily—"

He held up a hand. "I never told you this, but before I hired you I put in a call to Dr. Petrillo."

She stiffened. Her research mentor during her fellowship—the Grand Old Man of anabolic steroids. "What did he say?"

"What *didn't* he say! I couldn't get him to stop talking about you. He was overjoyed you were staying in research instead of 'wasting' your talents in clinical practice. So you shouldn't underestimate your abilities, Nadia. I'm certainly not. But as an extra incentive: if you stabilize the Loki molecule within the next four weeks, I am authorized to offer you a bonus."

"Really, that's not necessary."

He smiled. "You shouldn't say that until you hear the amount. How does one million dollars sound?"

Nadia was struck dumb. She opened her mouth but it took a few seconds before she was capable of coherent speech. "Did . . . did you say—?"

"Yes. A lump sum of one million. You can—"

Pat, a middle-aged tech with salt-and-pepper hair, knocked on the dry lab door before pushing it open. Fluorescent light streamed in from the hall.

"Excuse me, Dr. Monnet," she said, "but Mr. Garrison's on the phone."

Dr. Monnet looked irritated. "Tell him I'll call him back."

"He say's it's urgent. 'An emergency' was how he put it."

"Oh, very well." He turned to Nadia. "I'll be right back. Nothing is more important right now than this project."

I guess not, she thought. A million dollars . . . a *million* dollars!

The words kept echoing through her head as she waited, fantasizing what she could do with that amount of cash. She and Doug could get married right away, put a down payment on a house, get his software company up and running, jump out of limbo, and start *living*.

When a good ten minutes had passed and Dr. Monnet didn't return, Nadia stepped outside and signaled to Pat.

"Where's Dr. Monnet?"

She pointed toward the door. "He got off the phone with Mr. Garrison and hurried upstairs."

Nothing more important right now than this project, hmmm? she thought as she returned to the dry lab. Obviously something was. She hoped Mr. Garrison's emergency wasn't too serious or personal.

She stepped up to the imager and began rotating the 3-D Loki image back and forth, hoping the more she saw of it, the less discomfiting it would seem.

I'm going to beat you, she thought, staring at the molecule. Not for the bonus . . . this is the challenge of a lifetime, and I'm going to show I can do it.

But she wouldn't turn down that bonus. No way.

5

"We've been hacked!" Kent Garrison said as soon as the soundproof door was pulled shut and latched.

Kent, flushed, suit coat off, crescents of perspiration darkening the armpits of his bulging blue shirt, stood at the end of the table.

"Not true," Brad Edwards said. Dressed in a perfectly tailored blue blazer, he sat hunched forward in his chair across from Luc, twisting his delicate hands over the mahogany surface. "They said they think someone got past the fire wall, but they're not sure."

Stunned, Luc sank into a chair. "What? How? I thought we were supposed to have the best security available."

"Well, apparently we don't." Kent directed a venomous stare at

Brad who was responsible for the computer system. Kent tended to be full of bluster except when Dragovic was around.

"I was assured we had a state-of-the-art fire wall," Brad said. His usually perfect hair was in disarray, as if he'd been pulling at it. "But that was last year. Hackers learn new tricks too."

"Why aren't they sure?" Luc asked.

"They found evidence of temporary alterations in codes that could have innocent causes." Brad ran a hand across his mouth. "I don't pretend to understand it all."

Kent couldn't seem to stand still. He paced in an arc at the end of the table. "If it was some fourteen-year-old with too much time on his hands, I don't give a shit. He might have screwed up some data, but he'd never be able to make any sense of what he found."

"What if it wasn't a kid?" Luc said. "What if it was someone looking for something on us?"

"Like who, for instance?"

"One of our competitors. We're playing with the big boys now. Or maybe Dragovic hired someone. Or worse yet, a corporate raider looking for inside information before making a move on us."

Finally Kent sat down. He rubbed his eyes. "Oh, God."

Luc turned to Brad. "What countermeasures are we taking?"

Brad perked up at this. "The software people are going to link up to our system and monitor it. If anyone breaks in, they'll know, and they'll trace him."

"And then what?"

"We throw the fucking book at him," Kent said. "Unless of course it's our friend Milos, in which case we'll say pretty please don't do that anymore because it makes us very nervous."

Luc said, "But what if the hacker learns what we're doing with the money that's supposedly going to R & D?"

Silence around the table. An exposé would lead to an audit, an audit would eventually lead to Loki, and that would put them all behind bars for a long, long time.

Brad Edwards let out a long, tortured groan as he shook his head. "I don't know how much more of this I can take. I did not enter into this venture to become a criminal. We started with a straight honest business—"

"That was going down the tubes!" Kent said.

"And so we got in bed with the devil to save it."

"I don't see you hopping *out* of bed."

Brad stared at his hands. "Sometimes I wish the shit *would* hit the fan. Then this whole ordeal would be over. Maybe then I could sleep at night. When was the last time either of you had a decent night's sleep?"

Good question, Luc thought. If not for a few glasses of his best wine before retiring, he doubted he'd sleep at all.

"Cut the crap, will you?" Kent said, his face now nearly as red as his hair. "If you go up, don't think you'll be doing your time in some federal country club! We're talking drugs, here, and worse. With what they'll have on us, you'll spend the rest of your life in Rikers or Attica, where they'll pass you around as an after-dinner treat."

"Me?" Brad said, his lower lip quivering. "Just me? What about you?"

Kent shook his head. "I'll blow a big hole through my brain before it ever gets that far."

Luc wanted to scream. He'd heard all this before. "Can we return to the matter at hand? What do we do if this hacker breaks in and learns enough to bring us down?"

Kent did not miss a beat. "He gets the Macintosh treatment." He looked around, daring anyone to challenge him.

Luc had a flash of Macintosh's face as he died . . . the bulging eyes, the startled *O* of his open mouth. . . .

Not again . . . please, not again. . . .

"Let us hope we won't be faced with that choice," he said. "If it was indeed an intrusion, perhaps it was just a capricious stunt by an otherwise disinterested hacker who will target another system tonight."

"But if he doesn't," Brad said. "If he chooses to come back, we'll track him and find him."

They fell into silence. The meeting was over, but no one moved to leave. Luc didn't know how the others felt, but the world beyond their insulated, isolated, soundproof, bug-proof boardroom seemed full of danger and menace, a giant trap waiting to snap shut on him. He wanted to delay venturing outside this sheltering cocoon as long as possible.

6

Jack spent much of the late morning on his computer, designing an attorney business card. He'd used the program only twice before and still hadn't got the hang of it. He botched the first couple of attempts, then came up with a design that looked like the real thing. Running off a single sheet yielded a dozen cards. Plenty.

At one o'clock exactly, showered, shaved, dressed in a dark suit, white shirt, and striped tie, John Gavin, attorney-at-law, presented himself and his brand-new card to the doorman at the Millennium Towers on West Sixty-seventh Street. A call upstairs confirmed that he was expected, and he was pointed toward the elevator.

The Butler condo was on the twenty-first floor. On his way up Jack reviewed his options. He hadn't yet worked out just how he was going to handle Butler—hang him out the window for a while or maybe break his other leg—a lot would depend on how Jack felt when he saw him again. Right now he was in a pretty good mood. A shame to spoil it like this, but some things you could let slide; other things you couldn't.

A private nurse, her black skin seeming even darker against her white uniform, greeted him at the door. Jack recognized her accent from his phone call. She led him to the study and left him with Mr. Butler.

Jack felt the old fury scald his insides again as he stared at the bastard. Butler wore a Princeton sweatshirt and matching sweatpants with one leg cut off at midthigh to accommodate his cast. And he still looked like Porky Pig.

"Gavin, right?" he said, thrusting out a hand. "Bob Butler. Thanks for coming over." When Jack didn't shake hands, Butler said, "Something wrong?"

"Don't I look familiar?" Jack said.

"Not really." He smiled apologetically. "I assume you're a Barny if you're working for the alumni association, but I can't recognize some of the guys in my own class, let alone—"

"Last night," Jack said through his teeth.

Butler's smile faded. He averted his eyes. "Yeah. Last night. I suppose you want to know about that."

"I know all about it," Jack said. "I was there, remember?"

Butler looked up at him again. "You were?"

Jack leaned closer, pointing to his face. "Remember?"

"No," Butler said. "Everything's kind of a blur."

If he was lying, he was damn good at it.

Butler rubbed a hand across his stubbled jaw. "I remember being at the reception hall. Because it was our twenty-fifth, we mixed up a batch of our traditional 'everything punch.' We lugged in a galvanized tub and filled it with blocks of ice, fruit juices, and bottles of the cheapest vodka and rum we could find, just like in the old days. I remember downing a couple of glasses of that; I remember some of the guys getting loud and a couple of them even swinging fists at each other. After that . . ." He shrugged.

"You don't remember being in a mob that terrorized a bunch of people on the museum steps?"

He sighed and nodded. "I remember being in the street, then on some steps, fighting with . . . someone. But that's pretty much it. I don't remember details, though. I'm told I had a concussion. I woke up in the hospital with a broken leg and no idea how I got it. You say you were there. Did you see me?"

Jack nodded, watching for the slightest hint that he was lying.

"Did . . . did I do anything . . . bad?"

Jack forced calm. "You tried to kill an eight-year-old girl."

"*What?*" The depth of horror in Butler's expression could not be faked. "I did *what?*" His eyes pleaded with Jack. "Tell me she's all right! Please tell me I didn't hurt a child!"

"Somebody pulled her away from you just as you tried to chuck her off the top of the steps."

"Thank God!"

Butler's genuine relief cooled Jack's anger, but that didn't let him off the hook.

"You guys had to be doing more than cheap rum and vodka to mess up your heads like that."

"We were, but we didn't know about it. At least most of us didn't. But that bastard Dawkins did."

"Dawkins?"

"Yes. Burton Dawkins. Didn't you hear?"

"I'm afraid not."

"That's why I thought you were here—about Burt. The police were immediately suspicious that the punch had been drugged, so they tested it right away and found out it was. That's why we were released without being charged. They arrested Dawkins for spiking the punch." He shook his head. "Who would have thought a dweeb like him would do something like that. But the cops caught him red-handed with a whole bag of the drug."

"What drug?"

"They haven't said yet, but I called someone I know down at the commissioner's office, and he told me they think it's some new designer drug that's been popping up all over the country the past few months."

"What's it called?"

"He said it's sold under lots of names. They didn't have the lab report back yet, but he suspected it was a highly concentrated form called Berzerk."

"Sounds appropriate."

"I'm told it's spelled with a *z*."

"Like the old arcade game."

Butler flashed a smile. "Yeah. I remember that. Used to be my favorite when I was a kid. But there was nothing fun about this stuff. Potent as all hell. Between you and me, I smoked my share of weed in my younger days, snorted coke once or twice, did some speed-rite-of-passage stuff, you know? I've been high before, but I've never felt like I did the other night. I remember this sensation of awesome power, as if I were king of the world. It was truly wonderful for a while, but then it turned into this anger, this . . . this *rage* because this was *my* world and everything in it belonged to me and there were these other people around who were keeping me from what was rightfully mine." He grinned sheepishly. "I know it sounds insane now, but at the time it all made perfect sense. I felt like a god."

Jack hadn't heard of anything that did that to your head, but then he didn't hang with druggies.

"Sounds like you had a whopping dose of whatever it was."

"I guess so. I just know I don't want any more. Ever." He shook his head. "Imagine . . . trying to hurt a child. I've never even spanked one of my own kids—not once." He set his jaw. "Let me tell you something: Burt Dawkins is not going to get away with this. When the criminal courts are through with him, I'm going to haul him into court and sue his ass for every penny he's worth."

"You do that," Jack said, feeling deflated now that his anger had leaked away. He stepped toward the door. "Well, I've learned what I came for. I'll be in touch."

"Wait," Butler said. "You were there. Did you see how I got hurt?"

"Um, yeah. When someone grabbed the little girl from you, you, um, tripped and went down the steps yourself."

He paled. "I could have been killed. I guess I'm pretty lucky."

"You've got that right," Jack said, turning away.

7

"You're not hungry?" Mom said in her thick Gdansk accent. "Or you don't like my cooking no more?"

Nadia stared down at her half-empty plate. "You still make the best pierogies in the world, Mom. I'm just not that hungry."

Her mother sat across the rickety table from her in a kitchen where the smells of cooked cabbage and boiled *kiszka* permeated the walls. A thin, angular woman with a heavily lined face that made her look older than her sixty-two years, but her bright eyes still had a youthful twinkle.

Mom had already finished eating and was working toward the end of her second boilermaker. She nursed two of them every night, sitting there with a bottle of Budweiser and a shot of Fleischman's rye— "Fleshman's," as she said it—alongside. She'd pour an ounce or two of beer into a tumbler, sip it down, then pour a little more; every so often she'd nip some of the rye. Up until a few years ago she'd have been smoking a Winston as well. Nadia had got her off the cigarettes, finally convincing her that they were what had done Dad in, but Mom wasn't about to give up the boilermakers. This was how she'd learned to drink, and no one, not Nadia or anyone else, was going to change that.

"You have a fight with Douglas? That is why you're eating dinner with your mother on a Friday night?"

Nadia shook her head and pushed a pierogi around her plate. "No, he's just busy."

"Too busy for the girl he's to marry?"

"It's a project he's working on."

Doug had said he wanted to get back to his GEM mainframe hack before he got cold. He was determined to break through the final barriers tonight. She thought of him alone, hunched over his keyboard, not eating or drinking, totally absorbed in the data flashing across his screen. She'd been a little hurt, but then she realized she was developing an obsession of her own.

"Work, work, work. That's all you two do. That's all young people do these days. At least now that you are not in residency, you have off the weekends. You will see him tomorrow."

"Maybe."

Mom's eyebrows lifted. "Saturday he is working too?"

"Not him. Me."

Now her eyes fairly bulged. "You? This company is paying you by the hour?"

"No. It's salaried. But there's a project—"

"If they not pay you for going in on Saturday you should not go. See, if you were working as a real doctor with real patients instead of this research silliness you would make extra for doing extra."

"I will. I get a bonus if I complete the project before a certain date."

Mom shrugged. "A bonus? A big bonus?"

Nadia didn't want to tell her the million-dollar figure. She didn't want Mom working herself up with anticipation.

"Very big."

"A big-enough-to-be-working-on-Saturday bonus? Big enough so that after you get it you will quit this company and become a real doctor with real live patients?"

Nadia laughed. "Ooooh, yes."

"Then I think," Mom said, smiling, "that you should go to work tomorrow."

8

Sal Vituolo huddled on an East Hampton dune and wondered what the hell he was doing. Freakin' long ride to get here, and the sand being damp and chilly wasn't helping matters much. He hoped this was going to be worth all the trouble.

And expense. This Repairman Jack guy didn't come cheap. Sal had tried to pay him in car parts but it was cash—and lots of it—or nothing. He hadn't particularly featured handing over that much dough with no receipt, no guarantee. Guy could be a scammer and just take off, but sometimes you just had to put aside everything you'd learned in the school of hard knocks and go with your gut. Sal's gut said this Jack was a stand-up guy.

But maybe not wrapped too tight. Tires? What did he want with a freakin' truckload of old tires?

The guy had shown up this afternoon to pick up the rubber and his money. Then he told Sal to go out and rent a videocam, a professional model with the best zoom lens and low-light capabilities, and haul it out here to where he could see Dragovic's house. Keep your distance but get as close as you can without being spotted, he'd said. Sal wasn't sure exactly what that meant, but here he was.

He glanced around uneasily, hoping no one was watching him—

especially no one from Dragovic's crew. No telling what would happen
to him if he got caught spying on the party.

He checked his watch. Ten o'clock. Jack had said start taping at
ten, so Sal flicked on the power and settled into the eyepiece. He'd
been practicing with the videocam since he got here and had the work-
ings down pretty good. At maximum zoom, the telephoto night lens
magnified the light and the house to the point where Sal felt like he
was looking at the place from twenty feet away.

He'd peeped the party off and on. Looked like the Slippery Serb
was tossing a bash for his boys and his big customers. The crowd was
all guys, some in suits, some in sweaters or golf shirts. Sal knew the
type from their haircuts and their swagger—Eurotrash and local tough
guys, probably the kind Dragovic's lawyers would refer to in court as
"business associates."

Sal had watched them chow down on the best damn buffet he'd
ever seen—whole lobsters, soft-shelled crabs, a sushi chef, carvers
serving everything from prime-rib to filet, a raw bar, a caviar bar with
bottles of flavored vodkas jutting from a mound of shaved ice—until
he got so hungry he had to turn off the camera.

As he focused the scene now, he noticed something new going on
at the party. A bunch of bikinis were splashing around in the pool.
Where'd they come from? The guys were all hanging around the water,
sipping after-dinner drinks, smoking fat cigars, and watching.

Sal felt his shoulder muscles, knot. . . . He'd bet his life that somewhere in that crowd were the guys who splattered Artie all over Church
Avenue. He could be looking at them right now.

What am I doing videotaping a party? What for? And where do
Jack and my old tires come in?

Then he heard the helicopter.

9

"My, what interesting people," Cino said.

Her sarcastic tone irritated Milos. They stood in the corner where the main house joined its eastern wing. Drinks in hand—Ketel One for Milos, the ever-present Dampierre for Cino—they leaned on the railing of the highest tier of one of the multilevel decks and surveyed Milos's guests below.

Cino wore a high-collared embroidered kimonolike dress of red silk that clung to every curve of her slim body on its way to her ankles. With her dark bangs and jet eyes, she looked Oriental tonight.

"I'm sure you'll be more impressed with Sunday's guest list," he said. "The beautiful people are more your type. But these folk"—he gestured with a sweep of his arm—"are the ones who make this place and this party possible. My buyers, sellers, suppliers, and distributors."

"Distributors of what?" Cino asked with a mischievous grin as she leaned against him like a cat. She'd been hitting the champagne since midafternoon and her glittering eyes said she was feeling little pain.

Milos returned her smile. "Of the many items I import and export."

"What kind of items?"

"Whatever is in demand," he said.

"And the bathing beauties," she said, jutting her chin at the pool. "Are they part of your distribution network too?"

"Hardly. They're items in demand, which I imported from the city especially for the occasion."

He'd hired the best-looking girls from a number of strip clubs and vanned them out for the night. Their job was an easy one: party, have a good time, wear very little, and be *very* friendly.

"Ah," Cino said. "Window dressing."

"More like party favors."

Cino seemed to think this was very funny, and Milos enjoyed the ringing sound of her laughter as he watched the girls. Nature and silicone had provided them with fabulous bodies. They were on display now, but their real work would begin after they dried off. They had been instructed as to the pecking order of the guests and, keeping that in mind, were to pair off with anyone who was interested.

Tonight was supposedly a little bonus for the key people in the network of drugs and guns and currency that fed Milos's operations. Many races down there on the patio: Italians, Greeks, Africans, Koreans, Mexicans, all soon to be part of his growing empire. His was now an international business, and thus he had to be an international man and deal with everyone. Of course for his personal operations and security he used only full-blooded Serbs, hard, loyal men, blooded in battle.

But this gathering was more than just a party. It was a testimonial, an affirmation of sorts. They were here as Milos's guests. Some of them might harbor an inkling in the backs of their minds that they could be his equal, but tonight should lay that to rest. This wasn't neutral territory where equals meet. They had come to *his* place, where *he* called the shots; they were enjoying themselves on *his* tab and getting a good look at his impressive new digs. They were in a position where the fact that Milos Dragovic was *the man* was being pounded home every minute of their stay.

They were down there with the bimbos; he was up here with the supermodel. Didn't that say it all.

Forty-eight hours from now things would be very different. No business associates, no bodies in the pool. Sunday would be purely social, to establish and enhance his status among the big names out here.

"What's that noise?" Cino said.

Milos recognized the rapid *wup-wup-wup* that seemed to come from everywhere. "Sounds like a helicopter."

And then he saw it, maybe a hundred feet up, gliding in from over the ocean. A bulging net of some sort dangled beneath it. Milos couldn't see what was in the net, but it looked full of whatever it was. Some new way of fishing, maybe? But no water was dripping from the net.

Whatever he was up to, Milos thought, the pilot shouldn't be flying that sort of cargo over homes. If that net should tear . . .

"Oh, look," Cino said. "He's stopped right overhead."

That was when the first suspicion that something might be wrong flitted through Milos's mind. It became stronger when he noticed that the helicopter didn't have any numbers on it. He didn't know the exact rules, but every damn aircraft he'd ever seen had a string of numbers on the fuselage. Either this one didn't have any or someone had masked them.

Milos looked around and saw that the party had stopped dead. All his guests were standing still, looking up. Even the babes in the pool had stopped their splashing and were pointing at the sky.

"What do you think he's up to with all those tires?" Cino said.

Tires? Milos looked up again. Damned if she wasn't right. That net was full of tires. Must have been fifty of them at least.

What's that asshole doing dangling all those tires right over my house?

And then the net opened . . .

And the tires tumbled free . . .

And fell directly toward him and the house.

Cino let out a high-pitched scream.

"Get inside!" Milos shouted as he turned to do just that, but she was already on her way, moving remarkably fast on her sky-high high heels.

Milos dived through the door just as the first tires hit the roof with the staccato thudding of a giant doing drumrolls with telephone poles, accenting with the cymbal crash of shattering skylights. An instant later other tires landed directly on the deck-patio area, smashing railings, overturning tables, wrecking the greenhouse.

It wouldn't have been so bad if that had been it. But the tires on the ground didn't stop on impact; they kept moving, bouncing ten, fifteen feet in the air in all directions. The ones on the roof were even worse, caroming off the pitched tiles and sailing toward the pool.

Milos ducked as a tire slammed into a sliding glass door just a few feet to his left, cracking it but not breaking all the way through. Screams and panicked shouts rose from outside. Milos clung to the door frame, watching in horror as his party dissolved into chaos.

The girls in the pool were lucky—they ducked underwater as tires splashed around them. But the men on the decks and patio didn't have that option. They scrambled around, fleeing in all directions, bumping into each other, occasionally knocking each other down as the tires rained on them, flattening them, knocking them into the pool, upending tables, and sending food and flaming chafing dishes flying. The randomness of the assault, the unpredictable, helter-skelter nature of the trajectories added terror to the chaos.

Where was his security? He scanned the tumult and found a couple of them still upright. Splattered with an assortment of desserts, they crouched by one of the raised decks with their guns out and raised, eyes searching the sky. But the helicopter was nowhere in sight.

With the tires bouncing from the direction of the main house and the wings hemming them in on both sides, those guests still upright had nowhere to run except toward the beach. The tires bounced in pursuit, catching up to some and knocking them face-first into the sand.

It seemed as if the tires would never stop bouncing, but eventually, after what seemed like aeons, the last one wobbled to a halt. Milos stepped outside and gazed in horror at the shambles that had once been the pride of his grounds. Every square foot had suffered some damage. The girls were wailing as they crawled shivering and dripping from the pool. The cracked decks and patio were littered with debris and battered men struggling to their feet, some groaning, some cradling broken limbs, a few out cold and lying where they had landed. It looked like a war zone, as if a bomb had exploded.

But worse than any physical destruction was the deep, hemorrhaging wound to Milos's pride. Guests in his home, proud men here at his invitation, had been injured or—worse—caused to run like panicked children. Their humiliation while under his aegis was a double disgrace for Milos.

Who would want to do this to him? Why?

He searched above for the helicopter, but it was gone, as if it had never been.

Never had Milos felt so impotent, so mortified. He fought the urge to scream his rage at the moonless sky. He had to remain poised, appear to be in control—as much as one could be amid such havoc—and then his gaze came to rest on the tire that had almost smashed through into his living room. It was mud-stained and bald, so worn that its steel belts showed through in spots.

Junk! Bad enough that he'd been attacked in his home, but he'd been assaulted with garbage!

With a cry that was half roar, half scream, he picked up the tire and hurled it the rest of the way through the window.

As he watched it roll across his living room carpet, Milos Dragovic swore to find out who had done this and to have his revenge.

10

Sal's body was bucking so hard from repressed laughter he had to turn off the camera. If only he could scream it out, lie on his back and guffaw at the sky! Of course that might attract the kind of attention that would stop all laughs for good. He wiped his eyes on his sleeves and, still giggling, hurried off the dune toward his car.

Oh, God, that was wonderful. Those tires bouncing all over the place, tough guys running around like a bunch of cockroaches when the light goes on, screeching like little old ladies. The Slippery Serb's gotta be shitting a brick! And I got it all on tape!

When he reached his car he sat in the front seat and caught his breath. He stared out the window at the empty dunes.

Bad night for Dragovic, yeah, but was it enough for what he'd done to Artie? No. Not nearly enough.

But it was a start.

11

Jack crouched in the doorway across East Eighty-seventh Street from Monnet's building and listened to the radio on his headphones to pass the time.

He'd been on the Monnet trail for the past six or seven hours, following him from the corporate offices on Thirty-fourth over to the GEM production plant in the Marine Terminal area of Brooklyn, then to a warehouse down the street from the plant. Monnet had stayed late at the warehouse, returning home about an hour ago, and hadn't budged since.

Jack wasn't sure what he was looking for—something suspicious, something he could tag and follow up. So far he'd come up empty.

He spun the tuner dial to an all-news station in time to catch a story about a scandal in the police department. The drug seized in connection with the preppy riot had been stolen and an inert substance substituted in its place. Internal Affairs had launched an investigation.

So what does this mean now? Jack wondered. That classmate Butler had mentioned—Burt Dawkins, wasn't it?—walks? He shook his head. Great system. And he had no inclination to go after Dawkins himself. The link was too thin.

Jack's beeper vibrated through his pocket against his thigh. He checked the readout: one of the Ashe brothers. He went to the phone on the corner and used one of his calling cards to pay for the call.

Joe Ashe came on the line. "Twin Air."

"How'd it go?"

Joe started laughing. "What a pisser you are, boy! What a evil pisser! Frank was laughin' so hard he damn near put us in the drink! Those tires"—the word came through his Georgia accent as "tahrs"—

"was bouncin' ever' which way. You shoulda been there, Jack! You shoulda seen!"

"Oh, I'll see it," Jack said, hoping Sal had made a good tape. Exhilaration bubbled through him. It had been a wild idea, one that easily could have flopped. "I thought it might work, but you never know until you do it."

"Jack, it worked so well I don't know why the Air Force don't use tires instead of bombs next time we have another Gulf War or Yugo-slavia thang. You know how many tons and tons of old tires we got in this country that we gotta go out and bury or sink in the ocean ever' year? We could load 'em all into B-52s and drop 'em from fifty thousand feet. Can you imagine the commotion of a zillion tires landing after a ten-mile drop? Why, they'll be bouncin' right over buildings is what. Panic in the streets, man. If we'd thoughta this before, we coulda just *buried* Baghdad and Belgrade and got rid of a whole pile of junk to boot."

"I'd appreciate it if we kept the U.S. Air Force out of this for the time being," Jack said. "We're still set for another run on Sunday, right?"

"Set? We can't hardly wait! Almost seems a sin to be gettin' paid for this! Say, y'know, I was thinkin' maybe I'd add a little music on Sunday, y'know, like special for the occasion."

"Joe, I'd rather you—"

"You remember that ol' Bobby Vee song, 'Rubber Ball,' and the part where it goes 'Bouncy-bouncy, bouncy-bouncy.' Wouldn't it be cool if we could be blastin' that from some speakers while all those tires—"

Jack had to smile. "Let's keep it simple, Joe. Once we start em-bellishing, we start asking for trouble."

"The ol' KISS rule, huh? I gotcha. Just a thought."

"And a good one too, but let's do the second one just like the first, OK."

"You got it, boy."

Jack waited for Joe to hang up, then hit the # key to make an-other call.

12

His guests had gone now, most managing to exit under their own power, some needing assistance. After profuse apologies, Milos had seen the last one off, then got down to business.

He'd had Kim set up Cino in the theater room with the new Keanu Reeves film on the plasma screen and a fresh bottle of Dampierre in an ice bucket as her companion, then had put the Korean in charge of the caterer's staff to start them on the massive clean up job. That taken care of, Milos lined up his men in the security office in the basement.

This was his nerve center, crammed with state-of-the-art electronics. The feeds from all the surveillance cameras were monitored here; all outgoing calls of a sensitive nature were routed through here for scrambling. Milos had spent a fortune on this room so he could stay in the Hamptons and still run his operations with security. But tonight none of it had helped.

Sometimes for effect he acted like a madman, as he'd done in the GEM conference room yesterday. But tonight was no act. He stalked back and forth, red-faced, punching the air, screaming his rage at these men for allowing this to happen. He knew it was not their fault, but he felt he had to loose this pressure inside him or explode into a thousand bleeding, twitching pieces.

Finally he wound down. He stood staring at his silent, white-faced men. He knew what they were thinking: would he make an example of one of them as he had in the past?

Nothing Milos would have liked better—make someone the fall guy and shoot him dead right here. But that would be a waste of a good man, and if he was going to find out who did this, he'd need every one of them.

"Does anyone have anything to say?" he said when the silence had stretched to the breaking point.

More silence.

"Have any of you noticed anyone strange hanging around, anyone showing unusual interest? You, Vuk." He singled out an ex-corporal from the Yugoslav army who liked to bleach his hair. The man blinked but otherwise remained calm. "You've been on patrol this week. You see anyone paying too much attention to the house?"

"No, sir," he said. "Ivo and I ran off a man and his wife yesterday, but they were just walking on the beach. When they stopped to look, we moved them on. The wife didn't want to go, but the man gave us no trouble."

Milos nodded. "What is on the security cameras?" he said to Dositej, the surveillance man.

Dositej jerked a thumb over his shoulder at the half-dozen monitor screens in the surveillance booth. "I've been checking last week's tapes, sir. Haven't found anything yet."

"Nothing?" Milos said, feeling his anger rising again. *"Nothing?"*

Just then a phone rang. Dositej, anxious to duck the spotlight, hurried to answer it.

"It's Kim," he said after listening a few seconds. "Says you've got a call."

"I told him no interruptions!"

"He says it's from someone who wants to know if you got any old tires you care to part with."

Everyone started talking at once. Milos felt a sudden calm. He didn't have to search out the enemy; the enemy was coming to him.

Grabbing the phone from Dositej, he pointed to Mihailo, his balding, bespectacled communications man. "Trace the call." Then he spoke to Kim upstairs. "Put him through."

A crisp, WASP-inflected voice that sounded like a cross between George Plimpton and William F. Buckley came on the line. "Mr. Dragovic? Is that you?"

Milos could hear the same words echoing from across the room where their conversation was playing from a speaker on the communications console.

"Yes," Milos said, struggling to modulate his tone. "Who is this?"

"I'm the president of the East Hampton Environmental Protection Committee, Mr. Dragovic. Did you get our message tonight?"

"Message?" Milos said, playing along. "What message?"

"The tires, dear boy, the *tires.* Surely you noticed them, although considering the simply dreadful house you've built there, I suppose it's possible you might have missed them. Anyway, I'm calling just in case you've missed the point."

Milos felt his teeth grinding. "Just what *was* the point?"

"That you're not wanted out here, Mr. Dragovic. You are cheap and vulgar and we will not tolerate your type amongst us. You are a toxin and we are out to clean you up. You are garbage and your house a waste dump, and that is how we intend to treat it until you decide to pack up your trashy self, your trashy friends, your trashy lifestyle, and go back where you came from."

Milos clutched the receiver in a death grip and sputtered a reply. "Who *are* you?"

He heard an exultant "Yes!" from the communications console. He looked over and saw Mihailo giving him the OK sign. He'd traced the call.

"I believe I told you: this is not the militant wing of the LVIS, this is the East Hampton Environmental Protection Committee, and we mean business. Be warned, Mr. Dragovic," the man on the phone was saying. "We are quite serious. This is not a game."

"You think not?" Milos said, smiling. "I say it is—one that two can play." He hung up and turned to Mihailo. "Who is he?"

"Can't say," Mihailo said, adjusting his wire-rimmed glasses nervously, "but he was calling from the city—a pay phone in the East Eighties."

Milos cursed silently. He'd been hoping for a name, but he should have known the man would not call from his home.

"I think I've got something," Dositej called from the video monitoring room.

Milos stepped into the cubicle where Dositej was leaning close to a monitor, his nose almost touching its screen. "What is it?"

"I remember now. This car came by yesterday. Pulled right up to the front gate and stopped. I was about to send someone out when it pulled away."

Milos saw the grainy image of a man staring at the house from the passenger seat of an American-made sedan.

"I know him," said Ivo. "He's the one we chased off the beach."

Milos turned. Vuk and Ivo stood side by side. "You think he could be the one on the phone?"

Vuk shook his head. "Not the same voice. And the man we chased was too afraid of a fight to try anything like tonight."

"I'm not so sure," Ivo said, squinting at the screen. "We saw a man who did not *want* to fight, but I would not say he was afraid."

Milos considered Ivo the more perceptive of the two. And he did not bleach his hair, which was another plus. "We must find this man."

"No problem," Dositej said. Milos turned and saw the image of the car frozen on the screen. Dositej was pointing to the bumper. "There's his license plate."

Milos felt a grin spreading across his face as he stared at the numbers. Whoever you are, he thought, I will find you. And I will make you wish you had never been born.

13

Luc cradled the bottle of 1959 Château Lafite-Rothchild in his arms like a baby. He smiled at the thought. He and Laurell had had no children—thank God . . . she probably would have turned them into monsters just like her—but his wines were a consolation. Better, in fact. Each year, instead of costing you more, a good wine increased in value as well as flavor.

This Lafite, for instance. One of the finest ever produced, and never abandoned by its true parents. Every couple of decades or so Château Lafite sent over a team of experts from France to recork and top off its older vintages. This particular bottle had been recorked by the château in the mideighties; they'd even affixed a label as proof.

And a wine, unlike a wife or a child, will never break your heart.

When Laurell had sued him for divorce, she'd added injury to insult by demanding half of his wine cellar. The slut knew nothing about wine—she drank white zinfandel and wouldn't have been able to distinguish jug wine from premier *cru*. She wanted his only because she knew it was valuable and that splitting it up would break his heart.

She'd wanted to hurt him. She'd already forgiven him for two affairs, but the third had sent her over the edge. He'd tried to tell her that none of them meant anything to him, and that was true; he'd sworn that he loved her and only her, but that of course wasn't.

When was the last time he'd loved? Curious question. He *made* love, but that was different. He preferred brief, intense affairs, where both parties went their own ways afterward with no strings.

The ultimate had been that afternoon with Nadia. Such intensity, such abandon. He felt himself growing hard at the memory. Nadia hadn't wanted strings then and maybe wouldn't now. He'd love an encore, and he'd go for it if he were sure it wouldn't interfere with her work. He'd have to wait and see. Stabilizing that molecule was the top priority.

Another priority was packing this wine, the wine Laurell had coveted. She'd thought she'd crush him, but he'd anticipated her. As their marriage had deteriorated toward the breaking point, he'd methodically smuggled out his best bottles and substituted junk. Laurell wound up with a nice selection of *vin ordinaire*. She'd howled when she got the appraisal, but when asked which specific wines were missing, she hadn't a clue.

Luc gently nestled the Lafite into the excelsior-lined rack within the wooden packing crate, then took a sip of another wine and let it roll around on his tongue. He'd opened a 1982 Haut-Brion, a fabulous Graves, to help him through the ongoing chore of packing up his wine collection. All 600 bottles had to be removed from their temperature-controlled lockers and packed and ready to go within the next week or two.

He was not taking any chances. He had great faith in Nadia, but stabilizing the Loki molecule might be beyond her, might be beyond anyone. And if she failed, he did not intend to be around on June 22 when Dragovic learned that he'd just received his last shipment of Loki. No, Luc would be back in France, and his wines with him.

He hadn't told Brad and Kent. He smiled, wondering if they were in their own homes right now, making similar preparations. He doubted it. They both had wives and children to tie them down. And they didn't have anyplace to go.

He'd leave them to the Serb. They deserved it. After all, they were the ones who'd got the company into this mess in the first place.

He carried his glass out of the wine closet and through to his study. He would hate losing this grand place, but if as expected the creature died during the next few weeks, and if Nadia's work didn't show signs of real progress by mid-June, he would leave and never look back.

He almost wished that would happen . . . to force him to turn his life upside down and start it up again—in a new place, as a new person.

He picked up the vial of pale blue powder from his desk. This was it. A sample from the new batches being synthesized from last night's blood sample. Loki . . . the stuff that had made him rich, the stuff that could ruin his life.

Luc drained his glass. He would have loved another, but it was time to cab over to the warehouse and test the potency of this new batch.

Luc's stomach lurched . . . perhaps the last test he'd ever run. He wasn't sure whether he wanted to laugh or scream.

14

Jack hung up and rubbed the flesh in front of his ears. That Thurston Howell lockjaw accent was tough on the jaw muscles. But he thought the call had accomplished its two purposes: first, to get Dragovic thinking he was the target of some snooty locals willing to take extreme measures to get him out of the neighborhood—ludicrous, but it would serve to muddy the waters for the next few days; second, to set up

Dragovic for the call Jack would make after the Sunday night party; that was the pivotal point. If that call didn't work, the whole plan would fall apart.

He took one last look at Monnet's building. The doctor wasn't going anywhere at this hour. Time to head home for part *deux* of the Dr. Moreau festival: the Burt Lancaster–Michael York version from 1977. Not as atmospheric as *Island of Lost Souls*—Lancaster's Moreau could never match the oozing perversity of Laughton's—but Barbara Carrera's presence went a long way toward making up for that.

But as Jack turned to go he saw a cab pull up to the front entrance. The doorman opened the glass door and Dr. Monnet stepped out. Jack whirled and dashed up to Lexington where he'd parked the Buick.

The night wasn't over yet.

15

"I'm in!"

Doug pushed back from the keyboard and his chair rolled away on its casters. He felt like jumping up and doing a little dance but he was a lousy dancer. Instead he rose and headed for the kitchen, making a pit stop along the way. He grabbed another Jolt from the fridge, filled a bowl with Quisp and milk, and was back in front of his monitor in minutes.

He crunched the cereal as he studied his screen. The internal blocks around the financial files had finally yielded to his assaults. He was in. He'd routed the call through Washington, D.C., this time. No chance of a back-trace, should anyone be trying.

But now the real scut work began: making sense of all the numbers, finding the ones he wanted, and following the R & D money trail.

He rubbed his hands together. Just like the old days. A long night ahead, but he was wired and ready to go. With the right amounts of sugar and caffeine singing through his veins, he wouldn't have to stop until he'd tracked down what he wanted to know.

SATURDAY

1

Belly-crawling along a steel beam twenty feet off the warehouse floor, Jack stopped and pinched his nose to stifle a sneeze.

He could hear the building's resident pigeons cooing and rustling in the corners behind him. He'd upset them by climbing through the skylight during their sleep time, but luckily not enough to send them into panicked flight. Jack guessed they slept in the corners, but it was obvious from the droppings on the beam beneath him that they spent plenty of time right here. Good thing he was in raggedy castoffs. This getup was not going to be salvageable.

Jack had tailed Dr. Monnet from Carnegie Hill in Manhattan to its economic polar opposite in the old Marine Terminal area of Brooklyn, right off the BQE on the waterfront between Bay Ridge and Sunset Park. He hadn't liked the idea of using his own car, but counting on a cab to stop for someone dressed in his current ragman ensemble would have been an iffy proposition.

Monnet had stopped off at the GEM Pharma plant first, and Jack had been surprised to see the place lit up like Times Square. Its parking lot was crowded and the plant seemed to be going full tilt. GEM was running a third shift on a Saturday morning when every other factory around it was locked up tight. Business was evidently very good.

Monnet didn't stay long. Jack next followed him here, back to the same old brick warehouse he'd tailed him to earlier today. Jack had waited outside in the afternoon, and might have done the same tonight, but after watching one rough-looking down-and-outer after another being passed through what looked like a metal detector at the warehouse door, he decided he needed a look inside. Obviously the place was being used for more than just storage.

The building was sealed tight at ground level, with no way up to the roof. But the neighboring building was abandoned and all but leaning against it. Jack had been able to break through a window, make his way to the roof, and then jump the narrow gap to this building.

The interior was a single large open space, three stories tall, crisscrossed by supporting beams and girders, and mostly empty. Only one corner was occupied: a lit-up area covering less than a quarter of the floor had been walled off and partitioned but not roofed over.

Jack eased himself farther along the beam, closer and closer to this glowing island in a dark sea until he could peer down into the two sections of the enclosure. The nearer area was brightly lit. Half a dozen men—the ones he'd seen entering through the metal detector—stood around a small table, drinking from numbered plastic cups.

In an adjacent room beyond the far wall, the lights were lower; a number of indistinct forms huddled there, watching the front room through a cracked panel of tinted glass set in the wall that separated them.

A voice came through the speaker set above the glass.

"Be sure to finish all of your drink. We do not want you to become dehydrated during the test."

Monnet's voice? Jack had never heard him speak but had to assume that was him.

"Everybody finished?"

The men either held up their empty tumblers or said yes.

"Excellent. Now, each participant will take his spot at the test station that matches the number on his cup."

The men milled around, each eventually ending up before a "test station" that consisted of some sort of red vinyl cushion about the size of a bar pizza, set chest high into the wall; LED counters, each reading 000, rested at eye level over each.

Jack slid closer for a better view of the "participants."

"Good. Now, you've all been briefed on how the test works, but allow me to recap for you so that there are no mistakes. When the test is to begin, we will ring a bell. As soon as you hear the bell, you will begin punching the padded impact meter before you. This device measures the strength of each blow. The idea is to punch it as hard as you can as

often as you can. You are scored for strength as well as speed, and your cumulative score registers on the readout above your impact meter. The one who ends with the highest score wins an extra two hundred dollars. I must emphasize that there are no losers tonight. Everyone gets three hundred dollars no matter what the score. Please remember that. Is everybody ready?"

Nods and a chorus of grunts.

"Excellent. Now remember, don't begin until you hear the bell. Ready . . . set . . ."

The bell rang and the men began hammering their fists against the pads, some using one hand, others going at it left–right–left.

Jack, stretched out in pigeon guano, literally and figuratively above the fray, watched in bewildered fascination. What the hell was going on here?

The guys putting more power into their blows weren't matching the frequency of the ones with lighter, quick-shot styles, but for the first minute or so the scores stayed fairly even. Then Jack noticed one of the smaller fellows start to pull ahead. He had wide shoulders and short thick arms and was beating the crap out of his "impact device" with a rapid-fire two-handed assault.

This wasn't going unnoticed by the competition. Most of the men were glancing around, checking out their rivals' score, which didn't help their own. When they saw the little guy's, they upped their efforts, pounding harder and faster, but still craning their necks to see what the leader was doing.

He was pulling away, that was what he was doing. He was focused on that pad and he was going at it with everything he had.

Jack could see the frustration building in the others—read it in the hunching of their shoulders and the quick glimpses he had of their faces as they glanced around while they bashed furiously on their pads. But no one was catching up to the little guy.

Finally, one of the also-rans lost it. With a howl of rage he leaped from his station and began pounding on the little guy. As they traded powerful punches without seeming to feel them, they bumped into a third participant who immediately joined the fray. Within seconds all six were tangled in a wild, vicious brawl.

As Jack watched, agog, he was reminded of the mindless violence of the museum steps. But worse: these guys could fight.

Someone's going to get killed, he thought.

Then he noticed jets of yellow gas shooting from the walls. The mist enveloped the brawlers, making them cough, separate, and finally collapse. The gas settled over them like a heavy fog, then was drawn away through vents just above the floor line, leaving a tangle of unconscious forms.

Jack realized that this obviously wasn't the first brawl they'd had here and maybe not even the worst, considering the crack in the tinted observation glass, but the gas jets indicated that they had *expected* violence.

What the hell was Monnet up to? And who was in that control booth with him?

Jack slithered forward . . . just a few more inches to get a better angle on the control room. Had to be careful though. He was moving into the wash of light from the test room; he'd be visible from below if anyone looked up.

He stopped as the door to the test area opened and three men stepped through. Weird-looking dudes—heavyset, thick-shouldered with no necks to speak of, all with short hair, pug noses, tiny ears, and beady eyes. Some sort of security force? They looked like they'd all come from the same cookie cutter, and the identical turtlenecks only reinforced the impression. Reminded Jack of the Beagle Boys from the old Uncle Scrooge comics.

A lone figure remained in the control area. Jack could see him now: Monnet.

What are you doing here, Doc? What are you looking for?

Jack returned his attention to the worker types who were disentangling the unconscious brawlers and stretching them out on their backs. Where did Monnet find his "participants"? Better question: where had he found these strange-looking security guys?

As Jack pressed the back of his hand against his nose to stifle another sneeze, he noticed one of the security men look up and freeze. He grunted and pointed up, directly at Jack. The others followed his point.

They can't possibly see me all the way up here in the dark, Jack thought. Can they?

One of the three let out a cry that sounded an awful lot like the bay of a hound on the scent, and the three charged out of the testing area.

Shit, I guess they can.

Jack wasn't going to wait around to see where they were going or how they expected to get up here. Suddenly he was late for the door.

Did a one-eighty swivel on his belly and started crawling back the way he'd come. Moved as quickly as he could, scraping along through the guano, no longer worried about noise.

"Who's there?" called a voice, the same one that had given the "participants" their instructions, only now he sounded worried. Had to be Monnet. "Who's up there? Come down at once!"

Jack kept crawling. Movement below caught his eye. Three shadowy forms were racing across the floor, separating, each to a different wall where they leaped and began to climb.

Christ, they're climbing the walls!

No . . . not the walls themselves but the pipes and girders attached to them. These Beagle Boys were as strong and agile as they were strange-looking. And nowhere near as dumb as they looked. By splitting up they were reducing Jack's escape options to one: up.

Fortunately, that was where he wanted to go. But he'd never beat them at this pace. With a slow sick twist of his stomach, Jack realized that if he was going to escape he had to stand up and walk the beam— run, maybe. And he couldn't wait until he'd steeled up his nerve—had to get up and go now.

Wishing he'd taken gymnastics or at least balance-beam lessons somewhere along the course of his childhood, he pushed himself up to a crouch, one foot in front of the other, then rose to standing. Teetered for a heart-stopping instant as the beam seemed to tilt under him, then steadied himself. Arms out like a tightrope walker, he began shuffling toward the end of the beam.

Eyes on the beam, not on the floor . . . eyes on the beam, not on the floor . . . he made it a litany as he slid his feet along, coughing in the cloud of guano he was kicking up. He arrived at one of the vertical beams. He'd had a bad time getting around it on the way in when he hadn't been in a hurry; couldn't let it slow him up now. Trusting in his reflexes and the muscular toning from his regular workouts, Jack clenched his teeth and swung himself around the beam and kept moving. Had a hairy moment when he picked up too much momentum and felt himself falling forward but somehow managed to maintain his balance.

The wall lay twenty feet ahead; a narrow support ledge ran along it left and right from the beam. A brief dash to the left on that would take him back to the skylight. Chanced a quick glance around and saw two of the Beagle Boys making good time up the walls. The third was somewhere behind him and to his left. No way Jack was risking a look over his shoulder.

He all but ran the last three steps to the wall and didn't slow when he reached the ledge. With surer footing now he could move faster. Searched the shadows as he hustled toward the skylight and spotted the third Beagle far down the adjoining wall—just pulling himself up onto the ledge. Jack increased his speed. Had to reach that skylight first.

Didn't slow when he reached the corner—made the turn at his best speed and kept moving toward the skylight. The Beagle was on the ledge now, moving quickly—almost scampering—toward Jack. Didn't seem the least bit afraid of the height or of falling. If he got to Jack before Jack reached the skylight . . .

With a final desperation-fueled burst, Jack came abreast of the skylight and leaped off the ledge. Not a long jump—on the way in he'd been able to hang down and swing over to the wall ledge—but he had to be up and through before the Beagle Boy. Snagged the near edge backhanded and used his momentum to swing his legs up. When his sneakers caught the far edge he levered himself up and rolled out to the side. Soon as his body hit the roof he swiveled and slammed the skylight closed.

A howl of frustration filtered through from below. With nothing but air below the skylight, there was no way to open it from inside without a pole, and Jack hadn't seen one lying about.

"Sorry, Fido," he muttered; then he was on his way again.

He hopped the alley to the abandoned building and quickly made his way down to ground level. The street was deserted as Jack beat it to his car. Once in the front seat, locked inside, he allowed himself a moment to catch his breath.

What had he learned tonight? Had it been worth the risk?

Definitely. Monnet was testing a drug and, from the way he was going about it, not a legal one. The way the human guinea pigs reacted to it reminded Jack too much of the preppy rioters the other night for it to be anything but the Berzerk stuff Robert Butler had told him about.

Nadia wasn't going to be happy to hear that her beloved boss was dabbling with Berzerk. The way she'd spoken of Monnet had led Jack to expect a halo hovering over his scalp. But halos tended to dim when you started poking into someone's corners.

Was Dragovic involved? Had to be. Even if he was miles away tonight, the whole situation reeked of him.

Just as my clothes reek of pigeon guano. Jack started the engine. Time to get home and—

The car rocked as a heavy weight *slammed* against the driver door with alarming force, startling a shocked shout out of Jack. He had a quick impression of a dark shape hammering at the window inches from his face as another began pounding on the passenger door. A third landed on the hood as Jack fumbled for the gearshift.

The dog-faced security men had tracked him somehow.

As soon as his hand found the shift he rammed the car into gear and stomped the gas. The two flanking attackers hung on for a few yards but lost their grip as the car accelerated. The third remained, pounding on the windshield, but he slid off during a sharp swerve to the left.

Took a while for Jack's heart to stop hammering. Maybe he'd skip *The Island of Dr. Moreau* tonight.

2

"Did you catch him?" Luc said as the three roustabouts shuffled through the door empty-handed.

All three shook their heads in unison.

"Do you know who he was or what he was doing here?"

A trio of shrugs.

"Very well," he said irritably. He pointed to the test subjects who were beginning to stir to consciousness. "Get them on their feet, pay them, and send them on their way."

Luc returned to the control room so he wouldn't be seen. He slumped into a chair behind the tinted glass and tried to imagine who could have been spying on him. Not the police, certainly. If that were the case, the street outside would be filled now with flashing red lights.

One of Dragovic's men then? For what purpose? Dragovic knew that Luc tested the potency of each new batch of Loki but had never shown the slightest interest in the how or the where.

Perhaps just a common criminal, looking for something to steal. Lucky for him Prather's roustabouts didn't catch up to him.

Forget him. Who cares who he is as long as he's gone and keeps his mouth shut. I just want out.

The readouts indicated that tonight's strain of Loki was somewhat weaker than previous batches. He'd have to tell Dragovic to cut the new shipments less than the previous ones to maintain potency.

I don't care. I just want out.

As Luc watched the roustabouts rousing the test subjects, he realized that although he had every reason to be sunk chin deep in a black depression, he felt strangely jubilant.

Somewhere during the course of watching these lowlife creatures pummel each other, he had come to an unconscious decision that now bubbled on the surface: *I am getting out. No matter what, I am getting out.*

And that means I will never have to test another batch of Loki. Even if Nadia succeeds in stabilizing the molecule, I am walking away.

Of course, he would much prefer to leave behind a stabilized molecule. That would allow him to sell his shares and retire in plain sight. The alternative—should Nadia come up empty—would force him to go into hiding.

But one way or another, stabilized Loki or not, by this time next month Luc Monnet would be in France.

He found himself whistling contentedly—when was the last time he had whistled?—as he waited impatiently for the last test subject to be paid and shoved out the door.

Luc wanted to get home. He had wine to pack.

3

"This can't be true," Nadia said, her mouth going dry.

"Take it or leave it," Jack said with a shrug.

Nadia stared at him in dismay. Jack had dropped into the diabetes clinic unannounced this morning and said he had a progress report. Nadia had brought him back to her office where they could have privacy. He'd sat down and begun telling her this surreal tale about Dr. Monnet sneaking off to some warehouse in Brooklyn where he oversaw a group of men who bashed walls and each other. . . .

How could she accept such a bizarre tale from a near-stranger? It was too much. Insane.

Jack looked tired. She wondered if he might be into drugs, hallucinogens maybe. That would explain his story.

"I don't mean to doubt your word, but—"

"I think he was testing Berzerk," Jack said.

"What's that?"

"Street name for a new designer drug I've been hearing about."

"An illegal drug?" Nadia felt a surge of anger. She wanted to ask him if he'd been sampling some himself, but bit it back in time. "Oh, now you've gone too far!"

"I saw it in action the other night," Jack said. "During the preppy riot. The way Monnet's 'participants' acted last night reminded me of those homicidal preps I saw."

"But not Dr. Monnet!"

Jack shrugged again. "You wanted a connection between your doc and the Serb. There you go."

Feeling queasy, Nadia leaned back in her chair and squeezed her eyes shut. Milos Dragovic, reputedly dealing in anything illegal that turned a buck . . . Dr. Monnet, partner in a drug firm . . . a relationship between the two of them, hostile or not, what else could it be but drugs?

"All right," she said, opening her eyes. "If he is involved with this Berzerk stuff—and I'm not for an instant conceding that he is—it's because he has no choice."

"Whatever you say."

"You think he's a willing participant, don't you."

"I have no agenda here. I'm just telling you what I saw."

"And *I* saw Dragovic roughing up Dr. Monnet!"

"Could have been a disagreement over how to split the profits."

Nadia clenched her teeth to hold back a scream. "He is *not* in this willingly. Dragovic is holding something over him."

Jack leaned forward. "OK. I'll work on that end. But maybe you ought to be nosing into things at your end. If your guy is manufacturing something illegal like Berzerk, he's probably using company equipment to do it."

"All the production is done in . . . Brooklyn."

Jack was nodding. "Yeah. Right down the street from the punch 'em-up warehouse."

Nadia sighed. "It looks bad, doesn't it."

"It do. It do indeed."

"We have to help him." An idea began to take root. "What does this Berzerk do?"

"Not sure, but from what I've seen, it makes you act crazy violent."

"Really. Why on earth would someone want to take something like that?"

"A logical question. But logic doesn't enter much into the druggie world. If it feels good, do it—and screw the side effects."

"Can you get me some?"

Jack's eyes narrowed. "Why? You want to try it?"

"Not a chance. But I have a machine at work that can analyze anything. If I can identify this Berzerk, I can run a match for it in the company's database and see if there's any record of it."

"And if there is?"

She sighed. "Then we'll have one piece of the puzzle."

Jack pushed himself up. "I'll get on it. Call you when I find some."

A black mood settled over Nadia as she watched Jack go. Despite the warmth of her office she felt cold; she thrust her hands under her arms to warm them. Jack was supposed to help Dr. Monnet, yet he seemed to be gathering evidence against him. She had a bad feeling that this was not leading to a good place.

4

Doug couldn't help but laugh as he poured himself another shot of Old Pulteney fifteen year old. As a rule, eight o'clock in the morning was a tad early for scotch, but what did "early" mean if you'd been up all night?

He'd done it. It had taken him until dawn, but finally he'd tracked the GEM Basic R and D money to its final resting place.

"Ho-ho-ho!" he said, toasting himself. "You are a clever one!"

But what good is a triumph if you can't share it?

He called Nadj at the clinic. First thing every morning, rain or shine, weekday or weekend, that was where she could be found. But the nurse told him she'd already left. He tried her home but her mother said she was at the lab and expected to be there all day.

At the lab? On a Saturday? And then he remembered the million-dollar bonus offer. Yeah, he'd be working Saturdays *and* Sundays for something like that.

He called her extension at GEM but she didn't pick up, so he left her an enigmatic voice mail.

"Hi, honey, it's me. I did it. I found the answer to the question. I'll tell you the whole story at lunch. Meet me twelve-thirty at the Gramercy Tavern and we'll celebrate. Until then, think about hocking everything you own, begging, borrowing, and stealing every dime you can lay your hands on, and putting it all into GEM stock. Love ya. Bye."

He grinned as he hung up. That ought to pique her interest.

He yawned. Now for some shut-eye. God, he needed sleep.

Doug finished his scotch, turned off the computer, turned off his cell phone, disabled the ringer on the house phone, and headed for the bed.

No interruptions, just sleep, sleep, sleep.

5

"A dealer?" Abe said. "Plenty of dealers you know already. Why should you want to know another?"

He finished slathering margarine onto one of the kaiser rolls Jack had brought and took a huge bite.

"Not just any dealer," Jack said. "I need a guy who really knows his stuff. Somebody heavy into designer shit, who knows his chemistry and knows who's making what."

Jack had told Abe about his visit with Robert Butler and about the scene at the warehouse last night.

"A chemist, you say." Abe thought as he chewed. "The best man I can think of is Tom Terrific."

Jack had heard the name but never met him. "I thought he was mostly crystal meth."

"That's his mainstay, but he dabbles in other things as well."

"Think he'd know about Berzerk?"

"If it's out there and people are buying it, Tom has probably figured how to make it."

"Sounds like my man. Where can I find him?"

"Always a good question with Tom. He tends to keep on the move." Abe pulled a little notebook from his shirt pocket and flipped through it. "Here it is."

"You keep his number?"

"He's a customer."

Jack could see why a speed merchant would want to keep some firepower handy.

"What did he buy?"

Abe did his baleful stare over the tops of his glasses. "A pizza, what else."

"Come on, Abe. I just like to know what people are carrying out there."

"You want I should tell people what you buy?"

"Well, no, but—"

"Then such things you shouldn't ask. I am a priest and the basement is my confessional."

Jack made a face but said no more. It had been worth a try.

Abe dialed a number, spoke for half a minute, then hung up.

"He'll see you, but it'll cost."

"I've got to pay just to talk to him?"

"He says he's a busy man. A hundred for fifteen minutes. A consultation, he calls it. Two o'clock this afternoon. And he wants me along because you he doesn't know."

"A hundred for you too?"

"I'm free," Abe said, taking another bite of the kaiser and sprinkling poppy seeds all over the counter.

As Jack mentally ran over the rest of the day, he watched Parabellum hop around pecking up the black specks and idly wondered if birds got high on poppy seeds. If Tom Terrific was at two, he'd have time to get out to Sal's and arrange another shipment of party favors for tomorrow night's soiree at Dragovic's.

He wondered how the Serb's place had looked at first light this morning. Couldn't have been pretty.

6

It's still a shambles, Milos thought as he stood at his bedroom window and surveyed the grounds below. But not as much as it was an hour ago, and much more of a shambles than it will be an hour from now.

The workmen were making good progress. It hadn't been easy to find them. Milos had spent a lot of time on the phone last night threatening, cajoling, and calling in a slew of favors to get these men out here on a holiday weekend, not to mention offering triple time and a 30 percent on-time completion bonus.

But the place *had* to be fixed up in time for tomorrow night's party. He could not allow the beautiful people of the Hamptons to see his place in anything less than perfect shape.

And he could not allow a word of last night's madness to reach the press. He had sworn his staff and last night's guests to secrecy. Most of them would comply, the former out of fear, the latter because none of them had acquitted himself particularly well during the tumult.

As for today's workers, they would see the tires and the damage but he doubted they could reconstruct what had happened. They'd probably say that the Slippery Serb must throw some awfully strange parties.

Of their own accord, Milos's hands knotted in fists. *Who?*

The question had plagued him all night. That he'd been attacked by a group calling itself the East Hampton Environmental Protection Committee had seemed absurd at first; yet when he considered that the assault had been aimed at his pride rather than his person, it became more believable. Whoever had planned it had not only guts, but a cruel and crafty mind. And that would be more in line with a clique of outraged locals than one of his hard-assed competitors. They would have dropped napalm.

"May I come in?"

Milos turned at Mihailo's voice. He sounded excited.

"What is it, Mihailo?"

The communications man stepped through the doorway and glanced about through his thick glasses. Probably hoping to catch Cino undressed, Milos thought. But after watching her in that thong bikini she'd worn around the pool yesterday—and Milos had no doubt every male in the household had ogled her at one point or another—what was left to see?

"Remember that license plate we saw on the surveillance tape last night? I had a contact in the DMV trace it."

"And?"

"It's registered to a Gia DiLauro who lives on Sutton Square in the city."

"You mean Sutton Place."

"That was what I thought," he said, running a hand through his thinning hair. "So I checked. Sutton Square is a little cul-de-sac off Sutton Place at the very end of East Fifty-eighth Street. Eight town houses at most. Very exclusive."

"But didn't you tell me the call was made from a pay phone in the East Eighties?"

Mihailo shrugged. "That's where the trace went."

Milos remembered the drab Buick on the tape last night. "A very ordinary car for someone at such a fancy address."

"I know. Could be a live-in maid."

"Could be."

Milos pondered this. If the owner had been from Jackson Heights or Levittown, he'd have dropped it. But if this Gia DiLauro was rich enough or connected to someone rich enough to live in an exclusive spot on the East Side—only thirty blocks from where that arrogant shit called last night—she easily could be connected to someone with a place out here. So she or someone close to her could be involved with the so-called protection committee.

"Tell Vuk and Ivo I want to see them."

They'd seen the couple on the beach. He'd send them into the city

to check on this Gia DiLauro. If she was the same woman, they'd find
out the name of the man.

And if he or she was in any way involved . . .

Milos ground a fist into his palm until it hurt.

The phrase *scorched earth* lingered in his mind.

7

"*. . . Until then, think about hocking everything you own, begging, borrowing, and stealing every dime you can lay your hands on, and putting
it all into GEM stock. Love ya. Bye.*"

The words echoed in Nadia's head as she walked down a sunny
Park Avenue South—a different Park Avenue from the Waldorf neighborhood farther uptown. The sidewalks here were lined with office
buildings and businesses instead of luxury residences.

She'd listened to the message twice on her voice mail before de-
leting it. Doug had sounded so strange. He'd probably been up all night,
and that would explain it, but still . . . she wasn't sure she liked this
manic side of him.

And worse, this was distracting her from her work. Not that she was
getting anywhere. She'd spent yesterday and all this morning reviewing
Dr. Monnet's failed approaches, and it seemed to her that he'd exhausted every possible route. Then she'd reviewed her predecessor's
notes and seen that Macintosh had come up with new approaches, but
none of those had worked either. Where to go from here? It was frustrating the hell out of her.

Nadia walked along tree-lined Twentieth Street until she came to the
Gramercy Tavern. She wound her way through the crowded front room
with its bar, wooden floors, and bare tables, and spotted Doug waving to
her from the rear dining area. Carpeting and tablecloths back here.

She smelled scotch on his breath as he kissed her and pulled out her chair. His eyes were bright with triumph.

"How did you ever get a table?" she said as she sat.

The Gramercy was one of the city's hotter restaurants.

"Holiday weekend," Doug said. "All the regulars are out of town, I guess. Can I order you a chardonnay?"

Nadia shook her head. "Just an iced tea." She was heading back to the lab after this.

"Aw, come on," he said, grinning. "We're celebrating."

"Celebrating what, Doug?" she said, feeling an edge creep into her voice. "You call and leave this strange message, then when I try to call back I can't get through on any of your phones—"

"I pulled an all-nighter and was trying to get some sleep."

"I figured that, but meanwhile I'm left in the dark."

Doug reached across and took her hand. "Sorry. I've had tunnel vision for the last couple of days. A hack isn't something you can snack at—you know, do a little bit now, take a break, come back and do a little bit latter. It's like a supercomplex juggling act where you keep trying to get more and more balls into the air. Once you've got them moving and you've found the rhythm, you've got to stay with them. If you stop, even for a short nap, you lose the cadence and they all come crashing down. Then you've got to go back and start again with ball one."

The waiter arrived with their menus and a bread basket. Doug ordered Nadia's iced tea.

"But why go to all that trouble?" she said when they were alone again. "You're risking—"

"Because I've been lied to," he said, his mouth taking a grim turn. "They were keeping things from me and I was determined to find out what."

"And are you satisfied now?" Nadia said, squeezing his hand and praying he'd say yes.

He shook his head. "Not completely."

"Oh, Doug," Nadia said, feeling her heart sink, "you're not going to keep this up, are you?"

He grinned. "Nope. It's too wearing. I still don't know why the company's paying me commissions on sales I'm not making, but at least they're not cheating me, so I can let that go. And I did learn one answer

I was looking for—the one that concerns you—so I feel I can back off with my pride intact."

A twinge of alarm ran down Nadia's neck. "Me? What concerns me?"

"Your subsidiary. I found where all the research and development money is going."

Nadia couldn't help but ask. "Where?"

"Stock." Another grin. He looked like a little boy who'd found pirate treasure. "They're using every spare penny to buy back company stock." He leaned forward and lowered his voice. "And let's not mention the company by name, OK? Just in case."

Nadia glanced around. In case what? He didn't think he was being followed, did he?

"No, I'm not paranoid," he said, as if reading her mind, "but you never know." He straightened. "Anyway, I matched the timing of the stock purchases to a graph of the stock price, and it seems that every time the price takes a little dip, they buy up a bunch of it."

"Propping up the price? Why would they do that?"

"I can't imagine. But I *can* imagine why they'd be secretly hoarding a load of stock. Think about it: if you had insider knowledge that the stock price was going to jump, wouldn't you want to pick up as many shares as possible—without tipping anyone off, of course."

"But that's not only illegal, it's stupid. And as the principals in the company, they each must hold a ton of shares already."

He shrugged. "Since when does greed know limits? The important thing is that they must think the stock is going to be very valuable. And that, my dear, is a good thing to know."

Nadia caught herself running through the sources she might tap for a loan and pulled up short.

"Why?" She couldn't keep the note of reproach out of her tone. "So we can use this stolen information and load up on shares?"

Doug glanced away, then back at her. "Does sound tacky, doesn't it." He sighed. "Easy money . . . it's such a high. I suppose I'm as vulnerable as the next guy. Seemed like a great idea . . . get that start-up money and go to work for myself. Now, sitting here with you, it seems kind of sleazy."

"I can't quite take on the holier-than-thou role. For a few moments there I was thinking about how a windfall from a sure thing like that could affect my mother's standard of living—and my own."

"What's that make us?"

"Human, I guess. Though some people would call us *stupid* humans for not jumping on it."

Doug caressed the back of her hand. "I'll never feel stupid if I'm with you."

She laughed. "How many scotches have you had?"

He only smiled and she knew the love in his eyes was reflected in her own.

They sat in silence for a while. Finally Nadia voiced a question that had been bothering her. "What I'd like to know is what do they have up their sleeves that makes them so sure the stock is going to jump?"

"Only two things I can think of." Doug held up a finger. "They're expecting a takeover bid." Another finger popped up alongside the first. "Or . . . they're expecting a major breakthrough, like a new product that's going to take the market by storm." He pointed both fingers at Nadia. "Hey . . . maybe it's the project you're working on. Maybe *you're* the key to the company's future."

Me? A queasy feeling settled in the pit of her stomach. The best she could say about the status of the project under her captaincy was that it was becalmed and rudderless.

"If that's the case," she said, "I think we'd be better off leaving our money in the bank. And maybe I will have that chardonnay."

8

"I don't know how you manage it," Kent Garrison said with a note of hostility as Luc stepped into the conference room. Kent was stuffed into a pink golf shirt that matched the flush of his ample cheeks. "But somehow you always manage to be the last to arrive."

Up yours, Luc thought, but managed an ingenuous smile instead. "Just lucky, I guess."

Kent had called about an hour ago, saying, "We've caught the culprit," and that they needed an emergency meeting. He'd say no more, but Luc knew what he meant: the software people had tracked the hacker who'd broken into the GEM system.

Kent sneered. "What were you doing—counting your wine bottles?"

That brought Luc up short. Did they know? He glanced quickly at the usually dapper Brad Edwards. He looked terrible. Wrinkled shirt, half-combed hair, glazed eyes, slack expression—was he on tranquilizers?

"Counting his wine bottles," Brad said with a dull laugh. "That's a good one."

"I had to cancel plans," Luc said. A lie. His only plans had been to continue packing his wine. "Plus I was up late at the test session."

"Oh, right," Brad said, looking apologetic. "How'd it go?"

Kent held up a hand before Luc could answer. "Close the door first."

"It's Saturday morning," Luc said. "We're the only ones here."

Kent shook his head. "Not quite. Your new researcher is signed into the lab."

"Really?" Luc had to smile. "Amazing what the offer of a million-dollar bonus will do." He pulled the door shut and latched it, then sat down. "Couldn't we have discussed this in a conference call?"

"Our computer's been hacked," Kent said, leaning back and stretching the fabric of his golf shirt over the bloat of his belly. "How do we know our phones aren't tapped?"

The possibility startled Luc, especially in light of the uninvited guest at the test session. He told his two partners about it.

"Someone was spying on us?" Brad said, his lower lip jutting.

"I can't say for sure," Luc said. "He may simply have been some sort of squatter who thought the building was deserted. After all, we only use it once a month."

Brad turned to Kent. "Do you think he's connected to Gleason?"

"Gleason?" Luc said, alarm tugging at the inner wall of his chest. He knew only one Gleason. "You don't mean our sales rep, do you? What about him?"

"He's our hacker," Kent said.

Luc slumped back in his chair. "Oh, no."

"Yeah," Kent said, his face reddening. "One of our own."

"Whatever happened to loyalty?" Brad was saying, looking around as if the answer were going to pop out of the air. "First Macintosh, now Gleason. I can't stand it."

"Has he made any demands?" Luc said.

Kent shook his head. "Not yet. But he will."

"How do we know that?"

"He broke the financial codes."

"Damn it!" Luc said, anger burning through the alarm. "I thought the software people said they'd stop him!"

Brad fidgeted. "We told them to trace him, *then* stop him. They spent all night trying to trace him. The sysop in charge overnight said Gleason's very good. The only way they managed to identify him was through a signature code transmitted by his computer."

"I don't understand," Luc said.

"He was using a company laptop!" Kent shouted, hammering the table. "That's how he got through the fire wall. He used the goddamn computer *we* gave him, the sonovabitch!"

"Why would he do such a thing?" Brad said.

Luc ignored him. "Then you think he knows about the repurposing of the R & D funds?"

Listen to me, Luc thought. *Repurposing*. What an inane euphemism.

"Who knows?" Kent said. "The sysop said he was in the middle of all the numbers. If that was what he was looking for, he found it."

"What'll we do?" Brad said.

"Same thing we did with Macintosh," Kent said, fixing Luc with his gaze. "We hire your buddy Ozymandias Prather."

"No," Luc said. He wouldn't be a party to another death. "You yourself said he hasn't made any demands or any threats. He—"

"Only a matter of time," Kent said.

Brad was nodding. "Why else would he be snooping around in our computer?"

Luc didn't have an answer for that.

"I have a worse scenario," Kent said. "Gleason and the spy in the warehouse could be working together—for Glaxo or Roche or who knows."

"Aren't we getting a little paranoid?"

"With good reason!" Brad said. "We've got that crazy Serb on one side and the DEA on the other. We've got nowhere to turn!"

Kent slapped his hand on the table. "Look. It doesn't matter if Gleason's an industrial spy, a greedy bastard, or a goody-two-shoes potential whistle blower, he's got to go."

"You're talking about a man's life here," Luc said.

"Damn right I am!" Kent shouted, reddening as he leaned forward. "*Mine!* And if I have to choose between my skin and some disloyal nosy bastard's, guess who gets my vote!"

"Listen to us," Brad said softly as he pressed the heels of his palms over his eyes. "Voting on killing a man like we're voting on some minor corporate policy change."

"You know something?" Kent said. "It's not so hard the second time. We've done it once already. In for a penny, in for a pound, as they say." He raised his hand. "I vote yes."

Brad lifted his hand. "Me too, I guess. I don't see any other way." He shifted his watery gaze between Luc and Kent. "You know what we've become? We've all become Dragovics."

Luc's inability to deny the awful truth of those words sickened him. "I wish I'd never *heard* of Loki."

"*You* wish?" Kent said, jabbing his finger at Luc's face. "How about us? This is all *your* fault! If you hadn't started fucking around with that goddamn thing's blood, we wouldn't be in this mess!"

Luc's thoughts flashed back to the strange phone call he'd received last fall. Someone calling himself Salvatore Roma, saying he was a professor of anthropology and telling Luc he should pay a visit to a traveling "oddity emporium" that was stopped for the weekend in the village of Monroe on Long Island. Professor Roma had said there was an odd creature there with extremely interesting components in its blood. "Look into them, Doctor," the soft, cultured voice had said. "I guarantee you will find them *most* interesting."

Luc had made a few calls and had learned that indeed there was a tent show in Monroe for the weekend. Suspecting he was being hoaxed, but curious nonetheless, he'd made the trip and bought a ticket. When he saw the strange creature he assumed it was a fake, but it was an awfully good fake. So he introduced himself to Prather who seemed almost desperate to identify the creature. Because of this, he allowed Luc to take—for a fee—a sample of its blood.

And in that sample Luc found what he would later dub the Loki molecule. He isolated it, synthesized it, and began testing the blue powder on mice and rats. The results were disturbing. The mice, who usually clustered together in friendly piles for mutual warmth, began running around in bursts of frenzied activity and attacking one another. Their cages became miniature slaughterhouses. The rats, who were caged singly, would chew at the wire mesh of their cages until their mouths were bloody ruins, and leap to attack whenever one of the techs opened a cage door.

Luc had tried to reach this Professor Roma but could find no trace of him at any New York college. He cursed himself for not finding out how to contact the man.

Unknown to Luc, one of his research techs had a cocaine habit. To curry favor or perhaps to work a deal on a buy, the tech pilfered samples of the Loki powder and gave them to his supplier. These somehow found their way to Milos Dragovic.

Luc had known nothing of this at the time. As it was, he couldn't devote the time he needed to delve fully into the properties of this strange molecule, and perhaps he should have kept closer track of the Loki stock, but he'd been distracted by GEM Pharma's financial crisis.

"I also wish I'd never heard of TriCef!" Luc shouted, anger surging as he snapped back to the present. "*I* didn't put this company on the brink of financial ruin by wagering its future on the success of a single product!"

"The vote to invest in TriCef was unanimous," Brad reminded him.

"Yes, I went along," Luc admitted, "but only because I couldn't get on with my work with you two badgering me constantly."

GEM had been doing well, extremely well, with generic pharmaceuticals, but Kent and Brad wanted to boost the company from its small-time, also-ran status into a major. Luc had reluctantly agreed to their plan to buy world rights to a new third-generation cephalosporin that was supposed to blow all the other broad-spectrum antibiotics out of the water. They put the company deep into debt to launch TriCef. And TriCef tanked.

Then, to their shock, Milos Dragovic appeared and offered to buy the blue powder Luc had been experimenting with. He said he would take all they could produce for an undisclosed market overseas. They'd been wary, but not wary enough. What they'd known of Dragovic then came from the papers where he was portrayed as a rather glamorous if shady character. And he was offering a *lot* of money. . . .

"If GEM had been solvent when Dragovic approached us," Luc said, "we could have—we *would* have laughed him off. But as it was, we were faced with the choice of either throwing in with him or going Chapter Eleven."

The Dragovic money would pull them back from the brink, so they agreed to gear a percentage of their production facility to the stuff Luc called Loki.

"The proverbial offer we couldn't refuse," Kent said.

"We had a choice," Luc said. "We could have bit the bullet and refused. But we didn't."

Luc knew he had been right there on the line with his two partners, voting an enthusiastic yes—anything to save their financial hides.

Brad moaned. "But if we'd only known what the stuff could do, what he'd do with it."

"Let's not kid ourselves," Luc said. "You knew from my reports that it increased aggression tenfold in rodents; and none of us was so naïve as to believe someone like Dragovic had a legitimate use in mind."

Luc later learned that Dragovic had performed impromptu human studies with the samples. He'd discovered that a little of the blue powder imparted an intense euphoria, an on-top-of-the-world feeling. A larger amount elicited outbursts of mindless violence at the slightest provocation, sometimes with no provocation at all.

Dragovic had found an instant market in his gunrunning customers, so he sent the first shipments to his contacts in the various Balkan militias. Word spread like wildfire through the military underground and soon every military and paramilitary organization—from the Iraqis and the Iranians to the Israelis and Hamas—wanted a supply.

Dragovic set up a dummy corporation in Rome where he received bulk quantities of Loki shipped from GEM as TriCef. There his people filled capsules and pounded out tablets to distribute Loki throughout the world.

"Yeah," Kent said, "but we thought his market was a bunch of Third World military crazies who'd kill each other off and that would be it."

"Right," Brad said. "Who ever dreamed it would become a street drug right in our own backyards?"

Luc couldn't help laughing.

"What's so fucking funny?" Kent shouted.

"I ought to call Mr. Prather and see if he has use for ethical contortionists!"

"Don't push me, Luc," Kent gritted through his teeth.

"That's not fair," Brad said. "I've been *tortured* by this."

"Really?" Luc said. He didn't know why he was feeling so hostile. Almost as if he'd taken some of that damn drug himself. "I haven't noticed a big surplus in your draw account."

Brad averted his gaze.

The truth was that the huge profits from Loki had salved all their consciences. The drug had turned GEM Pharma into a money machine—a self-laundering money machine from which all the income derived from Loki was cleaned up by declaring it as profit from international sales of TriCef.

Kent had devised an almost perfect system. GEM synthesized the drug in its heavily automated Brooklyn plant where the few employees needed to maintain the production line thought they were manufacturing an antibiotic. GEM records showed bulk shipments of TriCef to Rome. From there the drug traveled such a tortuous path of cutting and packaging and repackaging that by the time the pills reached America their trail was so attenuated that it would be virtually impossible to trace them back to GEM.

Atop all that was the added safety factor of the unconsumed Loki spontaneously converting to an inert compound every new moon.

Loki had made them all very rich, but also guilty, trapped, and desperate.

And paranoid.

Dragovic's mercurial moods were not their only worry. A few months ago Brad had brought up the possibility of a hostile takeover by another corporation. The purchase of a controlling percentage of GEM stock would inevitably lead to exposure of their secret. To head that off they had been funneling the funds earmarked for basic research into the repurchase of their own company's stock.

What a catastrophic mess.

Luc sighed and closed his eyes; he pictured himself in a tiny rural café in Provence, sipping dark, rich coffee while the owner's cat basked nearby in a sunny window.

In three weeks I'll be out of this. Just three weeks.

But if Gleason blew the whistle . . . Luc's bucolic vision shifted from rural France to a jail cell right here in Manhattan.

He opened his eyes and fixed Brad, the company comptroller. "Prather will want cash, in advance. It's Saturday. How will you—?"

"I'll get it," Brad said. "Same amount as for Macintosh, I assume. I'll have it for you by this afternoon."

"One more thing we need to consider: Gleason has some sort of relationship with our new researcher."

Kent clapped his hands against the sides of his head and tugged on his red hair. "Aw, shit! How close?"

"I can't say. I do know he recommended her for the job, but beyond that . . ." Luc shrugged.

"Dear God," Brad said. "Can't *anything* be simple? What if they're close? We don't want to do anything to distract her from her work! You've got to find out!"

Luc rose. "I'll do my best."

"In the meantime," Kent told Brad, "get the cash together."

As Luc turned and reached for the door, Brad's voice was a low moan behind him. "How long can we keep this up?"

Brad was unraveling before their eyes.

Hang on just a little longer, Brad, Luc thought. Just a few more weeks. After that, you can dissolve into a quivering mass of Jell-O for all I care.

9

"If Abe vouches for you," Tom Terrific said, "that's good enough for me. But I'd like my consultation fee up front if you don't mind."

"Take a check?" Jack said.

Tom Terrific acknowledged the patent absurdity with a smile that revealed small yellow teeth spaced like kernels on a stunted ear of corn. His forehead went back even farther than Abe's, but he was much thinner, and the long salt-and-pepper hair growing off the rear half of his scalp was twisted into a single braid. He looked to be in his late forties, slightly hunched posture, painfully thin, wearing torn jeans and a sleeveless Mighty Ducks sweatshirt that revealed a showroom of tattoos up and down his arms. The Harley-Davidson insignia clung to his wasted left deltoid; a big red "1%" was engraved on his right. If Uncle Creepy had been a Hell's Angel, he'd have looked like Tom Terrific.

"I see you're into ink, Mr. Terrific," Jack said as he pulled a hundred-dollar bill from his back pocket. "You into bikes too?"

The massive rottweiler in the corner leaped to his feet and growled as Jack's hand moved toward Tom Terrific with the money.

"Easy, Manfred," he said without turning his head. "He's only giving Daddy some bread." To Jack: "Hey, call me Tom, Okay. The Terrific's just for kicks, y'know? And as for being a biker, yeah, I used to ride. Dropped outta Berkeley and rode with a Fresno gang for about ten years. Used to weigh in at an eighth of a ton too. But those days are gone. I now live the life of a pharmaceutical artiste."

Jack glanced around the basement apartment. Abe had led him down here to a narrow cobblestone street just south of Canal in Chinatown where Tom Terrific was probably the only non-Asian resident. His furnished apartment sat under a Thai restaurant, although *furnished* was probably a euphemism. The rug and furniture looked like the kind of stuff that people put out on the curb but nobody would haul away, not even the sanit men.

A long way from the digs of that other pharmaceutical artiste, Dr. Luc Monnet.

"What do you want to know?" Tom said as he tucked away the bill. "Looking to start your own operation?"

Jack shook his head. "Just want to know about Berzerk. Heard of it?"

"Heard of it?" Tom Terrific snorted. "Course I heard of it. Just wish I could make the damn stuff."

"Tom Terrific can't make it?" Abe said as he eased himself into a threadbare lounger. "I've always heard that if you can't make it, it can't be made."

"True up till this new stuff arrived. But lemme tell you, man, it's got me stumped." He grinned again. "But I'm not alone. Got the feds stumped too. They keep trying to class it as a CDS—"

"Seedy what?" Jack said.

"CDS—controlled dangerous substance—but they can't seem to pin down its molecular structure. Which, considering the equipment those fuckers got, must be *real* complex. But I'm not surprised. I mean, it's one fucking elegant drug from the distribution standpoint because it degrades into an inert substance after a while." He cackled. "Driving the feds and the cops nuts, man. They bust somebody with the stuff and by the time arraignment comes around, the evidence ain't a drug no more."

"The preppy riot guy!" Jack said, snapping his fingers. "They had to let him go because they said someone pulled a switch with the evidence."

Tom Terrific was shaking his head. "No switch. The stuff just changed. That's what happens, man: every bit, no matter where it is, goes inert at exactly the same time. Ain't it cool? You gotta use it or lose it. The dude who dreamed this one up has got to be the fucking Einstein of molecular biologists."

Jack couldn't help recalling Nadia's glowing praise for her hero, Dr. Monnet, about how brilliant he was.

The pieces were falling into place, but Nadia was not going to like the picture.

"If I was a customer," Abe said, "I should be pretty mad if my stuff goes dead on me like that."

Tom Terrific shrugged. "If it does, it's your fault. The stuff comes with an expiration date."

"But what *is* it?" Jack said.

"The million-fucking-dollar question. I can tell you what it's not, and it's not speed. Lemme tell you, I know everything there is to know about amphetamines, and this stuff ain't even a distant relative. Not an opiate or a barbiturate or a clone of PCP or Ecstasy either. Stuff's something entirely different. It magnifies whatever aggressive tendencies you have."

"And what if you don't have any?" Jack said.

"Everybody's got 'em. It's the beast in all of us, man; it's just that some of us are farther from the trees than others. I call it BQ: beast quotient."

" 'The stubborn beast flesh . . .' "

"What?"

"Just a line from a movie I was watching the other night."

"Yeah, well, lemme tell you, a normal-size hit'll send a guy who's already violence-prone—you know, with a high BQ—right over the edge. A heavy dose can make even Casper the Friendly Ghost blow his top. Nobody's immune."

"Just what the world needs," Abe said. "More blown tops. Who would make such a thing? For what purpose?"

"I hear it got its start in paramilitary units overseas but moved into the consumer market like *schnell,* man. And lemme tell you, whoever's marketing this shit is another kinda whiz. They're selling it in all shapes and sizes, with names geared to specific target markets. If they're going after the gangbangers and such, they call it Berzerk—that's their most popular brand—but it's also called Terminator-X, Eliminator, Predator, Executioner, Uzi, Samurai, Killer-B, and so on."

"How big a market can that be?"

"Not huge, but just the tip of the iceberg, it turns out. Once it caught on with the jocks and the suits—"

"Jocks and suits?" Jack said. "What the hell do they want with it?"

"Aggression, man. *Aggression!* You can be the new Air Jordan or John Elway or Warren Buffet or Bill Gates. All you need is an edge, and this stuff—in the right amount, of course, in a fine-tuned dose— gives it to you. The jocks are buying Touchdown, Goal, Slam-Dunk, Victory, Ninety-Yard-Dash, and TakeDown—different names, same shit. The stuff's replacing anabolic steroids as most abused substance in scholastic and professional sports. You heard about what happened at the Knicks game last night, right?"

Jack shook his head but saw Abe nodding.

"Can't believe you missed it, man. Leon Doakes, that new wide-body forward for the Knicks? He took the Pistons' little point guard— can't remember his name but he was driving the lane and floating past Doakes all night, making him look like a lead-footed jerk. Anyway, Doakes finally has enough so he just picks up this guard and tosses him into the stands. *Tosses* him! Guy landed in the sixth row!" Another cackling laugh. "I flipped around to all the news shows; caught the replay five times, man. It was awesome. And I'll bet you anything they were both ripped on Slam-Dunk."

"You said suits too?"

"Yeah. They get the mildest forms—I've heard of names like Success, Prosperity, CEO. Yessiree, lots of white-collar types are bringing it into the boardrooms. The stuff is spreading like wildfire. It'll be everywhere soon. The ultimate growth market. I'd love to hitch a ride on that train but it's just too tough a molecule for a small operation like mine."

"Who is making it, then?" Jack said.

Tom Terrific shrugged. "Don't know. I tried to find out, see if I could maybe get a line on its molecular structure, but I ran into a wall, man—a Serbian wall."

"Dragovic?"

"You got it. And that's when I stopped poking around. Lemme tell you, I ain't lookin' to mess with *him*."

Another piece falling into place.

"No other players?" Jack said.

"Dragovic's organization seems to have a lock on the supply. Near as I can gather, the source is in Europe somewhere. Makes sense, since that's where the stuff first appeared."

Here was a piece that didn't fit. If Monnet and his company were behind Berzerk, it seemed logical they'd be making it here in the U.S. where they had a plant. What better cover for illegal drug manufacturing than a legal operation?

"Got any you can sell me?" Jack said

"Berzerk? Nothing active. But I've got some in the inert state I was working on till it changed. When the preppy guy's turned, so did mine. I'll just give you some of that. No damn good to me anymore." He motioned Jack toward the back room.

"I'll stay out here," Abe said. "I want to take notes on your decor so I can maybe duplicate it in my own place."

The back room was Tom Terrific's lab. He was known to specialize in speed—ice specifically—and Jack had heard that his product got high marks from folks who were into the stuff.

When he turned on the light, a panicked horde of roaches scuttled for the corners and disappeared.

"Excuse the little guests, man. They weren't invited, but lemme tell you, they're a fact of life when you live under a restaurant."

Manfred the rottweiler had followed Jack and his master to the rear room but didn't enter. Jack immediately knew why. The place smelled like a high school chemistry lab with the drama club doing the experiments—a mixture of paint thinner and dirty cat litter. Trays of white paste sat on benches with fans blowing over them. An exhaust fan in the corner ran into a shiny new galvanized duct that ran up through the ceiling, but the room still stank.

"Just out of curiosity," Jack said, "what do you get for an ounce of the stuff you make?"

"Ounce? Hey, I sell it by the *gram*, man. My stuff is *pure*, and my tweakers know it's a long high." He gave Jack a sidelong look. "Why do you want to know?"

"Well, you're practically a legend. You've got to be able to afford better digs than this."

"Oh, I can, man, and someday I will. But creature comforts aren't the important thing now. I'm an artist, you see, and I need to stay close to my work."

Everybody's an artist these days, Jack thought.

"And one of the things about my art is that the, um, materials I use, especially the solvents, have got telltale odors that can bring the heat down on you PDQ. So what I've done is hooked into the hood over the stove in the restaurant upstairs. My fumes mix with their cooking odors and they all come out together on the roof. Pretty cool, huh."

"Very," Jack said. His eyes were burning from the fumes and he wanted to get out of here. "What about the Berzerk?"

"Right over here," he said and started fumbling through a pile of glassine envelopes. "I only deal to finance my art, you know, and lemme tell you, I'm working on something that'll make Berzerk last week's news. I call it Ice-Nine. One hit will give a smooth, utterly bodacious high that'll last a week. It's my Holy Grail. When I reach it, I'll be fulfilled. That's when I'll retire, but not a minute before. Ice-Nine or bust, man."

Right on, Sir Gawain.

"Here 'tis," Tom Terrific said, holding up a small clear envelope with a layer of yellow powder in its lower corner. "It's some sort of blue in its active state—"

"Just what kind of blue is 'some sort'?" Jack said.

"You know," he said with a wavering, uncertain smile, "I can't really say. Ain't that weird. I've been working with the stuff for the past coupla weeks, seen it every day, but I can't quite remember its color. But I know it wasn't yellow. Yellow means it's gone inert." He handed the envelope to Jack. "Here. Take it."

"All of it?"

"Sure. I was gonna throw it out anyway."

"How about some of the active form, just for comparison."

Tom Terrific's ponytail whipped back and forth as he shook his head. "Don't have any. There's always a lag in supply after the old stuff goes inert. The new stuff won't show up for another day or so."

"Strange way to do business," Jack said.

"Tell me about it. Was me, I'd have the new stuff out Day One after the old stuff crashed." He shrugged. "But who knows? Maybe they've got a good reason."

Jack stuffed the envelope into his pocket and turned to go.

"Wait," Tom Terrific said, holding up another envelope, this one half-filled with fine clear crystals. "Here's my latest—Ice-Seven. Want to try a taste?"

"No, thanks," Jack said, moving toward the door.

"On the house. You'll like it. Lasts about three days. Takes tired old reality and makes it *much* more interesting."

Jack shook his head. "For the last year or so, Tom, reality's been just about as interesting as I can stand."

10

Gia stopped her paintbrush in midstroke and listened. Was that the doorbell? She and Vicky had come out to the sunny backyard—Vicky for her playhouse, Gia to work on her painting—and they were a long way from the front door.

She heard the chime again, clearly now. With a glance at Vicky, who was setting a Munchkin-size chair before a Munchkin-size table by her playhouse, Gia wiped her hands and stepped inside.

As she headed through the house toward the front door, she wondered who it could be. Jack had said he'd be tied up most of the day, Gia hadn't arranged a play date for Vicky, and this was not a neighborhood where people popped in for a cup of coffee.

Despite the months of living in this grand old East Side town house, Gia still didn't feel she belonged here. Vicky's aunts, Nellie and Grace, had owned it but they were gone now, officially missing persons since last summer. But Gia knew the truth—the two dear old women were dead, devoured by creatures from some Hindu hell. If not for Jack, Vicky would have suffered the same fate. And thanks to Jack, the creatures were as dead as Nellie and Grace, incinerated on the ship that had brought them, their ashes sent swirling into the currents of New York Harbor. Vicky would inherit the house when Grace and Nellie were declared legally dead. Until then, she and Gia lived here, keeping it up.

Gia padded across the thick Oriental rug that lined the foyer floor and approached the front door as the bell rang again. Probably Jack and he'd forgotten his key, but just to be sure, she put her eye to the peephole—

And froze.

Gia's heart kicked up its tempo as she recognized the two men standing on her front step—from the other day on the beach in front of Milos Dragovic's house. No way she'd forget the obnoxious one with the bad bleach job.

What were they doing here? How had they found her? *Why?*

Jack. Had to be Jack. *Always* Jack. He'd been interested in Dragovic, and the objects of Jack's interest tended not to be the happiest bunch after he finished with them. But now Jack—and she as well, it seemed—had attracted the attention of the city's most notorious mobster.

Gia jumped as the bell chimed again. She looked back down the hall, hoping Vicky wouldn't hear it and come charging in expecting to find Jack. The best thing was probably to stay quiet and hope they'd conclude no one was home. Since the town houses here all sat cheek by jowl along the sidewalk, there was no way for them to go around to the rear. Maybe they'd just give up and go away.

She heard them talking on the other side of the door. It didn't sound like English.

Finally they walked back to the black Lincoln sedan at the curb. Gia breathed a sigh of relief as they pulled away, but they didn't go far. They parked at the end of the cul-de-sac and lit cigarettes.

They're watching for us. Damn them!

Gia felt a quiet anger begin to simmer beneath her uneasiness. She and Vicky were trapped in their own home. And they had Jack to thank for that.

She picked up the phone and dialed his beeper. He got us into this; he can damn well get us out.

11

"Whatsa matta?" Sal Vituolo said, giggling as he wiped the tears from his eyes. "You don't think that's funny?"

Sal had just run the tape of last night's raid on the little TV-VCR set in his office.

"I think it's perfect," Jack said.

Ten minutes ago he would have had some good yucks watching Dragovic's goons running and ducking as the tires chased them. That would have been before he'd spoken to Gia and learned that two of those goons were parked outside her door at this very moment.

He knew how they'd found her: had to be that hidden security camera by Dragovic's front gate.

My fault. Should have spotted it sooner. Must have recorded a picture of the car, and they traced her from the plate.

Damn! Never should have taken them along.

The good news was that Dragovic couldn't know that Gia had any connection to last night's rubber rain. He was just flailing about.

Trouble was, the man might get lucky.

Jack's first thought had been to tell Gia to call the cops and complain about two suspicious-looking guys lurking outside. That would chase them, but not far. They'd move, but they would not go away.

So he'd have to handle this but be careful as to how. His first reflex had been to take them out, permanently, leave the police to clean up the mess. Since they both work for Dragovic, everyone would write it off as a mob hit.

Everyone except Dragovic. He'd know why those two were there, and removing them would be like erecting a big neon sign over Gia's door saying, I'M INVOLVED.

No, this called for a more subtle approach. But what . . . ?

Sal's voice jarred him back to Staten Island. "I don't know how many times I've watched it already, but I crack up every time." He popped the cassette out of the set and held it up. "How many copies do I make and where do we send them? *Eyewitness News?*"

"No copies yet."

"Ay," Sal said, pointing to the new dual-deck VCR Jack had instructed him to buy. "Ain't that why I bought this? To make copies?"

"Right," Jack said. "But we need more. You've got to be on that dune to film the sequel at tomorrow night's party."

"I'll be there, but how about something better'n tires this time? How about glass? Yeah! I gotta shitload of broken glass around here."

He forced his voice to stay calm. "Tires are just phase one. Phase two is where he gets nailed."

"Nails?" He heard an unmistakable note of glee in Sal's voice. "You're gonna use nails? Now you're talkin'!"

Jeez. "No."

"Then what's phase two?"

"All in good time, my man. All in good time. Meanwhile, not to worry. I've got it all figured out."

"But we *done* tires. I don't want to do tires again. Tires ain't enough."

Jack chewed the inside of his cheek and resisted the urge to whirl and get in Sal's face and tell him if he didn't like what was going down he could take over and finish it himself.

That's the worry about Gia and Vicky, he realized.

It was getting to him.

He rose and stepped to one of the windows. Through the grime on both sides of the pane he could vaguely make out the mountains of old cars and scrap metal stretching behind the office.

"Gotta be something better than tires again," Sal whined.

"OK, Sal," Jack said, giving in. "Let's take a walk through your yard. If we find something better, we'll use it. If not—tires again."

And maybe I'll come up with a solution for Dragovic's goons.

As an ebullient Sal led him out into the sunny afternoon, Jack noticed a couple of men piling scrap metal onto the hydraulic lift on the rear of a battered old delivery truck, the same one Jack had used to deliver the tires to the Ashe brothers on Friday.

He watched the old truck's lift return to ground level after another load of scrap had been pushed into its interior. Its rear edge was beveled . . . like a knife. . . .

That gave him half of an idea. Jack scanned the rest of the yard and spotted some battered and rusted cars lined up against one of the fences. He pointed to them.

"Any of those wrecks drivable?"

Sal stopped and looked around. "Yeah, I s'ppose. Not legal-like. A coupla them'll getcha from here to there, but probably not back."

"I don't need to get back."

"Whatcha thinkin'?"

Jack was beginning to feel a little better now.

"I'm thinking I may take out some of my fee in trade after all."

12

"How long are we going to sit here?" Vuk Vujovic said, lighting another Marlboro.

All he'd done today was camp in this damn car in this rich neighborhood and smoke while they waited for this woman to show. He was stiff, restless, bored, and an unbroken chain of cigarettes had left his tongue feeling like soggy cardboard. The Lincoln was comfortable to drive, but he felt as if he'd moved into it. He checked his bleached hair in the rearview mirror. Dark roots were starting to poke through; he was going to need a touch-up soon.

"How many times are you going to check your hair?" said Ivo from the passenger seat. "Afraid it's going to fall out?"

"Not mine, old friend." He glanced at Ivo's dark but thinning hair. "I'll still have plenty when you're as bald as an egg."

"At least I won't look like a girlie-man."

Vuk laughed to hide his irritation at the remark. If anyone in this car was a woman it was Ivo—an *old* woman. "The ladies love the color."

Ivo grunted.

They'd met in the Yugoslav Army and later had gone through the Kosovo cleanup together. With the army and the country in shambles after that, they'd hired on with Dragovic.

Vuk stared at the woman's door. Look at this neighborhood. Elegant brick-fronted town houses on an almost private block that dead-ended at a little park overlooking the East River. No places like this back home, unless you were high in the regime. He tried to imagine what it cost to live here.

"I hate this waiting."

Ivo sighed. "Could be worse. We could still be in Belgrade waiting for our back pay."

Vuk laughed again. "Or waiting on line for a gallon of gas."

"Do you ever think about home?" Ivo said, his voice softer.

"Only when I think about the war." And he thought about that every day.

Such a time. How many woman had he taken? How many men, some KLA, most simply able-bodied males, had he marched into fields or stood against walls and shot dead? Too many to count. How powerful he'd felt—a master of life and death, surrounded by cries and wails and pleas for mercy, a master whose whim decided who lived and who died, and how they died. He'd felt like a god.

Vuk missed those days, missed them so much at times it nearly brought him to tears.

"I try not to."

Vuk glanced at his companion but said nothing. Ivo had always been soft, and now he was going softer. This was what happened when you lived in America. You went soft.

I'm going soft too, Vuk admitted. I used to be a proud soldier. Now what am I? A bodyguard to a gangster—a Serb by birth, yes, but more American than Serb—and sent on wild-goose chases like this one. But he knew he was better off than others of his generation still in Belgrade.

"Do you think this DiLauro *pizda* has any connection with last night?" Vuk said, reluctantly moving their talk back from the past to the present.

"Could be," Ivo said. "But even if she is, she seems gone for the holiday, just like everyone else around here."

All they'd seen in their many hours on watch were a few children with their nannies. Vuk had checked in twice with the East Hampton house to report that nothing was happening, hoping they'd be called back. Instead they'd been instructed to stay right where they were.

"We're wasting our time," Vuk said.

"You got us into this."

"Me? How?"

"You had to identify the man on the video." He mimicked Vuk's voice: " 'I know him. He's the one we chased off the beach.' You never know when to shut up."

Vuk had turned, ready to give Ivo hell, when he saw him straighten in his seat.

A delivery truck with no markings had turned into Sutton Square. It rattled toward them, then angled sharply toward the curb.

"He must be lost," Ivo said, easing back into his seat.

Vuk agreed. The truck might have been white once, but now it was so dented and scraped and covered with grime he could only guess at the original color. The driver had a thick white beard and wore a baseball cap pulled low over his forehead. His features were blurry through the windshield. Vuk watched him pull out a map and look at it.

Dumb, Vuk thought. How do you get lost in a city where the streets and avenues are all numbered?

But the driver apparently found what he was looking for, because he began moving again, pulling head-on into the opposite curb. As the truck began backing into the second leg of a three-point turn, Vuk noticed that its rear loading platform was lowered and riding about two feet off the ground. But instead of stopping or even slowing when it had reversed to the middle of the street, the truck picked up speed and kept coming.

Vuk leaned on the horn and pressed back in the seat as he saw the rear corner of the truck angle around and loom larger and larger in the windshield.

"He's going to hit us!" Ivo shouted.

Vuk covered his eyes and braced himself. The impact jarred him forward but wasn't as bad as he'd expected. When he opened his eyes he realized that the corner of the lift platform had punched into the grille. Their car had been spared the full impact of the truck itself.

"Sranie!" Vuk shouted.

Ivo too was cursing a blue streak as they pushed open their doors. This idiot driver was going to wish he'd never turned in here.

But the truck was moving again. This time forward.

"He's taking off!" Ivo shouted.

Vuk sprinted after it, but it was picking up speed too quickly. He motioned Ivo back into the car. The truck ran the red light across Sutton Place and headed up Fifty-eighth—wrong way against the traffic.

"He's insane!" Ivo cried as they watched the truck weave a zigzag course as it dodged cars in the oncoming traffic. Tires screeched, horns blared, but the truck kept going.

Vuk wasn't about to let some old *govno* in a rust-bucket truck outmaneuver him. "Jebi se!" he shouted. "So am I!"

High beams on and horn blaring, he gunned the Lincoln across the street and up Fifty-eighth. Luckily there wasn't much traffic, but still it was scary.

Up ahead the truck had made a right on First Avenue, and they got there just in time to see it make a left onto Fifty-ninth.

"He's heading for the bridge!" Ivo said.

Vuk followed and spotted the truck taking the on-ramp to the Queensboro Bridge.

He floored the Lincoln up the incline, screeched into the turn, and pulled onto the span.

Ivo pointed straight ahead. "There he is!"

Vuk grinned. Did this old fool really think he could outrun them?

He accelerated up behind the truck and was about to pull alongside when the car started bucking.

"What's wrong?" Ivo said.

Vuk looked at the dashboard and saw that the temperature gauge was into the red.

"We're overheating!"

The engine coughed, bucked, and, with an agonized whine, died. The Lincoln ground to a halt.

"Sranje!" Vuk pounded on the steering wheel. Through the haze of steam rising from under the hood he watched the truck disappear over the arch of the bridge. "Sranje! Sranje! Sranje!"

Ivo was already out of the car and moving toward the front. Vuk got out and joined him. Horns blared as traffic backed up behind them.

"There's the problem," Ivo said, pointing to the smashed-in grille. "Big hole in the radiator."

"Bastard!" Vuk shouted, slamming his hand on the steaming hood. "The lucky bastard!"

"Was it luck?" Ivo said, staring along the bridge to where they had last seen the truck.

"You think that old *govno* did it on purpose?"

"Why do you say old? Because he had a white beard? It could have come from a Santa Claus costume."

"You think it was the man from the beach?"

Ivo shrugged. "I'm just thinking, that's all. I'm thinking that if it was the man from the beach, and if he wanted to remove us from the front of his house, he succeeded very well, didn't he."

Vuk was fuming. He wanted to punch Ivo for looking so calm. Instead he spit.

"Sranje!"

How were they going to explain this to Dragovic?

13

Nadia was ready to call it quits for the day. As she waited for the molecular imager to go through its shutdown sequence, she checked her voice mail. One message: Jack wanted to meet her at the diabetes clinic at five. He had something for her. He left his own voice mail number in case she couldn't make it.

Nadia checked her watch. Almost five now. She dialed Jack's number and told him it would be easier to meet in front of the drugstore across from her office at a little after five. As she was hanging up . . .

"Such dedication."

Nadia jumped at Dr. Monnet's voice. She turned and saw him standing in the doorway of the dry lab.

"You startled me."

"Sorry," he said, stepping toward her. "I came in to pick up a package and noticed that you were still logged in."

"Just getting ready to leave, actually."

"I won't ask you if you've made any progress," he said. "That would be absurd at this early stage . . . wouldn't it?"

His last two words caught her by surprise. She studied him. Close up like this he looked tired. And well he should be if he'd been up all hours watching men punch each other as Jack had said.

But he seemed beyond tired—more like physically, mentally, and emotionally spent. And beneath the fatigue she sensed something akin to . . . desperation.

What is that hoodlum forcing to you to do? she wondered. What hold does he have on you?

"Yes," she told him. "Too early. I've only just finished reviewing your experiments. You covered a lot of ground."

He nodded absently, almost morosely. "I tried everything I knew. That's why you're here. For a fresh perspective."

Nadia looked down at the console and gathered up her notes to avoid facing him. How could she tell him she felt lost, that the things Jack had told her about his bizarre testing session in Brooklyn, and Doug's discovery of the secret stock buyback were upsetting her, making it almost impossible to focus.

Monnet cleared his throat. "There's another matter I need to discuss with you: Douglas Gleason."

Nadia stiffened. Oh, God. Does he know about the hack?

"What about him?"

"Word has filtered back that he's been in the research wing, even here in the dry lab with you. That's against the rules, you know."

Nadia relaxed and let out a breath. She turned to face him.

"I thought that only applied to people outside the company." A lie . . . but a little one.

"No. I believe I made it clear that this area is restricted to research personnel only. Are you two . . . close? Is that why you've been letting him in?"

Dr. Monnet seemed so intent on her answer. Why?

Nadia decided not to reveal that Doug had been letting *himself* in, and she remembered how Doug had been wary about letting on that there was any romance between them.

"Close?" She managed a smile. "No. We're just old friends."

"Do you see each other often? Do you discuss your work?"

Where was this going? "He's just a friend of the family." Another lie. "We have lunch now and then. He's just very interested in"—she almost said computers—"research. But I'm sure he'd never—"

"I am sure he wouldn't either," Dr. Monnet said quickly. Why did he suddenly look relieved? "But we must not forget that he's a sales-man, his business is talking, talking all day long, and one day in his enthusiasm he might slip and mention a product in a delicate stage of development. But . . . if he does not know about that product, he cannot slip. Do you see my point?"

"I do." It was a good point, one she could respect. She'd tell Doug about it when they met for sushi tonight. "And I promise you Douglas Gleason will not be seen in this department again."

Dr. Monnet turned and walked back toward the door. He left with-out a good-bye. She heard only a sigh and thought he said, "Yes, I know," but she couldn't be sure.

14

"Oh, no," Jack muttered as he followed Monnet onto the ramp off Glen Cove Road. "Don't tell me he's heading for Monroe."

This little jaunt had started in midtown after he'd returned from delivering a special party favor to the Ashe brothers on Long Island.

He rubbed his jaw from where the beard glue had irritated his skin. Had to admit he'd pulled a pretty damn efficient maneuver this afternoon with Sal's truck, leaving Dragovic's men stranded on the Queensboro Bridge.

He'd been in frequent contact with Gia since then and so far Dragovic's men hadn't returned.

He'd met Nadia in front of the Duane Reade across the street from her office as she'd suggested. He was just pressing a manila envelope containing the sample of inert Berzerk into her hand when he saw Monnet step out the door and start walking.

Jack had pointed him out and said, "There's your boss man. I'm going to see where he's off to."

Nadia was glancing nervously about as she stuffed the envelope into her shoulder bag. "Isn't this an illegal drug?" she whispered. "Can I get arrested?"

"No," he said, moving off. "It's not Berzerk anymore. Every so often the stuff turns inert—all at once. This stuff turned the other day."

Her eyes widened so much he thought they were going to bulge out of her head. *"What?"*

"I said—"

"I know what you said; it's just. . . ."

Jack had figured she thought he was nuts. "Hey, that's what I was told." Other people were coming between them now, and he'd moved far enough away so that he had to raise his voice. "Sorry I couldn't get you the active stuff. Maybe tomorrow or the next day."

Nadia had only stared.

He'd waved and hurried off to catch up with Monnet. But even now, almost an hour later, he was still puzzled by her expression. He'd expected disbelief, but hers had looked more like . . . anguish.

He'd followed Monnet to an Avis rental garage. As soon as he'd seen Monnet step through the door, Jack caught a cab back to the garage where he kept the Buick, then raced back to Avis just in time to see Monnet pull out and head toward the East Side. Jack had followed him through the Midtown Tunnel, along the LIE to Glen Cove Road. And now . . . toward Monroe.

After his near-death experience there last month, he'd hoped never to see that overly quaint little town again. But here he was, heading down the road toward Long Island's Gold Coast and the Incorporated Village of Monroe.

He took heart from the fact that Monnet was a scientist, a feet-solidly-on-the ground type, not the sort to be involved in the weirdness that seemed to gravitate toward Monroe. But what the hell was he doing out here?

They crawled along the main drag, done up as an old whaling village, which it once might have been, then continued east to a marshy area that curved around the harbor. Jack followed him down a rutted road that ran toward the Sound. The utility poles lining the road were plastered with posters Jack could not read in the waning light and arrows pointing straight ahead.

Jack's and Monnet's weren't the only cars on the road, and Jack was glad of that. Meant he wouldn't stick out if Monnet was headed for a secret meeting. Finally they came to a small cluster of tents ablaze with lights. A banner stretched between two poles proclaimed: THE OZYMANDIAS PRATHER ODDITY EMPORIUM.

A circus? Jack thought. He's going to a *circus?*

No, not a circus. The banner boasted pictures of a green Man from Mars, a Snake Man, a fortune-teller with three eyes, and other . . . oddities.

Oddities and Monroe . . . the combination set Jack's alarm bells madly ringing. A couple of human oddities from Monroe had damn near sent him on a one-way trip into the Great Beyond on his last visit here.

He tried to shake off the uneasiness by telling himself that this would be different, how it was a traveling show, just passing through Monroe . . . but he didn't quite succeed.

Jack watched as Monnet allowed himself to be waved into a spot in a grassy area roped off for parking; Jack parked three spaces away. But when Monnet got out of his car he didn't follow the meager flow of people toward the brightly lit arch that led to the midway. Instead, he struck off to the right toward a cluster of RVs, trucks, and trailers.

Jack allowed him a long lead, then followed in a crouch through the taller grass. He watched Monnet knock on the door of a battered old Airstream. The door opened and a tall ungainly figure was silhouetted in the doorway before stepping aside to let Monnet in. When the door closed again, Jack saw that it was labeled: OFFICE.

He crouched in the marsh grass, wondering what to do. Did this have anything to do with what Nadia had hired him for? Monnet had driven all the way out here for a sideshow—in a rented car, no less. He seemed to cab everywhere else; why hadn't he cabbed out here? Couldn't cost too much more than renting a car.

Unless of course he was trying to avoid any record of having made this little trip.

Time to do a little eavesdropping.

The moonless night was a bonus. He was about to rise and creep toward the trailer when he saw a couple of shadowy forms turn the corner of a nearby tent and move toward it. Something familiar about their shapes and the way they moved. . . .

When one of them stopped and sniffed the air, Jack realized with a start that they were a couple of the Beagle Boys who'd chased him from the warehouse early this morning. The one guy kept sniffing, turning this way and that, and Jack wondered, He's not smelling *me*, is he?

The breeze off the Sound was in Jack's face, which meant he was downwind.

Can't be me.

A few seconds later the pair resumed their course to wherever they were going, leaving Jack a clear field. But then someone else appeared and walked by the trailer. This rear area was a little too busy for his liking. Too much traffic and too likely a chance of being caught with his eye to a keyhole.

But what possible interest could a molecular biologist like Dr. Luc Monnet have in a traveling sideshow? Didn't seem likely it was related to what Nadia had hired him for, but experience had taught him that all too often the most disparate-seeming things could wind up connected.

He had to see this place in daylight. Tomorrow was Sunday. Too bad he couldn't bring Gia and Vicky along. He'd bet Vicks had never seen an "oddity emporium." But after spotting that Beagle Boy, no way. Tomorrow would be a solo flight.

He crept back to his car and pointed it toward Manhattan. Once through the tunnel, he swung by Sutton Square to see if Dragovic's men were back on watchdog duty but saw no sign.

He wondered if they'd be back tomorrow. They'd camped out all day without catching even a glimpse of Gia, so maybe they'd think she was away for the weekend and give up.

And maybe they wouldn't.

If they were back in the morning he'd have to deal with them again. He'd been cooking up an idea, but he'd need help.

Jack drove to the Upper West Side and, miracle of miracles, found a parking spot half a block from his apartment—had to love these holiday weekends. He walked over to Julio's.

The usual crowd was stacked at the bar, but the table area was only moderately filled.

"Slow night?" Jack asked as Julio handed him a Rolling Rock longneck.

They were standing by the window under the hanging plants. Jack's head brushed against one of the pots, causing a minor snowfall from the dead asparagus fern.

"Yeah!" Julio said, beaming and rubbing his hands together. He was wearing a sleeveless T-shirt as usual, and the motion caused muscles to ripple up and down his pumped-up arms. "Isn't it great. Just like the old days."

The yups and dinks were all out of town. The regulars at Julio's, working guys who had been coming in since he opened the place, weren't the type to leave on three-day weekends.

"I'm going to need a favor tomorrow," Jack said. "The driving kind."

"Sure. When?"

"Sometime between twelve and one will do."

"What I gotta do?"

Jack explained the details. Julio liked them, and so they agreed to meet around noon.

Jack walked home feeling as if the various situations around him might be under control. Not a comforting thought. Experience had taught him that the time you feel things are under control is the time you should start some serious worrying.

He managed to stay awake through the Lancaster-York *The Island of Dr. Moreau,* which somehow managed to make a fascinating story very dull. Barbara Carrera was gorgeous, but the luscious Movielab greens of the island sapped the atmosphere, and Richard Basehart didn't quite cut it as the Sayer of the Law. It was an official entry in the Moreau Festival, though, and he felt obliged to sit through it. A penance of sorts before the guilty pleasure to come: the hilarious Brando-Kilmer version from 1996.

SUNDAY

1

Oh, no, Nadia thought as she gazed at the shape floating before her. Oh please don't let this be true.

But how could she deny what was staring her in the face?

She hadn't slept much last night. She hadn't expected to after Jack dropped that bomb on her yesterday. *It's not Berzerk anymore. Every so often the stuff turns inert—all at once. This stuff turned the other day.*

Turns inert . . . just like the molecule Dr. Monnet wanted her to stabilize. His had also turned the other day . . . inert.

The first thing she'd done upon arriving this morning was prepare a sample of Jack's yellow powder for the imager. She'd inserted it a moment ago and now its molecular structure floated before her: an exact duplicate of the Loki molecule after it became inert.

If inert Berzerk equaled inert Loki, then the inescapable conclusion was that active Loki was active Berzerk. Dr. Monnet had her working on stabilizing a designer drug that induced violent behavior.

Amid a wave of nausea, she dropped into a chair. She had to face it: Dr. Monnet was involved with a dangerous drug. But to what extent? Was he manufacturing it for Milos Dragovic or merely trying to stabilize it for him?

And how willing was his participation? That was the real crux. Nadia couldn't help but notice how anxious Dr. Monnet seemed. That certainly was a good indication that he could be being pressured, even threatened. Or was she simply looking for excuses?

No. She had to have faith that he was not a willing party. And besides, logic said it couldn't be for the money. It made no sense for Dr. Monnet to be involved in illegal drugs when there was so much money to be made in the legal ones.

I should go to the police, she thought, but quickly changed her mind.

An investigation might or might not lead to Dragovic, but it would certainly expose Dr. Monnet's involvement. He could wind up in jail while Dragovic remained untouched.

There had to be another way. Jack was the key. She prayed he'd come up with something soon.

One thing she did know, though: she wasn't going to do another lick of work on this molecule until she had some answers.

2

Ivo had the wheel this time. Another day spent in front of the town house would garner attention, so they'd parked on the west side of Sutton Place this morning in front of a marble-faced apartment house, slightly uptown from Fifty-eighth Street and across from Sutton Square. From this spot he had a good view of the town house.

Yesterday's collision with the truck still bothered him: Accident or intentional? How to tell?

Their car today was another Town Car, but older. Since they'd parked Ivo had been noticing an odor.

"What's that smell?"

Vuk sniffed and ran a hand through his bleached hair. "Smells like piss."

"Right," Ivo said, nodding. "We got a car somebody pissed his pants in. Backseat, I'll bet."

Vuk smiled. "Someone was awfully frightened while riding in this car. Very likely his last ride."

"Well," Ivo said, "if a pee-stained car is our worst punishment, I'll take it."

Vuk laughed. "The boss was mad as hell, wasn't he. We're lucky we got off with our skins."

Ivo nodded. They could laugh now, but last night it had been no laughing matter. Normally Dragovic would shrug off an accident like a pierced radiator, but he'd flown off the handle, raging about the security area like a madman. He was still in a fury over the tire attack, wanting to kill somebody for it, but who? For a few moments Ivo had been ready to piss his own pants, fearing that he and Vuk would end up as surrogate whipping boys.

But then Dragovic had stopped abruptly, almost in midshout, and stalked from the room, leaving Vuk and Ivo—and no doubt many of the others present—shaken and sweaty.

Ivo remembered a sergeant like that in Kosovo. He'd had that same unpredictable, almost psychopathic streak. But at least the Army's rules and regulations had restrained him somewhat. Dragovic had nothing to hold him back. The rules were all his and he could change them whenever he pleased.

Ivo missed the Army, even though much time was spent sitting around waiting for something to happen or to be told what to do. Mostly he missed the structured existence. He did not miss the fighting.

He still had nightmares about Kosovo. He hadn't taken part in the cleansing. Never in a thousand lifetimes could he step into a home and shoot everyone in sight. Most of that had been done by the local police and paramilitaries. Some soldiers had participated—Vuk, for one—but most just stood by and let it happen.

That was my sin, Ivo thought. Turning my head. That and looting.

The looting had been so senseless—carrying off televisions with no way to get them back home. Only the officers had access to trucks, and they simply commandeered the most valuable items from the men under them and shipped them home.

The Ivo who left Kosovo was a far cry from the Ivo who had entered that hellish province. The night before boarding the transport out, he'd prayed that he wouldn't have to kill. But he'd returned with blood on his hands—the blood of a few KLA guerrillas, and civilians as well. But he'd killed civilians only when they'd asked for it.

His unit had been stationed in the area between Gnjilane and Ze-gra, and no one who was not there could ever understand what it was like. An old woman would hobble by a group of soldiers and, just before turning a corner, toss a hand grenade into their midst.

Sometimes you had to shoot first. Ivo knew fellows who hesitated. They went home in boxes.

Ivo had learned, and he'd returned to Belgrade in one piece. But the pale face and dead baffled eyes of a fourteen-year-old boy he'd shot, an unarmed boy who'd looked like he was armed but was only looking for a handout, had followed Ivo home and stayed with him.

At least in the Army you had the weight of the government behind you. Here, with Dragovic, the government was against you. But either way, you spent a lot of time waiting. Like now.

"Do you think the man from the beach was in that truck yesterday?" Vuk said, nodding toward the town house.

Ivo glanced at him. Why was he always paired with Vuk? He liked nothing about him. Too rash, always looking for trouble. Why look for trouble when it had so many ways of finding you.

"I suspect it, but I couldn't prove it."

Neither had mentioned their suspicions about the truck to Dragovic or anyone else last night. They'd have looked like fools for allowing themselves to be suckered, and they knew how the boss dealt with fools.

"One thing I do know," Ivo said, "is that after it happened, whoever lives there was able to come and go as free as they pleased. And that makes me—"

The car jolted and rocked as something *slammed* into the left front fender, knocking Ivo against Vuk.

"Sranje!" Vuk shouted as he was thrown against the passenger door.

Ivo straightened in his seat and looked around. His first thought: Not that truck again!

But instead of a truck he saw an old rusted-out Ford with its right front bumper buried in the Lincoln's fender. But no bearded man be-hind the wheel. This time it was a short, muscular Hispanic.

"Hey, sorry, meng," the man said with an apologetic smile. "This old thing don't steer too good."

"Govno!" Ivo yelled as he tried to push his door open, but the Ford was too close.

Vuk was already opening the passenger door, but by the time he'd reached the sidewalk, the Ford was screeching away, leaving them coughing in the thick white smoke from its exhaust.

"Get him!" Vuk shouted.

Ivo was already turning the key. As he threw the Lincoln into gear and hit the gas, it lurched forward a foot or so before swerving toward the curb. Ivo cursed and yanked on the steering wheel but it wouldn't budge.

"What's wrong?" Vuk said.

"Jammed!"

Vuk jumped out and ran around to the front of a car where he froze. Then his face contorted as he began swearing and kicking at the front tire.

Ivo got out to see what he was doing.

"Look!" Vuk shouted. "Look!"

In an instant he understood: the Ford had scored a direct hit on the wheel, leaving it cocked on its axle. Ivo turned and watched the battered old car dwindling in the distance on Sutton Place. Then he swung around and glared at the town house.

Vuk followed his gaze. "You don't think . . ."

"The man who hit us just now was *not* the man from the beach," Ivo said. "But still . . ."

Vuk turned back to the car. "Never mind him. What are we going to do about *this?*"

Ivo's anger faded to fear as he realized they were going to have to report another disabled car to Dragovic.

Vuk paled. The same must have dawned on him. "We'll have to get it fixed! Immediately!"

"On a Sunday?" Ivo said. "How?"

"I don't know, but we *must!*"

As Vuk yanked out his cell phone and began jabbing the keypad, Ivo's mind raced. If they could have the car towed, somehow get it repaired, they'd say nothing. As for watching the house . . . they'd lie . . . report no activity. No one was home anyway.

But they *had* to fix this damn car.

3

"One child," Jack said as he handed a ten to the guy in the ticket booth.

He was a beefy type, wearing a straw boater. He looked around.

"What child?"

"Me. I'm a kid at heart."

"Funny," the ticket man said without a smile as he slid an adult ticket and change across the tray.

Jack entered the main tent of the Ozymandias Prather Oddity Emporium and checked out his fellow attendees: a sparse and varied crew, everything from middle-class folk who looked like they'd just come from church to Goth types in full black regalia.

At first glance the show looked pretty shabby. Everything seemed so worn, from the signs above the booths to the poles supporting the canvas. Look up and it was immediately apparent from the sunlight leaking through that the Oddity Emporium was in need of new tents. He wondered what they did when it rained. Thunderstorms were predicted for later. Jack was glad he'd be out of here long before then.

As he moved along he tried to classify the Oddity Emporium. In some ways it was a freak show, and in many ways not.

First off, Jack had never seen freaks like some of these. Sure, they had the World's Fattest Man, a giant billed as the World's Tallest Man, two sisters with undersized heads who sang in piercing falsetto harmony—nothing so special about them.

Then they came to the others.

By definition freaks were supposed to be strange, but these went beyond strange into the positively alien. The Alligator Boy, the Bird

Man with flapping feathered wings . . . these "freaks" were so alien they couldn't be real.

Like the Snake Man. Jack couldn't see where the real him ended and the fake began.

Makeup and prosthetics, Jack told himself.

But the way he used his tail to wrap around a stuffed rabbit and squeeze it . . . just like a boa constrictor.

A good fake, but still a fake. Had to be . . . even if this was Monroe.

One aspect of the show that reinforced his feeling that these weren't real was that there was nothing sad or pathetic about these "freaks." No matter how bizarre their bodies, they seemed proud—almost belligerently so—of their deformities, as if the people strolling the midway were the freaks.

Jack slowed before a booth with a midget standing on a miniature throne. He had a tiny handlebar mustache and slicked-down black hair parted in the middle. A gold-lettered sign hung above him: LITTLE SIR ECHO.

"Hi!" a little girl said.

"Hi, yourself," the little man replied in a note-perfect imitation of the child's voice.

"Hey, Mom!" she cried. "He sounds just like me!"

"Hey, Mom!" Little Sir Echo said. "Come on over and listen to this guy!"

Jack noticed a tension in the mother's smile and thought he knew why. The mimicked voice was too much like her child's—pitch and timbre, all perfect down to the subtlest nuance. If Jack had been facing away, he wouldn't have had the slightest doubt that the little girl had spoken. Amazing, but creepy too.

"You're very good," Mom said.

"I'm not very good," he replied in a perfect imitation of the woman's voice. "I'm the best. And your voice is as beautiful as you are."

Mom flushed. "Why, thank you."

The midget turned to Jack, still speaking in the woman's voice: "And you, sir—Mr. Strong Silent Type. Care to say anything?"

"Yoo doorty rat!" Jack said in his best imitation of a bad comic imitating James Cagney. "Yoo killed my brutha!"

The woman burst out laughing. She didn't say so, but she had to think it was awful . . . because it was.

"A W. C. Fields fan!" the little man cried with a mischievous wink. "I have an old recording of one of his stage acts! Want to hear?"

Without waiting for a reply, Sir Echo began to mimic the record, and a chill ran through Jack as he realized that the little man was faithfully reproducing not only the voice but the pops and cracks of the scratched vinyl as well.

"Marvelous, my good man!" Jack said in a W. C. Fields imitation as bad as his Cagney. "Marvelous."

He moved off, wondering why he'd been afraid to let the midget hear his natural voice. Some prerational corner of his brain had shied away from it. Probably the same part that made jungle tribefolk shun a camera for fear it would steal their souls.

As he passed a booth with a green-skinned fellow billed as "The Man from Mars," he glanced up and stopped cold.

Dead ahead, a banner hung over the midway. Faded yellow letters spelled out SHARKMAN. But it was the crude drawing that had captured his attention.

Damn if it didn't resemble a rakosh.

After what he'd seen here already, he wouldn't be half surprised if it were.

Not that one of Kusum's rakoshi had a single chance in hell of being alive. They'd all died last summer between Governors Island and the Battery. He'd seen to that. Crisped them all in the hold of the ship that housed them. One of them did make it to shore, the one he'd dubbed Scar-lip, but it had swum back out into the burning water and had never returned.

The rakoshi were dead, all of them. The species was extinct.

But something here might resemble a rakosh, and if so, he was extra glad he hadn't brought Vicky along. Kusum Bahkti, the madman who'd controlled a nest of them, had vowed to wipe out the Westphalen bloodline; Vicky, as the last surviving Westphalen, had been his final target. His rakoshi emissaries had been relentless in their pursuit.

Passing a stall containing a woman with a third eye in the center of her forehead that supposedly "Sees ALL!" Jack came to an old circus cart with iron bars on its open side, one of the old cages-on-wheels once used to transport and display lions and tigers and such. The sign above it read: THE AMAZING SHARKMAN! Jack noticed people leaning across the rope border; they'd peer into the cage, then back off with uneasy shrugs.

This deserved a look.

Jack pushed to the front and squinted into the dimly lit cage. Something there, slumped in the left rear corner, head down, chin on chest, immobile. Something huge, a seven-footer at least. Dark-skinned, man-like, and yet . . . undeniably alien.

Jack felt the skin along the back of his neck tighten as ripples of warning shot down his spine. He knew that shape. But that was all it was. A shape. So immobile. It had to be a dummy of some sort or a guy in a costume. A helluva good costume.

But it couldn't be the real thing. Couldn't be. . . .

Jack ducked under the rope and took a few tentative steps closer to the cage, sniffing the air. One of the things he remembered about the rakoshi was their reek, like rotting meat. He caught a trace of it here, but that could have been from spilled garbage. Nothing like the breath-clogging stench he remembered.

He moved close enough to touch the bars but didn't. The thing was a damn good dummy. He could almost swear it was breathing.

Jack whistled and said, "Hey, you in there!"

The thing didn't budge, so he rapped on one of the iron bars. "Hey—!"

Suddenly it moved, the eyes snapping open as the head came up, deep yellow eyes that seemed to glow in the shadows.

Imagine the offspring from mating a giant hairless gorilla with a mako shark. Cobalt skin, hugely muscled, no neck worth mentioning, no external ears, narrow slits for a nose.

Spikelike talons, curved for tearing, emerged from the tips of the three huge fingers on each hand as the yellow eyes fixed on Jack. The lower half of its huge sharklike head seemed to split as the jaw opened to reveal rows of razor-sharp teeth. It uncoiled its legs and slithered across the metal flooring toward the front of the cage.

Along with instinctive revulsion, memories surged back: the cargo hold full of their dark shapes and glowing eyes, the unearthly chant, the disappearances, the deaths. . . .

Jack backed up a step. Two. Behind him he heard the crowd oooh! and aaah! as it pressed forward for a better look. He took still another step back until he could feel their excited breath on his neck. These people didn't know what one of these things could do, didn't know their power, their near-indestructibility. Otherwise they'd be running the other way.

Jack felt his heart kick up its already rising tempo when he noticed how the creature's lower lip was distorted by a wide scar. He knew this particular rakosh. Scar-lip. The one that had kidnapped Vicky, the one that had escaped the ship and almost got to Vicky on the shore. The one that had damn near killed Jack.

He ran a hand across his chest. Even through the fabric of his shirt he could feel the three long ridges that ran across his chest, souvenir scars from the creature's talons.

His mouth felt like straw. Scar-lip . . . alive.

But *how?* How had it survived the blaze on the water? How had it wound up on Long Island in a traveling freak show?

"Ooh, look at it, Fred!" said a woman behind Jack.

"Just a guy in a rubber suit," replied a supremely confident male voice.

"But those claws—did you see the way they came out?"

"Simple hydraulics. Nothing to it."

You go on believing that, Fred, Jack thought as he watched the creature where it crouched on its knees, its talons encircling the iron bars, its yellow eyes burning into Jack.

You know me too, don't you.

It appeared to be trying to stand but its legs wouldn't support it. Was it chained, or possibly maimed?

The ticket seller came by then, sans boater, revealing a shaven head. Up close like this Jack was struck by his cold eyes. He was carrying a blunt elephant gaff that he rapped against the bars.

"So you're up, aye?" he said to the rakosh in a harsh voice. "Maybe you've finally learned your lesson."

Jack noticed that for the first time since it had opened its eyes, the rakosh turned its glare from him; it refocused on the newcomer.

"Here he is, ladies and gentleman," the ticket man cried, turning to the crowd. "Yessir, the one and only Sharkman! The only one of his kind! He's exclusively on display here at Ozymandias Oddities. Tell your friends; tell your enemies. Yessir, you've never seen anything like him and never will anywhere else. Guaranteed."

You've got that right, Jack thought.

The ticket man spotted Jack standing on the wrong side of the rope. "Here, you. Get back there. This thing's dangerous! See those claws? One swipe and you'd be sliced up like a tomato by a Ginsu knife! We don't want to see our customers get sliced up." His eyes said otherwise as he none too gently prodded Jack with the pole. "Back now."

Jack slipped back under the rope, never taking his eyes off Scar-lip. Now that it was up front in the light, he saw that the rakosh didn't look well. Its skin was dull and relatively pale, nothing like the shiny deep cobalt he remembered from their last meeting. It looked thin, wasted.

The rakosh turned its attention from the ticket man and stared at Jack a moment longer, then dropped its gaze. Its talons retracted, slipping back inside the fingertips, the arms dropped to its sides, the shoulders drooped, then it turned and crawled back to the rear of the cage where it slumped again in the corner and hung its head.

Drugged. That had to be the answer. They had to tranquillize the rakosh to keep it manageable. Even so, it didn't look too healthy. Maybe the iron bars were doing it—fire and iron, the only things that could hurt a rakosh.

But drugged or not, healthy or not, Scar-lip had recognized Jack, remembered him. Which meant it could remember Vicky. And if it ever got free, it might come after Vicky again, to complete the task its dead master had set for it last summer.

The ticket man had begun banging on the rakosh's cage in a fury, screaming at it to get up and face the crowd. But the creature ignored him, and the crowd began to wander off in search of more active attractions.

Jack turned and headed for the exit. He'd come here hoping to explain Monnet's interest in a freak show, but that was all but forgotten now. A cold resolve had overtaken his initial shock. He knew what had to be done.

4

Luc had promised himself not to hover over Nadia while she was working—he knew how distracting that could be. She never would be able to give her scientific inventiveness and creativity full rein if she felt someone was looking over her shoulder every minute. But curiosity and just plain need to know had overcome him.

He'd been disappointed to find her signed out, but he'd come down to the dry lab to see what she'd entered into the computer. He tapped on the keyboard to retrieve the last image she'd been working on.

He sighed as a hologram of the too-familiar inert Loki molecule materialized in the air. He'd seen too much of *that*. He was reaching for the ESCAPE button but stopped when something on the monitor caught his eye. He stared in disbelief at the date on the screen, indicating that the image had been created at 9:20 this morning. Not recalled—*created*.

Impossible. Nadia could not have generated a fresh image without a sample, and he hadn't supplied her with any inert Loki. This had to be a mistake.

Luc checked the sample chamber and felt his chest constrict when he found a residue of yellow powder. How could this be? She must have used some inert Loki he'd left here—that was the only explanation.

But why couldn't he remember leaving it?

Stress. That had to be it. It sapped focus, the ability to concentrate. And he'd certainly had more than his share of stress lately.

And yet . . . Luc wished he could be sure. Was it possible she'd heard about a street drug that decomposed every month and had picked up a sample? Not Nadia. She wasn't the type to take drugs or have any interest in them.

Still, he couldn't mention this to Kent or Brad. They'd panic and want to do something rash on the chance that Nadia might link GEM to Berzerk. They'd become positively bloodthirsty.

No, he'd wait. Nadia was too valuable an asset.

But she'd bear watching. Close watching.

5

"Damn!" Nadia said as she hung up the phone, none too gently.

"Something is wrong?" her mother said from the kitchen.

Nadia stood in the front room. The little apartment was redolent of the stuffed cabbage Mom was simmering in a big pot on the stove. Since she knew how Doug loved the dish, she'd suggested that Nadia invite him over for dinner.

But how could she when his line was always busy?

"It's Doug," Nadia told her. "He must be on-line with that computer of his."

She'd left the lab early and had been trying to contact Doug all day—and not just to invite him for dinner—but his line had been busy every time she called. He wasn't answering his cell phone either, which meant he probably hadn't turned it on. He often didn't on weekends.

Or maybe Doug had lapsed into one of his programming fugues. Nadia had seen it happen before. He'd take the phone off the hook, bury it under a cushion, and start hitting the keys. Gradually he'd fade into a state of altered consciousness where he became one with his computer and nothing else existed beyond their union. It was spooky.

But why did he have to fugue out today of all days? She'd been in a blue funk ever since running the inert Berzerk through the imager this morning. Seeing that molecule floating before her had drained her enthusiasm for stabilizing it.

Oh, God! she thought, stiffening. I left the sample in the imager!

She'd been so shocked after recognizing the molecule . . .

She calmed herself. No one would be in the dry lab until Tuesday. She'd go back first thing tomorrow morning and clean up.

What she needed most now was to talk about this. Her mother might be good for any other topic, but not this one. Nadia needed Doug.

"Come, Nadjie," her mother called. "Eat. You'll feel better."

Why not? she thought with a mental shrug. Not much else to do.

But when she sat down she realized she wasn't hungry. As she picked at her food she noticed the beer and shot of Fleischman's sitting by her mother's plate.

"Mom," she said. "Would you mind pouring me one of those?"

6

Milos Dragovic gazed out upon the expanse of his grounds and was pleased. In less than forty-eight hours the army of laborers and craftsmen he had assembled had worked a miracle. And just in time. The final touches had been applied just minutes before the first guests arrived.

He watched them milling about the pool and clustering on the decks—the women mostly in black, the peacock men in coats of many colors. Quite a different crowd from Friday night's. Sprinkled among the glitterati he'd shipped in from the city were a fair number of Hamptons society. Not all the crème de la crème had accepted his

invitation, but more than enough to allow him to call the party a resounding success.

He smiled. To the uninformed, the acceptance rate to a party hosted
by a high-profile gangster might have seemed surprisingly high. But
not if Milos's invitation strategy were known. He had investigated
Hamptons society and divided the upper echelons into three groups.
He then sent out his invitations in three waves, all mailed locally two
days apart. When the first wave was received, he knew it would be
chatted up in the social circles. He could just hear them: Did you know
that boorish Dragovic fellow is having a party and he wants *me* to come?
Can you *ima*gine?

Of course the ones in the second and third wave were thinking,
Why wasn't *I* invited? Not that I'd even think of going, of course, but
why was I left out?

Then the second-wave invitation would arrive and there'd be a
sense of relief—*grateful* relief that they hadn't been passed over. The
post office's fault. Same with the third wave.

Thus the invitations would not be automatically tossed away. And
then the talk that it might be rather interesting to attend—Hamptons
slumming, you might say—and it will give us *so* much to talk and laugh
about afterward . . . we'll postmortem it for *days*.

But with everything at the party arranged and orchestrated by Kim,
seeing to it that only the very best of everything was served, and in the
most tasteful manner, the only fodder for their postparty conversation
would be how the affair had far exceeded their expectations.

The result would be that no one would turn down his invitations
next year.

And in time Milos saw himself winnowing the list, cutting those
who were not properly respectful. An invitation to the annual Milos
Dragovic soiree would become an object of envy, to be coveted and
striven for . . . like a membership at the Maidstone Club.

He wondered if any members of the self-styled East Hampton Environmental Protection Committee were present. If they hated him
enough to dump refuse on his house, how could they bring themselves
to attend his party?

Then again, there was the old adage: hide in plain sight. Milos's
enemy might assume he'd be above suspicion if he attended. But there
he was wrong.

No one was above suspicion. No one.

"Excuse me, Mr. Dragovic," said a voice to his left.

Milos turned and saw a tall, fair man. He stood with a glass of red wine in his left hand and his right extended. Milos recognized his face but the name eluded him.

"Jus Slobojan," the man said as they shook hands.

Of course. Justin Karl Slobojan. The wildly successful action-thriller director, worth a hundred million or so . . . originally a New Yorker, now living mostly in LA but still summering as much as possible in Amagansett.

"Mr. Slobojan," Milos said. "I've long admired your work." This was no lie. Even though his villains were often drug lords and gangsters, and always met a bloody end, Milos never missed a Slobojan film. "I am so very pleased to meet you."

And pleased he had come, especially after Mike Nichols and Diane Sawyer had turned him down.

"And I'm pleased to be here. This is a wonderful party." He leaned closer. "Did I hear that you had some trouble here the other night?"

Milos stared at the director. Could he be involved with this East Hampton Environmental Protection Committee? Unlikely. He spent too little time out here to get upset over who moved in. In fact, he was probably an outsider himself. Milos understood he'd been born in the Ukraine. In a way, that made them almost neighbors.

"A little vandalism by some locals," Milos said. "Nothing important."

"Good," Slobojan said. "Some of the rumors mentioned quite a bit of damage, but I can see now that they were exaggerated. You have a beautiful house for a party. The food is superb, and this wine . . ." He held up his glass. "If this is your house red, I'd love to see what you keep in your cellar."

"You know wines then?"

Slobojan shrugged. "A little. I dabble."

In Milos's experience, a person who downplayed his abilities as Slobojan was doing was most often a true expert.

"Then I believe I have a treat for you. Come."

He'd led the director halfway across the living room when he heard a sound outside. He stopped and turned.

"What's that?"

"What's what?" Slobojan said.

The sound grew louder as Milos hurried back to the doors. A helicopter! He was sure of it! With his intestines writhing into painful knots, he rushed outside and scanned the night sky.

"Is something wrong?" Slobojan said, coming out behind him.

"A helicopter! I hear a helicopter!"

Slobojan laughed. "Of course you do, old man. The Coast Guard runs up and down the beach all the time."

Already the sound was fading. Milos forced a smile. "The Coast Guard. Yes, of course."

Where the hell had the Coast Guard been Friday night when he was being bombed?

Milos relaxed. He'd thought about this all day and had come to the conclusion that he had little to fear from the so-called East Hampton Environmental Protection Committee tonight. This was a gathering of their peers. As much as they might hate him and his presence here in the center of what they considered their private preserve, they would not risk an assault on members of their own precious social circle. They'd know that if—more likely *when*—their identities were revealed, they would become instant outcasts, shunned by their own kind.

For tonight at least, his house was safe. But who knew after that?

That was why it was essential that he track down these bastards— especially the one who had called him on Friday night. Milos would deal personally with him.

He led Slobojan back into the living room where he had the 1947 Petrus breathing in a crystal decanter, the empty bottle beside it. As Slobojan bent to read the label, Milos turned the bottle.

"First you will try. And after you tell me what you think of it, I will show you the label."

"A blind taste test, ay?" Slobojan said. His smile looked uncertain. "OK. I guess I'm game."

Milos half-filled one of the decanter's matching crystal glasses and handed it to Slobojan. He watched closely as the director went through all the swirling and sniffing rituals, and wondered how he'd react when he finally tasted it. Here was a man who supposedly knew wine but had no idea if he was tasting something from France, California, or one of the dozen or so wineries right here on Long Island.

At last he took a sip. He made strange sucking noises, then swallowed. Justin Karl Slobojan closed his eyes as a look of beatific ecstasy suffused his features.

"Oh, dear God," he murmured. He opened his eyes and fixed Milos with a grateful stare. "I thought you were going to tell me you'd bought one of these so-called vineyards out here and this was your first bottling." He held up the glass and examined the ruby liquid. "But this is definitely French. An absolutely magnificent Bordeaux. I'm not good enough to identify the château, but I can tell you this is just about the best wine I've ever tasted."

Milos was delighted. He still didn't understand how people actually enjoyed drinking this acrid stuff, but at least he hadn't bought bad wine. He turned the bottle to show Slobojan the label.

The director's eyes lighted. "Petrus! I should have known. That's the—" His eyes fairly bulged as he noticed the date. "Nineteen-forty-seven! I was only two years old when this was grape juice!"

Milos handed the decanter to Slobojan. "Here. With my compliments."

"Oh, no. I can't. That must be worth thousands!"

Milos shrugged dismissively. "If one wants the best, one must be prepared to pay what is necessary." He thrust the decanter into Slobojan's hands. "Please. I insist."

"Then you must share it with me!"

Milos felt his cheeks pucker at the thought. "I have many more bottles. This one is for you. Share it with others here you know will appreciate it."

And will talk about it later, he silently added.

"Thank you," Slobojan said. "This is extraordinarily generous of you."

"It is nothing," Milos said as the director hurried away with his liquid treasure.

Yes, Milos thought, giddy with delight as he wandered back outside. The evening was progressing perfectly. This would indeed be a party to remember.

As he stood on the central deck he noticed an attractive young blonde and recognized her as Kirin Adams, the actress who had just co-starred in Brad Pitt's latest movie. She was standing alone near the end of the far deck, watching the ocean. Cino was not in sight at the moment, so Milos started toward her. He was almost to her side when he again heard the unmistakable sound of a helicopter.

He stopped. Coast Guard again or . . .

He looked out to sea but saw nothing. Then he realized the sound was coming from behind him. He turned and there it was, materializing out of the darkness on the far side of the house. He stood frozen as it glided over the roof like some giant black dragonfly.

Oh, no! They wouldn't dare!

One by one and then in groups, his guests stopped their eating, drinking, and talking to turn and stare at the approaching craft, to point at the strange-looking pod dangling from its undercarriage.

"No!" Milos screamed as the helicopter swooped a hundred feet overhead. He saw a door in the front section of the pod drop open, watched black liquid gush forth . . .

"Nooooooooo!"

He and his guests watched in mesmerized silence as the huge droplets fell in slow motion, dispersing in the air, their momentum carrying them forward. But when they landed, it was in accelerated time.

The black deluge struck, splattering the grounds and everyone gathered there. Women screamed in disgust and dismay; men shouted and cried out in anger. Milos himself took a faceful. Gasping, sputtering, he wiped his eyes and cleared his nose.

The smell: engine oil. Bad enough, but not clean engine oil, this was thick, black, filthy stuff. And it was everywhere. The entire yard was coated with it; even the pool showed dark splotches floating on the surface.

And then the sound of the copter was no longer fading but growing louder again. Milos looked up and saw that it had circled around and was coming in for a second pass. To his right he noticed a couple of his men drawing their weapons.

"Shoot it!" he screamed. "Shoot it down!"

But then pandemonium took charge. The sight of guns and the fear of another oily drenching sent the guests into wild panicked flight in all directions. But the oil had rendered the wood of the decks treacherous: all about him people were slipping, falling, or being knocked down. Even his own men were losing their footing.

It looked like a replay of Friday night—tables upended, food and glassware flying, people diving, rolling, floundering and gasping after being knocked into the pool. Except this time Milos was not watching from the safety of the house; he was down in the heart of a chaos of splashing oil, flying food, smashing glass, and beautiful people in flight. And worse—he was utterly powerless to stop it.

As the rear door of the helicopter's dangling pod dropped open above him, Milos spun and looked around for shelter. He noticed the blond actress crouching under a patio table. Good idea. He ducked and crowded in beside her.

"Get out of here!" she cried, pushing at him. "Get your own table!"

"This *is* my table!" Milos roared. "They're *all* my tables!"

Venting only a fraction of the fury boiling within him, he grabbed her by the shoulders and shoved, sending her rolling away. She ended up sprawled on her back on the decking.

She bared her teeth and screamed. "You bas—" she began, but then she stopped and her eyes widened.

Milos was just turning his head to see what had caught her attention when the tabletop came crashing down on his head and back, flattening him to the deck.

Through his pain-blurred vision he saw a whale of a man in an oil-soaked tuxedo groan and roll off the tabletop onto the slippery deck. And through the roaring in his ears he heard the actress's derisive laughter.

He lay prone, unable to move. It wasn't the table pinning him to the deck; humiliation and the feeling of utter impotence weighed him down. Instead of a scream of rage, the sound that rose in his throat was more like a sob.

7

Sal was grinning like an idiot as he stumbled away from the beach. Hard to believe, but tonight topped Friday night. And seeing Dragovic cowering under that table like an old lady, then getting flattened— *Madrone!* That alone was worth the price of admission. That walking piece of shit must be ready to die of embarrassment.

But that was nothing compared to how he was gonna feel when the local stations got hold of this videotape. Dragovic's Greatest Hits!

Had to hand it to Jack. Soon as he seen those barrels of old crank-case oil he knew exactly what he wanted to do, especially since Sal had a huge supply of the crud. Had to drain the crankcase of every heap that came into the yard and then pay some disposal outfit to cart it off. This was a *much* better way to get rid of it.

As for the hoity-toities at the party—served 'em right. The jerks deserved everything they got. More. Should've got busted bones and heads instead of walking away with nothing worse than messed-up clothes and a bunch of bruises and scratches.

Sal glanced back at where the lights from Dragovic's place filtered over the dune.

Hey, assholes, still think it's cool hanging with a murderer?

And you, Dragovic, Sal thought, patting the videocam. I got you right here, you murderin' sonovabitch. Everyone's gonna see what a pussy you are. You're gonna wish you was dead.

And yet . . . somehow it still wasn't enough.

8

The call came an hour later. Milos had cleaned up by then and was seated in the basement security area, waiting for it. So was Mihailo, manning his tracking computer.

"Mr. Dragovic?" said the too-cultured voice on the other end. "East Hampton Environmental Protection Committee here. My, my, I must say you do know how to show people a good time."

Milos had expected taunts and was prepared for them. He also had a plan of how to deal with these people.

"You surprised me," Milos said, his voice even. "I didn't think you would attack your own kind."

"*My* own kind? Ha! You are trying to insult me, aren't you, Mr. Dragovic. Those parvenus are closer to your kind than mine."

What is a "parvenu"? Milos wondered.

"A parvenu, by the way," the voice said, "is a Johnny-come-lately, with lots of cash, few social skills, and *no* breeding. But they are several cuts above you, Mr. Dragovic. And tonight they learned an important lesson: when one clusters around a cesspool, one risks getting splashed with slime."

Milos bit back a stream of profanity and launched into baiting his plan.

"You will not drive me out," he said. "I am looking for you. I will dedicate myself to turning over every rock on Long Island in search of you. And when you are found, do not think you will be handed over to police. No, you will be brought to me, and then we will see who is parvenu. Until then I will hold as many parties as I please, whenever it pleases me."

The caller laughed. "Excellent! I'm *so* glad to hear you say that. This has been too much fun to end after a mere pair of encounters. When's the next parvenu barbecue, as it were?"

"Tomorrow night," Milos said through his teeth.

"Excellent!" A pause, then, "You wouldn't be thinking of calling in the authorities on this, would you, Dragovic?"

"No! *I* am authority here!"

"Good. Because this is between you and us. And are we not men?"

What was this fool talking about?

"I do not know about you, but *I* am man, and I will have parties, many parties. Tomorrow night, and the next night, and the next night, and every night after until Labor Day. Do your damnedest!"

Milos slammed down the receiver and glanced at Mihailo on the far side of the room.

"He's calling from another pay phone," Mihailo said with a shrug. "Some place in Roslyn Heights."

"Where is that?"

"Almost back to Queens. I'll bet he pulled off the LIE and called from a gas station."

Milos hadn't in his most violent fantasies expected to be able to trap the man so quickly, but still he was disappointed.

"Very well," he told his men. "You all know what to do during the next twenty-four hours."

"What about us, Mr. Dragovic?"

Ivo had spoken. Milos turned and saw him and Vuk standing side by side. He was disappointed in these two. Both had been reliable men until now. But over the last two days their cars had been disabled twice—while they were sitting in them. They'd tried to cover up the second occurrence but he'd found out.

Two accidents in two days. Too much coincidence. Trouble was, the Sutton Square house appeared to be empty.

"You two will stay. I don't want you wasting your time—and another one of my cars." This drew laughs from the other men. Ivo and Vuk nodded and smiled uneasily. "We have too much to do here. The ones we are after will be coming to us tomorrow night. And I want us well prepared."

Milos rubbed his hands together. He had a hot reception planned for the East Hampton Environmental Protection Committee.

9

After finishing his call to Dragovic—which had gone just as he'd hoped—Jack left the gas station and headed up the highway to Monroe.

Parvenu . . . Abe had given him the word. A beauty.

In Monroe Jack parked at the edge of the marsh on a rutted road that ended a few hundred yards farther out at a tiny shack sitting alone near the Long Island Sound. He wondered who lived there.

A mist had formed, hugging the ground. The shack looked ominous and lonely floating in the fog out there with its single lighted window. Reminded Jack of an old gothic paperback cover.

Jack stuck his head out the window. Only a sliver of moon above, but plenty of stars. Enough light to get him where he wanted to go without a flashlight. He could make out the grassy area the Oddity

Emporium used for parking. Only one or two cars there. As he watched, their headlights came alive and moved off in the direction of town.

Business was slow, it seemed. Good. The show would be early bedding down.

After the lights went out and things had been quiet for a while, Jack slipped out of the car and took a two-gallon can from the trunk. Gasoline sloshed within as he strode across the uneven ground toward the hulking silhouette of the main show tent. The performers' and hands' trailers stood off to the north side by a big 18-wheel truck.

No security in sight. Jack slipped under the canvas sidewall and listened. Quiet. A couple of incandescent bulbs had been left on, one hanging from the ceiling every thirty feet or so. Keeping to the shadows along the side, Jack made his way behind the booths toward Scar-lip's cage.

His plan was simple: flood the floor of the rakosh's cage and douse the thing itself with the gas, then strike a match. Normally the idea of immolating a living creature would sicken him, but this was a rakosh. If a bullet in the brain would have done the trick, he'd have come fully loaded. But the only sure way to off a rakosh was fire . . . the cleansing flame.

Jack knew from experience that once a rakosh started to burn, it was quickly consumed. As soon as he was sure the flames were doing their thing, he'd run for the trailers shouting "Fire!" at the top of his lungs, then dash for his car.

He just hoped the performers and roustabouts would arrive with their extinguishers in time to keep the whole tent from going up.

He didn't like this, didn't like endangering the tent or anybody nearby, but it was the only scheme he could come up with on such short notice. He would protect Vicky at any cost, and this was the only sure way Jack knew.

He approached the "Sharkman" area warily from the blind end, then made a wide circle around to the front. Scar-lip was stretched out on the floor of the cage, sleeping, its right arm dangling through the bars. It opened its eyes as he neared. Their yellow was even duller than this afternoon. Its talons extended only partway as it made a half-hearted, almost perfunctory swipe in Jack's direction. Then it closed its eyes and let the arm dangle again. It didn't seem to have strength or the heart for anything more.

Jack stopped and stared at the creature. And he knew.

It's dying.

He stood there a long time and watched Scar-lip doze in its cage. Was it sick or was something else ailing it? Some animals couldn't live outside a pack. Jack had destroyed this thing's nest and all its brothers and sisters along with it. Was this last rakosh dying of loneliness, or had it simply reached the end of its days? What was the life span of a rakosh, anyway?

Jack shifted the gas can in his hands and wondered if he was needed here. He'd torch a vital, aggressive, healthy rakosh without a qualm, because he knew if positions were reversed it would tear off his head in a second. But there didn't seem to be any question that Scar-lip would be history before long. So why endanger the carny folk with a fire?

On the other hand . . . what if Scar-lip recovered and got free? It was a possibility. And he'd never forgive himself if it came after Vicky again. Jack had damn near died saving Vicky the last time—and he'd been lucky at that. Could he count on that kind of luck again?

Uh-uh. Never count on luck.

He began unscrewing the cap of the gasoline can but stopped when he heard voices . . . coming this way down the midway. He ducked for the shadows.

"I tell you, Hank," said a voice that sounded familiar, "you should've seen the big wimp this afternoon. Something got it riled. It had the crowd six deep around its cage while it was up."

Jack recognized the baldheaded ticket seller who'd prodded him back behind the rope this afternoon. The other man with him was taller, younger, but just as beefy, with a full head of sandy hair. He carried a bottle of what looked like cheap wine while the bald one carried a six-foot iron bar, sharpened at one end. Neither of them was walking too steadily.

"Maybe we taught it a good lesson last night, huh, Bondy?" said the one called Hank.

"Just lesson number one," Bondy said. "The first of many. Yessir, the first of many."

They stopped before the cage. Bondy took a swig from the bottle and handed it back to Hank.

"Look at it," Bondy said. "The big blue wimp. Thinks it can just sit around all day and sleep all night. No way, babe! Y'gotta earn your keep, wimp!" He took the sharp end of the iron bar and jabbed it at the rakosh. "*Earn* it!"

The point pierced Scar-lip's shoulder. The creature moaned like a cow with laryngitis and rolled away. The bald guy kept jabbing at it, stabbing its back again and again, making it moan while Hank stood by, grinning.

Jack turned and crept off through the shadows. The two carnies had found the only other thing that could harm a rakosh—iron. Fire and iron—they were impervious to everything else. Maybe that was another explanation for Scar-lip's poor health—caged with iron bars.

As Jack moved away, he heard Hank's voice rise over the tortured cries of the dying rakosh.

"When's it gonna be my turn, Bondy? Huh? When's my turn?"

The hoarse moans followed Jack out into the night. He stowed the can back in the trunk and got as far as opening the car door. And then he stopped.

"Shit!" he said and pounded the roof of the car. "Shit! Shit! *Shit!*"

He slammed the door closed and trotted back to the freak show tent, repeating the word all the way.

No stealth this time. He strode directly to the section he'd just left, pulled up the sidewall, and charged inside. Bondy still had the iron pike—or maybe he had it back again. Jack stepped up beside him just as he was preparing for another jab at the trapped, huddled creature. He snatched the pike from his grasp.

"That's enough, asshole."

Bondy looked at him wide-eyed, his forehead wrinkling up to where his hairline should have been. Probably no one had talked to him that way in a long, long time.

"Who the fuck are you?"

"Nobody you want to know right now. Maybe you should call it a night."

Bondy took a swing at Jack's face. He telegraphed it by baring his teeth. Jack raised the rod between his face and the fist. Bondy screamed as his knuckles smashed against the iron, then did a knock-kneed walk in a circle with the hand jammed between his thighs, groaning in pain.

Suddenly a pair of arms wrapped around Jack's torso, trapping him in a fleshy vise.

"I got him, Bondy!" Hank's voice shouted from behind Jack's left ear. "I got him!"

Twenty feet away, Bondy stopped his dance, looked up, and grinned. As he charged, Jack rammed his head backward, smashing the back of his skull into Hank's nose. Abruptly he was free. He still held the iron bar, so he angled the blunt end toward the charging Bondy and drove it hard into his solar plexus. The air *whooshed* out of him and he dropped to his knees with a groan, his face gray-green. Even his scalp looked sick.

Jack glanced up and saw Scar-lip crouched at the front of the cage, gripping the bars, its yellow gaze flicking between him and the groaning Bondy but lingering on Jack, as if trying to comprehend what he was doing, and why. Tiny rivulets of dark blood trailed down its skin.

Jack whirled the pike 180 degrees and pressed the point against Bondy's chest.

"What kind of noise am I going to hear when I poke you with *this* end?"

Behind him Hank's voice, very nasal now, started shouting.

"Hey, Rube! Hey, Rube!"

As Jack was trying to figure out just what that meant, he gave the kneeling Bondy a poke with the pointed end—not enough to break the skin but enough to scare him. He howled and fell back on the sawdust, screaming.

"Don't! Don't!"

Meanwhile, Hank had kept up his "Hey, Rube!" shouts. As Jack turned to shut him up, he found out what it meant.

The tent was filling with carny folk. Lots of them, all running his way. In seconds he was surrounded. The workers he could handle, but the others, the performers, gathered in a crowd like this, in the murky light, in various states of dress, were unsettling. The Snake Man, the Alligator Boy, the Bird Man, the green Man from Mars, and others were all still in costume—at least Jack hoped they were costumes—and none of them looked too friendly.

Hank was holding his bloody nose, wagging his finger at Jack. "Now you're gonna get it! *Now* you're gonna get it!"

Bondy seemed to have a sudden infusion of courage. He hauled himself to his feet and started toward Jack with a raised fist.

"You goddamn son of a—"

Jack rapped the iron bar across the side of his bald head, staggering him. With an angry murmur, the circle of carny folk abruptly tightened.

Jack whirled, spinning the pike around him. "Right," he said. "Who's next?"

He hoped it was a convincing show. He didn't know what else to do. He'd taken some training in the martial use of the bamboo pole and nunchuks and the like; he wasn't Bruce Lee with them, but he could do some damage with this pike. Trouble was, he had little room to maneuver and less every second: the circle was tightening, slowly closing in on him like a noose.

Jack searched for a weak spot, a point to break through and make a run for it. As a last resort, he always had the .45-caliber Semmerling strapped to his ankle.

Then a deep voice rose above the angry noise of the crowd.

"Here, here! What's this? What's going on?"

The carny folk quieted, but not before Jack heard a few voices whisper "the boss" and "Oz." They parted to make way for a tall man, six-three at least, lank dark hair, sallow-complexioned, his pear-shaped body swathed in a huge silk robe embroidered with Oriental designs. Although he looked doughy about the middle, the large hands that protruded from his sleeves were thin and bony at the wrist.

The boss—Jack assumed he was the Ozymandias Prather who ran the show—stopped at the inner edge of the circle and took in the scene. His expression was oddly slack but his eyes were bright, dark, cold, more alive than the rest of him. Those eyes finally settled on Jack.

"Who are you and what are you doing here?"

"Protecting your property," Jack said, gambling.

"Oh, really?" The smile was sour. "How magnanimous of you." Abruptly his expression darkened. "Answer the question! I can call the police or we can deal with this in our own way."

"Fine," Jack said. He upped his ante by throwing the pike at the boss's feet. "Maybe I had it wrong. Maybe you *pay* baldy here to poke holes in your attractions."

The big man froze for an instant, then slowly wheeled toward the ticket seller who was rubbing the welt on the side of his head.

"Hey, boss—" Bondy began, but the tall man silenced him with a flick of his hand.

The boss looked down at the pike where sawdust clung to the dark fluid coating its point, then up at the crouching rakosh with its dozens of oozing wounds. Color darkened his cheeks as his head rotated back toward Bondy.

"You harmed this creature, Mr. Bond?"

The boss's eyes and tone were so full of menace that Jack couldn't blame the bald man for quailing.

"We was only trying to get it to put on more of a show for the customers."

Jack glanced around and noticed that Hank had faded away. He saw the performers inching toward the rakosh cage, making sympathetic sounds as they took in its condition. When they turned back, their cold stares were focused on Bondy instead of Jack.

"You hurt him," said the green man.

"He is our brother," the Snake Man said in a soft sibilant voice, "and you hurt him many times."

Brother? Jack wondered. What are they talking about? What's going on here?

The boss continued to pin Bondy with his glare. "And you feel you can get more out of the creature by mistreating it?"

"We thought—"

"I know what you thought, Mr. Bond. And many of us know too well how the Sharkman felt. We've all known mistreatment during the course of our lives, and we don't look kindly upon it. You will retire to your quarters immediately and wait for me there."

"Fuck that!" Bondy said. "And fuck you, Oz! I'm blowin' the show! Ain't goin' nowhere but outta here!"

The boss gestured to the Alligator Boy and the Bird Man. "Escort Mr. Bond to my trailer. See that he waits outside until I get there."

Bondy tried to duck through the crowd, but the green man blocked his way until the other two grabbed his arms. He struggled but was no match for them.

"You can't do this, Oz!" he shouted, fear wild in his eyes as he was none too gently dragged away. "You can't keep me here if I wanna go!"

Oz ignored him and turned his attention to Jack. "And that leaves us with you, Mr. . . . ?"

"Jack."

"Jack what?"

"Just Jack."

"Very well, Mr. Jack. What is your interest in this matter?"

"I don't like bullies," Jack said.

It wasn't an answer, but it would have to do. Wasn't about to tell the boss he'd come to French-fry his Sharkman.

"No one does. But why should you be interested in this particular creature? Why should you be here at all?"

"Not too often you get to see a real live rakosh."

When he saw the boss blink and snap his head toward the cage, Jack had a sudden uneasy feeling that he'd made a mistake. How big a mistake he wasn't quite sure.

"What did you say?" The glittering eyes fixed on him again. "What did you call it?"

"Nothing," Jack said.

"No, I heard you. You called it a rakosh." Oz stepped over to the cage and stared into Scar-lip's yellow eyes. "Is that what you are, my friend . . . a rakosh? How fascinating!" He turned to the rest of his employees. "It's all right. You can all go back to bed. Everything is under control. I wish to speak to this gentleman in private before he goes."

"You didn't know what it was?" Jack said as the crowd dispersed.

Oz continued to stare at the rakosh. "Not until this moment. I thought they were a myth."

"How did you find it?" Jack said. The answer was important—until this afternoon he'd been sure he'd killed Scar-lip.

"The result of a telephone call. Someone phoned me last summer—woke me in the middle of the night—and told me that if I searched the waters off Governors Island I might find 'a fascinating new attraction.' "

Last summer . . . the last time he'd seen Scar-lip and the rest of his species. "Who called you? Was it a woman?"

"No. Why do you ask?"

"Just wondering."

Besides Gia, Vicky, Abe, and himself, the only other living person who knew about the rakoshi had been Kolabati.

"He referred to himself as Professor Roma. I'd never heard of him and haven't heard from him since. I searched for him afterwards, to see if he could tell me what he knew about the creature, but never found him."

Jack swallowed. Roma . . . figures.

"Something in the caller's voice, his utter conviction, compelled me to do as he said. Came the dawn I was on the water with some of my people. We found ourselves vying with groups of souvenir hunters looking for wreckage from a ship that had exploded and burned the night before. We discovered our friend here floating in a clump of debris. I assumed the creature was dead, but when I found it was alive, I had it brought ashore. It looked rather vicious so I put it into an old tiger cage."

"Lucky for you."

The boss smiled, showing yellow teeth. "I should say so. It almost tore the cage apart. But since then its health has followed a steady downhill course. We've fed it fish, fowl, beef, horse meat, even vegetables—although one look at those teeth and there's no question that it's a carnivore—but no matter what we've tried, its health continues to fail."

Jack now had an idea why Scar-lip was dying. Rakoshi required a very specific species of flesh to thrive. And this one wasn't getting it.

"I brought in a veterinary expert," Oz went on, "one I have learned to rely on for his discretion, but he could not help. I even had a research scientist test the creature's blood. He found some fascinating things there, but he could not alter the creature's downhill course."

Jack suddenly realized that the research scientist was Dr. Monnet. Had to be. And he'd found something "fascinating" in Scar-lip's blood.

Did Berzerk come from Scar-lip?

A drug that magnifies violent tendencies distilled from the most violent and vicious creature on earth . . .

A perfect fit.

"You're sure it's a rakosh?" Oz said, interrupting Jack's racing thought train.

"Well . . ." Jack said, trying to sound tentative. "I saw a picture of one in a book once. I . . . I *think* it looked like this. But I'm not sure. I could be wrong."

"But you're *not* wrong," the boss said, turning and staring into his eyes. He lowered his gaze to Jack's chest, fixing on the area where the rakosh had scarred him. "And I believe you have far more intimate knowledge of this creature than you are willing to admit."

Jack shrugged, uncomfortable with the scrutiny, especially since it wasn't the first time someone had stared at his chest this way.

"But it doesn't matter!" Oz laughed and spread his arms. "A rakosh! How wonderful! And it's all mine!"

Jack glanced at Scar-lip's slouched, wasted form. Yeah, but not for long.

He heard a noise like a growl and turned. The sight of one of the burly types from Monnet's warehouse standing in the exit flap startled him. He looked like he was waving good-bye to his boss. Jack turned away, hoping he wouldn't recognize him.

"Excuse me," Oz said and hurried toward the exit, his silk robe fluttering around him.

Jack turned to find Scar-lip staring at him with its cold yellow eyes. *Still want to finish me off, don't you. It's mutual, pal. But it looks like I'm going to outlast you by a few years. A few* decades.

The longer he remained with the wasted creature, the more convinced he was that Scar-lip was on its last legs. He didn't have to light it up. The creature was a goner.

Jack kept tabs on Oz out of the corner of his eye. After half a minute of hushed, one-sided conversation—all the employee did was nod every so often—the boss man returned.

"Sorry. I had to revise instructions on an important errand. But I do want to thank you. You have provided a bright moment in a very disappointing stop." His gaze drifted. "Usually we do extremely well in Monroe, but this trip . . . it seems a house disappeared last month— vanished, foundation and all, amid strange flashing lights one night. The locals are still spooked."

"How about that," Jack said, turning away. "I think I'll be going."

"But you must allow me to reward you for succoring the poor creature, and for identifying it. Free passes, perhaps."

"Not necessary," Jack said and headed for the exit.

"By the way," Oz said. "How can I get in touch with you if I wish?"

"You can't," Jack called back over his shoulder.

A final glance at Scar-lip showed the rakosh still staring at him; then he parted the canvas flaps and emerged into the fresh air again.

A strange mix of emotions swirled around Jack as he returned to the car. Glad to know Scar-lip would be taking a dirt nap soon, but the very fact that it still lived, even if it was too weak to be a threat to Vicky, bothered him. He'd prefer it dead. He vowed to keep a close watch on this show, check back every night or two until he knew without a doubt that Scar-lip had breathed its last.

Something else bothered him. Couldn't put his finger on it, but he had this vaguely uncomfortable feeling that he never should have come back here.

Flashes on the western horizon from the thunderstorm brewing over the city only accentuated his unease.

10

Still busy! Nadia wanted to hurl the phone out her bedroom window and let it crash four stories below on Thirty-fifth Street. Lightning flashed faintly through that window, but she heard no thunder.

Figuring a good night's sleep might help, she'd turned in early, hoping to wake up in the morning with a whole new perspective. But sleep wouldn't come, so she'd tried Doug's line again.

"He can't still be working," she muttered.

But she knew he very well could be. Sometimes he'd code all night. Either that or he'd conked out and left the phone off the hook.

"I'm going over there," she said.

She threw on some clothes and headed down the hall.

"You are going out?" her mother called from her bedroom where she was watching TV. "At this hour?"

"Over to Doug's, Mom. I need to talk to him."

"It can't wait until tomorrow?"

No. It couldn't. She needed Doug now.

"You think this is wise?" Mom went on. "Outside bad storm is coming."

"I'll be OK." Nadia pulled an umbrella from the closet by the door, then slipped back to her mother's room. "I shouldn't be too long."

She pecked her on the cheek and hurried down to the street. Thunder rumbled as she hit the sidewalk but the pavement was still dry. Across the street lay St. Vartan's Park, the tiny patch of green where she used to play when she was a child.

She walked down to First Avenue and caught a cab.

This actually might work out better than if Doug had come over for dinner, she thought after giving the driver Doug's address in DUMBO.

She wouldn't have been able to discuss Dr. Monnet's involvement with Berzerk in front of Mom. This way they'd have a chance to talk in private.

She smiled as another thought sent a warm tingle through her. And privacy meant they'd be able to engage in another form of communication. . . .

11

"Aw, no!" Doug said as his monitor went dead along with everything else electric in his apartment. Luckily he'd just finished a save or he'd have lost all the new code he'd just written for his tracking software. Still, he'd probably lost a whole screen's worth. Times like this he wished he'd invested in a BUPS unit.

He blinked in the sudden darkness; then a lightning flash strobed through the room, followed by a rumble of thunder. He'd been so wrapped up in his programming—he entered something like a Zen state when he worked like this—that he'd lost all track of time and surroundings.

"Damn," he muttered. "A storm."

He pushed away and went to the window. A cool breeze laden with the promise of rain washed over him. Another brighter flash of lightning with a louder thunderclap close on its tail. This was shaping up to be a biggie. Then he noticed that windows across the street were still lit up. How come they had power and he didn't? As a matter of fact, he couldn't remember the last time a storm had knocked out his power.

He picked up the phone to call Nadj but it was dead. Power *and* phone? How the hell had that happened? He wondered if Nadj had been calling him. Well, he always had the cell phone. . . .

Doug straightened as he heard the fire escape rattle. The wind picking up? Shouldn't be anybody out there. He went to the bedroom to see.

The window was wide open, just as he'd left it, the curtains billowing in the breeze. He stuck his head outside and checked upward— his apartment was on the top floor, so only the short length of 'scape to the roof lay above him. No one visible up there. And no one down. Probably the wind; a good gust would rattle the railings every so often. Far to his right, across the river, a brightly speckled sliver of Lower Manhattan was visible between two buildings.

The first drops of rain splattered him then so he backed inside and closed the window, then hurried to close the others.

Between the intermittent flashes and rumbles, the apartment was dark and eerily silent. Doug went to the kitchen for some candles. Once he had some light he'd hunt up his cell phone and give Nadj a call. He felt bad about neglecting her today.

He was searching through the miscellaneous drawer when he sensed—or thought he sensed—movement in the hallway. He stopped and squinted into the darkness. A lightning flash revealed nothing. He stepped down the hall and checked the apartment door—dead-bolted as always.

He decided the power failure plus the storm were giving him the creeps.

He went back to searching the drawer and finally found two half-consumed red candles, left over from the Christmastime dinner he and Nadj had shared last year. Now to find a match. One of the downsides to quitting smoking was that he never carried matches anymore.

But then he heard another sound above his rattling within the drawer . . . like a thump . . . from his bedroom.

Apprehension rippling across his back, Doug pulled a carving knife from the utensil drawer and stepped toward the bedroom.

"Somebody there?" he called, immediately thinking, What a stupid thing to say.

No reply—not that he'd expected one, and he'd have been shocked witless if anyone had answered. He assumed—*prayed*—that this was all nothing. It had better be. Because the knife was just for show. He wouldn't know what to do with it if he needed it. He didn't know a thing about fighting, wasn't sure he knew how to throw a punch, let alone stab someone.

He stepped into the bedroom.

"Hello?"

The shadows were deep here. And he noticed a faint musty odor that hadn't been present before. But it seemed empty. . . .

Then lightning flashed, illuminating two hulking forms pressed against the wall.

With a cry, Doug spun and ran for the front door. A blast of thunder engulfed his cries.

"Help! Hel—!"

He plowed head-on into a third hulk in the hallway and bounced back—like running into a lightly padded concrete wall. Doug almost fell but managed to keep his balance. He turned but lightning silhouetted the two figures approaching from the bedroom.

"I've got a knife!" Doug cried, holding it up.

Something slapped hard against his hand and the knife went flying. He opened his mouth to cry for help but thick fingers clapped over his lips, sealing them. Two more hands grabbed his ankles and lifted him off the floor. Despite his struggles, he was completely helpless as they carried him toward the bedroom like a thrashing, unruly child.

Why? his panicked mind screamed as his bladder threatened to empty. Who are they? *What* are they? And why do they want *me?* I've never hurt anyone. Why should anyone—?

The hack! They couldn't be from GEM, could they?

They carried him into the bedroom but then stopped—*froze* was more like it. They pinned him to the floor and held him there. They seemed to be listening. For what?

And then Doug heard a tapping. It took him a moment to realize it was coming from down the hall. Someone was tapping on his door.

His blood congealed into icy lumps as he heard a familiar voice call his name.

"Doug? Doug, are you in there?"

Nadia! Oh, sweet Jesus, it was Nadia. And she had a key. If he didn't answer she was certain to use it.

Got to warn her!

Hoping to catch his captors off guard, Doug suddenly began kicking and twisting, furiously funneling all his strength into wrenching his face free of the hand sealing his mouth. Had to warn her away, to run, call 911. . . .

Whoever was holding his feet lost his grip on Doug's right ankle. Doug lashed out with his free foot but connected with his floor lamp instead. His foot was recaptured as the lamp hit the floor with a crash.

Triumph turned to horror as Doug realized the noise would bring Nadia in sooner. He screamed against the muffling fingers, but only a whimper escaped. And then he felt a pair of fingers squeeze his nose and seal his nostrils.

As Doug fought for air and struggled to hold onto consciousness, he heard Nadia calling from the far side of the door.

"Doug? Was that you?"

Too quickly her voice faded with his strength and awareness, and all became nothing. . . .

12

"Doug, are you in there? Are you OK?"

Nadia had arrived at his door ready to give him a piece of her mind for staying incommunicado all day, but her pique was gone now.

Something's wrong, she thought as she clawed through her shoulder bag for her key ring.

She found it, fumbled Doug's key into the lock, and burst in.

But she stopped after one step. The place was completely dark.

"Doug?"

She found the light switch and flipped it but nothing happened. Leaving the door open so she'd have some light, Nadia walked down the short hallway to the front room. She found another wall switch and flipped that. Again, nothing.

Strange. The power was on in the hallway but seemed to be off in Doug's apartment.

She sniffed. What was that musty odor . . . like wet fur?

Nadia jumped as a flash of lightning lit the room and thunder rattled the windows. Creepy in here. She stepped back toward the hallway and used the light there to help her find her little penlight flash. She pressed the clip and frowned at the weak glow from the bulb. The batteries were just about dead, but they'd have to do.

She turned back toward the darkened apartment and hesitated. The smart thing would be to leave. If Doug was here, he would have answered.

But then, why *wasn't* he here? It was almost midnight.

She told herself he probably went out for a nightcap when his power failed, but she wouldn't feel right until she'd checked the apartment. And besides, she'd heard that sound, like something or someone falling. What if he'd tripped in the dark and hurt himself?

"If you're all right, Doug . . ." she muttered as she moved down the hall. "If you're perfectly fine and out enjoying yourself while I'm a worried wreck here searching your pitch-black apartment, I'm going to kill you."

She flashed the penlight's dim beam around the front room and found nothing out of place. Same with the second bedroom he used as an office. Odd to see his computer dark and dead. He hardly ever turned it off.

Nadia felt some of her prior annoyance creeping back as the penlight beam came to rest on Doug's phone. The least he could have done was check his voice mail before he went out. She idly lifted the receiver and put it to her ear.

Dead. That was odd.

Last stop was Doug's bedroom. The bed was unmade, but that was the rule rather than the exception, and everything looked pretty much the same as ever.

Then what had made that noise?

And why this deep cold apprehension gnawing through her? Why this vague feeling that she wasn't alone here?

Nadia moved toward the closet in his bedroom and had her hand on the doorknob when her penlight died.

That does it, she thought with a sudden stab of plain old fear as another flash of lightning blazed through the bedroom window, casting weird shadows into the corners. I'm outta here.

But first . . . she moved back to the blessed light of the hallway and scribbled on the pad of sticky notes she kept in her bag:

> *Doug—*
> *I was here. Where was you?*
> *Call me as soon as you get in.*
> *Love.*
> *N.*

Nadia hurried to Doug's office, stuck the note to his monitor screen, then dashed back to the hall. As she closed the door and locked the bolt, she was plagued by the strange sensation that she'd missed something in there, something important.

MEMORIAL DAY

1

Nadia snatched up the phone on the first ring. "Doug?"

A heartbeat or two of silence on the other end. A throat cleared and then a familiar voice came over the wire, but not Doug's.

"This is Dr. Monnet."

"Oh. Dr. Monnet . . . good morning."

Nadia leaned back on her mother's old sofa, straining to hide the crushing disappointment. She'd been trying Doug's number for hours—before she'd left for the clinic, and while she'd been at the clinic—but yesterday's busy signals had been replaced by a robotic voice telling her that the line was out of service.

"Good morning," he said. "I hope I'm not disturbing you."

"Not at all. I just got back from the clinic."

I just wish you were someone else.

"Such devotion."

"Well, as we both know, diabetes doesn't recognize national holidays."

"How true." He cleared his throat. "I was wondering if you were going to be in the lab today."

"I hadn't planned on it."

Actually she had, but only to remove the Berzerk from the imager's sample chamber. After that she might never go back, at least not until she had a good explanation as to why the inert form of a street drug matched the inert form of a molecule she'd been assigned to stabilize.

And then an alarming thought struck her. "Are you there now?"

"Yes. I stopped by. I thought if you were here we might discuss your progress."

Her heart fluttered in panic. She'd never dreamed Dr. Monnet would be there on Memorial Day. Should she run over? No. She couldn't go. Not until she contacted Doug and was sure he was all right.

"I . . . I have other plans."

"Oh. I see. Excuse me but did you . . . ?" His voice seemed to falter. "Did you say, 'Doug,' when you picked up?"

Yes . . . Doug. A pang of longing seized her. Where *are* you?

And now, after giving Dr. Monnet a lengthy cock-and-bull story Saturday about how they were just acquaintances, how was she going to explain this?

"Yes. He, um, asked me out to dinner last night and never showed up. And now his phone is out of service. I'm worried."

"Because he's an old friend."

Nadia wasn't sure if that was a statement or a question. Either way, Dr. Monnet's voice was rich with concern.

"Yes," she said. "I'm going over there to check on him personally."

"Do you really think that's wise?"

An odd question. "What do you mean?"

"I'll meet you there."

"No. That's not at all necessary. Besides, he's all the way over in DUMBO."

"DUMBO?"

"Yes. It's in Brooklyn—Down Under the Manhattan Bridge Overpass."

"That doesn't matter. Douglas Gleason is a valued employee. I insist. Give me his address."

Nadia didn't know what else to do. She gave him the address and he said he would meet her there.

This strange turn baffled Nadia, but at least Dr. Monnet would be leaving the lab. He hadn't mentioned the Berzerk in the imager, which meant he hadn't looked. Sometime today she had to get back there and clean up.

But Doug came first. . . . Her worry for him blotted out all other concerns.

2

Luc stood outside the brick-faced apartment building on Water Street, one of many along the block. He looked up at the blue underbelly of the Manhattan Bridge; he could hear the traffic rumbling across. An odd place to live, but he supposed one had to live somewhere. Perhaps the view of the city at night made it worthwhile.

He'd already been up to Gleason's apartment. He'd knocked and tried the door, but it was locked. Too bad. He was hardly eager to see Gleason's corpse, but if he'd been able to get in, he at least could have found the body himself, sparing Nadia the trauma.

Luc had told Prather he wanted Gleason handled differently this time. Macintosh had simply disappeared—bought a round-trip ticket to Chicago and never came back. He'd had no close friends, and when his family came looking, no one had any useful information, least of all his puzzled and concerned employers.

Gleason, on the other hand, was anything but a loner. And having a second GEM employee simply vanish—especially one with friends on the sales force, connections to dozens of doctors and their staffs, and a longtime relationship with Nadia—would make too many waves. It might even raise an official eyebrow, prompting an investigation into the whereabouts of both men. The last thing Luc wanted.

So Prather had been instructed to make Gleason's death look like a botched robbery. Very tragic and very final. And to cover all bases, Luc had requested a little vandalism as well—specifically, the theft of Gleason's company laptop and the destruction of his home computer if he had one.

That was why he'd insisted on meeting Nadia here—to help min-

imize the trauma of her finding an old friend dead. Even so, she wasn't
going to be much use as a researcher for the next few days.

And every single day counted, damn it!

Luc paced the sidewalk. He wanted to see Nadia face-to-face. He'd
experienced a moment of panic this morning when he'd checked the
office and learned that she hadn't signed in. Was it because of the
holiday or fatigue, or something else? He needed to look into her eyes.
He'd know in an instant if she suspected him of being connected to
Berzerk.

A cab pulled into the curb and Nadia alighted. Her face was drawn,
pale. She looked worried.

"Good morning," Luc said.

She nodded. "I hope it is," she said. "You really didn't have to—"

"Let's not discuss that anymore," he told her. "I am here. What
floor is Douglas on?"

"Top floor—the tenth."

At that moment she looked squarely at him and he saw no sign of
fear or distrust, only concern—not for or about him but for her missing
friend.

Deep concern. Warning prickles raced along his scalp and gathered
at the back of his neck. Too deep perhaps for someone she'd described
as "just a friend of the family"?

"How will we get into his apartment?"

"I have a key," she said, moving ahead of him.

As Luc followed her to the elevator, a lump in his gut told him that
there had to be more to this relationship than Nadia had let on.

At Gleason's door he hid his unease and waited as Nadia knocked
and called. Finally, when she inserted her key in the lock, he acted.

"Allow me," he said, gripping the doorknob as the bolt snapped
back. "Just in case."

"In case of what?" she said, blanching.

"Something may not be right here."

He pushed the door open and went in first, Nadia right behind him.
A few steps took him down the short entry hall until he could see the
overturned furniture in the living room. He turned quickly and gripped
her upper arms to keep her from coming any farther.

"Wait. Don't go in there. Something's happened."

"What?" Her eyes went wide and wild as she tore loose and fought past him. "What do you mean?"

Luc followed and almost plowed into her as she skidded to a stop on the living room threshold. The couch lay tipped over onto its back, a coffee table was flush against the opposite wall, and a floor lamp lay on the floor.

"Ohmigod!" she cried, hands to her mouth. "Ohmigod!"

Her shoulder bag tumbled to the floor as she darted off in another direction, moving deeper into the apartment, Luc at her heels. No stopping her. As she turned left into what looked like a bedroom, Luc wheeled right and found a room that looked like an office. As he heard doors slamming in the other room and then in the hallway, he noted briefly with satisfaction that the desktop computer's mini tower had been ripped apart, its contents strewn about the room. The hard drive lay bent and cracked open, damaged beyond repair.

As he turned to go, Nadia appeared and they almost collided. She must have found Gleason because she looked as if she were about to faint. He gripped her arm to support her.

"He's not here!" she gasped, panting as if she'd run a marathon. "I checked his bedroom and the kitchen and the bathroom and the closets but he's not here!"

Not here? He *had* to be here!

"Ohmigod!" she cried, lurching past Luc. "Look what they did to his computer! It wasn't like this last night! Jesus God, where is he? What *happened* here?"

That was what Luc wanted to know. Gleason was supposed to die here, not somewhere else. Or—his heart seized for an instant as a thought struck with the weight of a sledge—had Prather's men missed him?

Luc guided Nadia to a chair and helped her as she sagged into it. "It looks like just a robbery and maybe some vandalism."

"I don't see his laptop," she said, looking around. "And his living room rug is gone. Does that make any sense?"

It did if Prather's men needed a way to remove Gleason's body. But they were *not* supposed to remove it.

"No, it doesn't," he told her. "But you didn't see any blood, did you?"

He wanted her to say, Yes, oceans of it, but she shook her head.

He gave her shoulder a reassuring squeeze. "There. He's probably away for the weekend with—"

"He's not!" she said. Tears were sliding down her cheeks. "He would have told me!"

"Come now," Luc said. "Surely he has other friends. He probably—"

"We're engaged, damn it!"

Luc felt his knees go soft. Now he too needed to sit. "Engaged? But . . . but I thought . . ."

"Doug wanted to keep it secret. He had some idea that management might not approve of a close relationship between a sales rep and a researcher."

Gleason had been right, of course. Luc tried to frame a reply, but the only words that formed in his reeling brain were, *What have we done? What have we done . . . ?*

With her fiancé missing she'll be utterly useless in the lab—and not just for a couple of days.

That's it, then, he thought. Over. Done. *Fin.*

"I've got to call the police!"

Before Luc could stop her, she had the phone receiver to her ear—but only for an instant. She pulled it away and looked at it. "That's right. I forgot. Out of service."

She slammed it down and hurried from the room. Luc struggled to think of some way to stop her, some words that would convince her to hold off calling the police, but his mind was a blank. What could he say? Gleason was missing and his apartment showed unmistakable signs of foul play.

Nadia and the police . . . a potentially lethal combination. To determine *who* had broken in, she would have to ask *why* . . . and why they had stolen one computer and smashed another. Luc had to assume that Gleason had told her about his invasion of the GEM computer system. Would she make a connection? Nadia was too bright not to. And she would tell the police. And if she had any suspicions that Loki was a street drug, Luc sensed she would bring up those as well. And then the New York City Police and the DEA and the FBI would be dissecting GEM, and issuing warrants, and ending life as he knew it.

When Nadia returned seconds later, pulling a cell phone from her bag, he was tempted to snatch it away—but then what? Strangle her?

He thought of putting his hands around her throat and squeezing . . . watching her face mottle into blue.

No, he couldn't. And besides, a third missing GEM employee would *guarantee* an investigation. Nadia was as much a danger to him alive as dead.

His gut crawled as he watched her punch in 9-1-1. She paced back and forth as she waited for an answer, then wandered out of the room as she began talking to the operator or dispatcher or whoever handled those calls.

This tore it then. It was all over. He'd have to leave the country immediately. But what about his wine? He needed another two days to pack up the rest and ship it out—just one day if he worked all night. . . .

But what was the use? In France he could hide from Dragovic but not from the U.S. and French governments. He would be found, extradited, and Dragovic's contacts in prison would see to it that he never reached a courtroom.

There had to be a way to stop her. But how?

His nervous, restless, roving gaze came to rest on Nadia's shoulder bag and a plan crystallized. It was beautiful, perfect.

Quickly Luc reached into the bag and rummaged around. He felt a sweat break at the thought of Nadia wandering back and finding him up to his elbows in her personal belongings. He heard a jangle, reached for it, came up with her key ring, and shoved it into his jacket pocket a second before Nadia stepped back into the room.

"They're sending someone over."

She dropped the phone into her bag and stood there. For a moment she seemed lost; then her features twisted. She covered her face with her hands and began to sob.

"Where *is* he? Something's happened to him. I just know something terrible's happened!"

Moved by her anguish, Luc rose and put an arm around her shoulders. For a moment he regretted everything, then reminded himself that if Gleason had minded his own damn business, if he'd just kept his nose out of places it did not belong, Luc wouldn't be comforting this young woman while he planned her ruin.

"It'll be all right, Nadia. I know it will be all right."

And he meant that. Every word of it.

But for him, not her.

3

"This is too much!" Sal was saying. "Just too freakin' much!"

Jack had to smile as he watched the destruction of last night's party play out on the thirteen-inch screen. It *was* too much.

Holiday quiet outside the office. Except for the guard dogs padding around behind the fences, he and Sal had the junkyard to themselves.

"Now here comes the best part," Sal said, pointing at the screen. "I musta watched this a hundred times."

Jack watched Dragovic shove a pretty young woman out from under a table, then watched that table collapse under the impact of a tottering overweight party guest. Jack laughed. Beautiful.

Sal was almost falling out of his seat. "Can you imagine when that hits the airwaves? This guy ain't gonna be able to show his face in Burger King, let alone Studio 54!"

Jack started to tell him that Studio 54 was passé now but let it go. He knew what Sal meant, and he was right on the money.

"A fate worse than death," Jack said.

Sal hit the STOP button and turned to Jack. "I don't know about a fate worse than death. Not that all this ain't good an' all, but good as it is—"

"Yeah, I know. . . . Somehow it's not enough."

Sal smiled. "Yeah. Am I a broken record or what. But it's just . . . not. If you know what I'm sayin'."

"I do. But this has only been phase one. These first two hits are what you might call 'baking the cake.' In phase two we ice it."

"And when's phase two?"

"Tonight. This whole gig ends at tonight's party."

254

Jack was glad of that. After tonight, no more hard guys hanging around outside Gia's. He hoped.

"Tonight? Ain't no party tonight—least not according to my contact."

"Yeah, there is. Got it straight from Dragovic. Special party tonight, but your caterer friend won't be hired for this one."

"Well, we did tires and crankcase gunk," Sal said. "What next?"

"Something very special. You just make sure you and your camera are on that dune tonight. Be ready to shoot as soon as it's good and dark. This one will be the best yet."

"Yeah?" Sal wiggled his eyebrows. "Whatcha plannin'?"

"I'm planning to make a phone call."

"That's it? A call? To who?"

Jack wagged his finger at Sal. "If you knew that, you wouldn't need to pay me, would you. Just make sure you don't miss this party. And have the rest of my money ready. After tonight I don't think you'll be saying, 'it ain't enough.' "

4

"I thought we were going to see a parade," Vicky said.

"I did too, Vicks."

Jack stood on the curb between Gia and Vicky and gazed up and down Fifth Avenue. Saks and Gucci and Bergdorf Goodman lined the sidewalks but no marchers. Blue skies and mild weather, a perfect day for a parade. So where was everybody? Not even a single one of those pale blue wooden horses the police use to block streets to hint that a parade was expected or had already been by.

Jack did a full three-sixty scan, his eye out for more than marching bands. He'd done a careful reconnoiter of Gia's neighborhood before heading out to Sal's this morning, and then again a little while ago, and neither time had he found any signs of surveillance. Pretty much what he'd expected, but it didn't take him off alert. Jack had always found it more comforting to know where the bad guys were than where they weren't.

Since no one was watching them, and since he couldn't get hold of Nadia, he'd decided to take Vicky to a Memorial Day parade. But so far, no luck.

"God, it's good to be out," Gia said. "How much longer are we going to be under house arrest?"

To make the house look empty, Jack had advised Gia to stay inside and out of sight for the long weekend.

"We should be able to loosen up tomorrow."

She looked at him. "That means things come to a head tonight, I take it?"

"If all goes according to plan."

"Hey, look!" Vicky said, pointing. "More sailors."

Sure enough, a trio of young men of various shades—they looked like teenagers, and maybe they were—dressed in bell-bottomed whites and Dixie cup caps strolled their way from the direction of St. Pat's. As usual, the fleet was in for Memorial Day Weekend and white uniforms abounded.

"They're cute," Gia said. "But how do they get their whites so white?"

"Why don't you ask them?" Jack said.

Vicky put a hand on her out-thrust hip as they passed and said, "Hi-ya, sailor!"

The guys all but fell off the curb laughing, and Jack bit the insides of both cheeks to keep from doing the same. Gia turned scarlet and found something interesting atop the Saks building.

"What?" Vicky said, looking at her mother as the still-chortling sailors moved on.

"Where on earth did you hear that?"

"I saw it on MTV."

"There you go," Jack said, finally trusting himself to speak. "The root of the decline of Western civilization, such as it is."

"Well, young lady," Gia said, taking her by the hand and leading her across the street, "I think we're going to monitor your TV habits a little more closely from now on." She glanced back at Jack. "By the way, where are we going?"

"Let's try Broadway. Maybe they've got a parade there."

"You know," Gia said, taking his arm as they walked along, "I love the city on holiday weekends."

"You mean half-empty?"

She nodded. "It's like we've got the place almost to ourselves." She stretched out her arms and did a quick turn. "Look at that. I didn't hit anybody." She took his arm again. "I feel sorry for all these sailors. Of all times to get a leave in New York—one of the two big weekends a year when almost all the girls have left town for the beaches."

"I saw them checking you out pretty well as they passed."

"Don't be silly. I could be their mother."

"They weren't just looking—*ogling* is more like it. And I can't say as I blame them, what with those long stems sticking so far out of those shorts."

"Oh, pshaw."

"Pshaw? Did you actually say, 'Pshaw'?"

"Pshaw, and piffle," Gia said.

But Jack could see she was pleased she'd been ogled, and even more pleased that he'd noticed. But then he was always on watch around the two women in his life.

They came to Broadway. The deco front of the Brill Building gleamed in the sun across the street from them, but no parade flowed between.

Sharing a couple of oversize pretzels from a pushcart, the three of them wandered farther west. Jack slowed as they passed a defunct dance club in the midst of renovation. A sign on the double-doored entry proclaimed it THE FUTURE HOME OF NEW YORK CITY'S MOST EX-CLUSIVE NIGHTCLUB—BELGRAVY.

Dragovic's place. Jack understood that Dragovic had begun running his operation from a back office here—when he wasn't in the Hamptons.

One more move against Dragovic tonight and that chapter would be closed—he hoped. And as long as he'd be out on Long Island, he'd look in on the rakosh, just to make sure it was still fading away.

Jack was about to turn everyone around and head back when he saw an older man in a khaki Eisenhower jacket, blue twill pants, and a defiantly angled overseas cap limping toward them. Jack gave him a friendly wave as he came abreast.

"Hi. Isn't there supposed to be a Memorial Day parade?"

The man frowned. "There damn sure should have been. I hear there's a little one on Upper Broadway somewhere. Probably nobody watching it, though. We just had a ceremony on the *Intrepid* with hardly anybody there."

Jack took in all the medals on the right breast of the old soldier's bulging waist-length jacket. He saw a star that looked bronze and recognized a Purple Heart.

"You were in the Big One?"

"Yeah." He looked at Jack. "How about you?"

Jack had to smile. "Me? In the army? No. Not my thing."

"Wasn't my thing either," the guy said, his voice rising. "None of us wanted to be there. I hated every minute. But there was a job to be done and we did it. And we died doing it. My whole platoon, every one of my buddies, was wiped out at Anzio—everyone but me, and I just barely made it. But I did get back, and as long as I'm alive, I'll show up to remember those guys. Someone should, don't you think? But nobody gives a damn."

"I do," Jack said softly, surrendering to an impulse from out of the blue. He thrust out his hand. "Thank you."

The man blinked, then took Jack's hand and squeezed. His eyes puddled up and his lower jaw trembled as he tried to speak. Finally he managed a weak, "You're welcome." Then he limped away.

Jack turned to find Gia staring at him with red-rimmed eyes. "Jack, that was . . ."

He shrugged, suddenly uncomfortable.

"No, really," she said. "Don't shrug it off. That was nice. Sweet, even. Especially since I know how you feel about armies and governments."

"He isn't a government or an army. He's a guy. No matter what you think of any particular war, you've got to feel something for some poor guy ripped out of his life and handed a gun and sent somewhere to kill other guys who've been ripped out of *their* lives and sent to do the same thing, and while they're both shivering in their foxholes, scared they're not going to see another sunrise, all the fat cats, all the generals and politicos and priests and mullahs and tribal elders who started the whole damn thing, sit way to the rear, moving their chess pieces around." He jerked a thumb over his shoulder as he took a breath. "He got handed the dirty end of a dirty stick but he handled it. You've got to respect that."

"So it's another guy thing, huh?" Gia said, punching him lightly on the shoulder, guy style.

He glanced at her and saw the rueful twist of her smile. "To da moon, Alice!"

She laughed and turned to watch the receding Eisenhower jacket. She sighed. "Old soldiers . . ."

But Jack was back to looking out for some young soldiers, Serb vets. He knew that if and when they met again, they wouldn't fade away, and there sure as hell would be no handshakes.

5

The third key Luc tried worked. He opened the door, stepped inside, and quickly closed it behind him. The shades were down but enough sunlight filtered through to illuminate the waiting area of the diabetes clinic.

Now he could relax—a little. No one would be in for the rest of the day, especially Nadia, who was still with the police, giving statements and filling out forms. Luc had given a brief statement, then begged off, claiming a prior engagement. His involvement had been peripheral, after all.

At least to all appearances. But his brain burned with the need to silence Nadia and to learn why Prather had deviated from his instructions regarding Gleason.

Prather, however, had been infuriatingly vague when Luc finally had reached him by phone.

"Some unforeseen circumstances came up," was all he'd say.

When Luc had inquired—discreetly, of course—about "the remains," Prather had laughed and said, "Don't give that a second thought, Doctor! I've found an absolutely foolproof means of disposal!"

He'd sounded oddly excited.

The brief exchange had left Luc feeling frustrated and helpless. Taking a deep breath, he thrust Prather from his thoughts and looked around the front area of the clinic. He'd been here once during Nadia's brief recruitment phase, stopping by more out of nostalgia than the need to see her in action. He'd worked a clinic like this down in the Village during his residency. Lord, how long ago was that? Seemed like another epoch.

Maybe he could go back to something like this in France. Put some of his training to use again with people instead of molecules.

He shook off the distracting trains of thought. He was getting ahead of himself, and off track. If he didn't take care of Nadia, he could forget planning anything in France.

As he pulled on a pair of latex examination gloves, Luc noticed that his palms were sweaty. Tension coiled at the back of his neck. He kept imagining someone coming in and catching him here.

Let's get this over with, he thought as he moved toward the rear of the clinic.

No windows in the rear office, so he had to fumble for a light switch. As the overhead fluorescents flickered to life, he immediately spotted what he was looking for. Next to the empty Mr. Coffee sat a big black mug with NADJ printed in thick white block capitals across the front. He'd remembered it from his brief visit. He'd even remarked laughingly that no one could ever say they'd used her cup by mistake.

And there will be no mistake today, he thought grimly as he pulled a vial from his pocket.

He held it up to the light: Loki in its liquid form was odorless and tasteless, with only a hint of blue. He unstoppered the vial and poured about a tablespoon's worth into Nadia's mug. He rolled the thick liquid around, coating the inner surface halfway up the sides. The concentrate was drying already. In minutes it would be unnoticeable.

He'd estimated Nadia's weight at about one-twenty or so. A tablespoon of the concentrate was a hefty dose, and the effect would last a good four to six hours. He added a few extra drops for good measure.

He watched the sequence play out before his mind's eye. . . .

Nadia had few aggressive or violent tendencies, but within half an hour or so of finishing her coffee, whatever ones she possessed would be magnified ten-, twentyfold, turning her into a raging wild woman. She'd become uncontrollable, a jungle cat, raging about, smashing things, perhaps trying to smash people as well. Inevitably she'd be arrested for disorderly conduct and suspicion of drug use, but *only* suspicion, because the police labs had yet to figure out how to test for Loki.

But suspicion wouldn't be enough.

He stoppered the vial, returned it to his pocket, and came up with a small glassine envelope. He then stepped to Nadia's desk, pulled open the bottom drawer, and stuffed the envelope in a rear corner.

In act two, a police search turns up the envelope and the four Berzerk tablets within. Suspicion then becomes fact: Nadia is tagged with a record of drug abuse. Her credibility is destroyed and whatever suspicions she might raise about Gleason's disappearance or about GEM's connection to street drugs will be tainted . . . the ramblings of a brain-fried druggie.

The strength began to seep from Luc's legs and he dropped into Nadia's chair.

How can I do this to her?

Not only will her credibility go down the tubes, but her medical career as well. She might be able to retain her medical license after going through rehab, but her reputation as a reliable physician will be ruined.

Have I really sunk so low?

Luc gathered his strength and rose. He returned to the Mr. Coffee and picked up Nadia's mug. There was a sink in the washroom. He'd rinse it out, remove the pills from her drawer, and leave everything just as he'd found it. And then he'd look for another way to deal with this.

He started toward the door, then stopped.

What other way?

How else to keep her from accusing GEM, other than placing another call to Prather? That would be what Kent and Brad would want. As Kent had said, once you've ordered one death, ordering a second is easier. Ordering a third—Nadia's—would be a cakewalk for those two. But he had enough blood on his hands.

He stared into Nadia's mug. The concentrate was almost completely dry now. In a way, the Loki was by far the lesser evil. It might damage her future, but at least she'd be alive. And she'd have at least *some* sort of career.

In a way, he was saving Nadia's life.

Clutching that thought like a drowning man, Luc replaced the mug on the coffee shelf, turned out the light, and hurried for the door.

He had packing to do.

6

Milos strolled around the pool, acting like a host, but listening . . . straining his ears for the rhythmic pulse of a helicopter approaching through the night sky.

"Smile," he said to a trio of dapper Hispanics in bright-colored guayaberas. He'd brought them in from one of his Harlem brothels. "Look like you're having a good time. Make believe it's Friday night, before anything happened."

They smiled and nodded and dutifully lifted their glasses of ginger ale to him in salute. There would be plenty of time for the real thing after this was finished.

Everyone from Friday night's fiasco was here. Milos had invited them all back and promised them a chance to get even with the shit who had dropped garbage on them. To a man they had accepted— enthusiastically.

Milos noted with approval the bulges under their shirts. He patted their shoulders and moved on.

Milos's men had spent the bulk of the day doing what they could to clean up the grounds. The air still reeked of oil. He raged inwardly at how the filthy stuff had stained the decking and walkways. The entire area would have to be power-washed. But repairs would come later. He did not need the place to look perfect for what he had planned tonight.

In addition to Friday's guests he had brought in extra men and had them stationed in the oversize shrubbery with shotguns and rifles, all ready and eager for payback.

He rubbed his hands anxiously, wondering what those crazies would try to throw at him tonight. No matter. He was ready for them—ready to strike first and stop them dead in their tracks.

To that end, Milos had the lights low and the music off so he could hear the helicopter as early as possible. His instructions were simple: do not fire until you see the helicopter, but when you do, let loose with everything you have.

The voice on the phone had asked him if he'd been thinking of "calling in the authorities." Me, Milos Dragovic, call in police like some ordinary citizen who cannot handle his own problems? Never. No. You attack Dragovic, Dragovic attacks back, but ten times worse.

Of course, after tonight the authorities would be very much involved—no avoiding that after a barrage of gunfire and a downed helicopter—but he had top lawyers. A citizen was allowed to use deadly force in defense of his life, and that was what he'd be doing tonight: standing on his own property defending himself.

"I hear something!" one of the men on the beach shouted.

Everyone stopped talking at once. Silence abrupt and complete, like a power failure in a sound system. Only the sound of the surf . . . and then something else. No mistaking the *thrum* of helicopter blades beating the night air.

"All right!" Milos shouted. "It's coming! Get ready!"

All around him semiautomatic pistols and fully automatic assault weapons were slipping from holsters and pockets and held under jackets or behind backs as safeties were clicked off, rounds were chambered, and bolts were ratcheted back. He saw rifles and shotgun barrels rising into view among the bushes.

The choppy rhythm grew louder, clearer.

"Easy," Milos said, pulling his own .357 Magnum from its shoulder holster. "Easy. . . ."

And then, just as it became visible, something strange happened.

A bright beam of white light lanced downward from the copter. As it began to play back and forth across the sand, Milos was struck with a terrifying sense that things were about to go horribly wrong.

His shout of *"No!"* was lost in the deafening fusillade that erupted around him.

Milos saw the sparks of the bullets striking the helicopter's fuselage, watched it lurch, veer to the left and drop, then regain altitude and wobble away, trailing black smoke as it fled.

The guns had ceased fire almost as quickly as they had begun. No triumphant cheers rose from the stunned men.

They all could read English.

And then he heard the wail of sirens—many of them. He turned and saw chaotic red flashes lighting the night from the direction of the front gate.

Cops. Sounded like an army of them.

But how? How could they be here so soon? And in such numbers?

Milos Dragovic stood numb and frozen by his pool and asked himself over and over, Who is doing this to me?

TUESDAY

1

When Jack checked his voice mail in the morning he found three messages from Sal Vituolo, the gist of which could be summed up as, "Hey, Jack, call me. I gotta talk to ya, just gotta talk to ya."

So Jack called him from a pay phone.

"Jack! How'd you do it, man?" Jack couldn't see Sal but he sounded like he was dancing. "How'd you freakin' *do* it?"

"I gather it went off well?"

Jack had heard a few sketchy details on one of the all-news stations last night before turning in.

"Are you kiddin' me? He absolutely screwed himself, shootin' at a Coast Guard copter like that. But how'd you get it there?"

"Like I told you," Jack said. "I made a call."

"Yeah, but what'd you say?"

Jack had told the Coast Guard that a big shipment of this new drug that was making people go crazy was coming ashore at Dragovic's place in the Hamptons. He told them that was why Dragovic bought the place—so he could smuggle stuff ashore. The shipment was due shortly after dark—like between nine-thirty and ten.

But Jack didn't feel like going into all of that with Sal.

"I've got connections."

"You must, baby. I can't believe the heat that came down on that place."

According to reports on the news, state and Suffolk County heat had been duking it out with the feds over who had jurisdiction. Since they couldn't decide in time, they'd all shown up.

"I woulda got more tape but a lot of his muscle was haulin' ass outta there and some of them was comin' my way. So I did a little ass haulin' myself."

"But you got enough?"

"I got *plenty*. I hear the pilots are OK, but Dragovic's in deep shit for shootin' up their copter. Accordin' to the news they didn't find no heavy drugs in his place. Too bad, but at least some of his guys got tagged for possession. And of course he's up on all sortsa state, county, and federal weapons charges and even"—Sal snickered here—"disorderly conduct from the town of East Hampton!" His tone sobered. "But I bet the fucker's out on bail already."

"You can count on it. That's where the tapes come in. Did you send them off?"

"Made a shitload of copies last night, then went to the messenger service first thing this morning—did the locals, all the networks, CNN, Fox, even public access. If they got an antenna or a satellite, they got a tape."

"And you paid cash, right?"

"Course. Ay, I don't wanna be connected to this. No way."

"Good. Now just keep your eyes on the TV this morning."

"You kiddin'? I got the remote glued to my freakin' hand. I—wait a sec. Here's something! A special report. Turn on channel four, quick!"

"I'm not exactly near a TV," Jack said.

"This is it! They're showing it! Yes! *Yyy-essss!*" Jack was sure now that Sal was indeed dancing around. It was a sight he preferred to imagine rather than witness. "He's fucked! He is *so* fucked! He may be out on bail but he won't be able to show his puss in this town—hell, in the whole freakin' *world* again without somebody laughin' at him!"

"Now do you believe in a fate worse than death?"

"Yes!" Sal shouted. "Oh, yes!"

"And is it enough?"

"Yeah, Jack." Sal's voice softened as it dropped about a hundred decibels. "I think it is. And I think it's gonna be easier for me with my sister now."

"Jeez, don't tell her anything," Jack said quickly.

"Ay, I ain't stupid. I know how stuff gets around and I don't wanna wake up dead some morning. But at least I think I can finally look Roseanne in the eye now and not feel like a useless wuss. She won't know, but *I'll* know, and that's what counts, if you know what I'm sayin'."

"Yeah, Sal, I do."

2

"*Who?*" Milos screamed.

He stood in the center of his office in the rear of the unfinished Belgravy and stared at the remnants of a thirty-two-inch Sony TV before him. A brass table lamp jutted from the smoking hole of what had once been its Trinitron screen.

"*Who?*"

Who had done this to him? Who hated him so to publicly humiliate him this way? He couldn't believe that this East Hampton Environmental Protection Committee had done it. Truth was, he couldn't bear the thought of having been hooked, netted, and filleted for all the world to see by some raised-pinkie, tea-sipping, silver-spoon-sucking pussy from old-money Long Island.

He pressed the heels of his hands against his eyes and fought to focus his rage-scattered thoughts. He could feel his heart hammering inside his chest. He felt as if he were floating in space.

Think! Who!

The Russians . . . it had to be the Brighton Beach Russians. They'd been allies of his early on but lately they'd become jealous of his success. Only they would have the nerve to do this to him.

But this wasn't their MO. They preferred more direct methods—a

bullet or two in the face was their style. No, this had to be someone
with more control and calculation, someone who knew his weak points
and was not afraid to ram a blade into one and twist.

Who, damn it!

And why? Milos wanted to know that as badly as who. If he knew
why, he could figure who, and then he'd know what . . . what in particular he had done to make some sick *govno* set out to ruin him.

And that was what he was: ruined, pure and simple. Who would
deal with him again? Who would take him seriously? After that tape,
how could anyone fear him?

A ragged scream ripped from his throat and echoed off his office
walls.

The only solution was retribution. He had to find whoever it was
and destroy them. He had to send a message to the world that no one
fucked with Milos Dragovic and lived.

Even that would not restore his respect, but it would be a start.

But where to start? The only lead was a public phone in the East
Eighties and a man on a videotape, a man in a car owned by a woman
who lived on Sutton Place.

This man could be the key. He might not be the mastermind, and
most likely was not, but he could be the helicopter pilot. He could have
been scouting the house in the day to plan the best place to drop his
garbage at night. Or involved in some other way. If he could speak to
the man, Milos could make him tell.

Could be the man had no connection at all. If so, too bad. For him.

Milos was through with caution. Something had to be done, and
now. The Sutton Square house had been empty all weekend but the
holiday was over. Time to move. He stalked to his office door and
kicked it open.

"Ivo! Vuk! In here! Now!"

Milos watched the two men jump up and leave their paper coffee
cups on the cocktail table where they'd been sitting. They hurried toward him across the dance floor—or what was supposed to have been
a dance floor. He couldn't imagine opening Belgravy after what he'd
just seen. None of the people, the beautiful people he'd planned it for,
would show their faces. The place would wind up filled with smirking
hoi polloi hoping to catch a glimpse of the buffoon they'd seen on TV.

I'd sooner torch the place, he thought.

"Yessir!" Vuk and Ivo said, almost in unison, and Milos swore Ivo had started to salute.

They looked nervous, and well they should. They had avoided arrest by tossing their guns and extra clips into the pool at the first sign of the police. And they weren't the only ones. The illuminated bottom of the oil-stained pool had looked like an underwater armory.

And since it was his pool, Milos had been charged with possession of all those unregistered weapons.

But his lawyers could get him out of that.

The problem was who and what and why.

"This man you have been looking for over on Sutton Square. Bring him to me."

"Yessir!"

"And if he gives you trouble, shoot him. Do not kill him. Shoot him in the knees, then bring him to me. I wish to talk to him. He knows something and he will tell me."

"Yessir!"

As they turned to go, Milos added: "Do not return without him. And if something happens to your car this time, the only way I want to see you two come back is in a hearse."

They swallowed and nodded, then hurried for the street.

3

Jack had known something was way wrong the instant he stepped into Nadia's office at the clinic. She'd looked like she'd been on a two-week bender, and now, after listening to her story, he could see why. She'd broken down three times during the telling.

"So the last time you saw him was when?"

"Dinner on Saturday. Sushi . . . at the Kuroikaze Kafé." She sobbed. "Doug loved the spider roll there."

"Hey, Doc, you're using the past tense," Jack said. "Shouldn't do that."

She blew her nose and nodded. "You're right. I just . . ." She seemed to run out of words.

"Let's move to Sunday. You didn't see or talk to him all day—"

"I tried but his phone was busy."

"But you were there Sunday night and saw no signs of a struggle."

"No. At least I don't think so. It was dark, you know, with the power out and all. No, wait. I saw the computer and it was fine."

"That means the break-in took place after you left."

And what does that tell me? Jack wondered.

Absolutely nothing.

He could see a second-story man getting caught in the act during a break-in and losing it and killing the owner. It happened. But he'd never heard of anyone taking the body with him. A corpse wasn't exactly something you could slip into your pocket and stroll away with.

"Do you think it could be"—the word seemed to stick in her throat—"GEM?"

The question jolted him. "A big corporation? Taking someone out? Come on, Doc. They use lawyers for hit men. And why should they want to?"

"Well, I told you about Doug hacking their computer—"

"Yeah, but could they know about that? And even if they had caught on, how would they know what he'd found, if anything? I mean, it's not as if he was blackmailing them . . ." Jack caught and held her gaze. "Was he?"

She gave her head a vehement shake. "Never. Not Doug. He was thinking of picking up some GEM stock on the chance that what he'd learned meant it was going up, but I know blackmail would never ever cross his mind."

"You're sure?"

"Without a doubt."

Nadia could have been kidding herself, like the mother of the school's biggest pothead saying, Not *my* kid. But Jack didn't think so.

"So I doubt it's GEM."

"Don't be so sure," Nadia said. "Milos Dragovic is somehow con-

nected to GEM, and GEM is connected with"—she took a deep breath—
"Berzerk."

"Damn!" Jack said, slapping the table. "I knew it! That sample I
gave you matched up, I take it."

She nodded reluctantly. "It's my project at GEM, the very molecule
I'm supposed to be stabilizing. It's called 'Loki' there."

"Loki . . . makes you loco. And stabilizing it makes sense. The guy
who sold it to me told me about how it all changes to something useless
after a certain time."

Nadia rose from her seat and wandered out from behind the deck,
rubbing her hands in a washing motion. She looked agitated, too agitated to sit.

"Every twenty-nine days, twelve hours, forty-four minutes, and two-
point-eight seconds."

Jack blinked. "How—?"

She seemed to be on automatic pilot as she moved to the coffee
setup and grabbed the mug with NADJ across its front.

"And it's not just the molecule itself that changes. Every represen-
tation of the structure of the active molecule, whether it's a drawing,
a model, a computer file, even human *memory* of it, changes along
with it."

She stopped pouring her coffee and turned to stare at him, pot in
hand, as if waiting.

"Go on," he said.

"Aren't you listening?"

"To every word."

"Then why aren't you telling me I'm crazy?"

"Because I believe you."

"How can you believe me? What I'm telling you is impossible—or
should be."

"Yeah. And the same could be said for the beastie your buddy
Monnet gets his Loki from."

" 'Beastie?' You mean it comes from an animal?"

"Sort of."

"Sort of what?" Nadia was saying, and sounding a little annoyed as
she went back to pouring her coffee. Good. Better than crying. "It 'sort
of' comes from an animal, or it comes from a 'sort-of' animal?"

"A sort-of animal that doesn't follow any of the rules, just like this
Loki stuff."

Things were beginning to make sense now . . . sort of. Jack told her how he'd followed Monnet out to the freak show, and what the boss there had later said about a research scientist who'd found some "fascinating things" in the dying rakosh's blood.

"Doc, I'm willing to bet that one of those 'fascinating things' turned out to be Loki or Berzerk or whatever it's called."

She turned, holding her mug with both hands. "But what kind of animal—?"

"I wouldn't call it an animal—*animal* might make you think of a rabbit or a deer. I'd call it a creature or a thing. The only one of its kind left. And it's not like anything else that's ever walked this earth." He could have added that he had it on good authority that a rakosh wasn't completely *of* this earth, but he didn't want to get into that here. "Let's just say anything is possible where this thing is concerned."

"Even altering memories?"

Jack shrugged. "Nothing connected with that creature would surprise me."

Nadia looked at Jack, then at her mug. "Why did I pour this? I was too jumpy for coffee before and I'm way too wound up now." She half turned toward the door, then rotated back. "Do you want it?"

He'd already had a couple of cups, but it was always a shame to waste good coffee.

"How'd you make it?"

"Just black."

"Add a couple of sugars and I'll take it off your hands."

Nadia emptied two packets into the mug, then handed it to him. He noticed her hand was trembling. Looked like the last thing she needed now was caffeine.

"The good news is it's dying," he said.

"Dying?" Her hands flew to her face. "Oh, God! That's why he wants me to stabilize the molecule! He's going to lose his source!"

"And soon, I think."

"Dragovic's behind it all. He's forcing Dr. Monnet to do this. I know it, I know it, I know it."

"I don't," Jack said. He sipped his coffee: good and strong, the way he liked it. "And besides, Mr. Dragovic has other matters to occupy his mind at the moment."

Nadia brightened. "Yes! I heard about that." She narrowed her eyes as she looked at Jack. "You wouldn't happen to have anything to do with his troubles, would you?"

"His troubles are with the law and his image," Jack said and drank some more coffee.

"Anyway," Nadia said. "We've got to stop him, stop the drug."

"What do you mean 'we'?"

"All right, you. I wouldn't know——" She stopped as Jack began shaking his head. "What's wrong?"

"I don't do drugs . . . other than caffeine"——he hefted the NADJ mug——"and ethanol, that is."

"Well, good . . . great. . . ."

"But what I mean is I don't sell them and I don't stop other people from selling them."

"But Dragovic's forcing——"

"You don't know if Dragovic's forcing anything, Doc."

"All right then, forget force. The thing is, Dragovic has somehow involved himself in GEM and GEM is somehow behind this Berzerk poison."

"Which people are buying and ingesting of their own free will."

Nadia turned and stared at Jack, disbelief scrawled across her face. "Don't tell me you approve."

"I think drugs are stupid as all hell, and I think people who drug themselves up are dumb asses, but people have a right to control their own bloodstreams. If they want to pollute them, that's their business. I'm not a public nanny."

"You mean if you saw someone selling Berzerk to a twelve-year-old, you wouldn't do anything?"

"Never been there, but I might break his arms."

Jack thought of Vicky. And maybe his legs. And his face.

Nadia smiled. "So you *would* make it your business."

"We were talking adults before. Now we're talking kids. I'm not into crusades, but certain things I will not abide in my sight."

She cocked her head and stared at him. "*Abide* . . . that's a strange word from you."

"How so?"

"It's something I'd expect to hear from a southerner, and you're very much a northeasterner."

Good ear, Jack thought. "A man who taught me some things used to use that word."

She looked as if she wanted to pursue that but changed her mind.
Good.

"But back to Dragovic. His customers are committing crimes because of what he's selling them."

"And going to jail for them." Jack finished his coffee and stood. "As for me, I believe I've seen enough of Dr. Monnet and Mr. Dragovic for a long time."

"But it's not finished."

Jack sighed. "Yeah, it is. You wanted to know the connection between Dragovic and Monnet. It's this drug. You wanted to know what Dragovic has over Monnet: nothing. They're in this together, as in partners."

"I can't believe that."

"Monnet's the guy who discovered the stuff, he's the guy who's testing the stuff, and if you take a trip out the GEM plant in Brooklyn I bet you find he's manufacturing the stuff. Be objective for just two seconds, Doc, and there's no other conclusion."

Nadia half sat, half leaned on the desk and stared at the floor, saying nothing. Jack didn't like the job of telling her that her hero had clay tootsies, especially with her fiancé missing. . . .

"Tell you what, though," he said. "I'll ask around, see who's been boosting in the DUMBO area, and find out if anybody knows anything about Sunday night."

She looked up and smiled for the first time since he'd arrived. "Will you? I'd really appreciate it."

Jack left her with at least a little hope. He emerged onto Seventeenth Street with the morning sun warming the air and the traffic back full force after the holiday. Had the rest of the day pretty much to himself. So why not drop in on Gia? Vicky would be off to school by now. That meant they'd have the house to themselves.

Yeah.

Started walking east. Passing Stuyvesant Square he wondered if its heavy-duty spear-topped wrought-iron fence was meant to keep people out or in. Came to a cluster of medical buildings and wove through a throng of people in white coats with stethoscopes draped around their necks like feather boas. Why wear them out on the street?

Wassamatta? he thought. Afraid someone won't know you're a doctor? His irritation surprised him.

Hung a left onto First Avenue when he reached the faded brick slabs of Stuyvesant Village. Gia was about forty blocks uptown from here. A cab would be faster but he decided to walk it. Felt so full of energy—Nadia's coffee must have been superstrong—he'd be there in no time.

He was a good walker, had a stride that ate up distance. Strode up the east side of the avenue—one long strip mall—until he reached the Bellevue-NYU medical complex where every damn building seemed to be named after someone. That annoyed the hell out of him for some reason.

After he passed through the shadow of the brooding hulk of the Con Ed power plant, the street opened up into the UN Plaza with its big Secretariat building looking like something out of *2001*, towering over the swaybacked block of the General Assembly.

Jack remembered posing as a tourist in there last summer while following one of the Indian diplomats all over town. What a load of bullshit he'd had to suffer through while waiting for Kusum to leave. Tempted to make a detour right now, stop in there this very minute and tell them how to get their act together. First thing he'd have them do was move the big tombstone of the Secretariat, maybe lay it on its side so it didn't block the morning sun when he was walking by, or at the very least cut a hole in its center to let *some* light through.

Later. Maybe he'd straighten them out this afternoon. Right now he felt too damn *good* to waste even a second of this beautiful morning on those jerks.

But the flags—all these goddamn flags really bothered him. Rows of flags, blocks of flags, flags everywhere, wasting enough fabric to clothe most of Bangladesh. Reached into his pocket and grabbed his knife. Had a big-time urge to run up to those poles and start cutting the ropes—free the flags!

But no . . . take too long. Especially with Gia home alone. She was waiting for him, he knew. Jack was sure she could *feel* his approach, his growing proximity.

Moved on, passing a statue of Saint George killing some stupid-looking dragon on the other side of the fence, and there in the bushes, was that an elephant, a brown elephant? And then it was all blending together and then reversing direction and he felt like he was coming apart, pieces of him floating away, sailing into the air and then curving and boomeranging back to reassemble and fuse into something new and wonderful, the new Jack, King of the City.

After all, wasn't it known as New Jack City?

Energy bloomed in him as he picked up his pace. No matter that it was uphill all the way, he was strong, stronger, strongest. Came to Fifty-fourth and cut east one more block to Sutton Place South where he had a beautiful view of the sparkling East River. God, he loved this city, *his* city. Hadn't been born here, but that was OK. Meant he wasn't here by some accident of nature but here by choice. He'd come here and made it his own, explored every nook and cranny, knew highborn and low and every sort between. *Owned* this city, man, and no one was going to tell him any different.

Gia knew that, and that was why she loved him. And he loved her because she knew that.

Wait. . . .

Jack shook his head. Did that make sense?

Sure it did. Of course it did. Wouldn't have thought it if it didn't.

Breaking a light sweat, heavier in the small of his back where the Glock 19 rested in its nylon holster, and more around his ankle where he'd strapped the Semmerling, but he needed those guns, needed them because there were people in his city, not many but always a few, who might try to take the city away from him and make it their own, so he had to be vigilant, ever vigilant.

But not today, no worry about that today, because it was all his today and he felt *great*. Laughed aloud.

"Top o' da world, Ma!"

Guy coming the other way gave him a strange look but Jack glared at him, daring him to say something, anything, to say one single goddamn word. Guy looked away.

Smart. Nobody gives me looks in *my* city.

Felt a growing pressure in his groin as he turned into Sutton Square. Something flitted through his head, a thought about looking out for a car, a car with two men, but it was a slippery thought and avoided his grasp every time he reached for it.

Who cared about cars anyway. All he cared about now was getting to Gia. Gia-Gia-Gia. Oh, this was going to be good, so very-very good. Do it in the kitchen, do it in the living room, and maybe even in bed. Do-do-do. All day, and all afternoon until Vicky came home. Then he'd take them both out on the town, his town, and show them a great time, the best time of their lives, the kind of time only he could show them.

Knocked on the door. Couldn't wait to see the joy beaming from

Gia's face when she pulled it open and saw him, joy that would quickly turn to lust. And then he heard a child's voice, Vicky's, shouting on the far side of the door. . . .

"Mom! It's Jack! Jack's here!"

And suddenly a cloud moved over his sun and sucked all the heat from his body.

Vicky was home. Gia wouldn't . . . she'd never . . . not with Vicky around.

"Jack!" Gia said, her smile bright as she opened the door. "What a surprise!"

"Yeah," he said through his teeth. Tried to force a smile but couldn't, just couldn't. Could do just about anything in this city of his, but right now he couldn't smile. Stepped through the door. "Some surprise."

"Hi, Jack!" Vicky said, looking up at him with a big happy stupid grin.

Ignored her and turned to Gia. "What's she doing home?"

"She's got a sore throat and a cough." Gia's smile was gone and she was looking at him strangely.

"Doesn't look sick."

"Yeah, I got a bad cough," Vicky said. "Wanna hear it?" She started hacking.

Jack wanted to belt her—one backhand swipe to knock her into the next room. She was ruining everything. Maybe he ought to just grab Gia right here and do it in the foyer, right in front of Vicky. Be a good lesson for her.

"Is something wrong, Jack?" Gia said, concern growing in her eyes as she stared at him.

"Wrong?" he said, feeling fury building like a thunderhead in his skull. "Yeah, there's plenty wrong. First off, you coddle this kid too much—"

"Jack!"

"Don't interrupt me!" he said, his voice rising. "I hate to be interrupted."

"Jack, what on earth's wrong with you?"

There, she'd done it again. Interrupted him. She'd never learn, would she. Only one way to handle someone like that.

He balled a fist and raised his arm—

"Jack!"

The terror in Gia's eyes as she cringed away hit him like a kick in the gut, a bucket of ice water in the face. . . .

What am I doing? What's happening to me? Jeez, I was just about to punch Gia. What—?

And then in a flash of clarity Jack knew, and the realization struck like a knife through his skull.

Somehow, someway, he'd been dosed with Berzerk. The when and the where didn't matter right now. First thing he had to do was get out of here. Couldn't be with anybody, especially not Gia and Vicky.

Get . . . out!

Fighting panic, he turned toward the door. Remembered his guns— had to dump them. Mix a 9mm and a .45 with a snootful of Berzerk and a lot of people could wind up dead. Reached under the back of his T-shirt and pulled the Glock from its SOB holster, then ripped the Semmerling, leather straps and all, from his ankle. Shoved them into Gia's hands, then added his knife . . . and his wallet.

Immediately something made him want to snatch them back, pushed him to reach for them. What—was he crazy, giving his money and beloved weapons to this woman?

Forced himself to step back, to grit out words, "Something's wrong. Take these. Gotta go. Explain later."

She stared at him wide-eyed with fright and confusion. "What—?"

Didn't dare risk another word, another second here. Hanging onto control by his fingertips, could feel it wriggling away from him. Could maintain this grip only so long before it slipped away again. Wanted— needed—to be as far as possible from here when it did.

Turned and ran out the door.

4

"Let's go," Vuk said, reaching into his coat.

Ivo shook his head. He didn't want to do this. "Wait a bit. Maybe he'll come out."

They'd parked in a BMW 750iL up the gentle slope of Fifty-eighth Street from where they had a narrow-angle view of the door. A purely residential block. Not a single store and few pedestrians. They'd been here only a few minutes when they saw their man arrive on foot and enter the town house.

"And maybe he won't." Vuk took out his pistol, his tried-and-true 7.62mm M57 semiautomatic, and checked the action. "You heard what Dragovic said. If we see him, we take him and bring him in."

Ivo licked his dry lips. "The woman and child might be there."

"Hope so." He checked his bleached hair in the rearview mirror. "She's a beauty."

Ivo's palms were slick against the steering wheel. He'd sworn that his days of killing noncombatants were over. Vuk didn't care. Ivo doubted Vuk had ever given a second thought to what he'd done in Kosovo. He had to find a way to delay this.

"We need silencers," he said, grasping at the first idea to dart through his head. "Even a single shot in a neighborhood like this will bring the police."

"We'll have to risk it." Vuk reached for the door. "If we move fast enough, it won't matter."

Ivo grabbed his arm. "Wait."

He was trying desperately to think of something to say when movement by the town house caught his eye. The man was out again, almost running from the door.

"There he is!" he said, hoping the gush of relief was not apparent in his voice. "Moving fast."

"Don't let him out of your sight."

Ivo started the car and reached for the shift, then stopped. "He's coming this way."

The man broke into a jog as he crossed Sutton Place and started up the sidewalk.

"Coming right to us," Vuk said with a grin. "Perfect."

Ivo left the car in park and studied the approaching man. This was the first time he'd had a chance to see him since their brief encounter on the beach last week, and he looked . . . different. His expression was strange, somewhere between panic and rage. But his eyes . . . they'd been so mild last week. Now they were wild.

"Ready," Vuk said. The man would pass on his side. "You move when I do."

Ivo checked the street. Light traffic, only one or two pedestrians and none close by. When the man came to within a car length of their vehicle, Vuk opened his door. Ivo jumped out on the street side, drawing his own weapon, a FEG FP9, holding it low as he came around the rear bumper. He didn't chamber a round until Vuk had his weapon pointed at the man's chest.

"Into the car!" Vuk said.

Ivo pulled open the rear door with his free hand as the man skidded to a halt.

"What?" the man said.

"You heard!" Vuk said, gesturing with his pistol.

"You're the jerks from the beach. What are you doing in my city?"

"In!" Vuk lowered his barrel and pointed it at the man's legs. "Inside or I shoot your knees and drag you in."

The man's wild eyes darted from Vuk's gun to the one in Ivo's hand, then back again. No fear there or in his expression, just a brief baring of the teeth, very much like a snarl as he moved toward the open door. Ivo glanced around as he stepped back to let him in. No one was paying them any attention. Yet.

"Stop right there," Vuk said. He did a quick pat-down and grinned at Ivo when he found the empty SOB holster. "I think we have our man." To the man: "Where is your gun?"

"Home."

"Good place for it." Vuk shoved the man into the seat on the passenger side. "Do not move a muscle."

Ivo covered him while Vuk ran around to the other side and got in. He sat in the rear, facing their captive, while Ivo returned to the driver seat. Safe behind the wheel again, he let loose a breath he'd been holding. No one had noticed them. The whole operation had taken perhaps thirty seconds.

"So," Vuk said as Ivo pulled from the parking space, "you are man who wrecked our cars, yes?"

"*Your* cars?" the man said. "If you bring a car into my city, it's *my* car."

"Who are you?"

"You know very well who I am. I am Moreau. *Dr.* Moreau. Dr. *Jack* Moreau. I created you."

Something wrong here, Ivo thought. The man on the beach didn't talk crazy like this.

He adjusted the rearview mirror. The brown eyes flashed toward him, strangely glittering eyes. The eyes of a madman. Fear began to nibble at Ivo's gut. He felt like someone who had set a possum trap and wound up with a bear.

What have we let into our car?

"So it *was* you," Vuk said.

The man was shaking his head. "The beast flesh. . . . the stubborn beast flesh creeping back."

"Stop talking like fool. First you make fool of our boss, then you try to make fool of my friend Ivo and me too, yes?"

The traffic light on Sutton Place turned green as Ivo approached. He made a right and stopped at the red at Fifty-seventh.

"Ivo?" the man said to Vuk. "What kind of name is that? I didn't name him that when I created him from a dog. And you. I created you from a donkey, I think. An ass. But I did *not* give you that hair color. And why would I try to make a fool out of you when you do such a good job of it by trying to look like a carrot? Don't you own a mirror?"

Ivo could hear the strain in Vuk's voice. "I can shoot off your knees now, but that would mean I have to carry you inside to speak to our boss, and later I have to clean up the mess. But once we are inside, the boss will want you to speak, and I will be very happy to be one to make sure you tell everything he wish to know."

Ivo crossed Fifty-seventh, keeping as much of a watch in his rear-view as he did through the windshield.

"You would do well not to anger me by breaking the Law," the man said. "You remember the Law, don't you? Are you not men? Has the stubborn beast flesh crept back so far that you've forgotten the law? Break the Law and it's off to the House of Pain with you. I told you: I am Moreau."

"You are no one," Vuk said. "You are nothing. But you somehow manage to find yourself a fine-looking woman. Do you know what will happen after our boss is through with you? Ivo and I are going to come back and pay little visit to your woman. We are going to fuck her."

What is Vuk doing? Ivo wondered, anxiety building like a pressure in his chest. Why is he taunting him? Doesn't he see the man's eyes? Can't he tell that he's completely insane?

And an insane man is capable of anything.

As Ivo turned onto Fifty-fifth he said, "I think that's enough for now."

"No, Ivo. Not nearly enough. I want him to know how we will take turns with his woman and how she will love it because she has never had real man before. And then perhaps we move on to little girl."

Ivo felt the air within the car thicken, become charged, as if lightning were readying a strike.

"Vuk, please!"

"Vuk?" The man laughed. "That's a name? Sounds like someone puking. But I guess it goes with the rest of you, donkey-man. Dumb name, dumb hair, dumb ass."

Ivo sensed sudden movement behind him and knew, just knew that Vuk was swinging his pistol at the man's face. And he saw the burst of triumph in the captive's eyes that said this was just what he had been waiting for.

"Vuk, no!"

Ivo yanked the wheel to the right and slammed on the brakes. As the car lurched to a halt he pulled his pistol from his shoulder holster. But it was too late.

He heard the man roar, "You turn upon your creator?" The shot from the rear seat sounded like a cannon as warm droplets sprayed the back of Ivo's neck. "You two are beyond salvage!"

Ivo had his pistol on the rise, about chest high, and was swinging his head around when the muzzle of Vuk's M57 appeared, an inch from his right eye. As he gazed down that narrow tunnel to eternity, a flash bloomed in his vision and all became bright white light, engulfing him, consuming him.

5

Half blind with rage, he jumps out and aims Carrot Top's pistol at the car. Occupants already dead, which is just what they should be for threatening to harm his women.

A vagrant thought intrudes: *Wasn't I just thinking of harming them myself a few minutes ago?* but he brushes it aside. Yeah but that was different. What I do is one thing. Doesn't mean anybody else can do the same.

Took a supreme effort of his magnificent will not to tear their heads off as soon as they'd accosted him. But he wanted to give them a chance to redeem themselves. After all, he created them, and he is nothing if not a benign creator.

He is Moreau. Dr. Jack Moreau.

No fear is the key. A lesser being would have been afraid of the gun and the manlike thing holding it, but not him. He has no fear, and no fear means no hesitation, means no self-doubt, means simply doing what must be done, taking what you want when you want it with full knowledge that you can do it and that none of these lesser beings has the right or the means to stop you.

Oh, he was good in that car, so good, so fast, so much faster than the two creatures who dared to oppose him. But why should he be surprised? After all, hadn't he created them, transformed them from lower species? A shame to waste them, but they were reverting to their lower forms, the beast flesh had crept back so far that they forgot the Law, and forgetting the Law is punishable by death.

No, wait. Breaking the Law means a trip back to the House of Pain. Not death. He must have forgot. Oh, well.

So the manlike things he created are good and dead, but the Beamer must die too. Belongs to an enemy, someone who wants to take the city away from him. Can't send the car to the House of Pain, so he must execute it.

He pulls the trigger, shooting wildly, punching hole after hole in the fenders. Aware of screams, only a few, from up and down the street, and fleeing people dart through his peripheral vision, but he keeps yanking on the trigger.

Suddenly a wall of flame erupts from the rear of the car, knocking him off his feet and searing him with a blast of heat, peppering him with flying glass.

Half-dazed, he struggles to his knees, blinking, coughing, then to his feet. Notices that the dark hair on his arms is singed into tight, tiny pale curls and the skin is scorched and blackened. His shirt is torn and he's bleeding from a couple of spots on his already scarred chest. Shakes his head to clear the buzzing from his ears.

Across the street the Beamer is toast. Dead. Not merely dead, but clearly and sincerely dead, or however that goes. An evil devil witch car burning at the stake.

A weight in his hand. Carrot Top's gun—some sort of Tokarev clone. Barely remembers how he got it. Stares at the pistol. The slide is back, the empty chamber exposed. Spare clip's got to be in the car, which means this thing's no good to him anymore. Tosses it into the burning heap and looks around.

Where is he? Some sort of high-rise apartment building canyon. Oh, yeah. Mid-fifties—near Gia's. He spots a taxi stopped down the slope from the burning Beamer. Driver is twisted around. Seems to be trying to back up but the cars stacked behind him are preventing it.

Jack starts walking toward the cab. Driver turns and sees him. Eyes widen in his dark face and he tries to wave Jack off.

A cab, in my city, not wanting to give me a ride? What's happening around here? Has everyone gone crazy?

Keeps walking toward the cab. Driver has stopped waving. Doesn't appear to be the kind who believes in crosses, but from the look on his face if he had one he'd probably be holding it up to ward off this burnt-up and torn-up guy walking his way. Seems about to put the car in gear—Don't even think about it—then changes his mind. Jumps out and runs back toward First Avenue.

Jack stops and watches him go. Now doesn't that beat all. What's wrong with people today? First furious impulse is to run after the little bastard and teach him some manners, but the cab is before him, engine idling, driver door standing open almost like an invitation.

Looks like I'll have to drive myself.

But when he gets in he has second thoughts. Front section of the cab looks like a landfill—empty twenty-ounce Diet Pepsi and Mountain Dew bottles roll, Snickers and Dove Bar and peanut butter cracker wrappers flutter, and scattered all across the floor is a good half-inch layer of empty pistachio shells. Radio's playing some awful song in a foreign language—Farsi?—but at least the radio's still there. Can't say the same about the air bag; its compartment in the steering wheel is a gaping toothless mouth—either somebody stole it or it deployed some-time in the dim dark past and the driver never replaced it.

This is not, repeat, *not* suitable transportation for someone of Dr. Jack Moreau's stature but it's all he's got at the moment. Grabs the sticky gearshift, rams it into drive, and starts to move.

Wait. Move where?

Out of the city, zips through his brain. *Out of the city—fast.*

Doesn't remember why he should want to leave the city, but the idea is there, and it's insistent. But where out of the city?

Rage blooms anew as Jack passes the burning Beamer. He knows who owns it. Dragovic. That Serb bastard sent those two gooney boys to kidnap him and bring him—where? To his place in the Hamptons, of course, the place Jack trashed.

Now Jack knows where he's going.

"You want a face-to-face, Dragovic?" he shouts to the streaked windshield as he heads for the Fifty-ninth Street Bridge. "You got it!"

Rearview mirror is angled toward him and he starts when he sees a stranger in it. Face in the mirror is blackened with soot, eyebrows and hairline singed. And then he realizes the face is his own.

"Damn you, Dragovic!" he shouts, pounding the steering wheel. "You're gonna pay for this!"

Soon as Jack hits the bridge he puts his foot in the tank and cranks up the speed. Taxi doesn't exactly leap ahead, but it moves. Sunlight seems extra bright, but the birds fly more lazily than usual, and the other cars around him seem slow and ponderous, as if time is passing at a different rate for them.

Then it comes to him. He's not Moreau. He's gone beyond Moreau. His reflexes are superhuman now. He may have a crummy ride, but his newfound powers can more than compensate. He is a new deity.

King of the Road.

Traffic's not so heavy in this direction—most of it's heading into his city—but still pretty thick. The King begins weaving in and out, darting into openings where mere mortals would not dare, earning angry honks and gestures as he cuts across lanes and threads narrow divides.

Screw 'em.

Sees daylight ahead, a nice long stretch of open left lane, and the only thing blocking him from that direct line to infinity is a dark blue Volvo. Jack pulls up behind, riding its bumper. Sees the driver, a woman, idly twirling her hair with a finger as she dallies along in the lane, oblivious to him.

"Lay-deeee!" he shouts, honking. "King of the Road to lay-deeee! Listen to Joan Hamburg in another lane!"

But she makes no move to get over, gives no sign that she's even aware of the King's presence, and this only ups his rage.

He's boxed in, can't go around her, so he leans on the horn.

"Lay-deeeeeeeeeeee!" He feels like he's gonna explode now and he's shouting through clenched teeth. "Stop twirling your goddamn hair and get outta the King's way!"

But still no move to the side, let alone acknowledgement of his existence.

That does it. Jack stomps the gas pedal and it feels good, it feels *so* good when he rams her rear fender.

That gets her attention. The woman jumps as her car swerves left, then right. She glances quickly over her shoulder. Got both hands on the wheel now and she knows, god*damn* does she know, that the King is on her tail.

"Move! Move!" he's shouting as he waves his arm to the right.

But still she hangs in the lane, no blinker, no nothing. Jack leans on the horn and hits the gas again. She must see him coming because this time she swerves right just in time.

"Finally!"

As he pulls parallel he wants to sideswipe her, wants to slam into her lousy Volvo and send it careening all the way across the lanes—*bam!*—into and over the guardrail. And he should; he really should. As King of the Road he owes it to the other drivers on the bridge, owes it to other drivers everywhere in his asphalt domain to send her into screaming free fall, let her drink a little eau du East River, but he can't spare the time. For there's a larger blot on his world, a dark festering sore on the eastern horizon, a foul smudge named Dragovic, and it's Jack's divinely ordained mission to journey to East Hampton and clean it up.

So instead of ramming her he scoots by. You are spared, lady—this time. In his rearview he sees she's got a cell phone to her ear.

That's right, lady; call the cops. Call the fire department. Call anyone you want. Tell them the King of the Road moved you out of the left lane but spared your life. They'll just tell you how lucky you are. So learn from this, lady: the King catches you squatting in the left lane again, no more Mr. Nice Guy.

Makes good time from there and even does well on Queens Boulevard for a while, but he's still seething—at the woman, at the men who tried to kidnap him, at Dragovic, at all the damn cars on the road. Hates them all with equal intensity, which he's dimly aware shouldn't be, but somehow is.

But he's OK. Got it all under control. Saving it for Dragovic.

Then comes a traffic tie-up. Construction on Queens Boulevard, just before the Brooklyn-Queens Expressway. At least the sign *says* construction but Jack can't see a single soul working. No matter, the barriers are up, and all traffic has to funnel down to one lane.

Which has Jack steaming. If there was a way to drive this cab over the tops of the cars in front of him he would, but he's got to wait in line and crawl and merge, and then crawl and merge again. So humiliating for a king. Has to close his eyes and take deep breaths every so often to keep from ripping the steering wheel off the column.

A quarter-mile ahead he can see the cars cruising along the BQE overpass and he longs to be up there. Not much farther now. Just a few more car lengths and he can be up there too. A short jog south will put him on the LIE; he'll be trucking toward the Hamptons and Dragovic in no time. But right now he's got to—

Suddenly this big brand-new black Mercedes is angling into the gap in front of him.

"Where'd you come from?"

Obviously it scooted down the shoulder on Jack's left and cut in front of him while he was staring at the overpass. Jack is confounded . . . can't believe someone would do this to the King.

Instantly the world takes on this cranberry tint.

Venting an inarticulate cry somewhere between a scream and a growl, Jack hits the pedal and rams the Merc's front passenger door. The Merc rocks back and forth. And while the driver, vaguely visible through the tinted glass, is staring his way in shock, Jack reverses a couple of feet, angles the wheel a little left, and caves in the rear passenger door, but harder. Then he kicks open his door and jumps out of his cab.

Behind him he hears cheers and applause from other drivers, but he ignores them. He's focused on this sonovabitch with his blow-dried salt-and-pepper hair and his multi-thousand-dollar suit getting out of his Mercedes, guy who thinks he's gonna give the King some attitude. Well, listen, buddy, you don't know attitude, you've never seen, never dreamed attitude like you're gonna get right now.

Guy's eyes widen at his first glimpse of Jack, probably because with his singed hair, scorched skin, and torn bloody clothing he must look like someone who's just walked through a burning building for fun. And of course the fact that Jack is screaming and his outstretched hands are curved into claws does not make him look particularly amiable.

"You think 'cause you drive a Mercedes you can just cut in front of anybody whenever you damn well please? 'Snooze, you lose'—is that what you were thinking? Well this time you cut off the King of the Road and you do not *ever* cut off the King of the fucking Road!"

Jack jumps up on the Merc's trunk and comes for the driver. Wants to tear this guy apart with his bare hands and can see by the look on the guy's face, florid outrage blanching to oh-shit-what-have-I-got-myself-into? pallor, that the guy knows it. Leaps onto the car roof and slides across feetfirst as the guy ducks back in behind the wheel. Driver door is closing but Jack catches its upper edge with both sneakers, kicking it back open.

Now he's down inside the door with his feet on the pavement, pulling the guy out of the car, and the guy's kicking and clawing at Jack, whimpering please don't hurt him and how it was a mistake, a dumb careless mistake, and he's sorry, he's so terribly sorry.

Yeah, now you're sorry, Mr. Mercedes, but you weren't sorry a minute ago, were you, no, you weren't sorry at all then, and Jack wants to punch his face in but the guy proceeds to wet his pants and that's so pathetic and now he's burping and gagging and oh jeez he's gonna puke.

Jack turns the guy a quick one-eighty and lets him blow breakfast onto the concrete divider. Not gonna punch him out now, not with barf all over him.

All right, tell you what, Mr. Mercedes, we're gonna do a little trade, you and me. That's right, I'm going to be Mr. Mercedes now and you're gonna be Mr. Cabbie. Either that or you're gonna *walk* from here to wherever you're going.

Jack shoves him and sends him stumbling away, then gets in. Have a nice day. Slams the Merc into gear and peels rubber into the space that's opened up in the logjam while they've been having their little discussion. Smells good in here and it's cool. These are the sort of wheels he should always have, a full flash ride—except for the annoying little seat belt warning light. If he had one of his guns right now he'd shoot it out.

Seat belt? The King of the Road doesn't wear a seat belt.

Ooh, and looky here. Nifty little black driving gloves.

Slips them on, like a second skin, and thirty seconds later he's in the clear, gunning for the ramp to the BQE. And just like he knew, takes him no time to reach the Long Island Expressway. Once on that it's clear sailing.

Gets the Merc up to eighty and he's rolling maybe fifteen minutes like this when the sign for the Glen Cove Road exit looms large in the windshield—coming up in two miles.

Whoa. Glen Cove Road. That's the way to Monroe. And Monroe's where that dumb-ass freak show's keeping big bad Scar-lip the rakosh caged up.

Jack slips his hand inside his torn shirt and fingers the three thick scars that ridge the scorched skin of his chest. Scar-lip scars. Never paid back the big ugly for these. Matter of fact, went and stopped those two carny guys from poking him. Why the hell'd he do that? What was he thinking? Scar-lip scarred him—scarred the King. Can't let something like that go. What would people say? Got to go back and straighten it out, and now's as good a time as any. Yes, sir, overdue for a little side trip to kick some rakosh donkey.

Jack yanks the wheel to the right, cutting off a Lincoln and a Chevy as he zips across three lanes to the exit. But the going on Glen Cove Road is a lot slower. Pushes it as much as he can with his dodge-and-weave thing and makes decent time, but then the divided highway ends and it's down to two-lane blacktopville and he's steaming because nobody knows how to drive around here.

Hey, it's not Sunday afternoon you jerks so move your fat automotive asses or get offa my road!

And so he's riding bumpers, leaning on the horn, blinking his high beams, pushing the yellow traffic lights to the max, and zipping through a couple of reds until he sees other red lights, the bubble-gum kind, flashing in his rearview mirror.

A hick Glen Cove cop. Obviously he doesn't know who he's dealing with. You don't pull over the King of the Road.

Jack ignores him for a few blocks but then the guy has the nerve to hit his siren. Just a single *woop* but it sets off a rage bomb in Jack. Time to set this fool straight. Instead of slowing, Jack speeds up. Not too fast—doing forty in a twenty-five—but enough to make it plain that this big black Mercedes is giving Offissa Pupp an automotive single-digit salute.

Jack can't see the cop's face but he's got to be pissed because he's cranked his siren up to full blast now and not only are his flashers doing the dervish but his headlights are strobing like it's disco time as he crawls up the butt of Jack's Mercedes.

You like driving close? How's this?

Jack presses back against the headrest as he slams on the brakes and is jolted as the cop car plows into his rear bumper. Jack pauses long enough to see the cop disappear behind a billow of white; then he roars off, laughing.

Eat hot flaming air bag, Deputy Dawg!

But a mile or so farther on he's got another wooping flashing Glen Cove policemobile on his tail and it doesn't seem to matter that Jack's in Monroe now; the cop keeps coming. Jack speeds up, hoping to catch this guy same as the last, but Cop One must've put out the word because Cop Two hangs back. Jack's slowing down and speeding up, trying to reel him in, and maybe just maybe he's paying too much attention to the rearview, because when he focuses back through the windshield during the next speedup he sees this Pacer driven by an Oriental dude turning in front of him so he stands on the brake and hauls the steering wheel left and skids across the road and everything would be fine except this brand new Chevy Suburban the size of Yonkers is barreling down the other lane and it catches him broadside like a high-velocity ninety-thousand-caliber hardball, flipping the Merc onto its side and bouncing Jack in half a dozen directions at once around the front compartment. He's a human pinball between a set of power bumpers and as he sees the front right windshield post coming in fast for a face kiss he remembers the seat-belt warning light with sudden wistful fondness; then memory and consciousness take a breather. . . .

6

Luc fidgeted anxiously in his chair in his book-lined study and decided he could put it off no longer. He'd stayed home today but had been checking the employee sign-in list at the GEM offices via his home computer. Nadia's name was still absent.

He glanced at his watch. Almost eleven. If she hadn't signed in by now, she wasn't going to. Time to call the clinic. He punched in the number.

"Diabetes clinic," said a woman's voice.

"Yes. Is Dr. Radzminsky there?"

"No. She's gone for the day."

"Do you know when she left?"

"Who's calling, please?"

"This is Dr. Monnet. She works for me as a researcher."

"Of course. She's mentioned you."

Has she? I wonder what she said.

"Well, she hasn't shown up for work yet and I was wondering . . ."

Luc listened patiently while the receptionist related how Dr.

Radzminsky was upset because of her fiancé's disappearance and so on, and he made properly sympathetic noises. The important thing here was to establish his concern for a missing employee.

After learning that Nadia had left later than usual—almost nine-thirty—Luc told the receptionist to ask her to please call his office immediately should she return.

He leaned back and sipped his coffee and thought of Nadia's coffee. Undoubtedly she'd drunk from her NADJ mug by now and was presently wandering about somewhere, firmly in the grip of Loki madness.

Luc sighed with relief and a touch of regret as he wondered where she was and what she was doing. He confessed to a certain professional curiosity as to what behaviors the Loki would bring out in a sweet, even-tempered person like Nadia. He remembered reading about a meek mousy little housewife who, after taking a heavy dose from a well-meaning friend, cut her abusive husband to ribbons. Nothing so gory from Nadia, he hoped. Just enough to get her arrested and charged . . . and her credibility ruined.

He rose and returned to the living room. He surveyed the crates of wine neatly stacked and ready for shipment. He'd personally packed every one of them. Only four more to go.

He glanced at the television and saw that *Headline News* was re-playing the Dragovic videotape. Luc had already seen it three times but he sat down now, eager for a fourth viewing. He could not help grinning at the close-up of Dragovic firing wildly at the Coast Guard helicopter. Oh, this was delicious, utterly delicious.

He tried to imagine how small, how utterly humiliated Dragovic must feel right now and could not. He wondered who was behind this marvelous prank. Whoever he was, Luc could kiss him.

Much as he would dearly love to search the channels for more replays, he had to keep moving. The calendar on this, his last day in America, was pretty well filled. He had to finish packing the very last of his wine before the shippers arrived at three. Once the cases were safely on their way to France, he would have an early dinner, his last in New York, and then head out to the airport. A tingle of anticipation ran up the center of his chest. He was booked first class on the ten o'clock to Charles de Gaulle. A mere eleven hours and—

The phone rang. Luc checked the caller ID. If it was anyone from GEM, especially his partners, they could talk to his voice mail. His heart dropped a beat when he saw "N. Radzminsky" on the readout. He snatched up the receiver.

"Hello?" His suddenly dry mouth made his voice sound strange.

"Dr. Monnet, this is Nadia. I tried your office but—"

"Yes, Nadia. How are you?"

The question was not conversational routine—he truly wanted to know.

"I'm terrible," she said, her voice edging toward a sob. "I just got back from Brooklyn after spending an hour in the Eighty-fourth Precinct talking to the police. They've got *no* leads on Doug."

She sounded upset, her voice quavering, but she was undeniably rational. How could that be? The Loki . . .

"I'm so sorry, Nadia. Is there anything I can do?"

"Yes," she said, a hint of steel creeping into her voice. "I just got off the subway and I'm two blocks from you. I've got a few things I want to talk to you about."

Dear God! Coming here? No, she couldn't! She'd see the boxed-up wine, she'd guess—

"I-I was just leaving. Can't we—?"

"This isn't going to wait." Her voice grew more sharply edged. "Either I get answers from you or I have my new friends at the Eight-four do the asking."

Luc dropped into a chair, his heart thudding, the living room spinning. Was this the way her dose of Loki was taking her? Whatever the case, he could not allow her up here.

"I don't understand this. You sound so upset. I'll meet you outside. We can talk while I wait for a cab."

"All right," she said, then cut the connection.

Luc was wearing a light sweater and slacks. He threw on a blue blazer and hurried to meet her. He reached the sidewalk just as Nadia arrived. She wore a shapeless beige raincoat and looked terrible—puffy face, red-rimmed eyes—but not deranged.

But just in case . . .

"Walk with me," he said, taking her arm and guiding her up Eighty-seventh, away from his building. "What do you think I can tell you?"

"You can tell me if you had anything to do with Doug's disappearance."

Luc almost tripped. His first attempt at speech failed. On his second he managed, "What? How . . . how can you ask such a thing?"

"Because Doug knew things. He hacked into your company computers. He found out where your R and D funds were going."

"I had no idea!" Did he look surprised enough? "Why on earth—?"

"And I know things too. I know that Loki is being sold on the street. And I know you're involved with Milos Dragovic."

He glanced around at the lunchtime crowds beginning to fill the streets. "Please, Nadia. Not so loud!"

"All right," she said, lowering her voice a trifle. "But tell me . . . let me hear it straight from your lips: did you have anything to do with Doug's disappearance?"

"No! Absolutely not!"

Panic sent his thoughts caroming through his brain. Oh, dear God, she knows about Dragovic, about Berzerk and all the rest! How can this be happening? Not now! Not when I am almost free!

"How about Dragovic?" she said.

Think! Think! Think!

"Nadia, one of the downsides of going public is that anyone can buy your company's stock. Unfortunately, Mr. Dragovic owns a large block of ours and—"

"What's his relationship with you?"

Luc felt as if he were on the witness stand, being grilled by a prosecutor.

"It is very complicated, and I will explain it in full to you someday if you like, but suffice it to say that Mr. Dragovic could not be involved in Douglas's troubles because I doubt very much he even knows Douglas exists."

A long pause. They'd reached the corner of Lexington; he guided her left . . . downtown . . . toward her home . . . away from his neighborhood.

Finally she said, "I think I'm going to have to go to the police about Dragovic."

No!

Luc fought to keep the panic out of his voice. "Please don't be precipitous, Nadia. You will cause much misery and embarrassment for many people, and none of it will bring back your Douglas one minute sooner."

"I'm not so sure about that."

"Please give it a little more time, Nadia—at least until tonight, I beg you. Milos Dragovic is a vile, vile man, but I swear to you by all I hold holy he has no connection to Douglas. And if you've been watching the television at all, you must know he's had other matters on his mind."

Another pause, longer this time, then Nadia closed her eyes and breathed a deep, tremulous sigh. "Maybe you're right. I don't know. I'm so worried, so *frustrated*, I feel I've got to do *something!*"

"Wait. Just give it until tonight. I'm sure you'll hear something by tonight. If not, then do what you must. But give the police just a little more time."

"All right," she said, her voice barely audible. "Till tonight."

She turned and, without another word, continued walking downtown on Lexington.

Luc stepped to the side and leaned against the front of an appliance store. Somehow Nadia hadn't been dosed with the Loki. Or if she had she was resistant to its effects. Whatever, she was out and about and more dangerous than ever.

His eyes drifted to the TVs in the front window of the store where the Dragovic footage was playing again. A moment ago he'd tried to imagine how small and utterly humiliated Dragovic must feel. If Nadia went to the police . . . he had visions of stepping off the plane and finding officers of the Sureté waiting for him, of returning to New York in manacles, walking a gauntlet of photographers. . . . He would no longer need to imagine how Dragovic felt. . . . He would know first-hand.

He turned, found a public phone, and called a number he knew by heart. After three rings, Ozymandias Prather's deep voice echoed through the receiver.

"Prather, it's me." He needed to be discreet here. "I need your services again."

"Who is it this time?"

"A researcher. The fiancée of the last one. She suspects."

An odd laugh. "Do you warn people when you hire them that they might not have a future with your firm—or any future at all?"

"Please. This is an emergency. She could ruin everything."

"Really. That's a shame."

"Can you do it? Now?"

"In daylight? Out of the question. Too risky."

">

"Please!" He loathed begging this man but had nowhere else to turn. "I'll double the usual fee."

"Double, ay? And you say it's the fiancée of the last one. That presents possibilities. I'll need some information. . . ."

Flooded with relief, Luc gave Prather what he wanted: name, address, phone numbers, whether or not she lived alone. When he was finished . . .

"I will send someone by within the hour to pick up the payment."

"I'll have it ready." He'd pay for this himself, draw out the money immediately.

"Excellent. And since you're such a good customer, I believe I can work this one to cover for the last as well."

"Really? How?"

"You will see. Remember: money in an hour."

Luc hung up and headed for the nearby Citibank. Most of his money had been transferred to his Swiss account, but he still had more than enough left to pay Prather.

He stopped and took a few deep breaths. This is what he got for trying to find a humane solution. If he'd put Prather on it in the first place, he wouldn't be in this state.

He glanced his watch. Noon. Ten more hours. Maybe he could find an earlier flight. As soon as he settled with Prather he'd call his travel agent. New York was becoming too dangerous for him.

7

Took Jack a moment or two to realize he was in a hospital room. The IV running into his left arm pretty much clinched it.

A small narrow room, semiprivate, but the other bed empty. A dark dead television screen stared at him from the opposite wall a few feet beyond the edge of the bed. Cracks in the ceiling, in the walls, chipped paint on the doors. This place had seen better days.

So had his head—it was killing him. The rest of him didn't feel so hot either. Sat up and maybe that wasn't such a good idea—the room swam around the bed; his stomach heaved; pain shot through his left ribs—but he grabbed the side rails and hung on for the ride.

While he waited for the walls to stop moving he tried to figure out what the hell had put him here. Slowly, in brief bright flashes and glittery pieces, it came back . . . a succession of cars, shots, collisions, cops, all suffused with an overriding giddy exhilaration mixed with murderous rage. Psycho time, a berserko bender—

Berzerk. That's right. Remembered now, remembered that he must have been dosed with the crazy-maker stuff, and the only way it could have happened was in the coffee Nadia had given him. Didn't make sense that she'd do it. Which could only mean that the dose had been meant for her.

Jack had a pretty damn good idea of who had meant it. He'd figure out the why later. Right now he had to get out of here.

What time was it? No clock in the room. How long had he been here? Last thing he remembered was the cops chasing him and—

Cops . . . was he under arrest?

The near certainty of that sent a bolt of sick pain through his already throbbing head. Checked his fingertips—not the cleanest they'd ever been, but no sign of fingerprint ink. Yet. So far in his life he'd managed to keep his photo and fingerprints out of the criminal databases, and he desperately wanted to keep it that way.

He noticed a plastic wristband. "John Doe" had been typed in the patient name space. His admitting physician was a doctor named A. Bulmer.

John Doe . . . but you can call me Jack.

Next question: was he under guard?

Probably, but only one way to find out. Door to the hall stood open about a foot. A peek outside would give the answer.

Twisted the release on the side rail and slid it down. But as he swung his legs over the side, the room began to do the Harlem shuffle again. He let it finish, then eased his feet to the floor. Clinging to the IV stand for support, he stood. As the room swayed again—a slow dance this time—he felt cool air on his butt and realized that his shirt and jeans had been replaced by a light blue hospital gown with—check it out—full rear ventilation. MONROE COMMUNITY HOSPITAL ran in black along the hem.

Monroe again. Somehow he kept winding up in Monroe. Maybe he should move here.

Not a chance.

Didn't feature having his bare back end exposed to the world and hoped his own clothes were somewhere near, but first he had to check the hall.

With the IV stand as a rolling crutch, he shuffled to the door and peeked through the narrow gap on the hinged side. His heart sank at the sight of one of the local men in blue standing across the hall, talking to a nurse.

One cop. But what a cop. Size of a double-wide Kelvinator freezer. Badge on his chest looked like a refrigerator magnet. On a good day Jack might have been able to work something on him—maybe. But at the moment Barney Fife would have been a handful.

Only one other way out. Jack eased back and crossed the room toward the window. Legs were feeling a little steadier now but weakened again as he passed the mirror between the closets. The face reflected was a mess: fire-reddened skin, two black eyes under singed-off eyebrows, a swollen nose, and a wide bandage around his head. Lifted the gauze and winced at the sight of a four-inch row of sutures running up his right-front scalp. Worse, someone had clipped away the hair around the cut to give a clear field for the needlework.

The Frankenstein monster had looked better after his trip through the burning windmill.

Shook his head. A bad, bad day, and not getting any better.

Got worse when Jack reached the windows: he was in a third-story room overlooking the rear parking lot. And even worse news waiting when he checked the closets: empty, both of them. Maybe the cops had kept his clothes as evidence; more likely whoever had treated him had tossed them in the garbage. Either way . . .

Amid a sudden surge of anger Jack's fist cocked back to smash the closet door but he managed to hold it back. Barely.

What was this? Was he stupid? A noise like that would bring Officer Kelvinator running.

He realized he must still have a little Berzerk perking through his nervous system. The fluid from the IV probably had diluted it some, but he'd better be careful.

And as for the IV, that had to go. He undid the tape, pulled the needle from the vein, then slapped the tape back over the hole.

Back to the windows: a pair of old-fashioned double-hung storm types with the glass up and the screen down to let in the spring air. The weather had changed while he was out cold. The once bright skies were lidded now with gray, heavy-bellied clouds. Pulled up the screen and stuck his head through. A few feet down, a small ledge, half a brick wide, ran along the wall at floor level. The corner of the building was to his left; another set of windows sat six feet to the right.

Jack knew with sad sick certainty that those windows were his only option. What if he fell trying to reach them? What if the screen was locked when he got there? What if the room was occupied?

None of the what-ifs mattered, given the alternative. Could not allow himself to be arrested, booked, arraigned, whatever. Once that happened, life as he knew it would end. They'd do a background check and learn that he didn't have a background, did not even exist according to their records. And then the feds would get involved, wanting to know if he was a spy, and if not, then the IRS would want to know why he'd never filed a 1040, and on and on, smothering him. He'd never extricate himself.

Reaching that window was his only option, and if he didn't start moving now, he'd have zip options. Because as soon as Big Blue's nurse friend got called away, he'd be peeking in to see if his charge was conscious yet.

Jack suppressed a groan—part hip pain, part reluctance—as he swung his left leg through the opening. Slowly, gingerly, he straddled the sill until his foot found the brick ledge. The outer edge of his sole overlapped the ledge's three-inch width. He could have done with another inch but was glad for any ledge at all. Ducked his head through, biting back a cry as pain lanced along his ribs, then eased the rest of himself through.

Soon as he was outside, he pulled down the screen, which left him only the window frame to cling to. The next pair of windows was a mere half-dozen feet away, but it looked like the distance to the moon.

Arms spread, palms, chest, belly, and the right side of his face flush against the bricks, he began to move. Out of the corner of his eye he saw something white moving in the parking lot—an elderly woman with a cane limping toward the hospital from her car. Just then a gust flapped his hospital gown up around his shoulders.

Please don't look up, lady. Might make your day, but it'll ruin mine.

He edged along, left foot first, right foot following, inches at a time, and doing pretty well until he felt the building tip to his left. Knew it wasn't, couldn't be tipping, and hammered back the reflex to shift his weight to correct for it, a shift that would surely send him into free fall. Instead he pressed himself against the wall, creating a brick-and-mortar relief map on his right cheek; breath whistled between his clenched teeth as he dug his fingertips into the mortared grooves and hung on like a spider on the roof of a runaway train.

Finally the building steadied itself. He waited a few seconds to be sure, then moved on. Despite the breeze, he was bathed in sweat. When his leading hand finally touched the neighboring window frame, he resisted a sigh of relief; knew it was premature. Too many what-ifs still remained.

A few more inches and his fingers found the screen. No lip to grasp so he jabbed his finger through the mesh and pulled up. It moved. Great. And better still, no cries of alarm from inside. He'd lucked out—nobody home.

He slid the screen up and eased himself inside. Leaning on the sill, waiting for his racing heart to slow, he heard the snoring. He turned, slowly. The room was a mirror image of his, the near bed empty. The sound came from beyond the pulled privacy curtain. Jack padded to its edge and peeked around.

A heavy, balding, middle-aged man lay in the bed, IVs running into each arm, oxygen flowing into the right nostril, a clear tube snaking out the left into a collection bottle, wires running from his chest to a heart monitor, stained bandages across his abdomen. Looked like he'd just come from surgery.

Not good. Didn't know much about hospitals but figured they kept a close eye on postop patients, which meant a nurse could pop in any second.

Turned and opened the closets. Yes! Clothes. So to speak. Faded yellow-and-green checked pants, canvas slip-on boat shoes. ISLANDERS ran across the back of the satin jacket and NASCAR across the front of the cap, but Jack felt like he'd struck gold.

Everything but the hat was too big on him but he didn't care. Soon

as he had the cap snugged over his bandage, he peeked into the hall.
Big Blue was still yakking with the nurse, so Jack stepped out of the
room and strolled the opposite way.

Kept the brim low and his head down, looking up only to check
for exit signs. His heart was pounding again, his nervous system taut
as he waited for bells to start ringing and security men to come running
through the halls. But all remained quiet. Took the stairs instead of
the elevator, hurried through the lobby to the front entrance and into
the air.

Free. For the moment at least.

The wind was picking up and the clouds looked lower and heavier
than before. Rain coming. Wanted to get as far as possible from the
hospital so he started walking. Couldn't move too fast, though. Every
step sent a stab of pain down his left leg; something was using his brain
for an anvil and his scorched face tingled in the breeze.

Other than that, I feel just great.

But where was he? He'd been through Monroe a couple of times
last month but didn't recognize this stretch of road. All these post–
World War Two residential neighborhoods with their ranches and Cape
Cods and neat little lawns tended to look pretty much the same. Then
he spotted an arrow-shaped sign for BUSINESS DISTRICT and followed
that. He'd stand out less in a crowd.

Along the way he searched the pockets of the Islanders jacket and
found the hospital admission papers with the owner's name—Peter Harris—along with a few coins and two twenties.

Thank you, Peter Harris. I get out of this, I'll pay you back with
interest.

Downtown wasn't exactly chock-full of pay phones—maybe they
didn't blend with the old whaling port motif—but he found one in front
of a seafood restaurant and made a collect call to Abe.

"Abe, I need a ride."

"A ride to where?"

"Home."

"You can't take a cab?"

"I'm in a bit of a jam."

Abe sighed. "And where is this jam that you happen to be in?"

"Monroe. In front of a restaurant called"—he checked the sign—
"Memison's. When can you get here?"

"Oy. Monroe. You couldn't be someplace closer? OK. I'll pick you up in front of this Memison's, but don't figure on less than an hour and a half."

"Thanks, Abe. And listen—call Gia and tell her I'm all right. I'd call her myself but I don't want to hang in the open on this phone much longer. Tell her somebody dosed me with the same stuff that made the preppies crazy but I got through it OK."

"On the run and stranded in Monroe . . . this is OK?"

"Just tell her, Abe."

Jack hung up and looked around. An hour and a half to kill. The clock on the bank said twelve-thirty. Damn. He'd been out for hours, and by now the cops had to know he was missing. They'd concentrate on the hospital first, but when they were satisfied that he wasn't hiding there, they'd start sweeping the town. Where could he go for an hour where he wouldn't be noticed?

And then he knew.

8

The phone was ringing. Nadia didn't budge. It wasn't her cell phone—that was the only number she'd given the police—so she didn't care who was on the house phone.

She sat in her mother's front room, wiping her eyes. She'd found the little Quisp ring Doug had given her the other night. For an instant she saw him sitting at his computer in his boxer shorts, being so sweet, sexy, and silly at the same time, and she burst into tears.

Forcing herself to move, she rose and stepped to the window and watched the preschool children playing in St. Vartan's Park across the street. She felt lost, sapped of energy. Uncertainty about what to do or who to turn to had gnawed at her, leaving her all but paralyzed.

Doug, where are you? What happened?

"Nadjie!" her mother called from the kitchen. She sounded almost hysterical. "Praise God! My prayers have been answered. It is Douglas!"

Nadia scrambled out of the chair and almost tripped in her mad dash to the kitchen where she snatched the receiver from her mother's hand.

"Doug?"

"Nadia! How I've missed you!"

She burst into tears at the sound of his voice. It was him; oh sweet God it was him.

"Oh, Doug! Doug, where have you been? I've been worried sick about you!"

"I'm so sorry about that but this is the first chance I've had to call. I'm in trouble."

"What kind of trouble?"

"I can't go into that now. Let's just say I shouldn't show my face for another week or so."

"Oh, God! This is crazy!"

"I know it is. Look, can you help me out with a little cash? I don't dare use my ATM."

"Of course."

"Great. Can you draw out a thousand and meet me?"

"I don't think I have that much."

"Whatever you can spare."

"OK. Where do I find you?"

"I'm hiding out near a little town called Monroe. You know it?"

"Near Glen Cove."

"Right. Come there and wait near the pay phone in front of Memison's restaurant right on the main drag. I'll call you on that phone at two and tell you where to meet me."

"Doug, this sounds like something out of a bad spy movie."

"I know, and I'm sorry. But I don't have anyone else to turn to. Please, Nadia. Hang in with me on this one and I'll explain everything once we're face-to-face."

Face-to-face . . . God, she wanted that. More than anything in the world. She wanted to see Doug, touch him, make sure he was all right.

She glanced at the clock. Go to the bank, rent a car, drive out to Long Island . . . she'd have to get moving if she was going to make it by two.

"OK. I'm on my way."

"Thank you; thank you! I love you. And you won't regret this, I promise you."

She double-checked the name of the restaurant, then hung up and hugged her mother.

"He's all right! I'm going to meet him!"

"Where is he? Why can't he come here?"

"I'll explain everything later, Ma. The main thing is he's all right! That's all that matters!"

"Call me when you meet him," her mother said. "Just to let me know that *you* are all right."

"Sure! Soon as I give him a big fat kiss!"

She felt almost giddy with joy and relief as she ran to find her pocketbook.

9

The rain came in tropical style. One minute it was simply threatening; the next Jack was treading through a waterfall. Tried to run the remaining quarter-mile to the entrance but his banged-up legs and bruised ribs allowed for a trot at best. Arrived soaked and mud-splattered and in a foul mood. At least the main tent was still up, although the front flap was down and no one was selling tickets. Place looked pretty much deserted.

Jack slipped through the flap. The stale air trapped under the leaking canvas was redolent of wet hay and strange sweat. His feet squished within his wet deck shoes as he made his way toward Scar-lip's cage but stopped short, stopped stone-cold dead when he saw what was behind the bars.

Scar-lip, all right, but the creature he'd seen thirty-six hours ago had been only the palest reflection of this monster. The rakosh rearing up in the cage and rattling the bars now was full of vitality and ferocity, had unmarred, glistening blue-black skin, and bright yellow eyes that glowed with a fierce inner light.

Jack stood mute and numb on the fringe, thinking, This is a nightmare, one that keeps repeating itself.

The once moribund rakosh was now fiercely alive, and it wanted *out*.

Suddenly it froze and Jack saw that it was looking his way. Its cold yellow basilisk glare fixed on him. He felt like a deer in the headlights of an 18-wheeler.

He turned and hurried from the tent. Outside in the rain he looked around and found the trailer Monnet had entered the other night. Its canvas awning was bellied with rain. A plate under the OFFICE sign on the door read : "Ozymandias Prather." Jack knocked.

He stepped back as the door swung out. Prather stood staring down at Jack.

"Who are you?"

"And hello to you too. I was here the other night. I'm the 'Hey, Rube' guy."

"Ah, yes. The defender of rakoshi. Jack, isn't it? I barely recognize you. You appear to be a bit worse for wear since last we met."

"Never mind that. I want to talk to you about that rakosh."

Oz backed up a step or two. "Come in, come in."

Jack stepped up and inside, just far enough to get out from under the dripping awning. The rain paradiddled on the metal roof, and Jack knew he had about five minutes before the sound made him crazy.

"Have you seen it?" Oz's voice seemed to come from everywhere in the room. "Isn't it magnificent?"

"What did you do to it?"

Oz stared at him, as if genuinely puzzled. "Why, my good man, now that I know what it is, I know how to treat it. I looked up the proper care and feeding of rakoshi in one of my books on Bengali mythology and acted appropriately."

Jack felt a chill. And it was not from his soaked clothing.

"What . . . just *what* did you feed it?"

The boss's large brown eyes looked guileless, and utterly remorseless. "Oh, this and that. Whatever the text recommended. You don't really believe for an instant that I was going to allow that magnificent creature to languish and die of malnutrition, do you? I assume you're familiar with—"

"I *know* what a rakosh needs to live."

"Do you now? Do you know everything about rakoshi?"

"No, of course not, but—"

"Then let us assume that I know more than you. Perhaps there is more than one way to keep them healthy. I see no need to discuss this with you or anyone else. Let us just say that it got exactly what it needed." His smile was scary. "And that it enjoyed the meal immensely."

Jack knew a rakosh ate only one thing. The question was: who? He knew Prather would never tell him so he didn't waste breath asking.

Instead he said, "Do you have any idea what you're playing with here? Do you know what's going to happen to your little troupe when that thing gets loose? I've seen this one in action, and trust me, pal, it will tear you all to pieces."

"I assume you know that iron weakens it. The bars of its cage are iron; the roof, floor, and sides are lined with steel. It will not escape."

"Famous last words. So I take it there's no way I can convince you to douse it with kerosene and strike a match."

"Unthinkable."

Jack flashed on something a couple of the troupe members had said the other night.

"Why? Because it's a 'brother'?"

Oz didn't flinch from the term. "In a manner of speaking."

Jack leaned back against the door frame. This was beginning to make some sense, but not much.

"This is all related to the Otherness, isn't it."

That got a reaction. Oz did a long, slow owl blink and sat down. He motioned Jack toward the room's other chair but Jack shook his head.

"What do you know about the Otherness?"

"I've had a couple of people lecture me on it."

The Otherness . . . a force, another reality, inimical, implacable, impinging on this world, hungering for it. It had spawned the rakoshi and had almost killed him—twice. Still he didn't quite understand it, but he believed. After what he'd seen since last summer, he had no choice.

"And I've been up close and personal with a few rakoshi." He gestured through the door, toward the tents. "Your cast of characters out there—they're all . . ."

"Children of the Otherness? Not all. Some are merely accidents, victims of genetics or development gone awry, but we do feel a certain kinship with them as well."

"And you?"

Oz only nodded, and Jack wondered how the Otherness had marked him.

He took a gamble and said, "How did Dr. Monnet learn about the rakosh?"

"He received a call that—" Oz broke off and exhibited his crooked yellow teeth in a sour smile. "Very clever."

Jack pressed. "A call. Maybe from the same person who tipped you off about where to find the rakosh?"

"Perhaps yes, perhaps no."

Jack was pretty sure it was perhaps yes. Which gave everything that was going on a shape, the semblance of a plan: save the rakosh; cull a drug from its blood; spread that drug everywhere to cause a slow tsunami of violence and chaos.

And chaos was a bosom buddy of the Otherness.

"Does Monnet know about the turnaround in the rakosh's health?"

Oz shook his head. "Not yet. He finds its blood . . . interesting. He's terribly distraught over the fact that he's losing the source of that blood." He smiled. "Somehow I just haven't got around to telling him yet."

Leave him twisting in the wind, Jack thought. Serves him right.

"You seem to be remarkably well informed about this," Oz said. "But I don't sense that you are one of us. How does an outsider come to be so involved?"

"Not by choice, I can tell you that. Just seems that everywhere I turn lately I keep bumping into this Otherness business."

"Does that mean that you were here in Monroe last month when something . . . something *wonderful* almost happened?"

"Don't know about you, but I don't call a house disappearing 'wonderful.' And it didn't 'almost' happen—it's completely gone."

"I was not referring to the house but to what took it."

"Yeah, well, you might have a different opinion about that if you were there." Jack studied Oz's bright eyes. "Then again, maybe you wouldn't. But we're straying from the main subject here. It's got to go."

The boss's face darkened as he rose from his chair.

"I advise you to put that idea out of your head, or you may wind up sharing the cage with the creature." He stepped closer to Jack and edged him outside. "You have been warned. Good day, sir."

He reached a long arm past Jack and pulled the door closed.

Jack stood outside a moment, realizing that a worst-case scenario had come true. A healthy Scar-lip . . . he couldn't let that go on. He still had the can of gasoline in the trunk of his car. As soon as he was back in Manhattan he'd return to Plan A. And if he had to take the whole tent down to get it done, then that was how it would go.

As he turned, he found someone standing behind him. His nose was fat and discolored; dark crescents had formed under each eye. The rain, a drizzle now, had darkened his sandy hair, plastering it to his scalp. He stared at Jack, his face a mask of rage.

"You're that guy, the one who got Bondy and me in trouble!"

Now Jack recognized him: the roustabout from Sunday night. Hank. His breath reeked of cheap wine. He clutched a bottle in a paper bag. Probably Mad Dog.

"You look like shit, man!" he told Jack with a nasty grin.

"You don't look so hot yourself."

"It's all your fault!" Hank said.

"You're absolutely right," Jack said and began walking back in the direction of town to meet Abe. He had no time for this dolt.

"Bondy was my only friend! He got fired because of you."

A little bell went *ting-a-ling*. Jack stopped, turned.

"Yeah? When did you see him last?"

"The other night—when you got him in trouble."

The bell was ringing louder.

"And you never saw him once after that? Not even to say good-bye?"

Hank shook his head. "Uh-uh. Boss kicked him right out. By sun up he'd blown the show with all his stuff."

Jack remembered the rage in Oz's eyes that night when he'd looked from the wounded rakosh to Bondy. Now Jack was pretty sure that the ringing in his head was a dinner bell.

"He was the only one around here who liked me," Hank said, his expression miserable. "Bondy talked to me. All the freaks and geeks keep to theirselves."

Jack sighed as he stared at Hank. Well, at least now he had an idea as to who had supplemented Scar-lip's diet.

No big loss to civilization.

"You don't need friends like that, kid," he said and turned away again.

"You'll pay for it!" Hank screamed into the rain. "Bondy'll be back and when he gets here we'll get even. I got my pay docked because of you and that damn Sharkman! You think you look bad now, you just wait till Bondy gets back!"

Pardon me if I don't hold my breath.

Jack wondered if it would do any good to tell him that Bondy hadn't been fired—that, in a way, he was still very much with the freak show. But that would only endanger the big dumb kid.

Hank ranted on. "And if he don't come back, I'll getcha myself. And that Sharkman too!"

No you won't. Because I'm going to get it first.

Jack kept walking, moving as fast as he could back to town. When he reached Memison's he saw no sign of Abe's truck so he stepped inside.

"We're closed for lunch and we don't start serving dinner till five," said someone who looked like a maître d'.

"Just want to check the menu."

Taking in the sodden, ill-fitting clothes and muddy shoes, he gave Jack a please-don't-even-think-about-eating-here look as he handed him the laminated card.

Jack kept one eye on the street while he pretended to read about Memison's "Famous Fish Dinners." He saw a black-and-white unit roll by, the cop inside eyeballing everyone on the sidewalk. About ten minutes later Abe's battered panel truck of indeterminate hue pulled into the curb.

"Maybe some other time," Jack said to maître d' and handed back the menu.

The relief on the man's face said that Jack had made his day. Always nice to bring joy into someone's life.

Outside, Jack darted across the sidewalk and into Abe's truck.

"Gevalt!" Abe said when he saw him. "Look at you! What happened?"

"Long story." Jack slumped in the seat and pulled the cap low over his eyes, pretending to be asleep. Jeez, it felt good to sit. "Tell you on the way. Right now just get me the hell outta this place."

For the first time since coming to in the hospital he was reasonably sure he wouldn't be spending the next thirty or forty years in jail, and for the first time since that cup of coffee this morning he could sit and think. His thoughts were a mess. Aftereffects of the Berzerk maybe. His mind seemed to be lurching in all directions, emotions a roiling cauldron.

What had happened this morning?

He vaguely remembered racking up three cars, killing two men, but none of that bothered him. The events were dancing shadows in his brain. What he did remember, what kept looping in clear wide-screen surroundsound detail, was how close he'd come to slapping Vicky, how he'd wanted to punch Gia.

And that . . . that was unbearable . . . knowing he'd been *this* far from hurting them. . . .

Without the slightest inkling it was going to happen, he burst into tears.

"Jack!" Abe cried, swerving as he drove. "What's wrong?"

"I'm all right," he said, reining in his penduluming emotions. "It's this damn drug . . . It's still screwing with me. Did you call Gia?"

"Of course. A happy woman she's not."

"Where's your phone?"

Abe fished a StarTac out of his shirt pocket and handed it over. Before dialing, Jack funneled his thoughts ahead, forced his mind toward where to go from here.

First thing to do when he got back to the city was call Nadia and tell her to be careful what she ate or drank. Someone—Monnet most likely—was trying to drug her. Next he'd return here to take care of Scar-lip. After that, he'd have to make up for his behavior this morning with Gia and Vicky.

With that in mind, Jack punched Gia's number into Abe's phone. "Hi, it's me," he said when she picked up.

He heard a long, tremulous sigh. "Jack . . . what's happening to you?"

"That wasn't me," he said quickly. "Someone drugged me."

He went on to explain about Nadia's coffee and what the drug did to people, finishing with, "Even you'd be dangerous with a snootful of that stuff."

"I don't know about that, Jack," she said dubiously. "I do know that I never dreamed I'd ever be afraid of you."

That cut. Deep. "You've got to understand, Gia, that wasn't me; that was the drug."

"But what about the next time you show up unexpectedly? How can I be sure someone hasn't slipped you another dose?"

"Never happen."

"You can't guarantee that."

"Yes, I can. Oh, yes, I can. Berzerk is going to be yesterday's news."

Add one more task to his to-do list: Take down GEM, and Monnet and Dragovic with it. Tonight.

Fresh rage percolated through him—not Berzerk-fueled, his own vintage, the dark stuff he kept bottled in his mental cellars. This morning he'd told Nadia that he didn't care about drugs, that they weren't his business. But this was no longer business. This was personal now.

10

Nadia was running late. She'd missed a turn and found herself heading toward Lattingtown instead of Monroe. But now she was in downtown Monroe—a whole five blocks, from what she could see—and it was almost two and she couldn't find a trace of this seafood restaurant anywhere.

Wait . . . there . . . an old pub-type hinged wooden sign hanging over the sidewalk with a fish on a plate . . . and the name: MEMISON'S. And there was the public phone, right in front as Doug had said. But not a parking place in sight.

Then she saw a man in baggy clothes and a soggy-looking cap leave the restaurant and jump into an old panel truck. The truck pulled away, leaving her the open spot right in front of the phone. Talk about great timing.

Nadia pulled her rented Taurus into the space and hopped out. No sooner had she reached the phone when it began to ring. She snatched up the receiver.

"Doug?"

"Nadia! You made it! I knew I could count on you."

Thank God it was him. She looked around. Was he nearby? She felt eyes on her. "Where are you?"

"About a mile and a half away. I'm hiding in a tent show out on the marshes."

"A what?"

"Don't worry. I'm not running off with the circus. You can be here in a few minutes."

She memorized his directions, then hurried back to her car and made a U-turn. She followed the waterfront—sailboats and sport fishers in the water, blue-plastic weatherproofed craft still in dry dock, waiting to be launched for the season. After a quarter-mile she turned left. The houses and shops vanished first, then the pavement: she found herself on a dirt road running through a marsh. To her left a small harbor lay still and gray like pocked steel under the overcast sky. A small ramshackle cabin sat dead ahead at the end of the marching line of roadside utility poles; and to her right, a small cluster of tents, just as Doug had described.

He'd told her to look for a small red trailer beyond the rear of what he'd called the backyard. She saw a few cars parked in a makeshift lot that she guessed could be called a front yard, but no people about.

Where was everybody? The whole area seemed so still and empty, as if holding its breath. Creepy. The idea of wandering about alone on foot did not at all appeal to her, so she drove around to the rear of the tent complex. There she found a battered old trailer whose once proud chrome skin was scarred, dented, and painted a dull red, sitting far behind the tents and the rest of the show vehicles.

Was this where Doug was hiding? She couldn't see anyplace else that matched the description. Her heart bled for him. What had driven him to these extremes?

She parked her car nose-on to the side of the trailer and noticed that all the windows were boarded over. The door hung open. She called out as she stepped out and approached the dark opening.

"Doug?"

"Nadia!" His voice echoed faintly from the dark interior. "I'm so glad you made it."

"Doug, where are you?"

"Right inside. Come on in."

She felt hackles rising. Something wasn't right here. On the phone his voice had sounded perfectly fine. But here, without the filtering effects of wires and microwave transmissions, it sounded different. It sounded wrong. And then she realized that he had called her Nadia instead of his usual Nadj.

"Why can't I see you, Doug?"

A pause, then, "I'm on the couch. I'd really love to meet you at the door but I'm . . . I've been injured."

Doug . . . hurt. . . .

Without thinking Nadia found herself dashing up the two rickety steps and fairly leaping through the door. She stopped inside, looking around, waiting for her eyes to adjust to the dim interior. The air was mildewy and close despite the open door. She heard a rattling, rustling movement to her left.

"Doug?"

"Right here, sweetie," said his voice to her right—and from below.

She jumped at the sound and turned to see what she thought at first was a child, but then she noticed the mustache and the slicked-down hair. He looked like a midget from a barbershop quartet.

He grinned. "See ya later!"

Nadia watched in mind-numbed shock as the little man darted out the door.

His voice . . . he'd spoken in Doug's voice.

She was just beginning to move, just going into a turn, when the trailer door slammed shut, plunging her into darkness.

"No!"

The cry was a strangled sound as fear took an instant icy grip on her throat, choking off her air. She threw herself against the door, hitting it with her shoulders, pounding on it, shouting.

"No! Please! Let me out! Help!"

But the door wouldn't budge. She battered it and screamed for help even though she knew the trailer was too far from anything and anyone to hear her cries, but she kept it up until her voice was raw. Then she stopped shouting but kept pounding against the door, fighting the sobs that pushed up from her chest.

She would not cry.

And then she heard that rattle and rustle again from the corner and her frenzied panic turned to cold, cringing dread.

Someone, some*thing* was in here with her.

The sounds became more frenzied, and through the thrashing she caught muffled growls and whines, and whistling breaths. Whatever it was it sounded furious, but at least it wasn't coming any closer. Maybe it was leashed in the corner. Maybe—

Cell phone! Yes! She could call for help! She reached for her bag and then realized with a groan it was in the car. Now she truly wanted to cry.

More thrashing from the corner.

God, if she could only see! Slivers of daylight seeping through the boarded-up windows provided the only illumination, and what little there was only made matters worse as her eyes adjusted. Whatever was thrashing in the corner looked *big*.

Nadia felt around her and found a counter and a sink. She must be in the kitchen area. She found drawers and pulled them open, searching for a weapon or even a flashlight, but all she found were food crumbs and dust.

She turned and felt around behind her. A table and—thank you, God!—a candle, maybe three inches long, in some sort of glass holder. She ran her fingers across the tabletop and knocked something to the floor. Bending she patted around and came up with a plastic cylinder. A lighter.

Her initial joy quickly faded when she realized that light would reveal what they'd locked her up with. But as she listened to the hissing, whining, thrashing thing at the other end of the trailer she knew she had no choice. Not knowing was worse.

She flicked the wheel and held the flame before her. It revealed nothing, but all noise except for the hissing breaths ceased.

Was it afraid? Afraid of fire?

The silence was almost worse than the noise. She didn't know how much butane she had left, so she lit the candle. Then, holding it at arm's length before her, she edged toward the far end of the trailer, moving inches at a time.

And slowly on the right she began to make out a shape . . . and it was human-shaped rather than animal, stretched out on some sort of bed . . . and as she moved closer she saw that it was a man and he was bound hand and foot, spread-eagle on the bed . . . and she saw a mouth sealed with silver duct tape, and above the tape wide blue eyes glistening in the light. . . . She knew those eyes and the sandy hair falling over the forehead.

"Doug!"

The candle slipped from her fingers but she caught it again, barely noticing the splash of hot wax across her wrist as she leaped to his side. She was sobbing as she peeled the tape from his mouth.

"Oh, Nadj, I'm so sorry!" he half gasped, half sobbed. "I had no idea!"

She kissed him. "Doug, what happened? Why are we here?"

"I don't know," he said as she began to work on the knot on his right wrist. "I never got to see whoever snatched me."

"They stole your laptop and smashed your computer."

"Then it's got to be GEM."

"I think you're right."

Admitting that was a spike through her heart.

"I should have left their goddamn computer alone. But why you?"

Nadia had loosened the binding enough by then for him to wriggle his hand free. As he went to work on his left wrist and she tackled his right foot, Nadia told Doug about Loki-Berzerk and her suspicions.

When he was free he gathered her into his arms and she sobbed with relief and terror against his chest. His face was stubbled, his clothes wrinkled and smelly, but he was Doug and he was alive and holding her.

"I had no idea what they were planning when the little guy was talking to me," he said.

"The one who imitated your voice? He . . . he was uncanny."

"He came in with this big dog-faced guy and started talking to me, asking me if I needed anything and did I know why I'd been brought here. He didn't give me any answers, just kept asking questions. Now I know he was studying my voice."

Nadia studied his face in the flickering light. "Did they . . . have they hurt you?"

"Not a bit. They bring me food—plenty of it—and water." He jerked a thumb over his shoulder. "There's even a bathroom. Except for tying me up an hour ago, they've treated me pretty decently."

Nadia looked around, not seeing much. "And there's no way out?"

"None. Believe me, I've tried."

She stared at the candle flame. "What if we started a fire?"

"Thought of it, but who's going to send a fire alarm? These folks could probably put it out before anyone noticed, and even if fire trucks did show up, we'd probably be dead from the smoke before they got us out.

"OK," Nadia said. "No fire. Let's stay alive."

"That's what's got me. If what we know is so dangerous, why didn't they simply kill us?"

"If they haven't yet, they probably don't intend to. I can't think of any other reason to keep us safe and dry and well fed, can you?"

He shook his head.

Heartened by the simple logic of her reasoning, Nadia wrapped her arms around Doug and clung to him.

11

Milos Dragovic sat in the rear of his Bentley in sullen silence. The car glided uptown on Park Avenue, a black cocoon of steel-girded stillness amid the midtown cacophony. Pera, his driver, didn't speak—didn't dare. No music and certainly no news. Milos had heard enough news for the day.

Vuk and Ivo dead . . . he still could not believe it. How was such a thing possible?

He had seen it on the midday news—the burnt-out, bullet-riddled

husk of his car, the two bagged bodies being wheeled away on stretch-
ers, and still he could not accept it. And even less the story that it was
a lone assailant.

Witnesses said they had seen one man fleeing in a stolen taxi, but
Milos knew this could not be the work of a single man. The news was
calling the incident drug-related. It was not. These were the same people who had attacked him in the Hamptons. Now they'd moved to the
city. This had been an ambush, a well-planned execution carried out
with the precision of a military operation.

And that disturbed him the most. To ambush Vuk and Ivo like that,
someone had to know they were coming. But Milos himself hadn't
known where they were going until moments before he had sent them.
This left only two possibilities: either his office was bugged or he had
an informer in his organization.

The realization had chilled Milos's rage. If it was an informer, who?
He looked at the back of his driver's head. Pera, perhaps? No, anyone
but him. Pera had been with him since the gunrunning days. Pera would
never.

A bug then? He sighed. Either was possible. After all, Milos had
his own sources within rival organizations, even within the NYPD. None
of them seemed worth a damn at the moment. His rivals were laughing
at him and playing copies of the TV tape nonstop in their bars, but no
one, either publicly or privately, was taking credit.

The police were worthless, searching for this so-called lone assailant. They had no good description other than medium height, average
build, and brown hair, although some witnesses were disputing the hair
color. They couldn't agree on his facial features either except that he'd
been scorched by the flames from the burning car—Milos's car.

The police said he'd hijacked a taxi. That taxi was found abandoned
in Queens where he'd apparently hijacked a Mercedes. NYPD later
learned that while an all-points had been out on the Mercedes, the man
they sought was lying unconscious in a North Shore hospital. The local
police had considered him nothing more than a drunk driver. By the
time they realized that they held a suspect in a far more serious crime,
the man had vanished.

Milos wanted to scream: Not one man! He was a decoy, a set up
to make it look like one man could take out two of mine! It's all a plot,
a conspiracy to ruin me!

But he would be shouting at the deaf. The only ones listening were on the other end of the bugs in his offices, maybe even here in his personal car.

The thought made him hunger for fresh air.

"Pull over," he told Pera.

He got out at the corner of East Eighty-fifth. He saw Pera looking nervously about. He was spooked. Vuk and Ivo this morning . . . who would be next?

"Wait here," he said, and began to walk east.

He had decided to take the matter into his own hands. If he could not trust his men, his phones, his offices, his cars, that left him with one resource: himself. He would track down his tormentors and personally dispose of them. It was the only means left to him to salvage his honor.

But he possessed only one hard fact about his enemy: the first call from the so-called East Hampton Environmental Protection Committee had come from a phone on the corner of East Eighty-seventh Street and Third Avenue. That was it. The rest—the man in the car in the security video, for instance—was all speculation.

He reached Third Avenue and turned uptown. Two blocks later he was standing before the phone. He would deal soon, very soon, with the man in the video, and perhaps with his woman and child if need be. But Milos needed to do this first. He needed to be in this place, to stand where his enemy had stood and pushed these numbered buttons to dial his number and taunt him.

Why here? he wondered, turning in a slow circle. Why did you choose this particular—?

He stopped when he saw the high-rise co-op. He knew that building. Last fall he'd had one of his men look up the address. He'd barely glanced at the numbers before handing the slip to Pera and saying, "Drive by this address."

But the building was unforgettable . . . Dr. Luc Monnet's building.

Milos whirled and slammed his hand against the phone booth's shield, frightening an old woman passing by. He turned away before she could recognize him, and cursed himself for not being more attentive, for letting underlings do too much. If he'd been paying attention last fall he would have connected the location of the phone with Monnet last Friday. He could have brought all this to a halt that very night.

And then there would have been no second rain of filthy oil, no helicopter debacle, and no humiliating videotape playing and replaying nationwide today.

He calmed himself. That was in the past. That was done. He could not change it. But he could avenge himself.

Because it was all so clear now.

Monnet and his partners wanted him locked up and out of the way, leaving them a clear field to tie up all the Loki trade for themselves.

Fair enough. If Milos could have figured a way to produce the drug on his own, he would have cut them out long ago. That was business.

But to humiliate him so publicly. This went beyond business.

And all Monnet's idea, he was sure.

He ground his teeth. Monnet . . . Milos never would have guessed that prissy, pissy little frog had the turn of mind to conceive such a scheme, let alone the guts to execute it. But here was the evidence, staring him squarely in the face.

Motive and opportunity—Monnet had both.

Listen to me. I sound like a fucking cop.

But it was true. Same for Monnet's brother worms, Garrison and Edwards.

Time to turn the tables. Time to square accounts and balance the scales. Only blood would settle this.

Unfortunately that would mean a shutdown of the Loki pipeline— a slaughtering of the goose that laid the golden egg. Bad business. But his honor demanded this. He could put no price on it.

Besides, he had his millions stashed in the Caymans and Switzerland. Once he settled accounts he would disappear for a while, go abroad for a year or two. This city, this country had now been tainted for him by Monnet and his partners.

Milos began walking back the way he had come. So forget about the man in the security video now. Why waste time with him when he would only lead Milos back here, to the GEM Pharma partners.

The partners . . . Milos would have to think of a way to settle with all three. And since he no longer could trust anyone, he would have to do it alone.

He walked on, planning. . . .

12

"So, you're a hit man now?" Abe said, sliding the package across the counter.

Jack began peeling the masking tape from the tan butcher paper.

Once he'd pulled himself together on the ride back from Monroe, Jack had told Abe what had happened and what he needed. Abe had dropped him off at his apartment where he'd cleaned up as best he could. He'd put the muddied borrowed clothes aside; he'd return them to Peter Harris with a hundred-dollar bill when they came back from the cleaners.

Then he'd called Gia to explain things. He should have gone over in person but he didn't want Vicky frightened by seeing him scarred, battered, bruised, and burned.

Gia was not a happy camper. Once again Jack's line of work had put her and Vicky in harm's way.

No argument there.

When was it going to stop?

Good question. One he couldn't answer, one he could put off answering a little longer.

He hadn't brought it up, but they both knew that Vicky was alive now only as a direct result of Jack's line of work. Had he been a workaday member of straight society, she would not have survived last summer. He could still draw on that account, but he knew it was not bottomless.

The conversation had ended on a tense note.

Jack put those troubles aside for now. To take Gia and Vicky out of harm's way, a harm named Dragovic, he had to focus on the matter at hand. He unfolded the butcher paper, exposing the pistol.

"Looks a little like a Walther P-38."

Abe snorted. "If you should have very bad eyes and left your glasses at home, maybe a little. It's an AA P-98, .22 long rifle."

Jack hefted it, gauging its weight at about a pound and a half. Checked out the barrel: the front sight had been ground off and the last three-eighths of an inch were threaded. Then he picked up the three-inch-long black metal cylinder that Abe had wrapped with the pistol.

"Awfully small for a silencer. Will this work?"

"First off, a silencer it's not. It's a suppressor. You can't silence a pistol; you can only make it maybe less noisy. And will it work? Yes, it will work. It's a Gemtech Aurora. It uses the latest wet technology that will knock twenty-four decibels off your shots for up to two clips. After that it won't be so good."

"I figure I'm only going to need a couple, three rounds."

"Pretty much takes care of the muzzle flash as well."

Jack shrugged. "This'll be daylight."

"And here's what you should load." Abe plunked a box of .22 LRs on the counter. "Subsonic, of course."

"Of course."

No sense in using a silencer—OK, suppressor—if the bullet was going to cause a racket along its trajectory, a teeny tiny Concorde doing Mach Two and cracking the sound barrier all the way.

Jack noticed the FMJ on the box. "Full jacket?"

"Hollows or soft-points could be deflected going through the wipes inside the suppressor."

Jack grimaced. "Don't want that. And speaking of wipes, can I borrow your gloves a minute?"

Abe reached under the counter and produced a pair of cotton gloves, originally white, now gray with grime and gun oil. Jack slipped them on.

Abe was staring at him. "Those rounds have maybe someone's name on them?"

Jack said nothing. He poured out a dozen rounds and wiped them with the gloves. Then he began loading them into the P-98's clip. He routinely and obsessively collected his spent brass, but in certain situations it simply wasn't possible. In such a case, he didn't want to leave any fingerprints behind.

"Jack," Abe said softly. "You're mad at some people, I know, and with good reason. And you've got that look in your eyes that means big *tsuris* for somebody, but is this the way you want to go? This isn't you."

Jack glanced up at Abe, saw the concern in his face. "Not to worry, Abe. The target is cardboard."

"Ah. Now it's all clear," Abe said. "Especially the need for a suppressor. You're going to shoot a box and you don't want to startle its fellows. That's my Jack: always considerate. And where is this cardboard?"

"Brooklyn."

The last place Jack wanted to go tonight was Brooklyn. He had a throbbing headache, his scorched skin itched and burned, and the healing scalp cut stabbed periodic zingers down to his left eye. Add to that the general lousy feeling the drug had left in its wake, and the only place he wanted to go was bed. But he needed to settle this. Tonight.

He wiped the clip and slid it into the grip; it seated with a solid click. The last item in the package was a new SOB holster. He removed the suppressor, wiped and pocketed it, wiped the pistol, then slipped it into the holster, and the holster within the waistband at the small of his back. He let the rear of the extra-large turtleneck jersey fall back over it.

"Since when do you wear turtlenecks?" Abe said.

"Since an hour ago." The long sleeves and high collar covered his burns. And he might have another use for the rolled collar. "Check this out."

He pulled—gently—a floppy khaki boonie hat down low on his head, then slipped on oversize aviator glasses.

"How do I look?"

"Like a *Soldier of Fortune* subscriber. But it does cover a multitude of sins."

Jack had checked himself out at home. The getup hid his stitches and his black eyes. Didn't know if a police sketch of him was making the rounds after this morning's escapades or if the cops had issued a BOLO for a man with a scalp laceration and a scorched, banged-up face.

Jack headed for the door. "Breakfast tomorrow. I'm buying. What do you want?"

"Eggs Benedict, but with foie gras instead of ham."

"You got it."

"'You got it,' he says," Jack heard Abe snort behind him. "A fat-free bagel with tofu spread I'll get."

Jack stopped at a pay phone and dialed Nadia's cell phone for the third time since he'd been back. Still no answer, so he tried her home number. A woman with a thick Polish accent answered. Nadia wasn't home, she said. Jack picked up something in her voice.

"Is anything wrong, Mrs. Radzminsky?"

"No. Nothing wrong. Who is this?"

"My name is Jack. I . . ." He took a blind stab here. "I was helping her look for Douglas Gleason."

"Doug has been found. He call this afternoon."

Well, at least there was *some* good news today. "Did he say what happened to him?"

"My Nadjie go meet him, but she never call. She say she will call, and she always calls, but today she didn't call."

"I'm sure they're just so glad to see each other that she forgot."

"My Nadjie always call."

"I'm sure she'll check in soon."

But as he hung up Jack knew he wasn't at all sure. He'd never met this Doug but couldn't imagine a guy looking to develop his own software would smash his computer and then go out for a two-day stroll. According to Nadia, both she and Gleason knew damaging details about GEM. And now no one knew where either of them were.

Maybe he'd find out before the night was through.

13

Jack was on the leading edge of rush-hour traffic so he and the Buick made decent time over to the GEM plant in the Marine Terminal area. Found a parking spot a few blocks away and wandered back to the GEM loading dock. A ten-foot Cyclone fence topped with razor wire separated him from the action where two-hundred-pound barrels stamped with GEM PHARMA and TRICEF rode a conveyer belt into the rear of an 18-wheel semi. Heat-packing uniformed security guards patrolled the area.

Obviously a very valuable antibiotic.

Jack wished it were five hours from now with the sun down and night well settled in, but Nadia's disappearance was urgently bumping him from behind. Daylight did have certain advantages, though.

Jack returned to his car, pulled the P-98 from its holster, and fitted the silencer to the barrel. Drove back to GEM and double-parked by the loading area. A quick glance around showed nobody on the sidewalks. He chambered a round, raised the window to the height he wanted, rested the pistol on it—with the front sight gone he needed all the aiming help he could get. Took a bead on the leading edge of a cardboard barrel just starting its conveyor ride, made sure no one was standing behind it, pulled the trigger.

The *phut* sounded loud in the car, but he knew it had been swallowed by the ambient street noise. Saw the target canister wobble on the belt. Bull's-eye. Lowered the pistol and raised a pair of compact binoculars. Powder trickled from a tiny hole beneath the G in GEM. Blue powder. Berzerk blue.

To kill some time Jack drove around the area, wending his way through blocks of warehouses, under the BQE and back again, down to the rows of old docks. Couldn't see Manhattan from here—Red Hook got in the way—but had a nice view of Lady Liberty. The sight of her, standing tall and green out there holding her torch over the water, never failed to tweak some deep-buried part of him.

When he passed the factory again, the conveyor belt had been moved away and a guy who looked like the driver was closing and locking the rear doors. He and one of the security guards climbed into the cab. Another uniform opened the gate, and they were rolling.

Didn't matter what their final destination, they had to reach the expressway first. Jack got a head start, then pulled over next to a fire hydrant on the right. Leaned his elbow out the window to hide the pistol . . .

And had second thoughts.

This was so crude, not at all up to his standards. What he should do is follow a couple of trucks to their destinations, see where and how they off-loaded their cargo, then figure a way to get his hands on a load of Berzerk without anyone being the wiser. Do it with style.

Fuck style, he thought as the rig rumbled by. He pumped two quick rounds into the sidewall of the tractor's right front tire. No time for style this trip. Barely had time for crude, direct, and effective.

Like a massive beast that doesn't know when it's been wounded, the truck kept rolling, but its front tires were the only set not doubled. Eventually it would get the message that something was wrong.

Jack followed until the next corner, then turned off and parked in a tow-away zone on the side street—didn't plan to be long. Adjusted the boonie cap and shades, added a Saddam Hussein mustache, tucked the pistol into his belt under the loose shirt, and hurried after the truck on foot.

Found it half a block down, the driver and the guard standing by the flat tire, scratching their heads. Probably made a hundred of these runs without a lick of trouble, so they weren't expecting any. Jack slowed to a stroll, approaching along the sidewalk behind them, then ducked between two cars. No strollers about—this was strictly industrial and burnoutville—so he pulled the pistol, snaked his turtleneck collar up over his nose, and came up beside them on the right.

"OK, guys," he said through the fabric of his collar. "This is what flattened the tire." He held his pistol where it was shielded from the street but these two couldn't miss it. "And it will flatten you guys too without a peep if you don't play nice."

The driver, a twenty-something with a wispy blond goatee, jumped and raised his hands chest high, palms out. The guard was an older, heavier black. Jack saw the fingers of his gun hand twitch.

"You're thinking about doing a very bad thing, aren't you," Jack said quickly. "You're thinking, they're paying me to protect this shipment and that's what I've got to do. I respect that, my friend, but a word of advice: don't. Not worth it. I'm not here to hurt you or hijack your truck. I'm here just for a sample. So take off your gun belt, hand it to me gently, and we can all end the day with the same amount of blood in our veins as we started with."

The guard stared at him, chewing his neatly mustachioed upper lip.

"Hey, Grimes," the driver said, his hands shaking. "Come on, man!"

Grimes sighed, unbuckled the belt, and handed it over. Jack tossed it into the cab of the truck.

"Good. Now let's go get that sample."

At Jack's prodding, the driver led the way around to the rear of the semi. Jack kept both men ahead or to his left where he could cover them and keep the pistol out of sight. The driver unlocked and opened one of the doors, revealing canisters stacked four high, right to the edge. Jack noticed the guard eyeing him, looking for an opening, so he put him to work.

"Here," he said, handing him a medium-size Ziploc. "Fill this."

"With what?"

Jack quickly angled the pistol toward one of the barrels and snapped off a shot. The pop of the impact with the cardboard was louder than the bullet report.

The driver jerked back. Grimes only raised his eyebrows appreciatively.

Jack pointed to the fine stream of blue power dribbling from the hole. "Fill 'er up."

Grimes held the bag under the stream.

"Hell of a way to fill a prescription, man," the driver said.

When the bag was full, Grimes zipped it closed and tossed it to Jack.

Jack backed away and lowered the pistol.

"Thanks, guys. Sorry about the tire. I'd help you change it but . . . gotta run."

Before turning away, Jack raised his chin, causing the turtleneck collar to slip from the lower half of his face, exposing the mustache. Then he ran back the way he'd come, hiding the pistol under his shirt. He hopped into the car. He removed the hat, sunglasses, and mustache immediately, got rolling, and wriggled out of the turtleneck at the first red light. He had everything plus the pistol safely stuffed under the front seat by the time he reached the BQE ramp. The driver and guard hadn't seen his car, and any description they'd give would include a mustache, so no need to worry or hurry. He took the Brooklyn Queens Expressway north, obeying the speed limit all the way.

14

The intercom buzzed.

The limo already? Luc thought as he reached for the button. It's too early.

Raul's voice came through. "A package came for you, Dr. Monnet. I left it outside your door."

"Outside my door? Why didn't you ring?"

"I did but you didn't answer. Maybe the bell is broken. I'll have it checked tomorrow."

"Yes, do that." Do anything you want tomorrow. I will be long gone. "What sort of package?"

"A bottle from K&D."

Luc knew K&D well—a busy wine store over on Madison. Who would be sending him a bottle now?

Luc walked through the living room, skirting the three large bulging suitcases that waited by the door. The wine crates were gone—the shipper had wheeled out the last of them an hour ago—and the room seemed empty now without them. He just hoped to God DHL took good care of them. Some of those bottles were irreplaceable.

He unlocked the door and had pulled it open only an inch or two when it suddenly slammed back in his face, knocking him to the floor. He scrambled to his feet and stared in dry-mouthed horror at the intruder.

"Good evening, Dr. Monnet," Milos Dragovic said, grinning like a great white as he closed the door behind him.

"You . . . what . . . how . . . ?" Luc couldn't form a coherent thought, let alone speak it.

"How?" Dragovic said, his eyes taking in the living room as if he were cataloguing it. "My driver is keeping your doorman company for the time being. I made it quite clear to him that—" He stopped as his roving gaze came to rest on the suitcases. "Oh? Planning a trip? You've had your fun with me and now you're running off, is that it?"

What was he saying? "Fun with you? I don't know what you—"

He didn't see Dragovic's arm move but suddenly the thick back of his hand crashed against the right side of Luc's face. Pain exploded in his cheek and jaw, sent him stumbling, staggering back. He almost fell again. The room blurred through the tears in his eyes.

"It's too late for games!" Dragovic said.

Luc blinked and pressed his hands over his throbbing face. "What are you talking about?"

Two long quick steps and Dragovic was on top of him. Luc cringed, expecting another blow, expecting many blows. The thought of fighting back flashed through his brain, exiting almost before it entered. Luc didn't know how to fight. And if he tried he might only further enrage Dragovic.

But Dragovic didn't hit him. Instead he grabbed Luc by the back of his neck, wheeled him around, and steered him toward the large TV set at the far end of the room.

"There!" he said, pointing to the screen where the news was running. "How many times have you watched it?"

"Watched what?"

The grip on his neck tightened, fingertips digging deep into his flesh. The words spoken close to his ear were distorted by rage.

"You know exactly what! If we wait long enough they will show it again and we can watch it together!"

"You mean the film of you . . . from last night?" It had to be that.

"Yes!" The word hissed through clenched teeth and the pressure on his neck increased further. "The film you so cleverly arranged!"

"No! You can't believe that! No, it wasn't me!"

"Liar!" Dragovic shouted and gave Luc a violent shove.

Luc stumbled forward and fell against the television. Something popped inside and the tube went blank. His mind screamed, He's going to kill me!

"I swear!" Luc cried. "I swear by all that's holy I had nothing to do with it! Nothing!"

"You and Garrison and Edwards!" Dragovic said, his voice low and menacing. "You thought you'd get me out of the picture! Well, we'll see who's out of the picture!" He looked around. "Where's your phone?"

"In the kitchen."

"Find it! Now! You have some calls to make."

Luc glanced at his suitcases as he headed for the kitchen. So near . . . a few minutes more and he would have been on his way to the airport. Now he was sure he was headed for some lost corner of hell.

15

Jack hung up the pay phone at Eighty-seventh and Third. Nadia's mother still hadn't heard from her. The old woman said she'd left in the early afternoon, and was sure Nadia would have called sometime during those hours just to let her know everything was all right. She was worried.

So was Jack. He tried to think of reasons why this should be someone else's problem, anyone's but his. Didn't work.

OK. He figured he had scores to settle with both Monnet and Dragovic. But since he wasn't sure Dragovic was even in town, he'd chosen to settle with Monnet first. Now Nadia's whereabouts gave him an extra reason for a little tête-à-tête with the good doctor.

He turned and faced Monnet's building. The late-day sun reflected from the tall windows on its western flank. Was Monnet behind one of them? Wished he could find out. He'd called the GEM offices but they said he hadn't been in all day; all he got at Monnet's home number was the answering machine.

He'd parked his car nearby, blocking a delivery driveway that didn't look like it was going to be used soon. If it got ticketed, that was the breaks. He'd pay it tomorrow. He always paid his tickets. First off because the car was in Gia's name, and second because if he was ever stopped he didn't want the word *scofflaw* popping up when his plate was run through the computer.

The air lay warm and heavy after the earlier rain, too hot for the black-and-white nylon warm-up suit he was wearing, but he sensed a good possibility that tonight's work might turn wet, and nylon left no fibers. Had another reason for wearing the warm-up: zippered pockets. The Berzerk was in one, and his burglary tools—lock pick set, glass cutter, latch lifter—were scattered through the others. If Monnet didn't come out, Jack was going to have to find a way in. Not easy with a doorman, but he'd done it before.

Watched the Bentley idling before the front entrance. It had been sitting there when he arrived. He was wondering how much money he'd have to have before he even considered plunking down over a hundred large on a car when Monnet stepped through the front door.

Excellent.

And who was following right on his heels but Dragovic himself. Jack fought the urge to race across the street and put a pair of .22 LRs into his eyes.

The Serb had sent two men after Jack, but that wasn't the problem. It was understandable. After all, Jack had turned him into an international laughing stock, and when you dish it out you've got to expect some to come back to you. But Dragovic's men had threatened—no, they'd *promised* to rape Gia, and even Vicky. At least the one in the back seat with Jack had, and Jack had known from the dark joy dancing in the guy's eyes that he meant it, was looking forward to it.

Maybe going after noncombatants was Dragovic's policy; maybe it wasn't. Didn't matter. If the guys in the Beamer were typical of the kind the Serb had working for him, then Gia and Vicky would be in danger as long as Dragovic lived. Pretty much the same as leaving Scarlip alive and well in the city. Jack wasn't about to tolerate either.

He'd have to fix it . . . the alive and well part.

But he needed to talk to these two first. One of them was behind Nadia's disappearance. Her fiancé's too. Might be too late for both of them. If so, Jack wanted to know.

Patience, he told himself. Patience. You'll get your chance. And it'll be a twofer.

As a third guy came out and quick-stepped around to the driver seat, Jack hurried to his car. He followed the Bentley around to the FDR Drive where it turned downtown. Traffic wasn't so bad for six-fifteen in the rush hour. Made good time until they exited onto Thirty-fourth Street and began an excruciating westward crawl.

Only one place they could be headed: the GEM offices. That could present a problem. While waiting for Nadia outside the building the other day, Jack had noticed a guard in the lobby. Looked now like it was going to be quarter to seven or later by the time Monnet and Dragovic reached the building. The guard would pass them right through but was sure to want to see some ID from Jack before he directed him to the elevators.

But if Jack got there first . . .

He spotted a PARK sign and pulled into a garage. As he trotted along Thirty-fourth he put on his gloves, boonie cap, and shades, then ducked into a doorway and quickly stuck the mustache under his nose again. He'd have them all removed before he returned to the garage later.

He passed the Bentley within a block and easily beat it to the office building. He strolled into the lobby, all geometric chrome and marble, and went directly to the jowly middle-aged Hispanic sitting in the tiny security kiosk.

"Hi. Did Dr. Monnet arrive yet?"

The guard shook his head. "Haven't seen him."

Jack put on a relieved look. "Whew! That's good. I was supposed to meet him here and I'm running a little late. Traffic's murder out there."

The guard, whose name tag said GAUDENCIO, looked at him as if to say, What would Dr. Monnet want with you?

"I'm gonna be doing a little work in his office for him. You know, custom electronics. That's my thing."

The guard nodded. He'd bought it. "You doing work for the other partners too?"

"Who?"

"Edwards and Garrison. They're up there waiting for him. Sent everybody else home."

Jack did not have to fake it as he rubbed his palms together with relish. "No kidding? That's great! He's already bringing some other guy with him. Hey, this could turn out to be a very good day! Want me to sign in?"

The guard pushed a pen toward Jack. "Go ahead, but I can't let you up without clearance from upstairs." He reached for the phone.

"That's OK. I'll just wait and go up with the man himself."

After signing in as "J. Washington," Jack turned and saw the Bentley pull up to the curb out front.

"Here he comes now." He winked at the guard. "Don't say anything about how I just got here, OK?"

Monnet and Dragovic pushed through the revolving door as the Bentley pulled away.

"Evening, Dr. Monnet," the guard said.

Monnet nodded absently. His right cheek looked swollen, and he seemed to be a little out of it.

"How we doin' tonight, gentlemen?" Jack said with a big, vacant grin.

When neither acknowledged his existence, he fell in a couple of steps behind them and gave the guard a Who-can-figure-these-rich-guys? shrug.

The guard's answering shrug said he knew the type too well.

Jack followed them into an open elevator car. Saw Dragovic press 16, reached past him and pressed 18.

Again the urge to pull out the P-98 and finish it right here. So simple. But that wasn't going to do it, especially with the other two GEM partners waiting upstairs. One of them had to know what had happened to Nadia.

So Jack lowered his head and leaned in a far corner of the cab, watching.

Not a word out of either on the way up. Dragovic looked stiff with anger, Monnet almost limp with fear; the tension between the two of them flooded the cab. When they stopped on 16 and Jack saw Dragovic push Monnet out, he knew something heavy was going down.

He sidled over to the control panel and thumbed the DOOR OPEN button to watch a little longer. They stood before a glass wall etched with the GEM Pharma logo. He saw Monnet run a card down a magnetic swipe reader on the right, heard a buzz; then Monnet pushed open the glass door. The receptionist desk beyond the wall was empty.

Jack let the elevator doors close and rode up to eighteen. Once there he pressed the 16 button, and a minute later he was standing before GEM's glass wall.

No way to bypass the swipe reader with the crude tools he'd brought along. Same for the electronic lock in the brass-trimmed door: it was set solid, and even if he did manage to jimmy it, the door was alarmed—open it without swiping a card and all hell was sure to break loose.

That left the glass.

The panel opposite the free end of the door was untrimmed and maybe three-eighths of an inch thick. Jack pulled out his glass cutter and knelt. Leaning into the cutter, he scored an arc into the glazed surface, starting two feet up on the free edge and running down to the floor. Worked the diamond tip back and forth half a dozen times in the same groove, hot work that sweated up his hands inside the leather gloves. Next he cut a straight score along the floor line. That done, he lay back and gave the section a quick sharp kick. Once. Twice. On the third try the quarter-round piece of glass cracked along the scores and flopped inward onto the carpet.

Jack crawled through, then peeked into the main corridor to give it a careful twice-over. No visible security camera and no likely places to hide one. Good.

He straightened his warm-up and went hunting the lords of Berzerkdom.

16

"You didn't eat," the girl squeaked.

Nadia sat next to Doug on the cot and sized her up where she stood in the doorway of the trailer. She had a high-pitched voice and an undersized head, made smaller-looking by the tight ponytail she wore. She didn't seem too bright, and looked so frail Nadia was sure she could bowl her over and leap to freedom through the open door. But Nadia was also sure that even she and Doug together would never get by the pair of hulking dog-faced roustabouts standing a few feet outside.

"I can't," Nadia said.

Half an hour ago the girl had brought them each two hamburgers, two hot dogs, and large cups of fruit punch—all from the concession stand, Nadia was sure. Doug had eaten his, but Nadia could barely look at it.

"You must. Oz says so."

"It's too hot," Nadia said, hoping to keep her talking. The longer she lingered, the longer the door would stay open, allowing fresh air to waft through the stuffy interior. "And I'm scared."

"Aw," the girl said with what sounded like genuine compassion. "Don't be scared. Oz is nice."

"Who's this Oz?" Doug said, putting his hand on Nadia's thigh and leaning forward.

"He's the boss." Her tone said, Everybody knows that.

"But why did he kidnap us? Why is he keeping us here?"

A shrug. "I don't know. But he's feeding you good, right? And he gave you a nice trailer."

Nadia lowered her voice. "Can you help us out of here? Please?"

336

"Oh, no!" The girl's hand flew to her mouth and she started backing away. "I could never do that! Oz would be so mad!"

"Would he hurt you?"

"Us? No, Oz would never hurt us. He protects us; he helps us."

"Then help *us*. Please!"

"No-no-no!" she said. She turned and jumped through the door. "No-no-no-no-no!"

"Wait!" Nadia said, rising, but one of the roustabouts slammed the door in her face. Fighting back tears, she slumped back onto the cot and leaned against Doug. "What are we going to do?"

"Hang in there," he said, slipping an arm around her. "We'll think of—"

A clank from the front of the trailer cut him off. The floor tilted back a few degrees, then rocked forward. A chain rattled. Nadia rose and stumbled toward the noise.

Pressing her eye to a crack in the board over the window allowed her a slit view of the outside world. She saw the rear of a pickup truck. . . . Their trailer was hitched to it.

Suddenly the trailer lurched forward and she fell backward. Luckily Doug was there to catch her.

"What's happening?" he said.

"They're moving us."

"Where?"

"I don't know."

She had an awful feeling they were about to find out why they'd been abducted.

17

Who are they? Jack wondered. Houdinis? Where the hell did they go?

He'd crept around, peeking in all the offices and cubicles. He'd even checked the rest rooms and the small, well-equipped kitchenette but had found no one. Only area he hadn't explored was a short corridor near the center of the space. He'd avoided it after spotting a security camera set into the ceiling at one end. Hung there for all to see. Why?

Since the corridor was open on both ends, he was able to approach the camera from behind. Pulling a chair from one of the cubicles, he inspected the camera close up. No swivel mechanism. Aimed at the middle of the hallway. Interesting. Was it running? And if so, was anybody monitoring it? One way to find out. . . .

Jack used a roll of Scotch tape he'd borrowed from one of the desks and stretched three strips across the lens, then retreated.

When no one came to investigate, he moved back into the corridor. As he reached the midpoint, he heard a faint thump to his left. He turned and saw a door labeled: CONFERENCE ROOM. The sign was small, the handle recessed, and the door flush with the wall. Virtually invisible unless you were on top of it.

Conference room . . . of course. Where else would they be? He pressed an ear against the door and thought he heard raised voices—whether in anger or terror he couldn't be sure.

He stepped back. Soundproofed. And situated in the center of the GEM space, which meant no windows. Good thinking. If you need an electronic- and microwave-proof room, you don't want windows. The door had buried hinges and a recessed pull instead of a knob. That meant it opened outward. Gave it a gentle pull to test it. Wouldn't budge. Probably secured by a bolt on the inside.

Jack leaned back to consider his options. Can't kick down a door that opens out . . . didn't come prepared for this . . . have to improvise . . .

So what materials did he have at hand?

Took him about a minute to shape a rough plan.

Slipped back to the file room and rock-walked one of the smaller cabinets down to the door; then he returned to the kitchenette and picked through the utensil drawer until he found what he wanted.

18

"Lies!" Dragovic screamed, pounding the table with both fists. "You think I am stupid?"

How do I convince him? Luc thought as he cowered between Brad and Kent. Dragovic stood on the far side of the table, his back to the door, glaring at them like a maniac. He'd forced Luc to call an emergency meeting with his partners, telling them to clear both floors of all personnel.

And now he had the three of them trapped in this stifling room.

We are three, Luc thought. Why should we fear this one man? He may be armed, but after his arrest on multiple weapons charges last night he may be wary of carrying a pistol. The odds are on our side. If I give the word, the three of us could attack him. . . .

He glanced left and right at his two partners: sweat rolled off Kent in buckets, soaking his collar, spreading dark stains from his underarms; and Brad was almost in tears.

Then again, maybe not. . . .

"You've got to believe us!" Brad cried.

Dragovic's lips curled with scorn. "A strange creature gives us Loki, and now you say it's dying? I am to believe that?"

"Christ, please, yes!" Kent said. "If we were going to make up a story, we wouldn't make up something as crazy as that!"

Luc had hoped the unhappy truth about the creature would turn Dragovic from his paranoid fantasy, but it had only incensed him.

"I can show you the creature," Luc said. "You can see with your own eyes."

"Another trick!"

"No tricks. You'll see it; then you'll believe. And then you'll understand that it was not us who plotted against you. Think: why would we be trying to steal the Loki trade from you *when there will be no more Loki?*"

Dragovic stared at him for a few heartbeats, a flicker of doubt in his raging eyes. He opened his mouth to speak but was stopped by a knocking sound.

Everyone froze, listening. It came again.

Someone was pounding on the door.

Luc stepped away from the desk to the security console and turned on the hallway monitor. The screen lit but the image was blurred. Someone was standing outside the door but Luc could not identify him.

Dragovic motioned Brad toward the door. "See who it is!" he said, stepping away. "And no tricks!"

Luc noted with relief that he did not pull a weapon, a good indication that he didn't have one.

Brad pressed the intercom button next to the door. "Wh-who is it?" His voice would play through a speaker in the hallway ceiling above the door.

The reply was garbled . . . something about "security service" and "malfunction."

On the monitor, the blurred image of the man was waving at the camera. What security service? Luc wondered. And how did he get up here?

Dragovic pushed Brad away from the intercom and pressed the button. "Go away. We are busy. Come back tomorrow."

Another garbled reply, but one phrase came through loud and clear: ". . . the room may be bugged."

"What?" A chorus from four throats.

"More of your tricks?" Dragovic snarled, glaring at Luc. He turned to Brad. "Open it!"

Before Luc could protest, Brad's trembling hand fumbled the bolt back. He pushed on the door, and then things happened too fast.

The door was violently pulled open, almost catapulting Brad into the hall; then he suddenly reversed direction, stumbling backward against the conference table as if he'd been shoved.

And then Luc realized with a shock that he indeed had been shoved—by the odd-looking stranger who leaped into the conference room with a drawn pistol.

"Everybody hold still!" he shouted.

He was addressing all of them, but he kept his pistol—Luc noticed with alarm that it was fitted with a silencer—trained on Dragovic. Something familiar about him . . . the warm-up, the hat, the sunglasses. And then Luc recognized him: this man had shared the elevator with Dragovic and him a short while ago.

"Thank God!" Brad cried. "I don't know who you are, but you arrived just in time!" He pointed to Dragovic. "This man—"

"Shut up!" the stranger yelled, pushing Brad toward the end of the table. "Over there with your buddies." Then he turned to Dragovic. "You carrying?"

Dragovic stared at him. "Do you know who I am?"

"Yeah, now answer the question: what are you carrying?"

Dragovic sneered. "I have no need to carry."

"So you say. Take off your jacket and prove it."

"Go to hell!"

Without warning, the stranger's pistol coughed once and Dragovic fell back into a chair, his breath hissing between his teeth as he clutched his thigh. Luc saw that a splintered hole had appeared in the mahogany door of the cabinet behind him.

"Take off your jacket," the stranger said, "or the next one will go for the bone instead of creasing you."

Leveling a murderous glare at the stranger, Dragovic removed his suit coat, balled it in his bloody hands, and hurled it across the room at him.

"You are a dead man,"

"You already tried that once today," the stranger said, catching the coat with his free hand. "Now it's my turn."

Luc watched Dragovic's expression change from anger, to bafflement, then to . . . was that fear? Luc turned his attention to the stranger who was emptying the jacket pockets. He wished he could see the eyes behind those dark glasses. He seemed to be brimming with rage, more than Dragovic, if that were possible. What was it between these two? Luc glanced at Brad and Kent who looked as baffled and frightened as he.

A cold band tightened around his chest. Have we traded one madman for another—this one armed?

19

Jack had loved shooting Dragovic—took just about all he had to keep from pulling the trigger again—but relished the mix of terror and bafflement scooting across his face right now almost as much.

"You?" Dragovic said; then his eyes narrowed. "Yes, it *is* you! That mustache is fake. I have seen you!"

Jack found only a cell phone in Dragovic's suit coat. He dropped the phone on the table and tossed the coat back.

"No, you haven't."

"Yes. You were at my front gate!"

Damn security cameras, Jack thought.

"I knew it!" Dragovic shouted, purpling with rage as he pointed to Monnet. "You work for him, don't you! He hired you to humiliate me!"

Where'd he get that idea? Jack wondered, but decided not to straighten him out. This might work right into his plans.

"Just sit there and be quiet while I talk to these bozos," he said, dismissing Dragovic—which had to hurt him worse than another bullet. He turned to Monnet. "Where's Nadia Radzminsky?"

Monnet seemed jolted by the question. But maybe frightened too. Hiding something? Jack couldn't tell for sure.

"Nadia?" Monnet gave this nifty little Gallic shrug. "Why . . . home, I suppose."

"She's not. She's missing." He turned to the other two. "How about you guys? Any idea where I can find Nadia Radzminsky?"

"How should we know?" said the heavier, sweaty one.

"Radzminsky?" said the nervous ferret type. His eyes darted Monnet's way. "Luc, isn't that the new researcher we hired?"

"How do you know Nadia?" Monnet said.

Jack ignored him, concentrating on the other two. "How about Gleason—Douglas Gleason? He's another of your people who's MIA. Know anything about him?"

Bull's-eye, Jack thought when he saw the ferret's shocked expression. Here was a guy he'd like to play poker with.

Keeping a peripheral watch on Dragovic, Jack pointed his pistol at the ferret's head.

"Nice haircut, but I think the part would look better on the other side, don't you?"

The ferret clapped his hands against his scalp and ducked, crying, "Tell him, Luc! Tell him about Prather!"

Monnet closed his eyes and Jack stared at him, stunned. The only sound in the room was ripping cloth. Jack glanced at Dragovic and saw him tearing the silk lining from his suit coat and tying it around his wounded thigh.

"Tell him!" the ferret screamed.

"Shut up, Brad!" Monnet said through his teeth.

"Ozymandias Prather?" Jack said, and watched the three partners' faces go slack with shock.

"You know him?" Monnet said.

"I'm asking the questions."

"No-no," Monnet said, an excited look replacing the shock. "This is important! If you know him, then you must have seen the creature he calls the Sharkman."

"Yeah. Saw it a few hours ago." Where was this going?

"Then please tell this man," Monnet said, pointing to Dragovic. "Tell him how the creature looks, how it's at death's door."

"You kidding? It looks great—ready to bust out of its cage."

Monnet looked ill as Dragovic pounded his fists on the table and shouted something about liars and traitors, but Jack wasn't following because a sickening scenario was playing out in his mind.

He stepped closer to Monnet and pointed the pistol at his face. "You!"

The doctor cringed. "What?"

"What did Oz and his boys do to Gleason?"

"Nothing."

Jack jammed the muzzle of the silencer against Monnet's temple, hard enough to make him wince. "You've got three seconds . . . two seconds . . ."

"He made him disappear!"

"What's that supposed to mean?"

"I don't know!" Monnet cried. "He just said he'd found an 'absolutely foolproof means of disposal' and we'd never have to worry about him again. That's all I know; I swear!"

You bastard! Jack thought, aching to pull the trigger. You rotten lousy bastard. He'd bet all he owned that Oz's foolproof dispose-all had yellow eyes and a scarred lower lip.

"And Nadia? What about her?"

Monnet closed his eyes.

"Only one second left on your clock," Jack said, then held his breath, pretty damn sure he wasn't going to like this answer.

Monnet nodded. "The same." His voice seemed caught between a whisper and a sob.

"Aw, jeez."

It now seemed a possibility that the suddenly healthy rakosh hadn't lunched on Bondy as Jack had first thought. Oz must have fed it Gleason . . . and Nadia was probably next on the menu.

He backed away, trying not to give in to the increasingly insistent urge to redecorate the room with this son of a bitch's brains. That was too good for him. Too good for all of them.

"All right," he said. "I want all pockets emptied onto the table. Everyone. Now. Do it!"

The three executives got to it with gusto. Jack could see relief on their faces: Emptying pockets meant robbery. They understood that, and it sure as hell beat getting shot.

Dragovic didn't move. He simply sat there pressing a hand to his thigh and glaring at Monnet. Jack remembered his shouts about liars and traitors a moment ago. Looked like this little business arrangement was falling apart. He let Dragovic be—he already had what he wanted from him.

"Hurry!" Jack shouted, and meant it. Gleason was probably gone, but maybe he still had time to save Nadia. "I want all pockets turned inside out."

He didn't care about the wallets that landed on the table. The cell phones were what he wanted. Three more of them joined Dragovic's.

"You," he said, pointing to Mr. Sweaty. "Rip out every phone in the room and dump them here on the table." As Sweaty hopped to it, Jack pointed the ferret—the one Monnet had called Brad—in the direction of the wet bar at the far end of the room. "You bring me four glasses and a pitcher of water."

When all the phones had been collected, including the conference speaker-microphone in the center of the table, Jack wrapped them in someone's suit coat and tossed them out into the hall.

"Now," he said, tugging the Ziploc of Berzerk from his pocket and sliding it across the table to Brad. "Put a handful of that in each of the glasses."

The look on Brad's face left no doubt about his familiarity with the powder.

"W-why?"

"Just do it."

Brad's hand was shaking like a wino with the DTs, but he managed to get the job done.

"Now fill each glass halfway with water and pass them around."

A minute later, each of the four men had a glass of blue-tinged fluid before him.

"Bottoms up, gentlemen," Jack said.

Mr. Sweaty got sweatier. "No," he said shaking his head and staring at the glass like he'd been poured a shot of battery acid. "It'll kill us."

"Yeah, well, you gotta go sometime. Drink up; then I'm gone."

Dragovic snorted derisively, raised his glass as if he were toasting the room, and chugged the Berzerk. Then he hurled the glass across the table at Monnet, missing him by inches.

"I can't!" Brad wailed.

Jack put a bullet into the mahogany tabletop directly in front of Brad. The three executives all but jumped out of their seats; Dragovic was cool, though. Barely blinked. Under different circumstances, Jack could have almost liked him.

"I don't have time for this, so I'll tell you that we can do this two ways: you can swallow it, or I can shoot you in the gut and pour it in."

Mr. Sweaty drank his. He looked sick when he set his empty back on the mahogany. Brad choked halfway through his, and for a second or two Jack was afraid he was going to blow it all over the table, but he kept it down.

Monnet was the last. "Do you have any idea what this will do to us?"

"Firsthand. I got the dose you or Dragovic set up for Nadia."

"I have never heard of this Nadia," Dragovic said. "Who is she? Should I know her?"

"Then it was you," Jack said, staring hard into Monnet's eyes. He wanted so much to hurt this man. Instead he held up his free hand, the leather-clad thumb and index finger a hair apart. "This morning I came this close to hurting two people very dear to me because of you. I think you'd better drink up."

Monnet drank.

"Why?" Monnet asked when he'd drained the glass. "Why are you doing this?"

"Nadia hired me," Jack said, wanting to smash his teeth because Nadia was gone, maybe dead, because of this man.

"To do *this?*"

"No. To keep an eye on you." Jack pointed to Dragovic. "To protect you from him. She thought you were in trouble. She was worried about you. She cared about you."

He watched Monnet crumble. "Oh, my Lord."

He surprised Jack by dropping his face into his hands and sobbing.

Jack reached into a pocket, pulled out the paper-towel-wrapped collection he'd assembled in the cafeteria, and dropped it on the conference table.

"For your amusement. Just remember the Law: not to spill blood. Are we not men?"

He enjoyed their confounded expressions as he backed to the door and pushed it open. He couldn't resist aiming a Parathion shot at Dragovic.

"Got any old tires you care to sell?" he said in the Thurston Howell lockjaw accent he'd used on the phone. "Oily ones, perhaps?"

"You!" Dragovic cried, rising from his seat. "Why would you do that to me!"

"Nothing personal," Jack said. "I was hired to do it."

With that he ducked out and slammed the door closed. Immediately he tipped the filing cabinet, letting it fall against the door, wedging it against the opposite wall. Then he ran for the elevator, praying he could make it to Monroe in time.

20

Luc was vaguely aware of what was going on around him . . . Kent moving to the door, trying it, unable to open it . . . he and Brad futilely throwing their weight against it . . . their panicked cries about being trapped.

Other words had a death grip on his thoughts. . . .

. . . *She thought you were in trouble. She was worried about you. She cared about you* . . .

Each word, each syllable was a drop of acid eating through Luc's brain.

Poor Nadia. She was looking out for me while I was contracting her death. What have I become? What sort of monster am I? What brought me so low?

He raised his head from his pool of misery and found Dragovic staring at him from the far side of the table.

"So," the Serb said with a lopsided grin. "It is just the four of us again." He rose and moved along the table with a barely perceptible limp. The wound wasn't slowing him down. He pointed to the stranger's package. "Let's see what your man left us."

"He's not our man," Kent said. "We've never seen him before in our lives. At least I haven't."

"Me neither," said Brad.

"He said you hired him."

"Never!" Brad cried. "He said he 'was hired.' But not by us."

All eyes turned to Luc.

"You got rid of the Radzminsky woman without checking with us," Kent said. "Did you hire that man as well?"

Luc said nothing. He no longer cared what they thought.

Dragovic pulled at the paper towels wrapped around the stranger's package. They unrolled in one long strip until four carving knives fell free and clattered onto the table.

"Oh . . . my . . . God!" Brad whispered.

Dragovic picked up the longest and ran his finger along the edge. "Sharp," he said, grinning. He shoved the point toward Luc. "Want to feel?"

Luc gripped the front of his shirt and ripped it open, sending a button bouncing across the table. He thrust his exposed chest at Dragovic.

"Do it! Go ahead—*do it!*"

Luc was not bluffing. He was sick to his soul and could almost welcome ending it all right here.

"Don't dare me. Because I will—and your two partners as well."

"Don't even joke about something like that!" Kent cried.

"Who's joking?"

"Start with me," Luc said. "I don't care anymore."

It was something of a shock to realize that he truly did not care, and that granted him a bounty of wild courage.

Dragovic stared at him, his grin gone. "You will care when this bites into your throat."

"Stop this talk!" Brad said. "You can't get away with harming any of us. We're all trapped here until the cleaning service shows up." He glanced at his watch. "And they should be here within the hour."

"Right," Kent said. "You don't want them to find you here with a dead body and blood on your hands, do you? Even *your* lawyers won't get you off on that one."

Dragovic considered this, then shrugged. He tossed the knife onto the table. "Some other time, then." He leaned closer to Luc. "When you care. Because I want you to care."

"We've got to stay calm," Brad said. "That man, whoever he was, wants us to kill each other—*expects* us to kill each other. But we can outsmart him and have the last laugh if we just . . . stay . . . calm. We've all got Loki starting to run through our brains right now, enough to make half a dozen people crazy. But we're all intelligent men, right? We're smarter than Loki. We can beat it."

"Right," Kent said. "If we all sit quietly, saying nothing to upset anyone else, we can all survive until the cleaning service comes."

Brad moved to the far corner of the table and patted the chair there. "Milos, you sit here. Kent—"

"No!" Dragovic said, dropping into the chair opposite Luc. "I sit here."

"Very well," Brad said. "I'll sit here. And Kent will sit opposite me. That way we'll all be as far as possible from each other. Now: everyone be quiet and just . . . stay . . . calm."

Silence. Luc closed his eyes and listened to the faint hum of the air conditioning. After a few minutes he realized that his mood was lifting. He felt nowhere near as miserable as when the stranger first imprisoned them.

Thoughts of Nadia returned, but he found he could view them from a fresher, more realistic perspective. Absurd to blame himself for Nadia's demise when clearly it was her own doing. If she'd kept her attention focused on the task she'd been assigned, she'd still be alive and well. But no . . . she had to go sticking her nose where it didn't belong. If you play, you'd better be ready to pay.

And hadn't she lied to me about her relationship with Gleason? Damn right. Told me they were just friends when all the time they were engaged. Engaged! Serves the bitch right. Can't lie to me and get away with it.

Luc opened his eyes and found Dragovic staring at him.

"What are you looking at?" he said.

Dragovic sneered. "Dead meat."

"Please," Brad said from the far end of the table. "If we don't talk we won't—"

"Shut up!" Luc said. "God, how I'm sick of your whining, wheedling voice!"

"OK," Brad said, his face twitching as he pressed his palms flat on the table. "Fine. Let's leave it at that."

Luc bit back another remark. Brad was right. Tensions could soar under the influence of Loki. A casual remark could spark a war. He and everyone else had to keep quiet.

But *damn* he felt good! Hard to believe that just moments ago he'd been mired in some morass of guilt over what he'd done to Nadia. The Loki was letting him see the idiocy of expending even a nanosecond of thought, let alone guilt, on a nobody like her.

Loki . . . he regretted never trying it before. This was wonderful. His senses were turned to a higher pitch—he could feel the air, the individual oxygen molecules, hear the ticking of Dragovic's Rolex or whatever that garish contraption was on his wrist, feel the grain of the mahogany writhing beneath the varnish of the tabletop.

And his mind—so *clear.* He could see all the errors of his life, especially during the past few weeks, and how things would have been completely different if he'd had a little Loki to clear his vision.

He glanced around the table again.

Brad and Kent . . . what a pair of losers: the complete wimp and the flabby blowhard. How did I ever let myself become involved with them? And Dragovic—he's not so tough. Bigger and stronger, perhaps, but brawn carries you only so far. Even in a hand-to-hand fight, he'd be no match for my intellect. Why was I ever afraid of him?

He hated them all and wanted to be rid of them. The carving knives on the table beckoned to him, but no . . . too crude. Surely someone with his brain could think of a way to dispose of the three of them without drawing suspicion. Perhaps—

A shout interrupted his thoughts. Brad was on his feet, leaning over the table, jabbing his finger at Kent's face.

"Stop sweating! I can *hear* you sweating and it makes me sick!"

"*I* make *you* sick?" Kent said, leaping to his feet. "Listen, Twinkle-toes, if anybody around here makes people sick it's you and your pretty-boy clothes and incessant whining."

Brad's jaw dropped. "What? What are you implying?"

"I'm not implying a goddamn thing! I'm telling you you're—"

"Here!" Dragovic shouted.

He'd grabbed two of the knives and now he slid them down the table. They rotated lazily along their course and stopped between Brad and Kent.

Brad stopped, eyes wide.

"Look at him!" Kent laughed. "What a pussy!"

"Pussy?" Brad's face contorted with rage. His hand flashed out and snatched up one of the knives. "I'll show you who's a pussy!"

He leaped at Kent and they both went down beyond the far end of the table, out of Luc's line of sight. He heard thumping and thrashing and grunts and cries, saw Kent's bloody hand appear, watched it feel around, find the other knife, then disappear again.

Luc didn't stand, didn't move beyond turning his head toward Dragovic. It sounded as if Brad and Kent were killing each other, and he prayed that was the case. That would leave only Dragovic.

The Serb's eyes were on the battle playing out on the floor in front of him. He watched it avidly, grinning like a shark who smells blood and is waiting to feed on both the victor and the vanquished.

Then the thrashing stopped and a gasping and very bloody Kent Garrison struggled to his feet. Luc saw Dragovic pick up one of the two remaining knives and palm the handle upside down, rising and approaching Kent with the blade hidden against the underside of his forearm.

"Are you all right?"

Kent grinned. "Better than you'll be!"

Without warning, he slashed at Dragovic. But the Serb seemed to have expected it. He ducked back, then whipped his own blade across Kent's throat. Blood sprayed across the table as Kent dropped from view with a bubbling groan.

Luc's mind raced at light speed. Perfect! Kent gets blamed for killing Brad, Dragovic gets blamed for killing Kent, and I kill Dragovic in self-defense. He made no conscious decision: he was suddenly up on the table with a knife in his hand and in full charge toward Dragovic as the Serb turned toward him. . . .

21

Between the traffic jam at the Midtown Tunnel and the overturned tractor-trailer at the Springfield Boulevard overpass on the LIE, Jack felt almost lucky to reach Monroe in two hours.

His tentative plan was to drive across the grass in the darkness and pull right up to the tent, duck under the flap, splash Scar-lip with gas, light a match, and send it back to hell. Then, during the ensuing panic and confusion, look for Nadia.

But as he took the narrow road out to the marsh, he began to feel a crawling sensation in his gut.

Where were the tents?

Slewed his car to a halt on the muddy meadow and stared in disbelief at the empty space before his headlights. Jumped out and looked around. Gone. Hadn't passed them on the road. Where—?

Heard a sound and whirled to find a gnarled figure standing on the far side of his car. In the backwash from the headlights he could make out that the man was old and grizzled and unshaven, but not much more.

"If you're looking for the show," the man said, "you're a little late. But don't worry. They'll be back next year."

"Did you see them go?"

"Course," he said. "But not before I collected my rent."

"Do you know where—?"

"M'name's Haskins. I own this land, y'know, and you're on it."

Jack's patience was fraying. "I'll be glad to get off it; just tell me—"

"I rent it out every year to that show. They really seem to like Monroe. But I—"

"I need to know where they went."

"You're a little old to be wantin' to run off with the circus, ain't you?" he said with a wheezy laugh.

That did it. *"Where did they go?"*

"Take it easy," the old guy said. "No need for shouting. They're makin' the jump to Jersey. They open in Cape May tomorrow night."

Jack ran back to his car. South Jersey. Only a couple of possible routes for a caravan of trucks and trailers: the Cross Bronx Expressway to the George Washington Bridge would take them too far north; the Beltway to the Verrazano and across Staten Island would drop them into Central Jersey. That was the logical route. But even if he was wrong, the only way to Cape May was via the Garden State Parkway. Jack gunned for the Parkway, figuring sooner or later he'd catch up to them.

WEDNESDAY

1

Took Jack another two frustrating hours just to reach Jersey. Midnight had come and gone and Cape May was still better than a hundred miles away. The limit on the parkway along here was sixty-five. Jack set the cruise control on seventy and kept his foot off the gas pedal. If he had his way he'd be doing ninety, but that would put a cop on his tail and he'd had enough cops already for one day.

Some day. When was it going to end? He was pretty sure the Berzerk had cleared his system, but his aches and pains seemed to be getting worse instead of better. Especially his head. He'd had the radio on earlier and some station had played "You Keep Me Hanging On." Now it kept droning through his frazzled brain, Diana Ross's voice like a power saw hitting a nail.

And worst of all, he saw a good chance this whole trip might be for nothing. Had no idea how often or how much a rakosh ate, but if it had fed on Bondy first, then Gleason, he might still have a chance of finding Nadia alive. A slim one, but he had to give it a shot. Might have a hard time living with himself if he didn't.

He'd figured a train of freak show trucks and trailers would be next to impossible to miss, but he damn near did. He was too intent on an all-news station's big breaking story as he flashed by the New Gretna rest area. . . .

"*. . . mass murder in midtown: gangland figure Milos Dragovic, known in many quarters as 'the Slippery Serb,' is dead, apparently of stab wounds, along with three top executives of a pharmaceutical firm.*

357

The four were found locked in a conference room in the GEM Pharma
offices in midtown by a cleaning crew a short while ago. This is not
Dragovic's first appearance in the news today. He was—"

Jack was a good hundred yards past the rest stop, congratulating himself on how well that stunt had worked, when something familiar about the motley assortment of vehicles clustered in the southern end of the parking lot registered in his consciousness.

He slowed, found an OFFICIAL USE ONLY cutoff, and made an illegal U-turn across the median onto the northbound lanes. Half a minute later he pulled into the rest area and found a parking spot near the Burger King/Nathan's/TCBY sign where he had a good view of the freak show vehicles.

At this hour on a Wednesday morning in May, the rest area was fairly deserted. Except for a few couples straggling back from Atlantic City, Oz's folk had the lot pretty much to themselves. But why this rest area of all places? This was the only one Jack knew of that had a State Police barracks for a neighbor.

He slumped in the seat. Bad thought: if Oz was traveling with someone he'd abducted, this would be the last place he'd stop. Sick foreboding settled on Jack like a wet tarp.

But he'd come this far. . . .

He scanned the area. No way to sneak up on them, so he settled for a direct approach. Of course the smart thing to do was to dime Oz out to the New Jersey State cops a couple hundred yards away, but that didn't sit right. Never would. And besides, if Nadia had become rakoshi chow, the state cops would find nothing. And the Scar-lip problem would remain.

Jack opened the trunk and stared at the gasoline can. His plan had been Scar-lip first, then Nadia. He'd have to reverse that now. Find Nadia if possible, then go for the rakosh. He pulled the silenced .22 from where he'd hidden it beneath the spare, stuck it in the waistband under his warm-up, walked toward the Oddity Emporium vehicles.

Counted two 18-wheelers and twenty or so trailers and motor homes of various shapes and sizes and states of repair. As he neared he heard hammering sounds; seemed to come from one of the semi trailers. Two of the dog-faced roustabouts stepped from behind a motor home as Jack reached the perimeter of the cluster. They growled a warning and pointed back toward the food court.

"I want to see Oz," Jack said.

More growls and more emphatic pointing.

"Look, he either gets a visit from me or I walk over to the State Police barracks there and have *them* pay him a visit."

The roustabouts didn't seem to feature that idea. Looked at each other, then one hurried away. A moment later he was back. Motioned Jack to follow him. Jack lowered the zipper on his warm-up top to give him quicker access to the P-98, then started moving.

One of the roustabouts stayed behind. As Jack followed the other on a winding course through the haphazardly parked vehicles, he saw a crew of workers trying to patch a hole in the flank of one of the semi trailers. He pulled up short when he saw the size of the hole: five or six feet high, a couple of feet wide. The edges of the metal skin were flared outward, as if a giant fist had punched through from within. And Jack was pretty sure that fist had belonged to something cobalt blue with yellow eyes.

Shit! He closed his eyes and slammed his fists against his thighs. He wanted to break something. What *else* could go wrong today?

But his spirits suddenly lifted as he realized Oz hadn't wanted to park his troupe near the police barracks—he'd had no choice. Maybe Nadia was still alive.

The roustabout had stopped ahead and was motioning him to hurry up. Jack did just that and soon came to the trailer he recognized as Oz's. The man himself was standing before it, watching the repair work on the truck.

"It got loose, didn't it?" Jack said as he came up beside him.

The taller man rotated the upper half of his body and looked at Jack. His expression was anything but welcoming.

"Oh, it's you. You do get around."

Took most of Jack's dwindling self-control to keep from taking a swing at Oz right then and there. He was bursting to ask about Nadia but forced himself to stick to the rakosh. That was old news between them; he'd cover that, then press on.

"Had to feed it, didn't you? Had to bring it up to full strength. Damn it, you knew the risk you were taking."

"It was caged with iron bars. I thought—"

"You thought wrong. I warned you. I've seen that thing at full strength. Iron or not, that cage wasn't going to hold it."

"I admire your talent for stating the obvious."

"Where is it?"

For the first time Jack detected a trace of fear in Oz's eyes. "I don't know."

"Swell." He glanced around. "Where's that guy Hank?"

"Hank? What could you want with that imbecile?"

"Just wondering if he was bothering it again."

The boss slammed a bony fist into a palm. "I thought he'd learned his lesson. Well, he'll learn it now." He turned and called into the night. "Everyone—find Hank! Find him and bring him to me at once!"

They waited but no one brought Hank. Hank was nowhere to be found.

"It appears he's run off," Prather said.

"Or got carried off."

"We found no blood near the truck, so perhaps the young idiot is still alive."

"He is alive," said a woman's voice.

Jack turned and recognized the three-eyed fortune-teller from the show.

"What do you see, Carmella?" Oz said.

"He is in the woods. He stole one of the guns and he carries a spear. He is full of wine and hate. He is going to kill it."

"Oh, I doubt that," Oz said. "Going to get himself killed is more likely."

Jack understood taking a gun, but not the spear; then he remembered the pointed iron rod Hank and Bondy had used to torture it. Neither would do the job. If Hank ever caught up with the rakosh, he wouldn't last long.

He stared at the mass of trees rising on the far side of the parkway. "We've got to find it."

"Yes," Oz said. "Poor thing, alone out there in a strange environment, disoriented, lost, afraid."

Jack couldn't imagine Scar-lip afraid of anything, especially anything it might run across around here.

"On the subject of lost, alone, and afraid," Jack said, motioning Oz toward his trailer, "I need to ask you something."

Oz followed him until they were all but leaning on the battered wall of the old Airstream, out of earshot of the others.

"What?"

"Where's Nadia Radzminsky?"

Oz's eyes told him nothing, but the way his body tensed spoke volumes.

"Nadia . . . who?"

"The one Dr. Monnet paid you to eliminate. Where is she?"

"I haven't the faintest idea what you're—" Oz spotted the pistol Jack had pulled from his waistband.

"I have it straight from Dr. Monnet and his partners," Jack said softly as he began unscrewing the silencer. "They say they hired you to 'remove' Douglas Gleason and Nadia Radzminsky, so playing dumb won't cut it." He lowered the barrel, pointing it at Oz's right knee. "Now, I'm going to ask you again, and if you give me any more bullshit, I'm going to shoot you. Nothing immediately fatal, but it's going to hurt like hell. And then I'm going to ask you again. And if I don't get the truth, I'll shoot you again, and so it will go."

Jack had to hand it to Oz—he was cool. He glanced at a pair of his doggie roustabouts—how many did he have?—who had noticed the pistol. Low growls rumbled in their throats as they edged closer.

"They'll tear you to pieces before you get off that second shot. Perhaps before you get off the first."

"Don't count on it." Jack leveled the barrel at Oz's midsection. "I can pull this trigger *lots* of times before I go down. Any idea what a hollowpoint round, even a twenty-two, can do once it breaks up inside you?"

Jack's pistol was loaded with FMJs, but no need to tell Oz that.

"And don't think the shots will go unnoticed over there." Jack cocked his head toward the State Police barracks. "So not only will you be dead, but a bunch of troopers will be treating this whole area as a crime scene. They'll go through it with a fine comb. What'll they find?"

Oz's expression fluctuated between fear and rage. Jack pressed on, heading for home.

"You've gathered a nice little family around you, Oz. What will happen to them when you're gone and they've been broken up and scattered because of certain crimes you've committed? All because you wouldn't answer a simple question."

Jack hoped the bluff would work. He knew he'd be beaten to a bloody pulp if he pulled the trigger, and even if he survived, he feared police scrutiny as much as Oz. More. But Oz couldn't know that.

"Let's suppose, just suppose," Oz said, "that they were here. What happens?"

They? Jack fought to keep from showing the relief surging within him. "They leave with me and that's that."

"How do I know you won't stop at the first phone and report us?"

"You've got my word," Jack said. "I've got nothing against you, Oz. I have a business relationship with Nadia. If I get her out of this, you and me are even. I'm happy never to see or hear of you again, and I'm sure it's mutual."

"But what about them?"

"I think I can square it with them. Let's go ask."

Oz held back. "There's still the matter of Dr. Monnet. He—"

"He's dead."

The eyes narrowed. Oz wasn't buying. "Really." He drew out the word.

"Just turn on the radio. It's on all the news stations."

"You?"

"Never laid a finger on him. Dragovic, I'd guess."

"I see," Oz said, nodding. A small smile played about his lips. That obviously made sense to him.

"Monnet paid you to off them," Jack said, "but I assume you had other plans. Sushi for the rakosh, right?"

"The creature's eating habits appear to be similar to those of a big snake," Oz said, neither confirming nor denying. "It gorges itself, then doesn't eat again for days. I haven't had time yet to learn its cycle."

"And now that it's gone, you've got no use for the food you've stockpiled for it. Am I right?"

He nodded and sighed. "I suppose that settles it, then."

He led Jack toward the center of the vehicle cluster. Playing it safe, Jack followed close behind, his pistol trained on Oz's back. The roustabouts—three now—followed. Oz stopped before an exceptionally run-down red trailer.

Jack heard something thumping against the inner walls and faint cries for help. Oz pointed to the padlock on the door and one of the roustabouts unlocked it.

As the door swung open, Jack slid his pistol behind his thigh. An idea of how to make this a smooth extraction was forming, but it might not work with artillery on display.

The cries and pounding ceased. For a moment nothing happened; then a sandy-haired man poked his head out. He looked pale, haggard, uncertain, but Jack recognized him as Douglas Gleason from the photo Nadia had shown him. Then Nadia appeared beside him.

All right, Jack thought. All *right*. Now to get them out of here.

"Good evening, Dr. Radzminsky," he said.

Her head pivoted toward him and her eyes widened in recognition and relief.

"Jack!" she cried, her voice harsh and ragged from shouting for who knew how long. "Oh, Jack, it's you!"

"Jack? Who's Jack?" Gleason was saying, but Nadia shushed him.

"It's all right. He's a friend. Jack, how did you get here? How did you manage—?"

"Long story. Suffice for now that Monnet and his partners arranged for Mr. Prather here to kill you and your fiancé."

"Oh, no!" she said with more despair than shock.

"Knew it!" Gleason said. "Had to be him!"

"But why?"

"He and Dragovic were making Berzerk, and you knew it. But Mr. Prather is not a murderer," Jack said, nodding toward Oz, whose eyes widened in surprise. "So he merely kept you out of sight and out of harm's way until he could find a solution for your, um, predicament."

Jack was winging this. He glanced at Oz for a little backup.

"Yes," Oz said, barely missing a beat. "Dr. Monnet was blackmailing me, so I couldn't go to the police. I didn't know what to do. But now that he's dead—"

"Dead?" Nadia said. She looked at Jack.

"Milos Dragovic killed him."

"With him gone," Oz said, "it's safe for me to release you."

Jack said, "But there's one matter we have to settle first: This never happened. Mr. Prather needs your word on that."

Gleason needed about a second before nodding. "I can handle that."

But Nadia hesitated, frowning, not onboard yet.

"Come on, Nadj," Gleason said, putting his arm around her. "We weren't harmed. They even fed us."

"I've never been so frightened in all my life!"

"Yeah, but it's better than being dead. He could've killed us—he was *supposed* to kill us, and it would have been easier, but he didn't. We owe him something, don't you think?"

Come on, Nadia, Jack thought, trying a little telepathy. Say yes and we're out of here.

Finally she shrugged. "I don't know about *owing* him," she said, glaring at Oz. "But I guess we can keep it to ourselves."

Jack repressed a sigh of relief. He fished his car keys out of his pocket and tossed them to Gleason.

"My Buick's in front of the Burger King sign. Wait for me there. I've got one more matter to settle with Mr. Prather."

After Nadia and her beau had hurried from the scene, Jack turned to Oz.

"Where'd the rakosh break out?"

"About a mile back. Right near mile marker fifty-one-point-three, to be exact. We stopped but could not stay parked on the shoulder— we'd have the police asking what happened—so we pulled in here."

"We've got to find it."

"Nothing I'd like better," said the boss, "although I have a feeling you'd prefer to see it dead."

"You've got that right."

"An interesting area here," Oz said. "Right on the edge of the Pine Barrens."

Jack cursed under his breath. The Barrens. Shit. How was he going to locate Scar-lip in there—if that was where it was? This whole area was like a time warp. Near the coast you had a nuclear power plant and determinedly quaint but unquestionably twentieth-century towns like Smithville and Leeds Point. West of the parkway was wilderness. The Barrens—a million or so unsettled acres of pine, scrub brush, vanished towns, hills, bogs, creeks, all pretty much unchanged in population and level of civilization from the time the Indians had the Americas to themselves. From the Revolutionary days on, it had served as a haven for people who didn't want to be found. Hessians, Tories, smugglers, Lenape Indians, heretical Amish, escaped cons—at one time or another, they'd all sought shelter in the Pine Barrens.

And now add a rakosh to its long list of fugitives.

"We're not too far from Leeds Point, you know," Prather said, an amused expression flitting across his sallow face. "The birthplace of the Jersey Devil."

"Save the history lesson for later," Jack said. "Are you sending out a search party?"

"No. No one wants to go, and I can't say I blame them. But even if some were willing, we've got to be set up in Cape May for our show tonight. And frankly, without Dr. Monnet buying its blood, I can't justify the risk of going after it."

"That leaves me."

If Scar-lip got too much of a head start, he'd never find it which he could live with . . . unless the drive to kill Vicky was still fixed in its dim brain. Seemed unlikely, but Jack couldn't take the chance.

"You're not seriously thinking of going after it."

Jack shrugged. "Know somebody who'll do it for me?"

"May I ask why?" Oz said.

"Take too long to tell. Let's just leave it that Scar-lip and I go back a ways and we've got some unfinished business."

Oz stared at him a moment, then turned and began walking back toward his trailer.

"Come with me. Perhaps I can help."

Jack doubted that but followed and waited outside as Oz rummaged around within his trailer. Finally he emerged holding something that looked like a Gameboy. He tapped a series of buttons, eliciting a beep, then handed it to Jack.

"This will lead you to the rakosh."

Jack checked out the thing: it had a small screen with a blip of green light blinking slowly in one corner. He rotated his body and the blip moved.

"This is the rakosh?" Then he remembered the collar it had been wearing. "What'd you do—rig it with a LoJack?"

"In a way. I have electronic telltales on our animals. Occasionally one gets loose and I've found this to be an excellent way to track them. Most of them are irreplaceable."

"Yeah. Not too many two-headed goats wandering around."

"Correct. The range is only two miles, however. As you can see, the creature is still within range, but it may not be for long. Operation is simple: Your position is center screen; if the blip is left of center, the creature is to the left of you; below center, it's behind you; and so on. You track it by proceeding in whatever direction moves the blip closer to the center of the screen. When it reaches dead center, you'll have found your rakosh. Or rather, it will have found you."

Jack swiveled back and forth until the locator blip was at the top of the faintly glowing screen. He looked up and found himself facing the shadowy mass of trees west of the Parkway. Just as he'd feared. Scar-lip was in the pines.

But this'll help me find it, he thought.

And then something occurred to him.

"You're being awfully helpful."

"Not at all. My sole concern is for the rakosh."

"But you know I'm going to kill it if I find it."

"*Try* to kill it. The pines are full of deer and other game, but the rakosh can't use them for food. As you know, it eats only one thing."

Now Jack understood. He grinned. "And you think by giving me this locator, you're sending it a CARE package, so to speak."

Oz inclined his head. "So to speak."

"We shall see, Mr. Prather. We shall see."

"On the contrary, I doubt anyone will *ever* see you again."

"I'm not suicidal; trust me on that."

"But you can't believe you can take on a rakosh single-handed and survive."

"Wouldn't be the first time."

Jack headed for his car, relishing the look of concern on Oz's face before he'd turned away. Had he sounded confident enough? Good act. Because he was feeling anything but.

2

"Here he comes," Doug said.

Nadia lifted her head from his shoulder and glanced through the car window. Jack was about a hundred feet away, striding toward them. The sight of him elicited a warm glow against the deep chill that pervaded her. She couldn't remember ever being so glad to see someone as when she'd looked through the open door of that awful trailer and found Jack standing outside. She couldn't imagine how he'd tracked her down or why, but when she'd most needed someone he'd shown up.

"Good," she said. "Now we can get out of here."

She'd been huddled against Doug in the rear seat, feeling cold and tired, totally wrung out, but mostly sad.

Dr. Monnet wanted me dead.

She'd been forced to accept the truth of that, and yet . . . how could it be? Horrifying enough to learn that anyone wanted you dead, but Dr. Monnet . . . and after she'd been so worried about his well-being. It was too cruel.

To her surprise, Jack walked past the car and into the food court. Minutes later he emerged with a canvas shoulder bag emblazoned with ATLANTIC CITY in Day-Glo green letters.

"How's everybody doing?" he said as he slipped into the front seat.

"Better now," Doug said. "Thanks to you." He extended his hand over the seat. "I'm Doug Gleason."

They shook hands.

"Jack." He gave Doug's wrist a quarter-turn. "Is that a Quisp watch? Neat."

"You want it? It's yours."

Jack waved him off. "No, that's OK."

"I'm serious," Doug said. "I don't know how to thank you."

"You will in a minute."

Jack backed the car out of its spot but didn't drive far. To Nadia's dismay he parked in another spot in a far corner of the rest area by the RIDESHARE INFO sign. She wanted to go home.

"Aren't we going back?"

"Not yet." Jack pulled a couple of bottles of Snapple from the canvas bag and handed them back. "If you're thirsty, drink up; otherwise, dump it out on the pavement."

Nadia drank half of her lemon-flavored iced tea quickly. She hadn't realized how thirsty she was. Jack had opened his door and was emptying bottle after bottle into the parking lot.

"Shame to waste the stuff, I know," he said, "but it seems Snapple's about the only thing that comes in glass bottles these days."

Then he took out a glass cutter and began scoring the flanks of the bottles.

Baffled, Nadia said, "What are you doing?"

"Trick I learned from an old revolutionary. Ups the chances these'll shatter on contact."

Then he pulled an Atlantic City souvenir T-shirt and a newspaper from the bag. He began tearing up the shirt.

Nadia studied his face, his deft, sure movements. Where was the easy going fellow she'd seen off and on over the past few days? He'd been replaced somehow by this fiercely focused man whose sense of purpose radiated through the car. His expression was grim and the brown eyes she'd once thought mild now gleamed with intensity.

"What's going on?" Nadia said.

"One of Oz's attractions escaped. I have to go after it."

"He hired you?"

"No. This is my own thing."

"Why on earth—?"

"It may harm someone who matters to me."

"Can't you call the police?"

"They'll think I'm nuts, or trying to scam them with a Jersey Devil story."

Doug said, "This 'attraction' wouldn't happen to be a big, strange-looking creature with yellow eyes and dark skin."

Jack looked up. "You saw it?"

"Yeah. I think so. The night I was kidnapped they brought me into one of the tents and pushed me up against the bars of a cage with this huge guy in a stinking rubber monster suit inside."

"That wasn't a suit."

"Bullshit."

Jack focused those eyes on him. "Do I look like I'm bullshitting?"

"No." Doug swallowed. "And to tell the truth, afterward I got to thinking either that's the most convincing rubber suit on earth or I was face-to-face with a real live demon. So I kept telling myself that nothing like that ever existed in real life, so it had to be a suit."

"What happened when they put you up against the bars? Did it take a swipe at you, try to grab you?"

"No. It pretty much ignored me. It seemed more interested in getting out of its cage."

Jack simply stared at Doug.

"What?" Doug asked.

Jack shook his head. "When you get back home, do yourself a favor and buy a lottery ticket. If your luck's still holding, you'll wake up a multimillionaire."

He stepped out of the car, opened the trunk, and returned with a metal can and a flashlight.

Nadia remembered something. "Jack, is this the creature you told me about this morning—the source of the drug?"

"One and the same."

"I think I saw it when I was peeking through a crack between the boards over our windows. I saw them loading a big blue-black creature in a steel cage onto one of the trucks." And she remembered thinking at the time it had to be some sort of gimmick attraction because nothing that looked like that should be living and breathing on this earth. "That . . . that was real?"

Jack nodded. He squatted outside the car and began refilling the empty Snapple bottles from the big metal can.

Oh, no, Nadia thought, fighting a surge of panic as she watched him. He's not really—

But he was. Oh, yes, he was. The smell of gasoline was unmistakable.

Dizzy, she closed her eyes and hung on, wondering what had happened to her world in the past few days. She felt as if she'd tumbled down a rabbit hole into a nastily surreal Wonderland. The molecule she'd been assigned to stabilize had turned out to be an illegal drug, her fiancé had been abducted, a man she'd known for years and deeply respected, had even made love to, had ordered her death, and then he himself had been murdered. And now she was parked in a rest stop helping a man she barely knew make Molotov cocktails to go after some awful creature from a nightmare.

Nightmare . . . that's where she was right now.

She wished she'd never heard of Jack. If she hadn't hired him, maybe none of this would have happened.

She opened her eyes again and looked at him. "You're really going to chase after that thing? Alone? In the dark?"

He nodded. "Not exactly my idea of a fun time, but . . ."

"I'll go with you," Doug said.

Nadia wanted to punch him and scream, *How can you be such an idiot?* but held her tongue when she saw Jack immediately shake his head.

"This doesn't involve you."

"I could watch your back," Doug said, pressing. "I feel I owe you something."

Nadia wanted to kill him. The only hunting Doug had ever done was on a computer screen.

Jack finished tightening the cap on the last bottle.

"I appreciate the offer, but this is a one-man operation." He glanced at her and winked. "Good man."

"I know," she said, clutching Doug's arm. *And I want to keep him good and alive.*

Jack gently placed the six gasoline-filled bottles back into the canvas shoulder bag and worked sections of newspaper between them to keep them from clinking, then threw the pieces of T-shirt on top.

"What you *can* do for me is drive," he said, moving into the passenger seat.

Doug scrambled around, leaving Nadia alone in the back. They drove north through the New Gretna toll, then turned around and came back south through the toll again.

"We'll be stopping soon," Jack said. He seemed to be eyeing the mile markers closely. "After you drop me off, head back to the rest area and wait inside where you can hear the public phones. I've got the number of one of them. When I'm done I'll call you on my cell phone and tell you where to pick me up."

"How long do you think you'll be?" Nadia said.

"Can't say." He tapped the dashboard clock. "Just about two A.M. now. If you don't hear from me by six . . . go home."

"Without you?"

He cleared his throat as he scribbled on a scrap of paper. "If you don't hear from me by then it means things have gotten complicated. Go back to the city and call this number. A guy named Abe will answer. Tell him what you know. He'll take it from there."

Doug said, "But what—?"

"Whoa! Here's my stop."

Doug pulled over and Jack jumped out. He slipped the straps of the bag onto a shoulder and pulled the flashlight from a pocket.

"See you later," he said.

Nadia noticed how he limped as he hurried down the slope toward the trees.

I hope so, she thought as they pulled away. She felt a cold weight growing in her stomach. When she looked back, Jack had disappeared into the tall shadows.

3

Jack trained his flashlight beam on the scrub at the base of the slope, looking for broken branches. He found them. Lots of them. Something big had torn through here not long ago.

He stepped through and followed the path of destruction. He was glad he'd kept the boonie cap; without it the branches would be tearing at the sutures in his scalp. Already had a throbbing headache and a banged-up hip. Didn't need to start bleeding.

When he was sure he was out of sight of the highway, he stopped and pulled out the electronic locator. He was facing west and the blip was at the top edge of the screen. Had to move. Scar-lip was almost out of range.

He pressed forward until he came to a narrow path. A deer trail, most likely. Flashed his beam down and saw what looked like deer tracks in the damp sand, but they weren't alone: deep imprints of big, alien, three-toed feet, and work-boot prints coming after. Scar-lip, with Hank following—obviously behind because the boot prints occasionally stepped on the rakosh tracks.

What's Hank thinking? Jack wondered. That he's got a gun and maybe he learned how to hunt when he was a kid, so that makes him a match for the Sharkman? Maybe he's *not* thinking. Maybe a belly full of Mad Dog has convinced him he can handle the equivalent of taking on a great white with a penknife in a sea of ink.

Jack began following the deer trail, keeping one eye on the locator and turning his flashlight beam on and off every so often to check the ground. Scrub pines closed in, forming a twenty- to thirty-foot wall around him, arching their branches over the trail, allowing only an occasional glimpse of the starlit sky.

Quiet. Just the sound of insects and the branches brushing against his clothes. Jack hated the great outdoors. Give him a city with cars and buses and honking cabs, with pavements and right angles and subways rumbling beneath his feet and—best of all—streetlights. It wasn't just dark out here, it was *dark*.

His adrenaline was up but despite the alien surroundings, he felt curiously relaxed. The locator gave him a buffer zone of safety. He knew where Scar-lip was and didn't have to worry about it jumping out of the bushes and tearing into him at any second. But he did have to worry about Hank. An armed drunk in the woods could be a danger to anything that moved. Didn't want to be mistaken for Scar-lip.

The trail wound this way and that, briefly meandering north and south, but taking him generally westward. Jack moved as fast as the circumstances allowed, making his best time along the occasional brief straightaway, but his left hip felt like someone had lit a blowtorch in the socket.

The green blip that was Scar-lip gradually moved nearer and nearer the center of the locator screen, which meant he was gaining steadily on the rakosh. Looked like the creature had stopped moving. Why? Resting? Or waiting?

He guesstimated he was about a quarter-mile from the rakosh when a gun report somewhere ahead brought him up short. Sounded like a shotgun. There it was again. And again.

And then a scream of fear and mortal agony echoed through the trees, rising toward a shriek that cut off sharply before it peaked.

Silence.

Jack had thought the woods quiet before, but now even the insects had shut up. He waited for other sounds. None came. And the blip on the locator showed no movement.

That pretty much told the story: Scar-lip had sensed it was being followed so it hunkered down and waited. Who comes along but one of the guys who used it as a pincushion when it was caged. Chomp-chomp, crunch-crunch, good-bye, Hank.

Jack's tongue was dry as felt. That could have—most likely would have—been him if he'd gone after Scar-lip without the locator.

But that's not the way it's going to play. I know where you are, pal, so no nasty surprises for me.

He crept ahead, and the crack and crunch of every twig and leaf he stepped on sounded amplified through a stadium PA. But Scar-lip was staying put—eating, perhaps?—so Jack kept moving.

When the blip was almost center screen, Jack stopped. He smelled something and flashed his light along the ground.

The otherwise smooth sand was kicked up ferociously for a space of about a dozen feet, ending with two large, oblong gouts of blood, drying thick and dark red, with little droplets of the same speckled all around them. A twelve-gauge Mossberg pump-action lay in the brush at the edge of the trail, its wooden stock shattered.

Only one set of prints led away—the three-toed kind.

Jack crouched in the scrub grass, staring around, listening, looking for signs of movement. Nothing. But he knew from the locator that Scar-lip was dead ahead, and not too far.

Waiting to do to me what he did to Hank, no doubt. Sorry, pal. We're gonna play it my way this time.

He removed two Snapple bottles from the shoulder bag and un-screwed their caps. Gasoline fumes rose around him as he stuffed a piece of T-shirt into the mouth of each. Lifted one, lit the rag with a little butane lighter he'd picked up along with everything else, and quickly tossed it straight ahead along the trail.

The small flame at its mouth traced a fiery arc through the air. Before it hit the ground and *whoomph*ed into an explosion of flame, Jack had the second one in hand, ready to light.

Muscles tight, heart pounding, Jack blinked in the sudden glare as his eyes searched out the slightest sign of movement. Wavering shadows from the flickering light of the flames made *everything* look like it was moving. But nothing big and dark and solid appeared.

Something small and shiny glittered on a branch just this side of the flames. Warily, Jack approached it. His foot slipped on something along the way: the sharpened steel rod Bondy had used to torment the rakosh lay half-buried in the sand. Jack picked it up and carried it in his left hand like a spear. He had two weapons now. He felt like an Indian hunter, armed with an iron spear and a container of magic burn-ing liquid.

Closer to the flames now, he stepped over a fallen log and his foot landed on something soft and yielding. Glanced down and saw a very dead Hank staring up at him through glazed eyes. He let out an involuntary yelp and jumped back.

After glancing around to make sure this wasn't a trap, he took another look at Hank. Firelight glimmered in dead blue eyes that were fixed on the stars; the pallor of Hank's bloodless face accentuated the dark rims of his shiners and blended almost perfectly with the sand under his head; his throat was a red pulpy hole and his right arm was missing at the shoulder.

Jack swallowed hard. That could be me soon if I don't watch it.

Stepped over him and kept moving. The fire from the first Molotov cocktail was burning low when he reached the branch. Some of the brush had caught fire but the flames weren't spreading. Still they cast enough light to allow him to identify the shiny object.

Scar-lip's telltale collar.

Jack whirled in near panic, alarm clamoring along his adrenalized nerves as he lit the second cocktail, and scanned the area for signs of the rakosh.

Nothing stirred.

This was bad, *very* bad. In the middle of nowhere and he'd given himself away with the first bomb. Now tables were reversed: Scar-lip knew exactly where Jack was, while Jack was lost in the dark with only four cocktails left.

Dark . . . that was the big problem. If he could find a safe place to hide for a few hours, the rising sun would level the playing field a little. But where?

Looked around and fixed on a big tree towering above the pines ahead. That might be the answer.

Jack tossed away the locator and hooked the straps of the canvas bag around his shoulders, knapsack style. Spear in one hand, Molotov in the other, he edged ahead in a half-crouch, ready to spring in any direction. Sweat trickled down his back as he swung his gaze back and forth, watching, listening, but heard nothing beyond his own harsh, ragged breaths and his racing pulse drumming in his ears.

Hopped over the dying flames of the first Molotov and saw that the trail opened onto a small clearing with the big tree at its center. Good chance Scar-lip was somewhere in or near the clearing, maybe behind the tree trunk. One good way to find out. . . .

Tossed the second firebomb—another flaming *whoomph!* but no sign of Scar-lip . . . yet. Had to get to that tree. Angled around so he could see behind it—nothing. Clearing empty.

Dropped the iron spear—it would only get in his way—hustled over to the trunk, and began to climb.

Not fun. His hip shot pain through his pelvis and down his leg, and the effort worsened his headache.

Did rakoshi climb trees? Jack couldn't see why not. Doubted they were afraid of heights. Kept climbing, moving as fast as his battered body allowed, ascending until the branches began to crack under his weight. Satisfied that the far heavier Scar-lip could never make it this far up, he settled down to wait.

Checked the luminescent dial on his watch: just about 3:00 A.M. When was sunup? Wished he paid more attention to things like that. Didn't matter in the city, but out here in the sticks . . .

Tried to find a comfortable perch but that wasn't going to happen, and a nap was out of the question. At least his hip pain had eased now that it wasn't bearing his weight. And he found some solace in the realization that no way was Scar-lip going to catch him by surprise up here.

Through the leaves of the big oak he could see patches of the sandy clearing below, gray against the surrounding blackness. On the eastern horizon, a dim glow from the parkway and the rest area; but to the west, nothing but the featureless black forever of the Pine Barrens—

Jack stiffened as he saw a light—make that two lights—moving along the treetops to the west . . . heading his way. At first he thought it might be a plane or helicopter, but the lights were mismatched in size and maintained no fixed relationship to each other. His second thought was UFOs, but these didn't appear to be objects at all. They looked like globules of light . . . light and nothing more.

He'd heard of these things but had never seen one. . . . The Pineys called them pine lights but no one knew what they were. Jack didn't want to find out and would have preferred to see them heading elsewhere. They weren't traveling a straight line—the smaller one would dart left and right, and even the larger one meandered a little—but no question about it: those two glowing blobs were heading his way.

They slowed as they reached the clearing and Jack got a closer look at them. He didn't like what he saw. One was basketball size, the other maybe a bit larger than a softball. Light shouldn't form into a ball; it wasn't right. Something unhealthy about the pale green color too.

Jack cringed as they came straight for the tree, fearing they were going to touch him—something about them made his skin crawl—but they split within half a dozen feet of the branches. He heard a high-pitched hum and felt his skin tingle as they skirted his perch to the north and south. They paired up again on the far side but, instead of moving on, spiraled down toward the clearing.

Jack craned his neck to see where they were going. Toward Hank's body? No, that was on the north side of the tree. They were moving the other way.

He watched them hover over an empty patch of sand, then begin to chase each other in a tight circle—slowly at first, then with increasing speed until they blurred into a glowing ring, an unholy halo of wan green light, moving faster and faster, the centrifugal force of their rising speed widening the ring until they shot off into the night, racing back toward the west where they'd come from.

Good riddance. The whole episode had lasted perhaps a minute but left him unsettled. Wondered if this happened every night or if Scar-lip's presence had anything to do with it.

And speaking of Scar-lip . . .

Checked the clearing as best he could through the intervening foliage, but still nothing stirred.

Tried to settle down again and make plans for sunrise. . . .

4

Jack didn't wait for full light. The stars had begun to fade around four-thirty. By five, although still probably half an hour before the sun officially rose, the pewter sky was bright enough for him to feel comfortable quitting the Tarzan scene and heading back to earth.

Stiff and sore, he eased himself toward the ground, continually checking the clearing—still empty except for Hank. Soon as he hit the sand he opened the Snapple bottles and stuffed their mouths with rags. He kept one in hand and held the lighter ready.

The plan was simple: start at Hank's corpse and follow Scar-lip's footprints from there. He'd keep it up as long as he could. Didn't know how long he could go without food and water, but he'd give it his best shot. Right now what he wanted most was a cup of coffee.

As he approached the corpse, he noticed that the pinelands insects hadn't been idle: flies taxied around Hank's head while ants partied in the throat wound and shoulder stump. The thought of burying him crossed Jack's mind, but he had neither the time nor the tools.

A noise behind him. Jack whirled. Put down the bag and thumbed the flint wheel on the butane lighter as he scanned the clearing in the pallid predawn light.

There . . . on the far side, the spot where the pine lights had done their little dervish a couple of hours ago, a patch of sand, moving, shifting, rising. No, not sand. This was very big and very dark.

Scar-lip.

Jack took an involuntary step back, then held his ground. The rakosh wasn't moving; it simply stood there, maybe thirty feet away where it had buried itself for the night. Hank's arm dangled from its three-fingered right hand; it held it casually, like a lollipop. The upper half of the arm had been stripped of its flesh; the pink bone was coated with sand.

Jack felt his gut tighten, his heart turning in overdrive. Here was his chance. He lit the tail on the cocktail and stepped over the shoulder bag, straddling it. Slowly he bent, pulled out a second bomb, and lit it from the first.

Had to get this right the first time. He knew from past encounters how quick and agile these creatures were in spite of their mass. But he also knew that all he had to do was hit it with one of these flaming babies and it would all be over.

With no warning and as little windup as he dared, he tossed the Molotov in his right hand. The rakosh ducked away, as expected, but Jack was ready with the other . . . gave it a left-handed heave, leading the rakosh, trying to catch it on the run. Both missed. The first landed in an explosion of flame, but the second skidded on the sand and lay there intact, its fuse dead, smothered.

As the rakosh shied away from the flames, Jack pulled out a third cocktail. His heart stuttered, his hand shook, and he'd just lit the fuse when he sensed something hurtling toward him through dimness, close, too close. Ducked but not soon enough. The twirling remnant of Hank's arm hit him square in the face.

Coughing in revulsion as he sprawled back, Jack felt the third cocktail slip from his fingers. He turned and dived and rolled. He was clear when it exploded, but he kept rolling because it had landed on the shoulder bag. He felt a blast of heat as his last Molotov went up.

As soon as the initial explosion of flame subsided, Scar-lip charged across the clearing. Jack was still on his back in the sand. Instinct prompted his hand toward the P-98 but he knew bullets were useless. Spotted the iron spear beside him, grabbed it, swung it around so the butt was in the dirt and the point toward the onrushing rakosh. His mind flashed back to his apartment rooftop last summer when Scar-lip's mother was trying to kill him, when he had run her through. That had only slowed her then, but this was iron. Maybe this time . . .

He steadied the point and braced for the impact.

The impact came, but not the one he'd expected. In one fluid motion, Scar-lip swerved and batted the spear aside, sending it sailing away through the air toward the oak. Jack was left flat on his back with a slavering three-hundred-pound inhuman killing machine towering over him. Tried to roll to his feet but the rakosh caught him with its foot and pinned him to the sand. As Jack struggled to slip free, Scar-lip increased the pressure, eliciting live wires of agony from his already cracked ribs. Stretched to reach the P-98—spit balls would probably damage a rakosh as much as .22s, but that was all he had left. And no way was he going out with a fully loaded pistol. Maybe if he went for the eyes . . .

But before he could pull the pistol free of his warm-up pocket, he saw Scar-lip raise its right hand, spread the three talons wide, then drive them toward his throat.

No time to prepare, no room to dodge, he simply cried out in terror in what he was sure would be the last second of his life.

But the impact was not the sharp tearing pain of a spike ramming through his flesh. Instead he choked as the talons speared the sand to either side and the web between them closed off his wind. The pressure eased from his chest but the talons tightened, encircling his throat as he struggled for air. And then Jack felt himself yanked from the sand and held aloft, kicking and twisting in the silent air, flailing ineffectually at the flint-muscled arm that gripped him like a vise. The popping of the vertebral joints in his neck sounded like explosions; the cartilage in his larynx whined under the unremitting pressure as the rakosh shook him like an abusive parent with a baby who had cried once too often, and all the while his lungs pleaded, *screamed* for air.

His limbs quickly grew heavy, the oxygen-starved muscles weakening until he could no longer lift his arms. Black spots flashed and floated in the space between him and Scar-lip as his panicked brain's clawhold on consciousness began to falter. Life . . . he could feel his life slipping away, the universe fading to gray . . . and he was floating . . . gliding aloft toward—

—a jarring impact, sand in his face, in his mouth, but air too, good Christ, *air!*

He lay gasping, gulping, coughing, retching, but breathing, and slowly light seeped back to his brain, life to his limbs.

Jack lifted his head, looked around. Scar-lip not in sight. Rolled over, looked up. Scar-lip nowhere.

Slowly, hesitantly, he raised himself on his elbows, amazed to be alive. But how long would that last? So weak. And God, he hurt.

Looked around. Blinked. Alone in the clearing.

What was going on here? Was the rakosh hiding, waiting to pop out again and start playing with him like a cat with a captured mouse?

He struggled to his knees but stopped there until the pounding in his head eased. Looked around again, baffled. Still no sign of Scar-lip.

What the hell?

Cautiously Jack rose to his feet, his hip screaming, and braced for a dark shape to hurtle from the brush and finish him off.

Nothing moved. The rakosh was gone. Why? Nothing here to frighten it off, and it sure as hell wasn't turning vegetarian, because Hank's arm, the one Scar-lip had thrown at Jack, was missing.

Jack turned in a slow circle. Why didn't it kill me?

Because he'd stopped Bondy and Hank from torturing it? Not possible. A rakosh was a killing machine. What would it know about fair play, about debts or gratitude? Those were human emotions and—

Then Jack remembered that Scar-lip was part human. Kusum Bahkti had been its father. It carried some of Kusum in it and, despite some major leaks in his skylights, Kusum had been a stand-up guy.

Was that it? If so, the Otherness probably wanted to disown Scar-lip. But its daddy might be proud.

Jack's instincts were howling for him to go—*now*. But he held back. He'd come here to finish this, and he'd failed. Utterly. The rakosh was back to full strength and roaming free in the trackless barrens.

But maybe it *was* finished—at least between Scar-lip and himself. Maybe the last rakosh was somebody else's problem now. Not that he could do anything about Scar-lip now anyway. As much as he hated to leave a rakosh alive and free here in the wild, he didn't see that he had much choice. He'd been beaten. Worse than beaten: he'd been hammered flat and kicked aside like an old tin can. He had no useful weapons left, and Scar-lip had made it clear that Jack was no match one-on-one.

Time to call it quits. At least for today. But he couldn't let it go, not without one last shot.

"Listen," he shouted, wondering if the creature could hear him and how much it would understand. "I guess we're even. We'll leave it this way. For now. But if you ever threaten me or mine again, I'll be back. And I won't be carrying Snapple bottles."

Jack began to edge toward the trail but kept his face to the clearing, still unable to quite believe this, afraid if he turned his back the creature would rise out of the sand and strike.

As soon as Jack reached the trail, he turned and started moving as fast as his hip allowed. A last look over his shoulder before the pines and brush obscured the clearing showed what looked like a dark, massive figure standing alone on the sand, surveying its new domain. But when Jack stopped for a better look it was gone.

5

Jack became lost on the way out. His defeat and release had left him bewildered and a little dazed, neither of which had helped his concentration. A low lid of overcast added to the problem. The trail forked here and there and he knew he wanted to keep heading east, but he couldn't be sure where that was without the sun to fix on.

He'd called Nadia and told her he was on his way out and to hang in there. She'd sounded relieved. He'd call her again when he found a road.

But he didn't want to be caught carrying on that road, especially not a pistol that could link him to the bloody mess in the GEM boardroom. He pulled the P-98 from his pocket and opened the breech. He ejected the clip and, using his thumbnail, flicked the .22 long rifles free one by one, sending them flying in all directions. He tossed the empty clip into the brush. Then he kicked a hole in the sand, dropped the pistol into the depression, and smoothed sand back over it with his foot.

The gun was lousy with his fingerprints, but after a couple of rainstorms in this acid soil that wouldn't be a problem. No one was going to find it out here anyway.

He walked on, and the extra traveling time gave him room to think.

I blew it.

Defeat weighed on him, and he knew that wasn't right. Nadia and her fiancé were safe; Dragovic wouldn't be bothering Gia anymore; the world's supply of Berzerk would be useless powder in a couple of weeks, and its manufacturers wouldn't be making any more of it—or anything else for that matter; he'd made a guy named Sal very happy, happier than he'd intended; and he'd earned a nice piece of change in the process.

But the notion of Scar-lip roaming free remained a bone in his throat that he could neither cough up nor swallow. He felt some sort of obligation to let it be known that something big and dangerous was prowling the Pine Barrens. But how? He couldn't personally go public with the story, and who'd believe him anyway?

He was still trying to come up with a solution when he heard faint voices off to his right. He angled toward them.

The brush opened up and he found himself facing a worn two-lane blacktop. A couple of SUVs were parked on the sandy shoulder where four men, thirty to forty in age, were busily loading shotguns and slipping into Day-Glo orange vests. Their gear was expensive, top of the line, their weapons Remingtons and Berettas. Gentlemen sportsmen, out for the kill.

Jack asked which way to the parkway and they pointed off to the left. A guy with a dainty goatee gave him a disdainful up-and-down.

"What'd you run into? A bear?"

"Worse."

"You could get killed walking through the woods like that, you know," another said, a skinny guy with glasses. "Someone might pop you if you aren't wearing colors."

"I'll be sticking to the road from here on." Curiosity got the better of Jack. "What're you hunting with all that firepower?"

"Deer," the goatee replied. "The State Wildlife Department's ordered a special off-season harvest."

"Harvest, aye? Sounds like you're talking wheat instead of deer."

"Might as well be, considering the way the herd's been growing. There's just too damn many deer out there for their own good."

"And we're doing our civic and ecological duty by thinning the herd," said a balding guy with a big grin.

Jack hesitated, then figured he ought to give these guys a heads-up. "Maybe you want to think twice about going in there today."

"Shit," said the balding one, his grin vanishing. "You're not one of those animal rights creeps are you?"

The air suddenly bristled with hostility.

"I'm not *any* kind of creep, pal," Jack said through his teeth. Barely into the morning and already his fuse was down to a nubbin; he took faint satisfaction in seeing him step back up and tighten his grip on his shotgun. "I'm just telling you there's something real mean wandering around in there."

"Like what?" said the goatee, smirking. "The Jersey Devil?"

"No. But it's not some defenseless herbivore that's going to lay down and die when you empty a couple of shells at it. As of today, guys, you're no longer at the top of the food chain in the pines."

"We can handle it," said the skinny one.

"Really?" Jack said. "When did you ever hunt something that posed the slightest threat to you? I'm just warning you, there's something in there that fights back and I doubt any of your type can handle that."

Skinny looked uneasy now. He glanced at the others. "What if he's right?"

"Oh, shit!" said baldy. "You going pussy on us, Charlie? Gonna let some tree-hugger chase you off with spook stories?"

"Well, no, but—"

The fourth hunter hefted a shiny new Remington over-under.

"The Jersey Devil! I want it! Wouldn't that be some kind of head to hang over the fireplace?"

They all laughed, and Charlie joined in, back in the fold again as they slapped each other high fives. Jack shrugged and walked away. He'd tried.

Hunting season. Had to smile. Scar-lip's presence in the Pine Barrens gave the term a whole new twist. He wondered how these mighty hunters would react when they learned that the season was open on *them.*

And he wondered if there'd been any truth to those old tales of the Jersey Devil. Most likely hadn't been a real Jersey Devil before, but there sure as hell was now.

www.repairmanjack.com

FIC   Wilson, F. Paul
WIL   (Francis Paul)
C.1   All the rage.

11-00

DATE			